Raves for *Bl*

"Like the sexy derriere of its diva-femme protagonist Velvet Erickson, *Blind Curves* moves engagingly and with purpose. This clever and witty tale will appeal to mystery lovers and anyone who loves a game of cat and mouse."—Diana Cage, managing editor, *Velvetpark* magazine and author of *Girl Meets Girl: A Dating Survival Guide*

"Funny and fantastic whirl through a world of women as smart, savvy and sexy as we'd all like to be. The Blind Eye detective agency goes up against the murder of Rosemary Finney, the lesbian publishing magnate whom everyone loves to hate—especially her ex-lovers. Finney, with her 'ineffectual degrees in philosophy and women's studies,' has created difficulty for every in-dyke in San Francisco, including, after her death, the luscious femme-grrrl reporter Velvet Erickson, who is arrested for the murder but gets 48 hours' reprieve to clear her name. The two days bring a blitz of information and misinformation, mixed with dirty martinis and knee-trembling trysts. Cruising around the Bay Area following the sharp curves of plot, readers pick up delicious details of many subcultures—from Hollywood closets to New Orleans cops, from the psychology of losing vision to the fun of blind flirtation. The conflicting clues are filtered through the perspectives of the sophisticated, Japanese detective, Yoshi, and from the wheelchair of her apparently hapless assistant, ex-detective Bud. Only two questions remain: why can't life be like this? And, when's the next book?"—Gillian Kendall, author of *Mr. Ding's Chicken Feet*

"The Anderson-Minshalls have come up with a winner! With engrossing characters and an intricately planned plot, this first of a promised series of Blind Eye mysteries is not your average whodunit. Their intimate knowledge of the San Francisco Bay area, women's magazines, various disabilities and local protective services provide a richness beyond the scope of most mystery writers. Lots of romantic and sexual tension, career moves and the promise of medical miracles make me what to know not just who the killer is, but what happens next in these decidedly femme and butch characters' lives."—Lee Lynch, author of *Sweet Creek*

Visit us at www.boldstrokesbooks.com

BLIND CURVES

A BLIND EYE MYSTERY

by

Diane and Jacob Anderson-Minshall

2007

BLIND CURVES

ISBN: 10-digit 1-933110-72-4
       13-digit 978-1-933110-72-1

This Trade Paperback Original Is Published By
Bold Strokes Books, Inc.,
New York, USA

First Edition: March 2007

Credits
Editors: Jennifer Knight and Stacia Seaman
Production Design: Stacia Seaman
Cover Design By Sheri (GRAPHICARTIST2020@HOTMAIL.COM)

Acknowledgments

No author is an island. We're loosely paraphrasing Hugh Grant in *About a Boy*, rather than John Kennedy or whatever notable said it first. But in our case, it's apt. No author is an island, so we have many folks to thank: First and foremost, our publisher, Len Barot of Bold Strokes Books, without whom you wouldn't be reading this book now. BSB was our first choice in a publisher, and we haven't had a single regret about that. And many thanks to our lovely kiwi editor Jennifer Knight, who guided us through many sleepless nights of edits and spent more time than most would explaining to us the difference between omnipresence and third-person narrative and who often queried whether our word choices were esoteric, unconventional (and thus brilliant) ideas rather than, as was most common, horrible misspellings. Our cover designer Sheri suffered through our specific demands, and copy editor Stacia Seaman's detailed eye caught and corrected numerous would-be embarrassing mistakes. Any remaining errors in spelling, story or fact are all our own.

And, of course, we want to thank our family members—the Anderson, Minshall, Sherwood, Bolonos, Hernandez, Soria, Corcoran clans—who put up with hearing from us twice a year at best because we're stuck at our computers for months on end, and our dearest friends—Jeff, Athena, Angelina, Elisa, Corey, Erica—who get the same kind of shoddy attention while we play mad novelists instead of writing old-fashioned letters, attending cocktail parties, or throwing weekly *Noah's Arc* screenings (all things we'd love to do if only we could find the time).

Diane would be remiss if she didn't thank her boss, Frances Stevens, and her peeps at *Curve* magazine, who help keep her rooted firmly in reality. And big thanks to the women of publishing who have mentored her since she was thirteen, notably (and in no certain order): Darlene Allison, the editor of the *Independent Enterprise* in Payette, Idaho (who let Diane hang around long enough to discover writing was in her blood); Ann Crosby (a reporter at the *Daily Argus* in Ontario, Oregon, who told Diane that if she ever hoped to make more than $12,000 a year she should leave publishing right away—and she was right); and Ann DeBord, her long-suffering journalism teacher from Payette High School (who taught her how to balance her slavish devotion to the written word with the real world she was covering). And lastly, she thanks Jacob, her partner in crime and life, without whom she wouldn't do a vast number of things.

Jacob acknowledges that without his being injured at work and losing his ranger job, he might not have found time to write (or cook dinner, which Diane is most thankful for). In addition, he thanks the organizers of the National Novel Writers Month (or NaNoWriMo, as participants call it) and their challenge to write a novel in thirty days. With NaNoWriMo as the impetus, real events as our inspiration, and our love of mysteries and crime shows the driving force, we came up with Blind Eye Detectives and wrote what would become the foundation of Blind Curves. More personally, he offers his deepest appreciation for the many teachers who nourished his love of writing, those pioneers who have paved the way for transgender writers, and all the individuals who struggle with and overcome various kinds of disabilities—particularly his sisters Jennye and Michele. You are my heroes. And lastly, he thanks his wife Diane, for making every day worthwhile.

Dedication

As this is our first team effort, it seemed only fitting that we offer up more than one dedication. So this book is lovingly dedicated to our grandmothers, Annabel Biggs Anderson and Jennye Roberta "Keenie" Norman, both of whom were feminists ahead of their time, avid mystery readers, and overall rather tolerant broads. We're fairly certain they would both be proud.

And while this book is pure fiction, we've had people in our life who have inspired us to craft a story about betrayal, injustice, and greed. This book is for you as well. You know who you are.

Chapter One

Holy Fucking Hell. Between curses, Velvet Erickson flipped off a passing motorist. The driver of the blue Behemoth XL SUV echoed the bird with his own finger held high below his rearview mirror. He had come out of nowhere, suddenly on her ass, up her tailpipe, flashing his lights at her to get out of the way, when she was already driving ten miles over the speed limit. *What an asshole.*

Velvet thought he didn't deserve the alluring spectacle of her long nails, painted Corvette Red, waving an insult. She would never crop them to the nub like some utilitarian lesbians; she was, after all, a femme, and butches were an enterprising lot. They could just work around her nails. Her lovers—and they were legion—had never complained. In fact, they seemed to prize the scratch marks she tattooed down their backs. Some even showed them off to their friends.

She glanced in her review at the solid stream of cars behind her. As she darted in and out of the traffic, distant brake lights warned of problems ahead on the 101 North into San Francisco. Damn. It was barely six-friggin-a.m. How could there be a traffic jam already? She should have stayed on the 280. No, she shouldn't have come down here at all. She should have stayed in her warm San Francisco bed instead of hauling her ass out at three a.m. and traipsing down the Peninsula to some filthy parking lot just on the odd chance of catching Rosemary Finney red-handed.

What was that place called anyway? Wonderland? What a crock. Wonderland should be a Disneyland attraction, not some overgrown hiking trail in the boonies. Okay, Woodside probably didn't count as the boonies, not really. But it was, like, forty minutes south of the city down all these damn windy roads blacked out under a thicket of trees.

Velvet was exhausted. She felt like she'd been on some mythic quest, fighting her way through an enchanted forest searching for the princess trapped high in a castle tower. Except, Rosemary Finney was no princess. She was better suited for the role of wicked witch or evil stepmother. That woman was a bitch with a capital *B*.

Out the passenger window, past the empty darkness of the bay and above the East Bay's urban lights, the sun peeked over the hills like a shy geisha hiding behind her painted fan. San Francisco, still another ten minutes away, was stirring under a thick blanket of fog that would burn off early under the glare of the sun, leaving behind the Indian summer weather that was normal for October in the Bay Area.

Velvet loved the city in the fall. Temperatures were often in the seventies or eighties, permitting her to flaunt her buxom, kick-ass body in the tight, revealing outfits she preferred. By contrast, a typical summer's day was lousy, freezing cold with endless fog and winds that blew from the Bay to the breakers, forcing her to hide her curvaceous figure behind bulky sweaters.

Cresting the incline at Candlestick Park—she *refused* to call the professional baseball stadium 3Com Park or PacBell Park or eBay Park or whatever awful corporate shilling moniker they'd punished it with now—she gazed lovingly at the city spread out before her like a lover draped across her bed. Although she'd lived in San Francisco since she'd escaped from Los Angeles fifteen years earlier, she still felt a glow of euphoria each time she caught sight of its distinctive architecture. Rows of brightly painted houses undulated like waves lapping at the banks of the city proper. White stucco and pastel Victorians climbed high above the landscape, where they were, in turn, topped off by the grassy breastlike knobs of Twin Peaks.

Favored son, author Herb Caan, had described San Francisco as "Baghdad by the Bay." The staff at the *San Francisco Chronicle*, the newspaper where Velvet worked, had never quite gotten over the death of their most popular columnist. Even Stanley Wozlawski, the paper's editor in chief, who'd taken the position several years after Caan's passing, frequently waxed nostalgic about the good 'ol Caan days and invoked the man's name in times of crisis. "Herb Caan, save us," he'd exclaim, as though the columnist was now a saint enthroned at the foot of God, and he could put in a good word with the big guy in honor of his fellow journalists if he were so inclined.

Of course, Caan hadn't lived to see Bush destroy the real Baghdad, and now the moniker no longer seemed apt. Not compared to images of bombed-out streets and this stupid, never-ending occupation. Velvet had come to see Jerusalem as a more fitting comparison, with its white stone glistening in the sunlight as it climbed its way up a hill. From a distance San Francisco also appeared to have been cast in stone carved entirely from one quarry. While Jerusalem was a religious destination that beckoned people from around the globe, San Francisco was a gay Mecca that rivaled the Holy City's diverse demographics.

From the bowels of her old-school Louis Vuitton purse—no self-respecting dyke diva would carry one of those modern white and pastel bags—Velvet heard the muffled disco refrains of "More, More, More." Her cell phone was ringing. Who ever it was, was going to have to wait. Not that she was opposed to driving and talking at the same time, but she'd shoved the bag under the passenger seat when she'd gotten out of the car to follow Rosemary Finney and she couldn't reach it now.

Yet again Velvet wondered what she'd been thinking, driving out here. She'd sworn to avoid close contact with her ex-lover, but that was before the phone call last night. She'd just returned to her Bernal Heights shotgun house after driving home her latest conquest, Tucker Shade. It was after midnight and she'd heard the phone ring as she jiggled her key in the lock. Assuming at first that the caller was her booty call checking in, she had rolled her eyes. Lesbians could be so needy.

Velvet supposed she could have spent more time with Tucker after they'd finished their physical transaction, but she didn't like her sexual quarry to hang around. When they were done she wanted them gone. Velvet fancied herself a lesbian cougar: a member of the growing legion of middle-aged women who preyed on younger sport, though she was, admittedly, under forty.

The buzzing phone had fallen silent as she sauntered nonchalantly down the long hall. With a shrug, she dropped her keys on the kitchen counter, slid off her shoes, and shuffled barefoot into the living room. The house made groaning and creaking noises that she'd long since gotten used to. She ignored the sounds and settled into the soft cushions of the couch to watch disc four of *The Simpsons* season six.

The phone rang again just as Homer throttled Bart for some malfeasance.

Letting the DVD play, Velvet picked up the receiver and mumbled, "Hello?"

"Velvet Erickson?" The muffled female voice wasn't immediately familiar.

"Yes?" Velvet muted the Simpson family chatter.

"The reporter?"

"Yes."

"I have some information for you. About Rosemary Finney."

Velvet sat upright. That got her attention. "Who is this?" Maybe someone was playing a prank on her.

"I...I..." The caller stammered. "It's not important."

Of course it's important. Velvet shuffled through the entertainment magazines on her coffee table, looking for a pen and paper. If she switched on her recording device, the woman might get spooked and hang up.

"What kind of information?" she asked.

"It's about...let's say, illicit business practices."

The caller was a younger woman, Velvet decided, with a bit of an accent, like those corn-fed starstruck girls who poured off buses back home with nothing but an overnight bag and a fantasy in their heart. "Why call me?" Velvet asked. "Why not go to the police?"

"The police?" The caller scoffed. "You of all people should know that the Rosemary Finneys of the world aren't stopped by *police*." Though she emphasized it, the caller forced out the last word so quickly it sounded almost like "please."

While Velvet *did* doubt law enforcement's ability to enforce real justice upon those who could buy their own version of it, she didn't like the overt familiarity inherent in the caller's statement.

"What do you mean by me 'of all people'? Do I know you?" she wondered suspiciously.

"I'm familiar with your experience. You know, with Rosemary."

"Okay." Velvet allowed that to suffice as an answer. "So, what do you want to tell me about Rosemary Finney's business practices?"

"Uh, I..."

Velvet could hear the caller's dry voice cracking, and wondered what was making her so nervous. "Well?" she demanded impatiently.

She could really use hearing a juicy bit of gossip about her archrival and former lover.

"I shouldn't have called." The woman spoke abruptly. "Sorry—"

"Don't hang up!" Velvet's interest was piqued, her heart beating hard, her mouth watering. "After all that? You have to tell me." She'd never liked teases.

For a moment the line was so silent that Velvet was sure the mystery caller had already ended the call. Then the woman whispered, "It's not safe."

"What?" Velvet was surprised. "What are you afraid of?"

Words spilled out of the receiver in a rush. "It's not safe for us to talk. Just go to Wonderland Park in a few hours' time. You'll see. That's the lower lot. It's in Woodside, down on the Peninsula. Got that? Be there by five thirty a.m. Bring a camera. Oh, and Velvet?"

"Yes?"

"Be careful."

Velvet had wanted more information, but the line went dead and the dial tone buzzed in her ear. She looked at the caller ID, which, not surprisingly, read "blocked ID." Apparently she wouldn't be able to star 69 the caller or use the reverse directory to track her down. *Damn it.*

Still a little stunned, she looked at the paper in front of her. On the back of a used envelope, she'd jotted down a list of words: "Wonderland, lower, Woodside 530, camera, careful." She wondered what "illicit business practices" Rosemary might be involved in, exactly who the caller could be, and why she seemed so frightened.

Oh, Velvet knew what Rosemary was capable of. At one time or another she'd been the brunt of everything the woman dished out. But typically, Rosemary's preferred tools of torture tended to be emotional and financial more than physical. Rosemary Finney played with the emotions of friends, lovers, and employees, and she had a whole team of lawyers eager to impose the kind of pain people felt when their careers ended or they were forced into bankruptcy. Yet the woman on the phone had seemed afraid of something more tangible, the kind of something that might just lurk in the predawn darkness of a Woodside park.

Now, as Velvet jockeyed her way through the traffic near San Francisco's downtown exits, she thought about the pain Rosemary had inflicted on her and about her own revenge just a while ago. Sure, it was *schadenfreude*—a German term she'd picked up from *The Simpsons*.

She'd thought it meant "shameful joy" until her editor corrected her in front of the entire *Chronicle* staff. Although she'd been mortified with embarrassment at the time, Velvet had immediately gotten back on the horse and began using the expression's proper nuance: "malicious delight."

The term perfectly described her feelings right now. She knew she would relish this day for years to come. She *was* gloating over Rosemary's misfortune. And why not? Rosemary Finney had it coming. Velvet was glad, *glad* that she had been the instrument of that woman's undoing. It was about time.

The sound of shattering glass rose from the shrouded sidewalk as someone collected recycling from the curb outside Yoshi Yakamota's Richmond District home. In the darkness of her bedroom, Yoshi lay nestled beneath a thick goose-down comforter the color of desert mud, atop a low-slung Asian-influenced bed. Reluctantly, she felt for her bedside clock and pulled it toward her. She pressed a call button and a computerized voice that sounded a bit like Hal from *2001: A Space Odyssey* said, "6:57 a.m." in measured but staccato notes.

In other San Francisco neighborhoods, the early morning cacophony signaled the influx of entrepreneurial individuals who arrived under the cover of darkness, liberated glass and aluminum from plastic bins, and transferred them into waiting truck beds, car trunks, or shopping carts—thus preempting the city's pickup.

Yoshi respected the capitalist spirit of these people, many of them homeless, and did not understand residents who opposed it on the grounds that since they paid the city for recycling pickup, it was stealing when others removed the bottles and cans. These self-righteous citizens had even formed a political action group, the End Illegal Recycling Action Committee a.k.a. EIRAC, which pressured city officials to crack down on the early morning "thefts."

Yoshi didn't care who picked up the recycling, so long as it didn't end up in the local landfill. Of course she recognized that here in the Richmond, far from the poorer enclaves of the city, the odds were 60/40 that the din outside was actually the city's official recycling operation, not the entrepreneurs, although she had no idea why this was happening on a Wednesday morning instead of the usual Friday. Whatever the source, she wished she could just sleep through it. She used to be able to tune out the background sounds of the city. She used to be able to do a lot of things.

Yoshi sat up and swung her feet over the edge of the bed. Her toes inched sideways on the hardwood floor until they located the plush slippers tucked there. She pushed her feet in and shuffled slowly to the kitchen, where she pulled a mug from a bamboo-fronted cabinet and placed it in the sink. Keeping two fingers curled around the handle, she lifted the steel lever that turned on the tap and positioned the mug under the stream of cool water. Resting her index finger on the rim of the mug, she waited until the water moistened her finger before turning the faucet off. She then opened the ceramic container that held teabags, took one out, and dropped it into the mug's water and stuck the beverage into the microwave.

Her father would have been appalled. What respectable Japanese woman—or man for that matter—used a *bag* when they had access to fresh tea leaves? Her father had taught her to honor tea as far more than a beverage. It was a symbol of their cultural heritage, and the details of the Japanese tea ritual concealed lessons about one's connectedness to others, how to be present in one's actions, and the need to slow down and appreciate life's little moments. Having tea, in her father's sense of the word, bore little or no resemblance to Yoshi's current version: two minutes in the microwave and four quick gulps down as she rushed through her morning routine.

Yoshi pulled a smaller, handle-less Asian teacup from her cupboard and carefully poured some of her tea into it. She carried the cup into her living room, where she placed it on a diminutive bamboo table near an east-facing window. With her eyes closed, she bowed and then slowly backed away from the offering.

Maybe that would appease his spirit, she thought wryly. She missed him so much. Hiroki Yakamota's memory demanded more than an occasional cup of tea, and she knew it. But she did not want to think about that now, and the truth was, she missed the tea ceremony itself too. She yearned to have the slow-brewed tea infusing to perfection in one of her beautiful clay teapots. She had stopped using them recently when she nearly scalded her hand trying to fill one with boiling water fresh from the teakettle. Losing her eyesight had meant relearning even the simplest tasks. Yoshi silently promised herself that she would take the time to repeatedly practice pouring cold water from kettle to cup and move on to hot water when she had the procedure down pat.

She left the kitchen, her slippers slapping against the hardwood floor as she sauntered into the living room. She located the TV remote on the back of the quilted ecru divan, turned on the news, and went to her room to dress. She was buttoning a cap-sleeved blouse with oversized lapels when she heard the television newscast switch from traffic to a breaking news item. Yoshi listened for a few seconds, then gathered the rest of her clothes and rushed back into the living room.

"San Francisco publishing magnate Rosemary Finney, owner of the lesbian magazine *Womyn*, was found dead early this morning in a remote wooded area above Silicon Valley. We go live now to Marty Honda at the scene. Marty?"

Rosemary Finney? Yoshi fumbled around for the remote to amplify the volume. *Did he say Rosemary Finney?*

Reporter Marty Honda covered South Bay events for San Francisco's KTVU Channel Seven. Yoshi had met him once, ten years ago at the Cherry Blossom Festival. The annual event, held as the trees bloomed in April, brought hundreds of participants and onlookers to San Francisco's Japantown. There were parades and pageants, bonsai artists and calligraphers, tea ceremonies and kimono dance troupes of all ages, from grandmother to granddaughter. Seeing multiple generations of a family's women together always engulfed Yoshi in a storm of mixed emotions. It was beautiful and touching and cut her to the bone. Grandmothers and mothers, daughters and granddaughters, like an unbroken chain linking present with past.

It must, she imagined, be wonderful to be a part of such a lineage. Family meant so much to her people, and yet here she was without one, with only her father, a man who didn't even like to speak of his dead wife, let alone the extended family they had left behind in the old country. Hiroki Yakamota might have been a brilliant detective, but when it came to raising a girl he had no clue how to provide her with a feminine influence. He had raised her like a son. Maybe it was the obvious absence of maternal guidance in her life that had led some of the community's grandmothers to meddle in Yoshi's affairs. That had been the case on the particular blustery day in April when Yoshi had been introduced to the up-and-coming reporter Marty Honda.

"He's single," wizened Mai Lee whispered before shoving her in his direction, apparently not knowing, or not caring, that Yoshi was a lesbian.

Some of the elders in San Francisco's tight-knit Japanese community viewed lesbianism as a repudiation of their heritage and a naïve embracement of Western values. That or a meaningless activity a girl might engage in while "saving herself" for a proper Japanese husband. In Yoshi's case, it was also taken as proof of Hiroki's poor parenting skills. Without a husband, they reasoned, a woman could not have children. Without children a Japanese woman would have no family, no living proof of her achievements, no future generation to carry on her values—there would be no point to her life at all. After listening to this lecture repeated at each social function that Yoshi came to alone or with her father, she was actually relieved to speak with Marty Honda.

They were both single, but beyond that, they had little in common. While she was impeccably groomed, his black hair was unkempt and his suit wrinkled and reeking of cigarette smoke. She had wondered how he could be in television news looking the way he did. He had explained that when he was busy following a story he hauled his suit around with him in the news van, crumpled in a knapsack until he needed to step in front of the camera.

Yoshi had thought she might find Marty mildly interesting; after all, he was a reporter and she had recently become infatuated with a female journalist. But she had quickly bored of his penchant for name-dropping—the mayor played golf at the same club, he'd interviewed Steve Jobs—and his complete lack of interest in anything she had to say. As soon as his attention was diverted, she had skulked away into the crowd. Since then, she'd heard, he had gotten married, had a kid or two, increased his on-air time, and started losing his hair.

She adjusted the TV volume once more as Marty proclaimed with his customary swagger, "I'm here in the Santa Cruz Mountains, where the body of *Womyn* magazine CEO Rosemary Finney is being loaded into an ambulance. Ms. Finney, a longtime resident of Woodside township, was found dead on a popular Bay Area trail, apparently the victim of a homicide." He paused before asking someone, "Sir, can you tell us what happened?"

A young-sounding man replied, "I was just out on my morning run. Over there in the park."

Yoshi squinted, wishing she could see where he was pointing.

She could not. She could only make out two elongated blobs that she assumed were Marty and the eyewitness. Still squinting, she crept closer to the big TV, trying to catch a glimpse. The blur of dark greens resolved to vague shapes and shadows. She pressed her face against the monitor, feeling the little hairs on her cheek cling to the screen with static. Trees. A lot of trees. Tall trees. Flash of blue and red. Emergency lights.

"Santa Cruz Mountains—Highway 35!" Yoshi pronounced like a *Jeopardy* viewer confidently announcing the answer to television's deaf ears.

"I was on the Huckleberry Trail," the jogger continued.

"Wonderland Park." Yoshi concluded. There was only one Huckleberry Trail on the Peninsula.

"Anyway, it's kind of overgrown. They really should trim it back. That's why I didn't see her until I was almost right on top of her."

"Can you tell us what you saw?" Marty Honda prompted.

Yoshi collected her tea from the kitchen and returned.

"...not moving, and her shoes were gone, which was the damnedest thing. I kept focusing on how she didn't have any shoes, out here in the woods and the trail's muddy from the fog drip. I had to run all the way up here. I couldn't get cell phone service. I had to use that call box."

Yoshi imagined the man was pointing at one of the yellow boxes— strung up on telephone poles—that sprouted every few miles along the thin asphalt ribbon of Highway 35 that wound through the dark woods. If she recalled correctly, there was a call box just across the street from the top of Wonderland Park, near a row of mailboxes, tucked next to one of Midpeninsula Regional Open Space's brown metal gates. What was the name of that open space preserve? Skeggs? No, that wasn't its official name, just what people called it because they would park in the Skeggs Overview and dart across the highway, at a blind curve no less.

Yoshi remembered being afraid to cross the first time she had been there as a kid, when her father took her to see the Tafoni Caves. There was a large map on display in a wood and glass presentation—what had it said? She pictured it in her mind's eye. El Corte de Madera Creek Open Space Preserve. The Spanish name translated to "cut wood," which is what it had once been. Like most of the San Francisco Bay Area, the giant redwoods had long since been clear-cut and even the second growth harvested by the previous owner. Although half a dozen giants still dotted the preserve, most of the redwoods, while tall, bore fairly thin waists. Between them grew a thicket of tan oaks that blocked the sun on the western slopes angling down toward the ocean. The tan oak's bark was once utilized in the process of tanning leather, but loggers considered the species an inferior lumber and declared them unmarketable, which gave the weed trees further rein on the forest.

"Excuse me." Marty Honda sounded peeved about something.

A brusque voice interrupted the reporter's protestations. "No, *excuse me*. I need this gentleman to come with me."

That must be one of the law enforcement officers, Yoshi surmised. It might be a Midpen Ranger, or Woodside PD or maybe a county sheriff. It might even be CHP, the state highway patrol. Yoshi used to see their black-and-whites when visiting parks along the Santa Cruz Mountain's Highway 35, but primarily, she reminded herself, for traffic accidents.

"I'm sorry, Bob, it looks like that's it for now," Honda addressed the Channel Seven's news anchor.

"That was Marty Honda, live from Woodside's Wonderland Park, where the body of Rosemary Finney was discovered this morning. I think we have a photo here—do we? Yes, yes, here it is."

Rosemary Finney. Yoshi could picture the woman's visage clearly, even if she could not see the image filling the screen. Rosemary's long, dark ginger hair and tortoise-shell glasses were unmistakably familiar, and not just from the photo accompanying the monthly letter from the editor that fronted each issue of the lesbian magazine *Womyn*. The lesbian community of San Francisco was surprisingly incestuous, and only a few fresh dyke faces could not connect themselves to any other SF lesbo within six degrees of relationships.

But it was not six degrees that separated Yoshi from *Womyn*'s editor. It was one. *Velvet Erickson.*

CHAPTER TWO

By the time Tucker Shade arrived at the historic Flood Building in San Francisco's financial district, the fog had begun to lift, clinging to the rooftops of the taller buildings. The breeze ruffled her short hair and blew bangs the color of amber ale into her eyes. She brushed them aside, straightened her black and white striped tie, and smoothed her blue oxford shirt. Digging a set of keys from her jeans pocket, Tucker thought again how thankful she was for the dress code—not just at the agency, but in the San Francisco Bay Area altogether. It seemed like the whole city was on permanent casual Friday, especially the women in office work.

Back home in Idaho, she'd have had to wear a skirt to do this job. Tucker shuddered at the recollection. Her tall and gangly body looked ridiculous in feminine attire, or at least she *felt* ridiculous. As if dresses and skirts weren't bad enough on their own, wearing them meant wearing nylons. And no matter how hot nylons looked on a femme, Tucker couldn't bear the stuffed sausage sensation she'd gotten in pantyhose during events of enforced femininity, like weddings and funerals.

She took the ornate elevator to the fourth floor of the historic building, thinking about how nobody put this kind of effort into their work anymore, all cookie-cutter buildings thrown up overnight, without any character to them, inside or out. Although she'd never been out of the country, she'd heard that Europe had the kind of incredible architecture found in this building. She'd also seen it in some neighborhoods in New Orleans, where she'd spent a month before moving to the West Coast.

Exiting the elevator, Tucker strode to the fourth office on the right. For a moment she paused to stare at the company insignia appliquéd onto the door's frosted glass window. A large open eye stared back at her from the center of a gold badge encircled by the words "Blind Eye Detective Agency."

It was a strange name for a private investigation firm, Tucker noted, as she had most mornings since she'd gotten the receptionist job here three months ago. She'd always thought the phrase "turn a blind eye" meant to look the other way, which was sort of the opposite of "to investigate." But her boss, Yoshi Yakamota, insisted the name was appropriate.

"Everyone knows eyewitnesses are unreliable," she'd reminded Tucker last week. "At Blind Eye we use our other senses. We examine cases more thoroughly so we don't miss anything."

Utilizing her budding investigative skills, Tucker had uncovered a few interesting details about the agency and its small staff. Yoshi's father, Hiroki Yakamota, had chosen the tongue-in-cheek name when Yoshi had one blind eye. Now she was legally blind in both.

Mr. Yakamota had been one of the first Japanese American police officers to make detective in San Francisco. Then, years after he left the force and started his PI firm, he had gained notoriety for solving the infamous Bayside Murders. Tucker had the impression that he was the kind of father who never allowed his daughter to feel handicapped by her condition, which might explain why he had apparently pestered Yoshi into helping out at the agency while she was still a teenager.

When he was killed a few years ago, Yoshi took over his managerial role and inherited Blind Eye's other detective, Delbert "Bud" Williams. Tucker thought Bud Williams had probably been a pretty good cop, but she could imagine him being overly aggressive, or a little too delighted by the chance to use his authority. Maybe being shot in the back, landing in a wheelchair, and being forced into a disability retirement had changed him. Maybe he hadn't been this way as an officer.

Bud had stayed with Blind Eye after Mr. Yakamota's death but Tucker had the feeling he wasn't entirely comfortable at the agency. She wondered if he resented working for a woman, even one as bright as Yoshi, and if he was just hanging around until he could get his own agency off the ground. She was sure that he would never admit it, but she thought Yoshi was the only agency head that would let him work in the field, being in a wheelchair and all.

Tucker contemplated her own role as she let herself into the office. She screened calls, processed mail, kept the filing system organized, and did some preliminary research on cases. Although she hoped to be more, in her estimation she was barely part of the team at all. She flicked on the light switch, dropped her knapsack next to the metal desk, and hung her oversized men's jacket on the coat tree tucked in the corner. So her computer and the copy machine could have time to wake before she needed them, she turned them on immediately. A combined laser printer, scanner, and fax machine shared the cupboard top with the copier, and Tucker collected several faxed pages from the printer tray.

Retrieving an archaic Dictaphone from the cabinet beneath the office machines, she took it and the two-page fax addressed to Yoshi and set them both on her own desk. Then she continued her morning routine, filling the glass carafe with water from the small sink and pouring it into the coffeemaker. Although she would make coffee later for potential visitors, Tucker began each day by brewing a pot of tea for herself and Yoshi. Their electric kettle had just died, and she hoped the hardware store would call soon about the new one she'd ordered. Yoshi had been polite about the improvised tea-making yesterday, but Tucker didn't want to try her patience.

While the water was gurgling its way through the contraption, she sat on her wheeled office chair that was built like a wasp with two separated cushions connected by a metal backbone. After clearing the answering machine, she plugged in the Dictaphone and began reading aloud from the latest fax.

"Office of Marin County Coroner. Autopsy performed five, twenty-four, o-six, eight thirty a.m. by Lori Singh—that's L-o-r-i S-i-n-g-h—MD. Assistant Ann Marie Sherwood. Summary report autopsy for Kristal Tarnoff." Tucker spelled out the full name and continued: "Coroner case number 2006 dash 114."

Not nearly as squeamish as some girls, Tucker didn't mind reading the autopsy reports for Yoshi's audio research files. The reports, which came in from all the Bay Area counties, utilized similar formats and provided the standard information like height and weight of the victim and whether that was consistent with the norm for their age, any visible ligature marks, lab results that included toxicology and trace evidence, and a rundown of the condition of each major body system: skeletal, gastrointestinal, and central nervous systems. They concluded with a final opinion that offered estimated time of death, a.k.a. TOD, and cause of death. In Kristal Tarnoff's case, TOD was between 7:30 and 9:30 the night before the medical exam, and cause of death was asphyxia due to ligature strangulation.

When she'd finished, Tucker took the cassette into Yoshi's office and set it in a rich chocolate leather, velvet-inlaid tray on the large dark cherry desk. Carefully arranged on the desktop were three low profile brunette platters, a clean black phone, and a slim iMac computer. The wood's high-gloss finish was so shiny Tucker could see her features reflected there. Her strong nose, thin lips, high forehead, cool blue eyes, and light hair exhibited her Nordic heritage. She wasn't yet fond of her face, but she had grown accustomed to it.

With a quick parting glance around the office to convince herself that she hadn't disturbed anything in Yoshi's private retreat, she returned to her own desk and began the tedious task of deleting penis enlargement and diet pill ads from her e-mail. She was still working her way through the in-box when she heard a knob turning.

Yoshi, she thought, and glanced up to see a shadowy figure behind the frosted glass of the office door. The soft scent of apple, grapefruit, white amber, and sandalwood, which was Yoshi's signature perfume, drifted on the air. Tucker smiled and nervously ran her fingers through her hair as the well-dressed Japanese American woman paused inside the door and folded a telescoping white cane, which she then hung on the coat rack. Silky smooth brown loafers swaddled her delicate feet and she wore a fitted pantsuit.

Yoshi didn't remove her toffee-colored jacket, but Tucker could see that underneath was an ivory cap-sleeve blouse. A few months ago she wouldn't have even known what a cap sleeve *was*, but Velvet Erickson had been schooling her in fashion and entertainment—among other things.

Tucker had been raised in a world without fashion, where one wore clothing not for style or comfort, but functionality. Even her mother's wardrobe consisted primarily of worn jeans, plaid flannel shirts, and hiking boots. Nobody in her small farming community would've recognized couture clothing if it bit them on the ass. Yoshi, on the other hand, might not see the photos in fashion magazines any longer, but obviously she knew enough about designers or fabrics to stay in style. Or maybe she had one of those personal shoppers.

"Good morning, Yoshi," Tucker said.

Not turning toward her, Yoshi nodded slightly, acknowledging the greeting. "Any messages?" She crossed the small reception cube on her way to the inner office.

"Just Mr. Snodgrass asking about the photos."

Yoshi paused at the office door with her name etched on the fogged glass. "Nothing from Velvet?"

"Uh, no." Tucker said, suddenly sheepish. She worried about the day Yoshi would find out that she was dating her best friend, Velvet. Tucker wondered whether she was more afraid that Yoshi would be disappointed, or that she might not give a hoot.

"Put her through immediately."

"Of course." Tucker wished Yoshi would turn toward her, just once. But she stepped inside her office and shut the door behind her without looking back.

Yoshi kept her door closed a lot. Velvet had offered Tucker a whispered explanation once, when she was visiting. Yoshi was new to this being blind thing. That is to say, she'd been losing her sight for a long time, but it was only recently that it had gotten this bad. She was still learning blind tricks, like looking up when someone spoke. Even though she couldn't see, the speaker would want to see her eyes when they talked, otherwise they'd feel ignored. Like Tucker did.

Maybe Velvet was right; maybe Yoshi didn't look at Tucker because of the degenerative disease attacking her optic nerve. It had robbed her eyes of both sight and pigment, and left her with striking pale blue irises. Yoshi's eyes reminded Tucker of those hot pools in Yellowstone National Park that looked so inviting but which the park rangers warned were deadly and could instantly scald any person or animal that fell in. She wouldn't mind drowning in Yoshi's waters, Tucker mused, then she looked around nervously as if, were Yoshi close enough, she might read her mind.

Despite Velvet's reassurances, Tucker still wondered if Yoshi *was* avoiding eye contact with her deliberately. Even though she was losing her sight, Yoshi might fear that if Tucker gazed into her eyes, she'd be transfixed. If that happened, neither of them would be able to look away. Their feelings for each other would spill over and they'd fall into each other's arms, and…well, obviously, Yoshi was too much of a professional to allow that kind of thing to happen with her receptionist. Which was why Tucker was going to become a detective.

She'd already started taking night classes at the Sam Brown School, a San Francisco institution that trained private investigators, and when she was done she would become a PI herself. Then she'd be Yoshi's colleague, not her subordinate. Of course, Tucker was only ten hours into the intensive 212-hour Investigative Career Program, and after completing the required courses, she would still need to accumulate 6,000 hours working with a licensed investigator before she could qualify for a license of her own. That was 6,000 hours. 150 weeks. 38 months. Two and a half years. Three years from now, Tucker figured, she and Yoshi could finally give in to their attraction for each other.

Unless, Tucker worried again, unless she had already blown any chance that Yoshi could ever think of her *that* way.

❖

Slumped down behind the wheel of his baby blue 1960 Chevy Impala, barely visible over the dash to any passersby, Delbert "Bud" Williams had his eyes trained on the front door of the Enchanted Towers. A luxury apartment building catering to upscale young couples, the Towers had recently opened in the south of Market area of downtown San Francisco. Bud had been here two hours waiting for his mark, Rebecca Brown, to leave the privacy of her enchanted apartment and enter his less-than-charmed world.

Brown's husband, sure that his wife was sabotaging the success of their fertility efforts, had hired Blind Eye to shadow her. In his desire to catch the missus in the act, he'd also wired his apartment with surveillance cameras that downloaded to his laptop in a 24/7 live feed. To monitor Rebecca's activities outside of that love nest, Bud was tailing her.

He had been on this detail for three days and he was bored to tears. His jeans were slung low under his recently cultivated beer belly, and his navy blue T-shirt was stained with spill-back from the many coffees he'd imbibed to stay awake. A dress shirt and suit jacket folded on the backseat provided him with professional attire that he could exchange for his stakeout clothes in an instant. Yoshi demanded that he be able to look presentable at any given moment, regardless of how long he'd been on surveillance.

Not that he was tempted to do so. He *was* tempted to ball the fresh garments up into a pillow and take a nap. Despite her relatively hip zip code, Rebecca Brown seemed to lead the monotonous life of a suburban housewife, with regular trips to the grocery, hair salon, and trendy boutiques. Her secrets were even more boring than most: she pored over the gossip tabloids but threw them away before going home; instead of shopping at the street level Whole Foods she took a cab to Grocery Outlet; and when she met a mother with child she made cooing noises and her eyes glistened with tears. Bud had photos of the entire spectacle. It made him nauseous.

The bench seat next to him was buried under a layer of trash. Wadded candy wrappers and crumpled In-N-Out Burger bags mingled with newspapers, empty film boxes, and his case notes. His 8 megapixel 15x zoom Samsung Pro815 shared seat space with a padded carrier cushioning his three thousand dollar, top of the line, old-school Nikon F6 SLR 35 millimeter plus 50mm, 70-150 and 70-210mm zoom lenses. In the backseat, his folded wheelchair leaned against his headrest. Rather than give up his favorite vehicle, he'd used his insurance settlement to upgrade the Impala with special controls that allowed him to operate gas and brake pedals despite his useless legs. At the same time, they refitted his once-original classic with a bench seat, headrests, and seat belts.

Bud reflexively stroked his cheeks, relishing the roughness of the stubble that was part of his general f-you to Yoshi Yakamota's restrictive grooming standards. She preferred him to be clean-shaven, and had said as much more than once. But he wasn't going to let some broad tell him what to do, especially when she wasn't even his wife—back when he *was* married.

Bud looked at the gold retirement watch cinched around his wrist. It hardly seemed worth the bullet he'd paid for it. 8:35 a.m. He'd seen Mr. Jason Brown roll out at 8:15 in his silver BMW and he still had another twenty minutes before the wife exited the front door to slide into a prearranged taxi. God, this gig was dull. It was so mind-numbingly boring that he'd actually *prefer* watching *Brokeback Mountain* on a ten-story IMAX screen while sitting next to some guy beating his stiffy. Okay, maybe not. But this was still pretty fucking dull.

CHAPTER THREE

"Good morning, Blind Eye Detective Agency, how may our senses be of service?"

"Good morning, Tucker." The smooth voice was unmistakable.

"Oh, hi, Velvet. Yoshi's been waiting for your call."

"Yoshi?" Velvet sounded hurt, but still managed to purr her next query. "What about you, *mon cheri*? Don't you miss me?"

Tucker felt the heat rush to two specific points of her body. One was her cheek, the other was much lower. She squirmed. "I-I'm sorry. I just assumed...of course I'm happy. I—"

Velvet chuckled. "I'm playing with you, Tuck."

"Oh." Lord, she felt so stupid.

"Do you know what it's about? Yoshi sounded so concerned on her message."

"Uh, no. She just got in. I mean, we haven't talked. I don't know."

"Okay, okay. Pass me through. And Tucker?"

"Yes?"

"Can you get away for a quick lunch? Sushi?"

Tucker blushed again at the sexual innuendo. She lowered her voice. "I can't. Not during work. Tonight?"

"You have my number. Call me," Velvet suggested.

"Right, of course. Hold on. I'll see if Yoshi's available." Tucker patched Velvet through to Yoshi even though she'd have preferred to chat with the femme herself.

She wondered why Yoshi's response was curt. Was her boss mad at her? There was no mention of please, or thank you. Yoshi could come across cold sometimes, but she was *always* polite. Something must really be wrong.

After Tucker hung up, she could hear low murmuring from Yoshi's office but couldn't make out what was being said and it was rude to eavesdrop, anyway. She went back to decoding Bud's physician-scrawl-style notes so she could type them into the computer to be translated into printed Braille for Yoshi.

The cherry flame of Yoshi's extension stayed lit for a very long time before her disembodied voice crackled over on the intercom, still abnormally brusque. "Get Bud in here right away."

"He's on assignment," Tucker reminded her tentatively.

"This is more important. It is *essential* that he come back here. No, scratch that. Ask him if he has an in with the Woodside Police or San Mateo County Sheriff. Have him get on that immediately. It is essential that we ascertain all we can in regard to Rosemary Finney's murder."

Wow. Murder. They hadn't had a case like that at Blind Eye while Tucker had been there; it was mostly just skip traces and cheating husbands.

"Please drop what you are doing as well," Yoshi continued. "I would appreciate your completing a background on the victim. Rosemary Finney was the publisher of *Womyn* magazine."

"Was she the one they found in the hills this morning?" Tucker asked.

"Yes," Yoshi confirmed.

"Who's our client?"

Yoshi didn't answer immediately, which was odd. She always provided Tucker with the details to complete the client information paperwork. Was it Velvet? Tucker instantly dismissed the idea. Just because Velvet had been on the phone directly preceding Yoshi's instructions didn't mean anything. Velvet couldn't be involved with a murder. Could she?

"For now, let us just say we are looking into it for a friend." Yoshi gave a rare political answer.

Tucker dialed Bud's cell, holding the phone between her shoulder and ear so she could start an Internet search on Rosemary Finney.

The results popped up and one caught her eye immediately: a photo of Rosemary Finney looking overly intimate with a buxom brunette. Tucker didn't have to read the fine print to identify the other woman. It was Velvet. Her Velvet.

❖

When the factory-installed ring tone notified Bud that he had a call, he shuffled through the papers on the bench seat of the Impala feeling for something of weight and substance. All the while, he kept his eyes trained on the apartment building's front door. He hadn't sat out here for two hours only to miss his quarry because some moron had rung the wrong cell phone number or the kid at the office needed her hand held to get some paperwork done.

The phone rang three times before he found it and punched the answer button with his thumb. As the pad of his thumb spilled over onto several other buttons, he wondered how kids these days did all that texting. Maybe it was a genetic thing, some evolutionary change that gave today's teenagers more flexible thumbs.

Holding the small black box awkwardly between his ear and his mouth, wishing he could stretch it until it cradled his neck the way a landline receiver did—the way a phone was *supposed* to fit—he barked, "What?"

"Good morning, Bud," the office girl responded pleasantly.

"Yeah," he grunted. "What's up?"

"Yoshi wanted to know if you have any contacts down in Woodside or San Mateo County."

"Which one?"

"Both. I mean either."

She was the type that flustered easily. It made Bud want to toy with her. There was something annoyingly naïve about the kid. It made him want to crush her spirit, for her own good. The world wasn't a nice place; it chewed up the innocent and spit them out before breakfast. Life sucked and then you died, and that girl needed her eyes opened before something really dangerous came along.

"Yeah. I got guys I could talk to. What's up?"

"We've got a new case. The Rosemary Finney murder."

"Is that the stiff they pulled out of the woods this morning?" Bud asked.

"Yes. Yoshi wants you to go on a fishing expedition, find out what evidence they've got, what they think happened, any witnesses and suspects, that kind of thing."

"And I'm just supposed to ditch this?" For chrissake, the bitch he was tailing would be leaving the building in five minutes.

"Sorry, Bud. Yoshi said to drop everything."

"Whoa, that must mean good money. Who's our client?"

"She wouldn't tell me."

"She wouldn't tell you? *Fuck*."

"What?"

"Oh, right, excuse my French," Bud apologized.

"No, why do you say that? Does that mean something bad?"

"Who was in her office this morning? Or who called?"

"Just Velvet—you know, from the paper."

Bud grew tumescent at the mention of Velvet. *Back in the day*, he thought, *I could've called her a sex kitten or a minx and not lose my job.* He cleared his throat. "Yeah, that's not good. See it means either there's some *story* there and Velvet is hoping for a Pulitzer or she's a suspect. Either way we're not getting paid shit."

Predictably, Tucker got all defensive on behalf of their boss. It was so obvious the girl had a crush on Yoshi, and equally apparent she wasn't in the league of the Japanese princess. "I'm sure there's—"

"Yeah, I know. Whatever. I'm going. Does her majesty need me to drop by the office? No? Good. I'll head south and give her a buzz later."

Bud hung up before he heard a goodbye.

❖

When Tucker put down the receiver and actually focused on the screen before her, she figured out two things. One was that she'd somehow entered her search in the images file, and the other was that although the Internet might have the memory of an elephant, it also had a way of flattening time by offering up current and out-of-date references on the same page. The photograph of Rosemary with her arm around Velvet was from 1994, back when the two worked together. The picture had been published in *Womyn*'s ten-year anniversary issue and made it online in a piece about *Womyn*'s early history.

Tucker clicked back to the search engine and renewed her hunt. After the requisite "Books by Rosemary Finney" Amazon ads, the first twelve mentions Google spat out for Rosemary Finney were for a singer fronting the New Zealand alt-rock band Suddenly Spring. The Rosemary Finney that Tucker was looking for apparently didn't have a personal Web site, at least not one that came up on the first few pages of results.

There were articles authored by Finney and numerous interviews about her publishing company and its popular lesbian magazine *Womyn*.

Tucker clicked over to Womynmag.com. Under the tagline "a feminist review of lesbian culture" were images of the latest cover, featuring the cast of the *Isle of Lesbos*, the hot lesbian cable show. NOT JUST PLAYING GAY, screamed a headline. Below, smaller text teased, "The *Lesbos* Cast Comes Out," and provided a link to the story. Not having a television of her own, Tucker had only seen a couple of episodes of the nighttime soap critics called a "lesbian *Sex in the City*," but she did read all the reviews and insider gossip about the show mentioned in Velvet's well-worn copy of *Entertainment Weekly*. Most of *Lesbos* was filmed on a soundstage in Hollywood, but the producers increased authenticity by shooting scenes in San Francisco's lesbian neighborhoods of Bernal Heights and Noe Valley, and hotspots like the Lexington Club. Various high-profile local lesbians had also appeared as extras.

Tucker wondered whether Rosemary, being the well-known face of a San Francisco–based lesbian magazine, had ever been on *Isle of Lesbos*. There were several pages of the *Womyn* site dedicated to *Lesbos* facts and trivia. Tucker skimmed these for any mention of *Womyn* staff members or even the magazine itself showing up on set, but she found nothing. Not having a San Francisco lesbian publication mentioned on a lesbian show set in the city seemed odd to Tucker and she wondered if it was some kind of a snub by the show's producers. She'd have to ask Velvet, who was much more knowledgeable than she about the inner workings of Hollywood.

As she read *Womyn*'s most recent article about *Lesbos*, Tucker found references to three supposedly straight actresses who the article described as closeted lesbians.

That *was* big news.

Not only were the young actresses of *Lesbos* culled from the hot up-and-coming Hollywood leading ladies but Jennifer Garcia, who played a sultry lesbian rock star, had recently announced her engagement to Tinseltown heartthrob Keith Ridger, about whom there'd been so many gay rumors that the tabloids clung to the story like drowning rats to a log. Tucker located the byline and found Rosemary Finney listed as the author. The rest of the article was a feminist diatribe about the negative political and psychological ramifications of straight actresses portraying lesbians. Especially actresses who were, Finney argued, closeted lesbians playing straight women playing lesbians.

Tucker jumped in her seat at a soft noise behind her. "Oh, Yoshi, you scared me. I didn't hear you come in."

Yoshi did not apologize—having nothing to apologize for. Perchance her own actions would illustrate that it was not essential for women to act contrite.

"I'm sorry," Tucker apologized.

Okay. Perhaps not. "Have you found anything interesting?" She stared over Tucker's left shoulder at the computer screen. She couldn't really see it, but some habits die hard.

"Oh, wow. How'd you know I'm surfing the Web?" Tucker asked.

"I can hear the computer on, and the way you are sitting indicates that you are gazing at the screen, although I do not hear you typing. You are simply shifting the mouse."

"Oh, right," Tucker acknowledged. "That makes sense. So, mostly I've just been making a list of people to follow up with. You know, I was thinking?"

She ended the sentence with a lilt in her voice, as though she was asking a question. It was something she frequently did, though more so when she first joined the Blind Eye team. Yoshi wondered if Tucker was aware that the consequence of this particular speech pattern was that Tucker appeared hesitant and unsure of herself. "Yes?" she prompted.

"You know that before I started working here I spent a month down in New Orleans helping with Katrina recovery efforts, right? Well, one of the people I helped when I was down there was this seventy-year-old grandmother, Miss Latisha, who lived in the Ninth Ward."

Yoshi noticed lately that when she drew within close proximity to Tucker, the younger woman became physiologically nervous, her breathing increased. Not so much that it would be obvious to someone else, but Yoshi, concentrating on sounds the way she had since losing her sight, heard Tucker's breath catch as though it were a record skipping once and shifting to a elevated RPM. If she remained there for a prolonged interval, she could smell the sweet musky odor of perspiration forming in the hollow of Tucker's underarms. Was it a good or bad thing that she elicited such a response?

"Anyway," Tucker continued, "one of her granddaughters, AJ, moved out here after Katrina. She's a police officer. You know, one of those that stayed through the hurricane and tried to help everyone but lost her home and came out here to work so she could send money back to help her family. AJ, she's one of the reasons I moved to the Bay Area. See, I used to read her letters to Miss Latisha—she's got cataracts, you know, and has trouble reading—and AJ wrote such great things about the area."

Tucker had a just-off-the-farm ingenuousness, which made sense, given that she had only recently relocated here and originated from Idaho or Utah or another Midwestern state—Western, Yoshi reminded herself; Tucker was particularly indignant about being referred to as a Midwesterner.

"*Mid*west?" Tucker had exclaimed once. "It's *one* state over from California! Just because it isn't on the coast doesn't mean it's not still the West!"

Yoshi had nodded conciliatorily rather than voicing the snippy response that darted into her head: "Japan is just west of here, but you do not hear me becoming distraught and correcting everyone who signify it as the Far East, do you?" Directional locations were so relative.

Tucker's gullibility concerned Yoshi, but the girl's innocence had its charm. At the same time, Tucker's easygoing demeanor sometimes seemed to be a false front obscuring some hidden pain, and if you listened intently or, Yoshi imagined, gazed deep into her—blue? green?—eyes, you would find a wounded puppy there, quivering in fear, desperate for a tender caress but flinching at any outstretched hand.

"One of Miss Latisha's relatives is renting me that room over in Oakland."

Yoshi did not find all of Tucker's country girl characteristics endearing. How long would it take her to get to the point? She meandered through stories like someone on a Sunday drive turning randomly down streets to view Christmas lights. For Yoshi, time was a valuable commodity not to be squandered.

"Tucker," she interrupted. "The point?"

"Oh, gosh, I'm sorry, Yoshi. So anyway, AJ? I think she's working for Palo Alto PD now—that's down on the Peninsula, right? Is that in the same area as where this murder happened?"

"Yes, actually, it is. Can you call her and establish whether she is acquainted with Woodside officers?"

"Yeah, that's the thing. I have her number, but it's at home. Maybe I could go out over lunch or something."

"Certainly, let us have you do that. In the meantime, tell me more about your list of POIs." Yoshi used the acronym for person of interest.

She was starting to weave insider police jargon into her conversations with Tucker. It was time for the PI wannabe to step up her game.

"Oh, sorry. Did you know Rosemary just *outed* Jennifer Garcia?"

"Who?" Yoshi asked.

"Jennifer Garcia. She's on *Isle of Lesbos*."

"I don't subscribe to HBO."

"It's Showtime, actually," Tucker corrected, before rushing on. Maybe she had seen the impatience on Yoshi's features. "Anyway, she's a big television star. Latina. She used to go out with that basketball player. Uh, what was his name? Oh, and she's engaged to Keith Ridger now."

"Really?" Much to her über-hip friend Velvet's dismay, Yoshi did not keep up with Hollywood's hot list, but you'd have to live in a cave not to know who Keith Ridger was. He'd been *People* magazine's Sexiest Man just a year ago, and his antics spawned a cottage industry of tabloid speculation, particularly about his sexuality.

"They are engaged? But, I thought he was—"

"Gay? No." The blurry dark shape that was Tucker's head moved from side to side.

"According to whom?" Yoshi snorted.

"Keith. He says those are just rumors." Tucker sounded like she believed him. Yoshi wondered if the younger woman had never had her trust broken. What would it be like to deem everyone truthful and without hidden agendas?

"Certainly, if his fiancée is a lesbian, that damages his case, does it not?"

"Probably. So, I guess that makes him a suspect too, since that gives him motive." The click of computer keys told Yoshi that Tucker was adding Keith Ridger to her list.

"Not a suspect," Yoshi corrected. Tucker hadn't absorbed Yoshi's private eye lingo. She reined in her frustration; after all, Tucker had only been with Blind Eye a few months. "Remember that we consider them people of interest—POIs—until we have had the opportunity to rule them in or out."

"Oh, right, sorry. And I've got Jennifer Garcia down, since this could really damage her career, too."

"Did you not just say that she portrays a lesbian on the *Isle of Lesbos*?"

"Yeah, so maybe it doesn't matter. But then if she's not in the closet, why would she be engaged? I don't know, do you think it still hurts a big actress's career if she comes out?"

Yoshi was not convinced that Jennifer Garcia was a "big" actress, now that she had finally associated the name with a face. She certainly had not been nominated for an Academy Award—although she had supporting roles in a few successful films, as far as Yoshi could recall. Obviously Garcia's publicist was paid to ensure gullible youngsters such as Tucker were wildly impressed. Image was more important than substance these days, and not merely in show business. She found herself a little disappointed that Tucker was so readily sold on appearances. If she ever hoped to become a PI she would need to develop skepticism and a desire to probe beyond the obvious.

In a neutral tone, Yoshi said, "It is difficult to determine what effect coming out might have on a career. Continue your effort and ensure that you track down contact information for the people on your list. Also, include the staff and former employees of *Womyn*."

"Right, that makes sense, 'cause she worked there," Tucker affirmed.

"She was the employer," Yoshi amended. "And not a well-liked one, from what I understand."

"Oh?"

Yoshi did not answer the question inherent in the response. She was reflecting on the other controlling interest at *Womyn* magazine, Rosemary's partner Karen Friars. With Rosemary out of the picture, Karen would be the sole surviving owner of the lesbian publication. Yoshi was quite interested in speaking with the widowed publisher who stood so much to gain from Rosemary's demise. In addition to the magazine itself, Yoshi understood that Rosemary had bequeathed her substantial fortune to Ms. Friars. Yes, Karen Friars was absolutely a POI.

CHAPTER FOUR

Protected by her cubicle from the noisy news floor of the *San Francisco Chronicle*, Velvet Erickson slumped against her desk with her head in her hands wondering what the hell she was going to do. Her black pinstripe skirt was riding high, shorter than usual, above her black stockings and patent black pumps. The collar on her tight white blouse was rumpled at the edges, a rare less-than-perfect day for Velvet, and her fitted pinstripe jacket, which had lost a button while she was out in the field, was now crumpled up in the corner.

In front of her, the desktop was piled high with haphazardly stacked spiral notepads, dozens of scrawled-upon Post-it notes, and single sheets of paper that constituted her research on the dozen articles she was currently juggling. On top of all of it lay a tattered copy of a Bay Area Career Women newsletter, open to a page of attorneys.

Velvet was no longer high from her early morning escapade. Now it was all crashing down on her. The realization that she was in big trouble had washed away her glee at giving Rosemary her comeuppance. She was wondering who might have seen her this morning at Wonderland Park. Were the cops ripping through her Bernal Heights home right now, armed with a hastily written search warrant? During their call, Yoshi had advised her to get a lawyer. Velvet fretted that would just make her look guiltier. She didn't even know if the cops suspected her, so wasn't it premature to be hiring a lawyer? Yoshi had been insistent, especially after Velvet admitted that she'd had a public row with Rosemary at the Liberty Café just two days ago, a confrontation that could make her look bad.

The Liberty was a small upscale eatery in the Bernal Heights district of San Francisco. Standing on the Cortland Avenue sidewalk, in the darkening fall evening, Velvet had spotted her old friend, and business associate, Marion Serif through the restaurant window. Marion was waiting for her at one of the petite square tables near the back of the narrow dining room. Velvet waved but didn't get her attention, so she squeezed past the line into the faintly French-feeling bistro, with its hardwood floors, lemon-colored walls, and adorable white wainscoting.

As usual, the restaurant was fairly packed, even early on that Tuesday evening. Velvet had been eating there since the place opened twelve years earlier; she and Rosemary Finney and their soon-to-be exes at the time had one of the first tables. The city's foodies and the denizens of Bernal Heights kept Liberty a must-visit eatery, which infuriated Velvet since the posh spot still didn't take reservations. She pointed out Marion to the maître d' and then pushed her way down a tight corridor that was narrowed by guests spilling from their too-small seats.

The venue wasn't *her* choice. She and Marion met for dinner every month and the choice of eatery alternated between them. Velvet never picked the Liberty, even though it was in *her* neighborhood and they did make the city's best chicken potpie. Sure, Velvet enjoyed the food—she considered herself a well-schooled connoisseur of good eats, after all—but she also enjoyed feeling full when she'd finished a $23 entrée. Paying that much for a petite, if delectable, meal like tuna confit with currants, pine nuts, and saffron-soaked onions always made her feel embarrassed about grabbing a Big Mac on the way home to quiet her unsatiated hunger.

So the truth was, Velvet had arrived late because she'd already eaten. Tonight she'd stopped down the street at Zante's and quickly gobbled down a slice of Indian pizza—an only-in-SF specialty made of naan bread crust, spicy spinach sauce with tandoori chicken, and cauliflower. Marion would have never approved.

"Sorry I'm late," she said as she sat down and picked up the menu. "What are you having?"

"Savory vegan polenta with asparagus flan and field greens," Marion said, ever the food snob. Velvet shivered at the words "asparagus flan."

"Ah, cornmeal mush," she joked, "food of my people."

At least that's what she suspected: that her people, her ancestors, ate cornmeal mush. Her lily-white Scandinavian last name hid the truth of her multicultural roots. Velvet was adopted. As far as her parents were told, she was some mix of Native American and Hispanic peoples. Beyond that, who knew? She had the kind of features that coded her as ethnic, but the subcategorization was anyone's guess. She'd been taken for Italian, Greek, Palestinian, Spanish, Latin American, and a member of nearly every Native American tribe. And it wasn't just WASPs who wanted to tag her with an ethnicity. Ethnic people were always claiming her as one of their own. It was a compliment that others saw her as one of them, a member of whatever tribe they hailed from. Velvet felt it helped make her a better writer, the right person to chronicle the lives of San Francisco's diverse populace.

She peeked at Marion over the menu and thought again how she was glad not to be the other woman. As much as she envied the sense of ritual and belonging Jewish dykes shared, at this one moment she was relieved to be religiously ambiguous—especially when it came to her unlimited food choices. She didn't envy Marion's dietary restrictions, which were compounded by her allergy to all things dairy. One time, after they'd shared a vegan ice cream sundae at this lesbo-hipster ice cream shop called Maggie Mudds, Marion had to go to the hospital and have her stomach pumped because their server accidentally used the same scoop on the vegan ice cream that he'd used for the regular kind. What a terrible waste, Velvet thought to herself as she decided on lemongrass-skewered Kobe beef and new potatoes.

She set down the menu. The athletic Marion, always a stunning butch, was snappily dressed in her typical designer wear, in this case a black pantsuit in a richly textured fabric that showcased attractive Mediterranean features framed by her short but well-groomed dark hair. Velvet decided the suit was Armani. She prided herself on keeping up with the latest fashion and recognizing by sight the work of top designers. Her education predated *Sex in the City*, but her nearly slavish devotion to the cable show further refined her tastes. Like Marion, she couldn't afford to fill her entire wardrobe with the latest couture, but over the years she'd collected prime basics and peppered in essential accessories like a few pairs of Manolo Blahnik shoes.

Tonight Velvet wore a black A-line skirt with a complementing black and white corset top accented by billowy sleeves. She felt like Johnny Depp from *Pirates of the Caribbean* every time she wore it. There really was nothing better than a film based on her favorite

Disneyland ride. At least before politically correct management had neutered the ride by ruthlessly discarding the lecherous drunkards and bawdy wenches.

"How's the magazine business?" Velvet asked. Marion published *Bend*, the first national lesbian publication, and primary rival of Rosemary Finney's *Womyn*.

"As interesting as usual. Are you sure you don't miss it?"

Velvet took a drink from her triple extra-dirty martini, a very simple drink she too often had to explain to cocktail servers, and swirled it around in her mouth. The truth was, she did miss the pace of magazine publishing. She missed writing for lesbian audiences, and she missed the camaraderie of an all-woman staff. She set her glass down and looked Marion in the eye with a smirk.

"You mean the low pay, the politics, the constant battle to get celebrities to talk with you? No."

Marion smiled and shrugged. "Well, there *is* that. But no, I meant the entertainment part. I know you're doing great work now. I saw you were nominated for another award. Something about sex slaves, wasn't it?"

Velvet nodded. "Yeah. I did an investigative piece about this creep landlord in Freemont who was shipping women in from India."

"Sure, money matters, but don't you ever wish you were back critiquing movies and interviewing Oscar winners?" She held Velvet's gaze, daring her to lie.

"Okay," Velvet admitted. "God knows I love pop culture. It's pathetic really. You *know* I still watch practically every movie that comes out or you wouldn't keep asking me to write a review column."

"You can't blame me for trying."

Their meals arrived, models of minimalism. Velvet pointed at her plate. "A graphic designer's wet dream. Lots of white space."

Marion laughed. She picked up her fork and knife and attacked the small square of cornmeal. "How's that other piece going?" she asked without looking up.

Velvet knew exactly what Marion was speaking of. She finished chewing a flavorful bite of Kobe beef and replied, "It's coming along, although not as fast as we'd like it to."

"Did you see the latest issue of *Womyn*?"

Velvet shook her head and applied her attention to her martini. She delicately bit half the blue-cheese-stuffed olive off the skewer and swirled the other half in the vodka. Small pieces of blue cheese crumbled into the liquid.

Something pressed against Velvet's leg. Often equating the effects of alcohol with ensuing sexual gratification, her first thought was that Marion's hand was caressing her knee. She'd promised herself to keep their relationship limited to business, but her limb quivered under the light touch.

She looked down at her lap, expecting to glimpse Marion's neatly manicured fingers climbing up her thigh. Instead, she discovered a magazine that Marion had judiciously slipped there. She smiled at her own disappointment, which she experienced physically, like a flower opening to the sun only to shrivel back into itself at a sudden eclipse.

Business, she thought, getting back on track. She inched the magazine closer for inspection. It was the latest issue of *Womyn*, with a headline blaring NOT JUST PLAYING GAY: THE *LESBOS* CAST COMES OUT. She looked back up at Marion and raised her eyebrows.

Marion nodded. "They've stolen our cover. Again."

Velvet sighed and bit her lower lip. "You had this?"

"We had the quote from an interview we did with an actress who had a walk on part. She said most of the women on the show were lesbians in real life. We have it on tape but we could never get confirmation from the studio. I mean, it was more than that actually. The executives vehemently denied it. Our source was reliable, but we felt without confirmation…"

"Right." Velvet nodded. Without confirmation, saying someone was gay could get a publisher sued, an actress fired, and unfortunately a whole lot of people in hot water. Even for actors and actresses willing to play gay on film, the stigma of actually *being* queer could still ruin their career. Velvet was surprised that *Womyn* had been willing to risk the fallout, even for the great newsstand sales the story would generate.

"Oh fuck," Marion wheezed, and the color drained from her attractive face.

Velvet whipped her head around to the door where Marion was staring and found Karen Friars entering Liberty with her partner Rosemary Finney, the bitch herself.

"Jesus." Velvet flipped back so fast she nearly fell over. She shoved the magazine under her generous ass and hastily drained the last half of her martini.

"I can't believe *they*'re here." Marion hid her face behind the dessert menu and lowered her voice to a whisper. "I didn't even have a chance to tell you. They're *suing* me."

"What?" Velvet gasped, and the sharp inhalation of air propelled the final piece of blue-cheese olive into her windpipe, choking her. A few solid coughs dislodged it before her tablemate had to resort to the Heimlich maneuver.

Velvet shot a look of silent thanks to a man who was eyeing her apprehensively. He was balanced on the edge of his chair as if eager to jump and wrap his arms below her ample breasts, all in the name of saving her life. "I'm fine," she mouthed and smiled. As a long-haired, big-breasted, round-assed femme, she frequently felt the object of men's openly sexual stares. Velvet sighed. If only butches would notice as often. Instead many of *them* seemed, at first glance, to mistake her for a hetero.

"Can you believe that?" Marion whispered. "They've stolen our last three cover stories. And they have the *nerve* to claim I'm putting them out of business?"

"Wait? Out of business?" Velvet was stunned. "Are you saying *Womyn*'s actually going out of business?"

"I know. I'm as surprised as you. I had no idea they're even having difficulty, but I get served with this lawsuit the other day claiming my 'immoral and illegal business practices' are forcing them to shut down and declare bankruptcy, and therefore I should be found personally liable for three million dollars."

"Three million." Velvet whistled. She leaned forward in her chair until she practically met Marion in the middle of the table. "Are they crazy? Immor—"

"You cunts!" A shrill voice interrupted their mumblings.

Velvet jumped back in her chair.

Rosemary Finney stood next to their table, her hands clenched at her sides, her navy blue pantsuit taut across her chest. Behind the rims of her vintage glasses, her wide sea green eyes bored holes into Velvet, and her shoulder-length crimped hair, as though loosened from its restraints by anger, puffed out wildly around a face splotched purple and red.

Velvet's immediate reaction was one of fear. She found herself sliding away from her former friend, lover, and business partner and pressing against Liberty's cool cinder-block wall, hoping it would open up and swallow her whole. She'd never known Rosemary to be violent, but at that moment she had no doubt about the possibility.

Rosemary Finney was one of those kids born suckling a diamond-encrusted pacifier. She grew up in Woodside, a tony town where Jaguars and Hummers lined driveways and a proliferation of mall-like mansions cut into the wooded hills, causing environmentalists instant aneurysms. The elder of two girls, Rosemary had been shipped off to private boarding school in Switzerland and then to Yale where she earned ineffectual degrees in philosophy and women's studies. By the time Velvet met her thirteen years ago, she was a poor little rich girl in crisis, slumming it in a funky San Francisco loft. She didn't have a job, but she had perfected trust fund living.

When she wasn't working her way through the city's fuckable lesbians, she spent her days doing lunch, writing poetry, and exploring her political-protest-of-the-week club membership. Velvet met her when Rosemary hooked up with the sales director at *The Monitor*, the gay magazine where Velvet worked.

Rosemary was smart and chic, a sexy and rich lesbian with feminist flavoring. Velvet was quickly enamored. Perhaps *duped* was the word she was looking for. Rosemary had waxed eloquently about crafting underground, counterculture lesbian utopias and smashing the patriarchal system—all the while looting vaults that generations of Finneys had filled by oppressing the working class. Rosemary's father, an ultraconservative congressman from California, wasn't amused by her antics and she became Daddy's dirty little secret, somehow eclipsing her younger sister who had run off and joined the circus as a performer with Cirque du Soleil.

Launching a lesbian magazine had probably been the furthest thing from Rosemary's mind. But when Velvet and Nikki, Rosemary's lover, walked away from *The Monitor* after another row with their publisher over lack of lesbian visibility, it didn't take long before the three women were drunk with possibilities. Fueled by appletinis, they mapped out a new publishing empire by, for, and about gay women. They were going to take the lesbian nation by storm. It would be a lesbian publishing revolution.

And it was. It took just four years, and by the time *Womyn* was flourishing, they were so discombobulated and their lives so strained from the pressure that there was nothing left of their shared ideals.

During a dyke-drama-laden breakup, Nikki had left in a huff just months after the initial planning meeting. Rosemary and Velvet had subsequently played at being lovers but they could never seem to agree on the rules of the game, and Velvet didn't like the protective gear she was forced to wear.

Then Rosemary met Karen Friars, cofounder of a well-known investment firm that was making zillions in the dot-com boom. All of Rosemary's dozens of other lovers fell by the wayside. Karen became the star running back of Rosemary's life, and her blue-blood origins seemed to serve as a catalyst for Rosemary's reconciliation with her biological family. That was when the real problems began.

Reclaiming the Finney name seemed to peel away Rosemary's feminist ideals. Velvet realized that the antipatriarchy sentiments so dear to herself were merely baubles to Rosemary Finney. Worn for years, they could be suddenly cast aside when she bored of them. Velvet's friendship, and later her very person, was discarded just as ruthlessly. Suddenly Rosemary stopped using her money to subvert the system and used it instead to buffer herself from the needs and concerns of common folk. Karen even convinced her to abandon her funky loft in exchange for their very own Woodside McMansion. Even worse, in Velvet's opinion, Karen became *Womyn*'s biggest investor. It was cash the business desperately needed for expansion, but for Velvet, it came with a steep price. Within weeks of investing, Karen wangled her way into the daily management of the magazine, taking over the role of publisher, and became Velvet's boss.

Velvet was livid that someone without qualifications, even if she was rich, could just walk in off the street and not only order *her* around, but also initiate an avalanche of changes, like axing investigative pieces and letting advertising impact the editorial content. Sure, they got more funding from advertisers, but Velvet couldn't stand running stories that praised a product they were being paid to promote. That wasn't journalism. To top it all off, the advertisements Karen seemed to attract were for cigarettes, beauty products, and weight-loss gimmicks—all paid for by companies the magazine had originally refused to promote.

Velvet vowed to keep the magazine she'd helped start from becoming everything she hated. Too broke to hire an attorney, she spoke with a law school friend who said, in legalese, that she was screwed. Her sweat-equity investment in *Womyn* meant nothing. Velvet felt like a 1950s-era housewife seeking a portion of her husband's earnings in a divorce. Her commitment to the magazine might be lauded, but it was not to be rewarded, either financially or in editorial control. She had no more power than any other hired staff member.

One day, after a particularly heated argument with Karen about the magazine's direction, Velvet took her case to Rosemary, appealing to their friendship, and to logic and feminism, and a sense of justice. But those values were no longer of concern to Rosemary, and she accused Velvet of undermining Karen's authority. In the politest, not-personal manner Velvet could muster, she appealed to the one thing Rosemary now prized: money. Risking her wrath, she detailed the ways in which Karen's presence cost the company cold hard cash: high staff turnover, lost subscribers, offended writers, lowered industry respect.

Rosemary flew into a rage at the suggestion that Karen was less than perfect. It was hard to tell what she was screaming because her voice cracked and shrilled. Recognizing she'd sparked a powder keg, Velvet quietly recommended that, in accordance with their employee contract, they set aside the argument and appeal to an outside mediator.

Rosemary laughed. It wasn't a pleasant laugh. She was so furious, her hands shook, capillaries burst in her cheeks, and the vein in her neck bulged. "You mean this?" She threw the contract at Velvet. "Ha. It's not legally binding."

As Velvet stood stunned, her mouth agape, Rosemary began a diatribe, claiming it was Velvet, not Karen, who'd been bad for the company. That it was Velvet, not Rosemary, who'd ruined their friendship, and that it was Rosemary, not Velvet, who'd created *Womyn,* from initial conception through all the work in between. She topped off her rant by repeatedly demanding, "Get out, bitch," in rising decibels.

Back then, Velvet had shrunk from Rosemary's irrational rage just as she was now, huddled into the bricks and mortar of the Liberty Café. She could remember the rest of that day's events as if from a distance, refusing to grant them the power to make her tremble with shock and anger again. She had locked herself in a restroom stall to sob, and when she'd finally pulled herself together, she'd returned to her desk.

Karen had greeted her with a brusque but pleased, "You're *so* fired."

Disbelieving, Velvet had wanted to hear it from Rosemary. She got her wish as her former friend roughly escorted her to the door and quite literally *threw* her out of the office and locked the door after her. Shortly afterward, Karen had emerged and dropped a lidless file box at Velvet's feet. It was her personal effects.

Like that wasn't enough, Rosemary had then filed for an official restraining order explicitly prohibiting Velvet from coming within five hundred yards of the company that she'd helped build. It could take battered wives months or even years to collect the evidence needed for such an order, but the Finney legal team had made it happen in under an hour.

If there is one thing that life has taught me repeatedly, it's to know when I'm beaten. The apt words had come to Velvet's mind when she was served, courtesy of Principal Skinner on *The Simpsons*. Unable to find a way around the legal maneuvering of the Finney offense, she'd been forced to give up her efforts to get partial custody—or even visitation rights—of her beloved *Womyn*.

And here was Rosemary, standing in Liberty, blaming anyone but herself for the demise of the magazine Velvet had considered her baby. She could hardly believe her eyes when the irrational publisher yanked the dessert menu from Marion's hands, yelling, "You bitch. I knew you were sneaking around trying to ruin me."

Karen pulled on Rosemary's shirtsleeve. "Let's just go."

Rosemary snatched her arm back and turned on Velvet, hissing, "I should have known *you'd* be in on this." In one smooth motion, she reached onto the table, snatched someone's water glass, and flung it at Velvet.

Velvet saw the flash of movement and ducked just as the glass sailed over her head and shattered against the wall. She felt something like snowflakes on her face and reached up to brush aside the melting water. Her fingers came away streaked with blood. Flying glass had nicked her face. Enraged by the injury and relieved at having escaped worse—like a shard in her eye—Velvet sprang at Rosemary, yelling, "You bitch!"

Karen already had one of Rosemary's arms, and the gentleman who'd gallantly been ready to offer Velvet the Heimlich was rushing to grab the other one. As though having an out-of-body experience, Velvet found herself inches from Rosemary's face, not knowing how she'd gotten there. It was almost as if she was watching herself from somewhere high on Liberty's walls. Suddenly she looked down and was surprised to discover her hands were pressed against the exposed flesh of Rosemary's neck, her bright red nails barely visible against Rosemary's crimson skin. Although disturbed by her own desire to throttle the woman, Velvet was pleased to see fear slowly wash over Rosemary's face, dousing the rage in her eyes. As though possessed by the spirit of Homer Simpson with Rosemary standing in for the disobedient Bart, Velvet's hands began to close into a choke hold around Rosemary's neck.

Before she could constrict Rosemary's breathing, Marion and several interfering patrons tackled her, breaking her grip. As she tumbled back under their combined weight, Velvet spat at the equally engulfed Rosemary, "You come at me again and I'll kill you. You got that, bitch? I'll fucking kill you!"

The words had barely escaped her before Velvet regretted saying them.

Now, just days later and with the benefit of hindsight, she was petrified. At least thirty restaurant patrons could testify that she'd made a death threat that night. The police weren't stupid. Once they found out she'd also driven to Woodside the morning of the homicide, they would add two and two and in no time she'd be wearing an orange jumpsuit.

So yeah, she could not deny there had been moments when she wanted to kill Rosemary Finney. But then, so, she speculated, had about a third of the lesbians in San Francisco. Which one had done it? Who finally took the unsinkable Rosemary Finney down? When she found out, would Velvet want to shake a murderer's hand?

She stared at the mushroom-colored polyester-and-rayon walls of her cubicle at the *Chronicle* and mentally rehearsed what she was going to say to the defense attorney when she hired one. *I'm innocent.* Like that would convince anyone.

CHAPTER FIVE

W hen Bud Williams rolled his wheelchair into the Mission District Police Station where he'd spent most of his twenty years on the force, none of the detectives looked at him. Oh, they glanced up when the door opened, but once they realized it was him their gazes plummeted to the floor and remained glued there for the duration of his visit.

Some of their avoidance had to do with his current place of employment. It wasn't as adversarial as, say, becoming a defense attorney or a prisoner rights advocate, but working for a PI firm was still sleeping with the enemy. However, in his case, their eyes had begun avoiding Bud long before he took the job at Blind Eye Detective Agency. It started when he was first out of the hospital and confined to desk duty. He seemed to make the other detectives uncomfortable. His physical presence had a way of clearing a room.

It hadn't taken him long to figure out the problem. His coworkers were filled with revulsion at his handicap because it reminded them of their own frailties. He knew the feeling; he'd had it himself when a guy was hurt on the job a few years back and condemned to limited duties. Injury stalked cops around every corner, especially as they got older. Disability was like Death's younger brother and, like his sibling, he was a mob boss you could avoid for a while, but eventually, he'd track you down and break your legs.

Disability had a way of emasculating a man. Bud's former coworkers treated him like his weakness was contagious, and he'd started to wonder whether these guys were really as strong as he'd thought. Maybe they were hiding their shortcomings behind the shield.

Maybe they'd all become cops to put distance between themselves and their weaknesses or the powerlessness they'd felt as kids—the kind of helplessness that fills you with rage and the pure certainty that when you're a man you won't take shit from anyone, not your old man or the bully down the street. Only once you grow up, the bullies get bigger and your father's belittling voice is now in your head and you find yourself searching for something to shield you from all of it.

Guys would come up, stare at the floor, and tell him how it sucked that *this* happened. They never named the thing that had occurred, never spoke the words "gunshot" or "disabled," as if by verbalizing those words they would jinx themselves. They'd simply tell Bud how brave he was and how, if it was them, they just couldn't do it. More than one detective confided that their lives would be *over* if something similar happened to them.

Bud recognized the inference. The manly response to such castrating paralysis was to eat his gun. Only he'd had to turn in his service weapon—the Glock 9mm semiautomatic beauty that had been his faithful companion—when he became a desk jockey. One morning after he'd been riding the desk for three months and it was obvious he wasn't going to get better, he opened his top drawer and found a handgun resting comfortably on a stack of lined yellow paper pads. It was an untraceable throwaway with its serial numbers filed off, a gift from one of his brothers in blue. It didn't come with instructions. It didn't have to. He knew all too well what was implied.

At home that night Bud found himself on high alert, almost expecting one of his friends to show up and put a cap in his head from a misguided sense of loyalty. The next day he called Human Resources and asked about disability retirement. He was gone in two weeks. And it was obvious that his old cronies would prefer it if he stayed away. Which was why he didn't bother speaking with them. He was at the station house to chat with one of the new generation detectives, Chico Hernandez, who Bud could see now, ducking down the hall toward the restrooms.

Fuckin' Chico. On one hand, the young detective was his major source of information in the department, but on the other, Chico was a thorn in Bud's side, a constant reminder of everything Bud didn't have. He was the son Bud never had, and his father, Jesus Hernandez, Bud's former partner, was not only still walking around but still married, and still on the force. In fact, Jesus had gotten himself transferred to San Jose years ago and now the bastard was that city's flippin' chief of police. Bud remembered how happy it'd made him when he found out that Chico was gay. It was such a relief. It sort of evened things out.

As he rolled his chair down the hall, he could see Chico crouching down by the water fountain, his dark eyes darting back and forth like a trapped rabbit's. Damn, the guy was built. Bud remembered that joke he'd heard about gay guys needing all those muscles to pin another dude down—now *that* was funny. Course, Bud's guns weren't anything to shake a stick at now that his arms powered him around. But his jeans didn't hide the fact that his legs were skinny stork sticks. That's why old Ironside had a blanket draped over his lap, Bud thought, recalling the TV show from his younger days.

Chico Hernandez's muscles rippled under the bright body-hugging T-shirt he wore beneath a dark suit jacket, styling like that *American Idol* sissy, Ryan Seacrest. The guy was lucky he worked in San Francisco, where he could get away with that kind of casual shit. Bud suspected that Chico wore tight jeans, too. He didn't know for sure because he kept his eyes above the belt, thank you very much, even when that meant craning his neck. He hated the way the wheelchair lowered his eye level, making it so he always had to go out of his way to avoid staring at some guy's package.

"What do you want?" Chico muttered.

"Good to see you too, Chico."

"You know the guys razz me for talking to you."

"They *razz* you? Poor baby. They razz me too. It's really funny being disabled." Bud's sarcasm didn't get a rise out of the detective.

"...after that Reynolds case," Chico continued. "Chief read me the riot act about leaking information to a civilian."

"Civilian?" Bud spat out the distasteful word. "Don't insult me. What's the news on the peninsula murder? That editor chick?"

"That *chick*?" Chico sputtered angrily.

Bud smiled to himself. He loved to dick with politically correct assholes.

"She's—she was—" Chico persisted undaunted, "Rosemary Finney."

"She a friend of yours or something?"

"No, not a friend." Chico sighed. "Acquaintance. But she's very well known in the local LGBT community. Her death is a big deal. Everyone's talking about it."

Bud rolled his eyes. He didn't get the younger generation's propensity for giving themselves all these complicated "identities" and then turning around and shorting it all to an acronym. To Bud, *B*, *L*, and *T* had nothing to do with queers and everything to do with a great sandwich.

"Are they saying anything useful?" Bud asked.

"No, just speculation."

"Oh really? And who do 'they' say might have done this?"

Chico shook his head. "Despite whatever stereotypes you might have, Bud, I don't base my investigations on rumor and gossip."

Bud rolled his eyes under lowered lids. "What*ever*. What do you know about it? How was she killed?"

"Sounds like she was strangled, but there's no autopsy report yet."

Bud tried his luck. "I'd like to see that report when you have it."

"What's your interest?" Chico whispered suspiciously. "You just got hired by the suspect or something?"

Bud shifted in his chair, trying to move closer. Years on the force and endless hours at the gun range—most of it before they mandated ear protection—had limited his hearing range. "Shit. There's a suspect? That was fast." Bud tried a nonchalant shrug as he lied, "Just looking into it for a friend of a friend. Who do you guys like for it?"

"Shh. You wanna get me in trouble?" Chico cast a furtive glance down the hallway from where they spoke by the men's room.

Bud wondered if Chico would feel more comfortable *in* the bathroom. Maybe he was the kind of gay man who had sex in public restrooms. Bud had always wondered about the attraction of glory holes. He imagined sticking his dick through a hole in a bathroom stall to be mouthed by a stranger. *Okay,* he could see the appeal. Like an amputated arm, sometimes his dead penis fairly ached. What would he do if he had it back? If he could get hard? If he could come? He'd do anything, Bud thought. He'd do everything. He'd stick his dick in every hottie that walked by. He wouldn't waste all those years trying to be monogamous. He'd be like one of those ball players who'd fucked a thousand girls. Maybe *he'd* even try a glory hole.

It made him mad that he still thought of sex all the time, his brain making its own random connections even though he couldn't do anything about it physically. He felt like he was just getting hornier and hornier as the years passed since that last time with his wife, and he had no way to relieve it. Ever.

"There's this journalist," Chico was whispering. "Chief just got off the horn with the San Mateo district attorney…"

The D-fuckin-A? The case was only five or six hours old. This early in the game, having the DA involved could only mean one of two things. And since they hadn't found someone standing over the body with a bloody knife, Bud was guessing that Rosemary Finney wasn't just a big shot in the gay community. She, or someone close to her, was straight up *connected.*

"…at the *Chronicle.*"

"Wait. The *Chronicle*? Fuck me." Bud shook his head. He hated feeling played.

"Why?" Chico asked.

Bud spun his chair in a 180 and whispered, "I wasn't here. You didn't see me."

"Wait, I don't get it. What did I just say?"

Bud ignored the young detective. He knew who their new client was; there was only one person at the *Chronicle* that Yoshi would go all out for. Velvet Erickson. Yoshi wanted to play this game? Not tell him what was really going on? Fine. He could play too.

He was still contemplating exactly how he was going to show Yoshi what a real detective was made of when she phoned him.

"What do you have so far?" None of the teasing pleasantries that could make a guy feel good about himself. No. She was always about business.

Bud was opening the Impala door. He let go of the handle and said, "She was strangled." He didn't let on that he knew more than she wanted him to know about who they might be working for.

"What else?"

"Hey, I've only been on it for a few hours."

"I need to rule out a couple of persons of interest," she said.

Bud rolled his eyes. "Shoot."

"Rosemary Finney was trying to out an actress. Jennifer Garcia. She just got engaged to Keith Ridger."

"The actor, right?" Bud didn't see a lot of movies. Ridger was in a spy thriller last year wearing skintight spandex. The guy was always primping and grooming himself. Meterosexual was just another word for queer. "I thought he was gay."

"I have no idea," Yoshi said. "But I want to know if there is any way they could be involved."

That figured. If Velvet had gotten her ass in trouble, Yoshi would be looking to point the cops in another direction. "I'll talk to them," he said, like it would be no problem to get past security and lawyers and ask a couple of celebs if they killed a woman for calling them queers.

"Let me know as soon as you have anything," Yoshi said.

Before Bud could answer, she'd hung up. He tossed the phone into the car and fought his way in after it. He would get around to talking to the celebrity couple when he was good and ready. But first he needed to find out a whole lot more about the crime. Real detectives got their facts together before interviewing anyone.

❖

When Blind Eye's round wall clock held its hands straight up like a robbery victim, Tucker poked her head into Yoshi's office. "I'm heading out to lunch now," she said. "I'll be going all the way out to Oakland and back, to get that cop AJ's contact information. So it'll take a while. I'll try to get back by three."

Yoshi's dark hair brushed over her shoulders as her head bobbed in assent. "Of course. Thanks for reminding me. I will see you when you return."

"Great," Tucker replied, then immediately berated herself as she closed Yoshi's door. *Great?* What an idiot. Why couldn't she be more eloquent when speaking to Yoshi?

Tucker pulled the suit jacket from the coat tree's branches and slid her arms into its well-worn interior. She'd bought it during college and it quickly became her favorite, and not just because she thought it looked cool. Tucker loved that in addition to the external pockets, the inner lining had numerous cubbies for her daily essentials. She'd never been one to carry a purse. But she did like being able to carry her overnight needs, in case she had a hookup, without always having to lug around her bulky backpack.

She exited the Flood Building onto Market Street and was immediately engulfed by the lunch-going business crowd. She battled to keep her feet and struggled to get up to speed before being trampled.

Tucker was still learning how to let go and allow the herd to carry her along with their momentum. She feared she'd end up somewhere unexpected, like deep in the Tenderloin, and get stuck there while the rest of the mob slid by.

Fighting her way down the stairway that descended to the Bay Area Rapid Transit subway station, Tucker reminded herself that she *liked* working at Blind Eye. Without the repetition, she didn't think she could continue subjecting herself to this psychological torture. She was used to the wide open spaces of Idaho, where the only thing to block her view were mountains and where other people were more likely to avoid her than press up against her. With the crowd jostling her and their closeness robbing her of air, her olfactory senses overwhelmed by the pungent odor of sweat and perfume, she could find herself panicking.

BART rides were the worst part of her day. To get through them, she closed her eyes and pretended that she wasn't trapped in a sardine can which itself was trapped inside a tubelike tunnel that ran beneath the San Francisco Bay. What if the train broke down? What if the tunnel gave way? Her shrink had her meditate through much of the ride, a habit that Tucker credited with making her appear a much more normal person than she felt inside.

"Normal" had been a label thrown around during her childhood, and she bore the burden of being the only ordinary kid in the family. Well, until she came out, anyway. Then her mother sobbed, "I just wanted *one* normal child, but I guess that was too much to ask."

Tucker had never felt *normal*, though. She felt like the girl in that Ferron song, "White Wing Mercy," the one that talks about fearing her family will realize she's crazy and lock her away. That'd been one of her childhood fears, that one day they'd discover she was even sicker than her siblings and she'd be sent away. Like her mom had talked about doing with Tucker's little brother, Hunter. When he was first born and the doctors said he'd never be normal and they might as well just send him to an institution right then.

After her first introduction to San Francisco's downtown, Tucker had vowed she would avoid the area in the future. All those people pressed together like feedlot cattle. All those tall buildings blocking out the sun, making you feel like you were at the bottom of the Grand Canyon. All the scary homeless junkies and prostitutes. But then the temp agency she worked for sent her to Blind Eye and she'd never wanted to leave.

When Yoshi offered her a full-time position, Tucker hadn't hesitated in accepting. She felt at home at the office after a mere two days. Bud came off gruff and everything, but she'd grown up around opinionated, brusque rednecks and it put her at ease. Bud reminded Tucker of her dad, her real dad, not the stepfather she'd lived with since she was eight. Tucker's father was strict and never said I love you, but he'd showed his affection for her with nighttime games of catch and by inviting her to fix cars with him on the weekends.

Even though she'd never mention it, she knew another reason she'd taken the job was because both Yoshi and Bud were differently abled. She'd seen how the world dumped on the disabled and she wanted to feel like maybe she was making some small difference.

As the train thundered the rest of the way through the Bay tunnel, Tucker ate her sack lunch of white bread egg salad sandwich and a ziplock bag of potato chips. She exited at the Lake Merritt station and walked the three blocks to Oakland's Chinatown.

Despite the glowing descriptions that policewoman AJ Jackson had written her grandmother, Miss Latisha, Tucker hadn't taken easy to Oakland. Maybe for lifelong New Orleans residents like AJ, Oakland was a great city. When Tucker had read AJ's letters to Miss Latisha in the candlelit darkness of Katrina-torn New Orleans, the San Francisco Bay Area had seemed like a faraway mecca where everything was possible. If she'd been home, instead of volunteering in a hurricane war zone, AJ's imagery might have held little interest and Tucker wouldn't have moved here at all.

As it was, she'd managed to retain her sanity only by orchestrating her life so that much of it was spent within walking distance of the Lake Merritt BART station. On weekends, she languished at the lakeside park, watching Italian gondolas cruise across the dark agate and puce water, kids in paddleboats tossing about with laughter, and California brown pelicans cawing and diving for fish in the middle of this indisputably urban area. Sometimes Tucker watched the Ladies of the Lake, a women's sail club that she found out started in 1916, as the gray-haired old birds glided across the lake buoyed by their shared love of water.

And though nighttime adrenaline-fueled sideshows had become a nuisance to the police, Tucker was oddly compelled by the mostly African American young folks who gathered in parking lots and city streets to play music, show off their cars, and do vehicular stunts. She'd been to a few, even though she hung back behind the crowd. Although they had a wholly hip-hop, Oakland feel to them, the sideshows reminded her of cruising back when she was in high school.

Tucker's tiny apartment smelled a little like the damp earth of planting season back home. She leased it from the Johnsons, an amiable old black couple who happened to be Miss Latisha's nephew and his wife. The Johnsons seemed to genuinely love having a wannabe PI under their roof. They kept inviting her to dinner and Mrs. Johnson often packed Tucker lunches in brown bags with her name scrawled on the front in marker and left on the kitchen counter. Tucker had her own toilet downstairs but shared the family's upstairs shower and kitchen area.

AJ's phone number was on a scrap of paper at the bottom of the cardboard box that served as Tucker's underwear drawer. Tucker was too embarrassed to tell Yoshi that in addition to not having a Palm Pilot, a cell phone, or even a planner, she didn't have her own landline. She was still living like she was in college—quite the opposite of AJ, who was only a few years older than her.

Miss Latisha had given her AJ's number and told Tucker to call her when she got to Oakland. When Tucker didn't get to it on her own, the Johnsons had invited both women for dinner and Tucker had taken an instant shine to the dyke cop from New Orleans. AJ was strong, smart, butch, and working class—all things that immediately put Tucker at ease. Though they were merely years apart in age, Tucker looked up to her and felt like she wanted to *be* AJ when she grew up.

Chapter Six

O fficer Angela Joy "AJ" Jackson gazed out over the still waters of the San Francisco Bay. God, she missed New Orleans. If she squinted her eyes just so, she could almost fool herself into thinking she was on the shores of Lake Pontchartrain and that the distant San Mateo Bridge, spanning the Bay and leading back to her stuffy East Bay studio apartment, was instead the Lake Pontchartrain Causeway.

There were echoes of her hometown in the geography of the San Francisco Bay, but not in the land itself. In New Orleans, if you went up the elevator in one of the higher downtown buildings, nothing blocked your view and you could see forever. But not here. Before she came out West, the only hill she'd ever seen was when her grade school class took a field trip to the Audubon Zoo. They'd taken turns playing on Monkey Hill, the bare dirt hill built by the WPA during the Depression, which still towered eight feet above sea level. Their teacher read a brass marker about how the mound was built so that the kids of New Orleans could know what a hill was.

The mountains that rose on all sides of her now were something like three hundred *times* as high as Monkey Hill, and they made her feel trapped with no way out.

The abandoned vehicle parked next to her, wheels gone, windows shattered, and sprayed with graffiti, lent another degree of authenticity to AJ's New Orleans fantasy. It was this vehicle, AJ was pretty sure—along with the smell of salt water drifting through her rolled-up windows—that had got her homesick again. She'd been in the Bay Area ten long months, and still the smell of café au lait and beignets lingered in her nostrils like she was standing in Jackson Square right this very moment.

Goddamn, she missed her hometown food. Her mouth watered at the thought of fried chicken and spicy red beans and rice. Thank God she'd recently discovered a Popeye's Chicken joint in Hayward. But not on the Peninsula. And there wasn't no frozen daiquiri drivethroughs or breakfast joints serving grits. And she'd kill for a pot full of red mudbugs boiled in Tony Chachere's Creole spice. Instead, East Palo Alto offered up only fast food chains and a few Mexican cantinas. Venturing farther afield she could get a diet of greens that the locals called California cuisine. After a lifetime of heavy sauces and spicy dishes, California cuisine—especially the strange obsession with adding avocado to everything—felt like grazing on the area's green grasses and weeds. Every salad she ate reminded AJ that she wasn't a fucking cow or whatever naturally ate that kind of crap.

With a sigh, she reached into the small paper bag next to her and pulled out a cylinder bound tightly in tin foil. Slowly unwrapping the super-sized burrito she'd gotten from a nearby taqueria, AJ glanced toward the potholed city street that led to the dirt parking lot. Fifteen minutes ago, dispatch had radioed asking her to meet a Midpeninsula Open Space ranger at the Ravenswood parking area. The guy hadn't shown, then she got another call telling her to make the meeting tomorrow instead, so it seemed like common sense to eat her lunch now that it was almost two in the afternoon.

Refrains of Crazy Town's hip-hop tune "Butterfly" wafted through the air, reminding AJ of the one that got away. She sang along, thinking of Chantal, the way her perspiration would pool on the small of her back and moisten her round ass while they were dancing together, barely touching in all the right places, at the Rubyfruit on a rare night when hip-hop brought the city's black dykes to the white bar. That was before the hurricane, and before Chantal broke her heart.

AJ's mind wandered until the song went away and came back again and she remembered it was the ring tone on her cell phone. She made a mental note: change ring tone to a New Orleans rapper like Juvenile and kill two birds with one stone. She remembered her high school music teacher telling students that both jazz and hip-hop originated in her hometown. He was a brother from New York and he'd falsely assumed that the teens didn't know that fact. But they had, they'd all known since they was younguns that their favorite music style started on the same streets they played in. There was something rewarding about the overlooked city spawning a global phenomenon.

She swallowed the bite of burrito, washing it down with a swig of Coke, then answered the phone. People here told her she'd lose the unmistakable drawl of the South after living in the Bay Area for a few years, but AJ wasn't sure she wanted to lose what she considered the official vernacular of the African American nation. She wasn't even sure she wanted to stay here that long. She'd only planned to be away until New Orleans was resuscitated, and the police department did some damn housecleaning.

"Hi, AJ?" the voice on the other end of the phone asked.

"Yeah, who's that?" She knew from the pause at the other end that her response sounded like "who dat?" In the dialect of Louisiana, "dat" was often used for "is that," and though her new colleagues found her use of it confusing, the habit was hard to break.

"Tucker Shade. You know…"

Ah, the cute little white girl that was staying with AJ's cousins over in Oakland, the one Grandma Latisha thought so highly of. Before Tucker arrived in town, AJ had gotten instructions to be nice to her. "Hey, Tucker."

"I'm not bothering you, am I?"

"Naw, I'm on lunch."

"Oh, good. Hey, the reason I'm calling is, well, I don't know if I told you that I work for a private investigator?"

"Yeah, you did." Over dinner at the cousins', AJ had thought the two of them would converse about law enforcement and investigation, but it turned out the Shade girl was just the receptionist.

"Well, we got this case, it's down in your area, actually in the woods near Woodside, but I thought maybe with you being with Palo Alto PD…"

"*East* Palo Alto," AJ corrected.

"Wait, what's the difference?"

AJ laughed. "Girl, it don't get much different than that! I've only been here six months and even I be knowin' that."

"Oh." Tucker sounded embarrassed. "I've never been south of San Francisco. Can you explain it to me?"

"Sure 'nough. It be like the diff' between Audubon Place and Ninth Ward," AJ explained, using New Orleans's points of reference.

"I never saw New Orleans before Katrina. And everywhere I went looked pretty much the same. Flattened rubble. I don't think I even got uptown, just to the Ninth Ward and East New Orleans."

"Hmm. Okay, Palo Alto. That where Stanford University be? Like there ain't no crime. Just richy-rich white folk with mad cribs, clean streets, and snobby restaurants you got to dress up for."

"Oh, okay."

"East Palo Alto. That where I'm at, and we got ourselves high murder rates and full-up crooked police shit."

"Like New Orleans used to be?"

"Yeah, some. NOPD get a bad rap but it ain't all bad." Or at least it *wasn't*, AJ thought. "East Palo Alto's like East LA, or some shit. Latino ghetto with turf wars between rival gangs and—" AJ cut herself off. She could mention the problems she'd had since she joined the EPA PD, but she'd been burned before. She didn't know this kid well enough to trust her with the details.

"You really work for your money." Tucker sounded deflated. "I was hoping maybe…I mean,…"

"So spill. What's your business up in here?"

This seemed to raise Tucker's spirits and the younger woman quickly relayed what she knew, which was not a whole lot, about the murder of some rich white lady. A murder that would no doubt get priority and resources because of the victim's money and the color of her skin.

AJ wanted to care but her ability to trouble herself over someone who wasn't black had been washed away by the New Orleans flood, when she saw bloated bodies rotting in the streets and her people fighting for their lives while the fucking politicians acted like it wasn't happening. Those bastards in Washington DC had watched New Orleans drown. They'd known exactly what it would take to save the city and they hadn't just failed to provide it, they'd *decided* to withhold it. They wanted the city to die. After all, what was New Orleans to the Republican Party? A bunch of black folk?

They think we nothing but murderers and hos. And they talk like N'awlins the modern-day Sodom and Gomorrah. President Bush and his redneck cronies probably done watched us on TV, holding babies in the air and begging for water, and they probably laughed, clappin' themselves on the back for a job well done, then gave the order to blow the levees and drown the Ninth Ward.

She didn't give a shit 'bout no dead white girl.

"That park. What's it called?" AJ asked, driven partly by guilt at her own lack of interest. Tucker'd been a godsend for her grammy

Latisha, and AJ's manners demanded that, in return, she help the girl out.

A pause. "Wonderland. It's in Woodside."

"Well, I might be able to help y'all," AJ said. "I'm supposed to take a meeting with this ranger here tomorrow. I'll let y'all know what I find."

When Velvet saw the uniformed officers exit the elevator to the *Chronicle*'s second-floor editorial department, she thought about running.

Everybody runs. Tom Cruise said it in *Minority Report.* Velvet was most aware of her movie-junkie habits at times like this, when lines from films popped into her head. Like the running commentary of a voice-over, she'd think in dialogue borrowed from cult B-movie favorites, highbrow independents, lowest-common-denominator blockbusters, Oscar winners, and even obtuse foreign flicks.

She experienced her motion-picture obsession as a brand of collector's madness. Like fanatical Beanie Baby owners' the world over, her passion spilled from one room to the next until it threatened to engulf her entire home. Her living room housed three floor-to-ceiling shelves packed tight with DVDs carefully arranged in alphabetical order by title. Rather than displaying fine art, the hallway and bedroom walls were devoted to her extensive collection of movie posters. As her own private curator, Velvet regularly rotated compilations through the framed and lighted displays. Currently showing were the refined works of Polish artists who individually hand-designed movie posters for American classics including *Taxi Driver, Sunset Boulevard*, and *The Fly.*

Velvet tried not to stare conspicuously at the two cops loitering by the cubicle nearest the elevator. Ever helpful, Rachel Heinz stood up and pointed in Velvet's direction. *Moron.* Why was it that the girl could barely remember her name on most occasions but today could pinpoint her location from fifty yards? How did Neo escape from *his* cubicle office? Oh, right. *The Matrix* hero didn't; he climbed out the window but got scared on the ledge. Wuss. Of course *she* couldn't go around clinging to window ledges. It had nothing to do with her fear of heights. She just didn't want anyone looking up her skirt. The skirt—Velvet thought of that cute, sexually harassed secretary in *Bridget Jones*—was also the reason she couldn't crawl out of her cubicle hoping that her profile was low enough to avoid detection.

"Velvet Erickson?" The two cops blocked the mouth of her shoebox stall, one in front, and the other back a little to the right.

Velvet sighed. She should have taken Yoshi's advice and hired a lawyer. From her seated position, her eyes were level with the officers' black leather duty belts. One, a woman, produced a pair of handcuffs. For one brief, glorious second Velvet thrilled at the erotic trappings: leather, cuffs, and uniforms. Then she remembered where she was.

"Turn around, please, miss," the other cop, a man, commanded gruffly.

Velvet's titillation was quickly replaced by mortification. "You don't have to cuff me, I'll come willingly."

"Please turn around," the cop repeated, ignoring her plea.

Velvet reluctantly turned her back to them. Her right arm was yanked roughly behind her and the cold metal snapped around her wrist.

"Velvet Erickson." The policewoman was equally officious. "You are under arrest for the murder of Rosemary Finney. You have the right to remain silent."

Velvet's left arm was wrenched back and secured. Grabbing the link between the two metal bracelets, the female officer propelled her out of the privacy of her cubicle and into full view of the hallway. *The perp walk is* supposed *to happen at the courthouse*, Velvet thought, her cheeks flushing. Lights flashed as one of her enterprising coworkers snapped photos.

"You have the right to an attorney."

Velvet's workplace march of shame seemed to last a lifetime. She focused on the threadbare charcoal gray carpet in front of her, trying to ignore her gawking colleagues.

"If you cannot afford an attorney…"

Finally, they were at the elevator. Velvet thought about pushing the call button with her nose, just to hurry things up.

"One will be appointed for you." The cop stopped her recitation as she pressed the button. The doors slid open immediately.

Thank God. Velvet hurriedly entered and sighed in relief when the door closed behind them. As the elevator drifted down and the officer concluded reading her rights, Velvet swore she could still feel her coworkers' eyes on her. At least some of the startled onlookers wouldn't be disappointed to witness her humiliation. A handful of seasoned old newsmen thought a former magazine editor had no place in the *Chronicle*'s newsroom.

Chapter Seven

It was after three p.m. when Bud pulled his Impala into the gravel California Transportation Park-and-Ride turnout across from Crystal Springs Reservoir. The man-made lake stored drinking water for San Francisco residents. It was fed by local runoff and the long system of pipes that stretched all the way across California's Central Valley to Yosemite National Park, and siphoned Lake Hetch Hetchy.

Like many local residents, Bud had been here as a kid on a school field trip. He didn't remember much about Crystal Springs, except that it sat directly on the San Andreas Fault and as a kid he'd imagined the ground opening up and the whole lake draining like a bathtub. Most of the land around the reservoir was a protected refuge closed to everyone but a handful of water tenders and political bigwigs. Bud had read a newspaper article a few years back that said the water district rangers made, like, seventy-thousand dollars a year, lived in fancy lakeside houses, and hosted big-shot guests like former San Francisco Mayor Willie Brown and Senator Diane Feinstein.

Fucking snobs. The place should be turned into a recreation area. He wouldn't mind buzzing around on his Jet Ski out here on the rare occasions he still got to play like a big kid. There was something so freeing about being on the water. He could almost forget about his crippled legs. But now he had to haul the thing all the way to Nevada to have any fun. Damn environmentalists had outlawed Jet Skis on the bay and local waterways. Bastards.

Bud pulled alongside Sheriff Deputy Roy Freeman's patrol car, so each faced the opposite direction, front end to rear and vice versa. This automotive sixty-nine allowed two drivers to speak through open windows without leaving their seats. It was a classic law enforcement meeting style in San Francisco Bay's smaller cities and rural areas. He unrolled his window and stuck his arm out into the space between the cars. "Hi, I'm 16D5, Bud Williams, retired detective," he offered as he saw Deputy Freeman suspiciously eying the unmarked vehicle.

Bud had a Motorola 2 wave radio system that allowed him to scan local emergency traffic and speak directly to personnel when he needed to. Most dispatchers would quickly sniff out amateur users and remind them that radio traffic was reserved for official and emergency business. But if you knew the lingo, especially if you were previously a law enforcement officer yourself, you could slide under the dispatch's radar. So Bud had simply asked to get a 10-87, a meeting, with the deputy involved in that morning's 10-55—coroner's case, a.k.a. dead body. When asked who he was, he used his old radio call sign, SFPD 16D5.

"You're here about the murder at Wonderland?" Deputy Freeman asked.

Bud nodded.

"What's your interest in the case?"

"I'm with Blind Eye Detectives. We were hired to find the killer." Bud kept his answer vague, allowing the deputy to assume Blind Eye was there at the behest of grieving family.

"That's a shame," Deputy Freeman commented while shaking his head. "Nobody trusts us to do our job anymore."

"I hear you," Bud empathized.

"I mean, what is it, only half a day since time of death and the DB's family's already hired a PI? No offense to you, but you know, I think Woodside PD is already gunning for someone. They might just wrap this up before you even get started."

"You're kidding me, right?" Bud affected surprise.

"Those Woodside boys work fast." Freeman winked at Bud, indicating he didn't chalk their speed up to brilliance. "Guess when you have your first murder in twenty-five years, you've got to act speedily, else all those rich residents wouldn't feel safe." He pulled a soft pack of Marlboro Reds from a breast pocket. "Your being here's proof they're right."

"You think there's rushed judgment going on?" Bud asked.

Freeman tapped the cigarette pack against the dashboard. "Could be. Could well be. Like I said, I'm betting there was a lot of pressure on someone to wrap this up and *quick*."

"Pressure," Bud echoed, thinking about Yoshi's persons of interest, the queer celebs.

"You know how it is." Freeman looked like he had a bad taste in his mouth. "There's rules for us, then there's rules for *them*."

"I hear you." Bud nodded. "Who was first on scene? Woodside?"

"No. One of those Midpen rangers. It came in as a medical call first."

"Midpen?" Bud wasn't familiar with the name.

"Midpeninsula Open Space, something like that. They've got these parks all along Highway 35, up on the hill." Deputy Freeman pointed past the reservoir to the winding road that disappeared into the tree-shrouded Santa Cruz Mountains. "But they call 'em preserves, not parks. Being all wooded and such. Then they got some land down south near Cupertino."

Deputy Freeman reached out of his window, holding the Marlboros out to Bud. The pack was open and one filtered end stuck up, begging to be accepted. Bud shook off the proffered cancer stick. "Gave it up."

It was technically true. He didn't smoke cigarettes anymore, not since he left the force. Now he had a pipe in the glove compartment and a little packet of sweet-smelling tobacco leaves. You had to have *something* to do on stakeout. There was only so much time you could spend consuming snacks and reading the *Chronicle* sports section. Still, it seemed a little weird for someone his age and a law officer to boot, so he kept it tucked away.

He blamed Tucker Shade for its presence, actually. He'd scrawled something in his notes one day about needing a smoke, or maybe he'd doodled lit cigarettes. Anyway, Tucker shoved a package at him one morning and stuttered something about how it belonged to her dad and she thought he might like it. She was always trying too hard in that way, doing stuff for people like some desperate little kid hoping for friends. She went bright red as usual and babbled on about buying a new mouthpiece. The whole time Bud didn't know what the hell she was talking about.

Later he'd cracked open the small rectangular box and found a beautifully hand-carved cherry-colored pipe and a pouch of scented tobacco. It looked like something a dweebish college professor would have hanging from the side of his mouth. Bud had shoved it back in the box and tossed it on the floor. He wasn't that guy.

A few days later when he was ready to scream in boredom and had another nicotine craving, he remembered the pipe, packed the bowl with tobacco, and lit up. He'd been surprised to find that he actually liked the pleasant aroma, the sensation of the pipe between his lips, and the sweet smoke curling in his mouth.

"So the rangers were already there?" he commented. "I thought it was really early. Before dawn."

"Yep, that's right." Deputy Freeman mumbled past the cigarette in his mouth.

"They've got rangers on around the clock?" Bud was impressed. Most park and open space systems couldn't afford twenty-four-hour patrols.

"Nothing like that." Deputy Freeman flicked open a Zippo and lit up. "It's just that some of those rangers, they live on the hill. I guess they're on call 24/7." His exhaled smoke drifted through Bud's window.

"Got it. So, when did you arrive on scene?"

"I didn't head up there until they called for the coroner," Freeman admitted sheepishly. "We don't get a lot of murders up there. Just the occasional body dump. You know, someone gets killed over drugs or something and the perp wants to ditch the evidence. They figure the best place to unload it is in the woods."

Bud nodded absentmindedly. Watching the other guy smoke was giving him cravings of his own, but he didn't dare pull out his pipe. He couldn't risk losing the deputy's respect. Not yet.

"'Course, sometimes you get lucky. Like a few years back when that Palo Alto student went missing?" Freeman looked at Bud for confirmation.

Bud nodded. He remembered the story. It made headline news because she was a Stanford student. She'd supposedly been biking over the mountain to the ocean, and just disappeared. It came on the heels of several high-profile abduction cases.

"We had search parties all over the woods up there at the time because we were following up on a tip. Some chick sold out her boyfriend to get out of a drug charge. Supposedly, he killed another female and the two of them drove up there and dumped the body."

A radio squawked inside the patrol car. Deputy Freeman stopped to listen, took another inhalation, and continued, smoke curling out of his mouth like a dragon. "We brought that broad up there two days in a row but she couldn't pinpoint the spot, then those Stanford kids trip right over it. It was pretty decomped by then and I guess they thought it was their missing friend. Shit, she'd only been gone a week. How'd they think she'd rotted away so fast? I guess those Stanford kids aren't so damn smart after all."

"I thought the Stanford girl *was* found."

Freeman took a last puff on his Marlboro and then crushed it out in his ashtray. "Yeah. She killed herself up in a park near Palo Alto. One of the rangers found her swinging from a tree. That's what we always say when we're doing searches up there—don't just look at the ground. Look up. Look for the swingin' feet." He laughed.

Bud smiled. He missed the gallows humor of the force, but he needed to lead the deputy back to the subject of today's murder. "Did you go down to where this DB was found? The Finney chick?"

"And hump all the way back up the hill? The EMS team probably trampled the evidence anyway, so no point. I just took a statement from the reporting party and checked the jurisdiction with the fire chief. It's Woodside's case and no one's stepping on *those* toes nohow."

Bud knew what he was saying. Woodside had a reputation. With some cities, good working relations applied and officers on the scene could investigate until the detectives showed. But others, like Woodside, once jurisdiction was confirmed, officers just secured the scene until they arrived. He thanked Freeman and stayed where he was until the deputy drove away. If Woodside PD was already gunning for someone, did that mean they actually had something on Velvet Erickson? Could that loudmouthed bombshell actually be guilty?

Bud needed to speak with the first respondents—these Midpeninsula rangers Freeman mentioned. He could hardly wait to find out what Woodside had on her.

Following directions given him by Deputy Freeman, he drove up Highway 92, rising with the twisting road until it peaked high above Silicon Valley. When he turned onto Highway 35, the vantage point gave Bud a panoramic view, with the bay on one side and the Pacific Ocean on the other, stretching toward the horizon and disappearing at the curve of the earth. He didn't pull over to enjoy the view. Soon the narrow highway dipped into the cover of trees—burnt orange trunks, crammed next to looming evergreens. His perspective disoriented by all the foliage, Bud began to feel like he'd never see daylight again.

Although the afternoon sun was shining brightly in the valley below, up here under the branches of tall redwoods it was drizzling. It took him a few minutes to realize that the beads of water on his windshield weren't raindrops. It was the fog. Of course he was familiar with fog. He lived in San Francisco, after all, but he'd never before seen it drench an area so completely. It was almost like the tall trees were pulling the water from the sky, as though they'd pierced a cloud and caused it to rain.

As he continued along, the fog drifted down until it enveloped his Impala in a ghostly haze. His tires losing their grip on wet pavement and the glare of the fog reducing visibility, Bud was forced to slow to a snail's pace. He was so irritated by the sluggish momentum that when he saw a pullout to his left, he swerved into it, even though a sign warned him not to. Darting in front of oncoming traffic sent his heart racing. He parked near two outdoor crappers, unrolled his window and retrieved his pipe from the glove compartment. He unfurled the little Baggie of tobacco, took a pinch out, and packed it in the bowl. Holding the pipe in his left hand, with the other he dug in his right pocket, shifting in his seat until his fingers closed around cold metal. He extracted the Zippo, flicked it open, and, sucking on the mouthpiece, lit the pipe's tobacco.

As the cool damp air wafted through his window and the sweet smoke curled up his nose, Bud began to relax. After he smoked the bowl, he tapped the ashes out of the open window. While he was here, he decided he might as well take advantage of the porta-potty. Who knew when he'd get a chance to piss again. He unlocked his seat belt, opened the car door, and swung his hips sideways. The move dragged his feet across the floorboard but didn't get them outside. To do that, he lifted each immobile leg in turn, using his arms to drop them when his feet were over pavement.

He opened the rear door, gripped the top with both hands, and, with a grunt, lifted his whole body from the edge of the seat and swung himself around like a trapeze artist. Swiftly following his body with one hand and then the other changing positions on the door frame, Bud was able to land his butt cheeks onto the edge of the backseat.

A little winded by the relocation effort, he swore at his weak-ass body and sat there for a minute, regaining his strength. Then he jerked the wheelchair from its position, swung it in front of himself, and folded it open. He flipped the lock on the wheels so the chair wouldn't roll away and hoisted himself onto the padded seat. He released the brake, rolled back, and slammed the Impala's doors closed. He didn't lock the car but he took his keys with him. If some asshole ripped off his gear despite his handicap placard, he'd hunt them down and beat the hell out of them.

Rolling into the disabled pod, he thought how it was shaped like the transportation device in *The Fly*. He wouldn't mind being able to teleport on days like this.

When he was done and rolled back out to the parking lot, he discovered a vehicle had arrived while he was busy. Two young men stood next to a metallic green two-door Mazda removing mountain bikes from a rack on the vehicle's trunk. They wore tight spandex, matching yellow and blue jerseys, and shorts so revealing that when they turned toward him, Bud swore he could tell the men were circumcised. He snapped his gaze away from them and rolled toward his Impala. Just as he was starting to open the door, he noticed a sign posted at the other end of the lot, barely visible through the fog. Although he didn't give a shit about rules or educational material it might pronounce, he was curious about where exactly he was, so he took a moment to find out.

The plaque described the turn out as Skeggs Point Overlook, and indicated that beyond the heavy layer of fog, Silicon Valley stretched out below. If you had a zoom lens, you'd not only be able to locate larger landmarks like the Stanford University's giant telescopic dish but also correctly identify a coed's bra size. He made this last part up because a close-up of a scantily dressed college girl was about the only thing that would make the excruciating drive up here worthwhile.

The two bike riders whizzed past him and darted across the highway where they were swallowed by the fog. He hoped they'd be blinded by the haze and ride off a cliff. It didn't seem right that these punks could be up here in the middle of the day flaunting their mobility. He'd been like them once, so sure of his invincibility. They probably had no idea how tenuous their hold on physical abilities could be, having been hurt and healed a hundred times. Then something as benign as a rock in the trail could send them flying over their handlebars and break their neck.

He didn't wish paralysis on anyone. Just a broken arm or fractured collarbone.

It took him several minutes to get back to the Impala and cram himself and his chair into their respective spots, and he exited the overlook the way he'd come in. He hadn't driven more than thirty or forty seconds when he spotted a row of mailboxes that had been invisible through the mist until he was almost parallel to them. He braked hard and veered off the road. He was glad that the sheriff had given him directions or he would've driven right past the spot.

In his rearview Bud could see the yellow call box that the witness had used to call for help that morning. Across the two-lane highway was an entrance to the Wonderland Park. This was sandwiched between two roads that came at opposite angles and intersected with Skyline Boulevard, leaving a small strip of undeveloped land in between that was the upper corner of the park. Although he could see the sign for Bear Gulch, the roadbed itself wasn't visible from his vantage point as it apparently dove sharply down to the left. The second road, marked Mountain Meadow, inclined up to the right.

Bud sifted through the debris on his bench seat until he located his cell phone. He'd been putting off calling the Blind Eye office but he figured that by now the police would be questioning Velvet and Yoshi was probably on tenterhooks, wondering what was going on.

Bud chuckled to himself as he watched the image displayed on the LCD spool endlessly, searching for service. Unsuccessfully. Probably could have guessed he wouldn't get a signal up here in the cover of the forest. He shrugged. Oh well, let Yoshi get mad when he didn't check in. He was pissed at her anyway because she hadn't told him of Velvet's involvement in this case.

Still, he did like fiery women, and on Yoshi that fierceness seemed particularly hot, contrasting as it did with her cool Japanese refinement. First glance, you might think her a shrinking violet or demure innocent like a lot of Asian women seemed to be. He'd heard Asian broads were the preferred trophy wives of dot-com types. And who could blame them? American babes had gotten far too bossy and *liberated*. That might be kind of hot for a good fuck, but you didn't want to marry a woman like that, not if you wanted to wear the pants in the family. It was easy to get taken in by the way Yoshi looked down all the time. But Bud figured that must be less about modesty and more about embarrassment, like she worried everyone could tell she was blind by the color of her eyes. They were this startling translucent blue, really unusual on an Asian chick.

Yoshi was like one of those kung-fu-fighting, kick-ass Asian girl assassins he'd seen on movies. Under that sweet exterior was a no nonsense B-I-T-C-H. He'd never wanted a broad for a boss, and he found ways to be a less-than-perfect employee. But there was something about Yoshi's attitude that he respected. You needed to be hard as nails in this business, but sometimes the camouflage of her soft shell elicited cooperation in a way his harsh words didn't. Not that he'd ever admit that out loud.

He dropped the phone back into the pile and hauled out his 35mm camera and 70mm lens. Thankful there was still enough daylight for decent exposures, he snapped off a stream of wide-angle location shots before moving on to more detailed work. Opening the Impala's door, he took close-ups of the ground directly below. The dirt was muddy from the fog and there was a jumble of tire tracks. The thick tread of off-road four-wheel-drive trucks crisscrossed the fat six-inch-deep ruts left by fire and emergency vehicles. Bud concluded these were left that morning when the DB was hauled up from Wonderland Park. The newer tracks of passenger cars and SUVs probably belonged to the nearby residences because they swung in close to the mailboxes.

With the door still open, he switched to a medium-distance lens and took close-ups of the soft shoulder across the highway, starting at the entrance to the park, which was a mishmash of footprints, and slowly pulling back from the log fence. Closer to the pavement were more tire ruts. He swung the camera northward, focusing on the soft shoulder and keeping it zoomed so he could clearly see individual pebbles. The ground was pretty thrashed until he got about twenty feet away from the access point.

From then on it was relatively undisturbed, and Bud was able to discern the tracks of a thin tire running parallel to the highway. It was the tread of a mountain bike, and since it wasn't visible closer to the park entrance it most likely predated the morning's emergency crew, but it seemed to be headed straight for Wonderland. Bud veered his attention back to the entrance and took a photo of a small square sign posted there. It showed a bike surrounded by a circle with a cross through it. *No bikes*. Whoever'd ridden to the park had probably left their vehicle in the Skeggs lot seventy-five yards down the road. But since there was only one set of bike tracks, they hadn't come back this way. *Interesting.*

Bud let the Impala drift slowly backward toward the yellow call box while he continued snapping images of the wide soft shoulder. Rather than collecting roadside trash or making casts of the tire impressions, he preferred photographs. Less mess to deal with and he could blow up the images to make tread comparisons.

A two-story rustic barnlike house stood twenty yards back from the road to the west. Bud reversed into the driveway that led to it and took photos out the passenger window. The late-afternoon shade was so deep under the trees that he wasn't certain if he'd exposed the film. He switched to his digital and moved closer. He'd learned that digital cameras captured more information than the 35mms. A picture that would have previously seemed too dark to keep could now be manipulated in Photoshop until it was totally clear. Of course, he didn't do that work himself. Couldn't stand to learn that new shit. But with young guns like Chico harping on him for being a Luddite, whatever that was, he'd finally given in and found a service bureau to do the work for him.

It looked like the house had been subdivided into apartments. That explained at least two of the six mailboxes lined up by the highway's pavement. Above one screen-doored entry, an external stairway led to the second level. Bud wondered if the guy upstairs was an early riser and whether he'd seen anything that morning. Cracking his driver-side door, he scooped up a handful of driveway gravel and flung it at the second-floor window. The pebbles scattered, striking randomly against the wood paneling but not hitting the glass or garnering a response from the resident. Maybe the guy was at work.

He scraped another fistful of the small rocks and threw them against the building. They hit with the rat-a-tat-tat of automatic gunfire, and at least one bounced off the windowpane. Rather than rousing the upstairs resident, this attracted the downstairs neighbor. A woman emerged from the doorway, wearing slippers, a terry cloth housecoat, and hair curlers. Bud was surprised by the look on her face. She didn't seem scared, or concerned about this strange man throwing rocks at her house. Just eager to help.

"You looking for Warren, the park ranger?" she asked. "He moved away."

"Oh? When was that?"

"Couple months ago, I guess it is."

"Who lives up there now?" Bud asked.

She shook her head. "No one. Won't be anyone there until they hire a new ranger. Way that they work, it could be six months or something."

"Did you hear or see anything unusual early this morning?"

"Ah, you mean when that woman was killed at Wonderland? Maybe if Warren had still been here she might've made it. You know, because he would have gotten there quicker? You with Woodside PD?"

"No, I'm a *private* investigator."

"Oh, okay." She nodded.

In the background, a baby started to cry. The woman glanced over her shoulder and back at Bud.

He thanked her for her time and as she ducked back into her apartment, he turned the car around near a squatty outbuilding with four garage-style doors. One of the doors was open. Rather than being the kind of door that rolled back into the building, it stuck straight out like a razzing tongue. Brown corrugated cardboard boxes rose to the ceiling and spilled out of the storage unit. Bud photographed this for good measure, then made a five-point turn and drove back to the highway.

Looking across Skyline Boulevard at the Wonderland entrance, he imagined Yoshi yelling at him to get his ass out of the car. He briefly considered the idea, reviewing the muddy shoulder, gravel driveway, and the highway's blind corners.

"Seriously," he explained to an imaginary Yoshi, "it wouldn't be safe. My chair's wheels would get stuck. It's not meant for four-wheeling, you know."

He thought of the wheelchairs that were now designed specifically for trail travel with fat tires, deep tread, and hardier suspensions. Until now, he could never imagine why someone would need one. He didn't spend enough time outside the city limits to make that kind of purchase worthwhile. He'd sooner buy a mechanized wheelchair or set his Impala up with a series of hydraulic lifts that would spit the chair out at the touch of a button. Besides, few things made him want to get out of his car these days. Sometimes he felt like he was just on autopilot, going through the motions well enough to keep his job, but not really engaged, not like he used to be as a detective.

"I might tip over." He made up excuses for the continued argument with Yoshi in his head. "If I tried to cross the road I'd probably get killed by a passing truck." As if to illustrate the point, a motorcycle whizzed by at half the speed of light.

Bud pulled cautiously out of the driveway and continued down the road. A few minutes later, the tightly knit canopy of trees opened to reveal the small, unincorporated burg of Skylonda and its smattering of houses, a roadhouse restaurant, an archaic gas station, and a shoebox convenience store. On the right, next to the wooden A-frame that was Alice's Restaurant, a sign marked the entrance to the local California Department of Forestry Fire Station. Bud slowed but didn't stop. He would call later pretending to be Deputy Freeman. He'd make up some story about losing their report and ask them to fax him another copy. The CDF was too well organized and savvy to hand their paperwork over to a PI or a civilian, and in person, in his chair, he wouldn't pass for an active-duty detective.

As he drove slowly past, Bud glanced at the sandwich board detailing the day's specials at Alice's. He briefly contemplated the tables and mismatched chairs alongside the patio and the bikers parked in the lot, weekend warriors on rice rockets and full-timers on old-school Harleys. His stomach growled but he forced himself to drive on, continuing on Highway 35 past the intersection of Highway 84 that bisected the Santa Cruz Mountains east to west. In his younger days he would have stopped in a heartbeat, but now, what was the point? Any stop entailed another protracted struggle to get his wheelchair from the car.

Instead Bud dug through the pile on the bench seat next to him until his fingers closed around a Snickers. Thank God for candy bars. Maybe he should get that black canvas bag out of the trunk. Designed to hang over the seat and organize his stuff, it had a large section for files and big pockets on the sides where he could store his cameras and snacks. He'd been a little surprised when Tucker gave it to him last month on his birthday, even more so when she mentioned she'd been looking for something like it for a while. He didn't really understand why she went out of her way to be so nice to him when he'd never made an effort to befriend her. He had surmised that the girl had some serious daddy issues.

"What the hell am I supposed to do with this?" he'd asked when she pushed the bag at him. "Who asked you to get this in the first place? I have my own system."

An enormous "Stop trying to change me" billboard had popped up in his head, surprising him a little since it wasn't like Tucker was his ex-wife or anything. She was just trying to be nice. When her face fell in disappointment—a look that hadn't helped matters—he took the thing, to shut her up, and stuffed it in his trunk. Since then, he'd seen her walk past the Impala and peek in at the front seat. She seemed a little saddened that the organizer wasn't there, but she hadn't mentioned it.

At least once a week Bud thought about the bag and how it might make it easier for him to find things while driving, but he was too entrenched in his position to actually relent and use it. If he gave in now, she'd think she'd guilted him into it, wouldn't she? That's what women were like. Once they found out you had a soft spot, they'd aim right at it, sending arrows of tears and looks of disappointment, and talking of their hurt feelings.

Crying shouldn't be allowed at work. It should be outlawed, plain and simple, a fireable offense. Bud firmly believed that *feelings* didn't belong on the job. The workplace used to be the one sanctuary where men didn't have to deal with those *feelings* you had to tiptoe around at home. Nowadays women brought all that baggage to the office. Even the boys in blue, who had once been allowed to be men, swearing and pulling pranks on each other, and not worrying about fucking *feelings*, even cops had to go through all this touchy-feely sensitivity training. The world had become a dangerous place for old-school men, one where a wrong word or gesture could get you disciplined, fired, or even sued.

He considered heading into the office, but Yoshi hadn't phoned him again, which meant she had plenty to do without his input, and she'd probably gone home for the day by now. There was no point starting to dig dirt on Keith Ridger and Jennifer Garcia, either. That could wait until tomorrow. Of course, there was always his Enchanted Towers surveillance stint, but the jealous hubbie would be home at any moment and Bud could do without the guy sticking his head in the window and baring his soul for another hour. He stared out into the fading light. No one would miss him if he wanted to spend all night in front of his TV with a pizza and beer.

He put a call in to Yoshi and informed her voicemail that he could be reached at home if anything came up. It was a safe bet nothing would, and even if it did, he'd be the last person she would call unless she had no choice. Yoshi only used him for the work she couldn't handle, or didn't want to handle, and there was just enough of that to keep him in a job. Bud supposed he could be thankful for that. Things could be worse. A lot worse.

CHAPTER EIGHT

Yoshi disguised a yawn and wondered how much longer it was going to take for Velvet to be escorted from lockup. Yoshi had waited at the police station until late the previous evening, only to learn that her friend was not going to be released immediately. The police did not seem to realize that they had made an error, and Velvet was to be arraigned first thing in the morning. Yoshi had not been permitted to see her, so she had gone home for practical reasons. She needed sleep, a shower, and fresh clothing.

A little after eight in the morning she had returned to the station, to occupy one of their uncomfortable chairs until she could walk out of here with her best friend. At least Velvet had not been required to pay a compulsory overpriced bail to obtain her freedom, Yoshi thought. She was fortunate that the judge at the arraignment was a *Chronicle* reader and had apparently recognized Velvet as a respected journalist. Or perhaps she'd recognized Velvet as having once edited the lesbian magazine *Womyn*. Or maybe they had even shared a bed. Who was to say that her honor was not a lesbian? Whichever it was, Velvet had been afforded a rare forty-eight-hour window to clear her name and avoid having to surrender herself to the San Francisco justice system for a preliminary hearing.

When Yoshi heard the front desk clerk step away, she ducked through the door and wandered out of the public waiting area into the bullpen, the large open office in which desks where paired in twos and threes. She had been inside the Mission Police Station a few times and remembered the layout.

When she first walked into the room the voices of half a dozen officers seemed to mingle together into a thunderous roar. It was true that when you lost your eyesight your other senses heightened to fill the void. But it was not instantaneous or absolute. When she was faced with this type of cacophony from all directions, it took Yoshi a moment or two to filter out the background noises and focus on a specific conversation. It was similar to staring at a wall of forest green, where the vegetation is shades of the same color. At first glance, it appears uniform, but then your eyes focus and you can separate out trees, grass, and bushes.

Yoshi narrowed her interest to two conversations. One was a man's voice talking in the distinctive pattern of telephone communication.

"I understand that," he was assuring the person on the other end of the line. "I'd still like to come down and speak with you in person."

There was a pause for the response. Yoshi heard a rustling of paper, as though he were preparing to write down information.

"965 Mission. Thank you. I'll see you later today, then."

Yoshi made note of the address and focused her concentration on the other conversation of interest. Two men were speaking in low voices farther in the room. Yoshi strolled in their direction.

"…just the shoes."

"No murder weapon?"

"Maybe…to lab…comparison."

"Witnesses?" As Yoshi drew closer, she recognized the gravelly tenor of Detective Ari Fleishman.

"Still canvassing—"

"Whoa." Ari cut the other guy off. "PI—don't say *anything*."

Yoshi smiled to herself. Detective Fleishman was not a bad guy. They had worked together on several cases. They respected each other. She could hear papers shuffling on the desk as one of the men buried something below documents. Just because she and Ari played well together did not mean they showed each other their cards.

"Say anything about what, Ari?" Yoshi asked. Turning toward the other man present, she outstretched her hand, "Yoshi Yakamota, Blind Eye Detective Agency."

"Detective Packard of the Woodside police." His hand closed around hers and pumped vigorously.

"Detective," Yoshi acknowledged. "Did your mother not teach you that it is rude to hide important papers from blind girls?"

He dropped her hand. Yoshi could almost hear the crimson of embarrassment flush his cheeks. "Oh no, I was just—"

"Ari?" she requested, ignoring Packard's discomfort. "Do you have a moment?"

"Certainly." He moved a chair noisily across the floor as an invitation to sit.

"But this is my case," the Woodside cop complained as if she weren't there.

The air rippled and the chair squeaked as Ari straightened from his seated position and moved a hand toward his face. Yoshi imagined him holding a finger up in front of his lips, motioning Packard to hush.

"I'll just be a minute," Ari insisted.

Packard sighed and shuffled away in the direction of a harsh coffee aroma.

"He is going to be disappointed," Yoshi said as she took a seat.

"What? Why?" Ari sat down in his rolling office chair, which creaked and groaned slightly under the weight.

"You are out of coffee."

"Oh, come on, how could you possibly know that?" He swiveled in his chair.

"Fresh coffee has a distinctly different odor than coffee that has been congealing for hours. By now, the burnt coffee smell suggests there is only a thin layer of sludge at the bottom. Not enough for a full cup, I imagine."

"You aren't here about our coffee, Yoshi. You don't even drink the stuff. So what do you want?"

"The Rosemary Finney case. What do you have on Velvet?"

"Enough."

"Come on, Ari, give me something. I know you haven't acquired the murder weapon, the body has only been cold for, what, twenty-four hours? Have you even obtained the ME's report yet? Have you looked at other suspects? What evidence do you have that substantiates an *arrest*?"

Ari pivoted his chair around and rolled closer.

"Look." He lowered his voice. "It wasn't my call, okay? Woodside's all gung-ho to wrap this up. But I can tell you this—it might have been hasty, but your client is looking very good for this. A witness reported seeing her car at the crime scene. Get an explanation for that, and who knows." He rose abruptly. "It looks like your client's anxious to leave."

"Really? I simply cannot imagine why." Yoshi stood and thrust the chair out of her way. "Oh, one more thing," she said, intentionally mimicking Columbo's parting shot. "Where did you locate the shoes?"

"You heard that. Damn it! Fine—they were in the Dumpster at Velvet's workplace, right next to where she parked her car." He touched Yoshi's forearm. "I'll walk you out."

❖

Velvet embraced Yoshi and kissed her on the cheek. "God, am I glad to see you!"

"Are you?" Yoshi looked suspicious. "You seem surprised."

"I thought maybe you'd send Tucker."

"You sound slightly disappointed. What is that about?"

Velvet deflected the question as she glanced around at her surroundings. "Can we go? I'll feel a lot better when we're out of here." She took Yoshi's arm in her own. "I saw you talking with the detective—what's his name—Fleishman? Did he tell you anything?"

As soon as the two women stepped out onto the sidewalk, they were hit by air thick with the pungent, unmistakable aroma of Mission Street. It wafted up from the sidewalk stinking of used wine blended with slow-cooked taqueria beans and deep-fried Chinese dishes. Homeless mingled with Latino day workers, while skateboarding urchins darted between the steady flow of vehicles and pedestrians who seemed locked into a serious competition for right of way.

Velvet raised her voice to be heard over the din. "Wow, there's a cab—how lucky is that? Taxi!" She frantically waved her arm, which was already toting a cell phone in a pink fuzzy poodle-shaped holder and a recycled rubber messenger bag.

The yellow cab stopped four feet from the curb. Velvet opened the back door for Yoshi, who slid in and gave the address for the Blind Eye offices.

"No, no," Velvet said as she climbed in and closed the door. Leaning forward in the seat, she demanded, "901 Mission."

Yoshi raised an eyebrow. "The *Chronicle*?"

The cabbie quickly darted into traffic to prevent second thoughts. "Feel free to speed," Velvet told him.

On cue, the bored Pakistani driver slammed on the gas and roared through the busy streets like a post-heist getaway driver. Fighting the g-force vortex within the cab that threatened to slam her into Yoshi, Velvet grabbed the door's armrest to keep herself in place and explained, "I've got to get back to work."

"Work? You were arrested yesterday. Surely no one is expecting you to report for work as usual."

"I know, you'd think that'd give me some leeway, but Stan sent explicit orders to get right back there this morning. Can you believe they cuffed me right there in the office? God. How humiliating."

"Who is next door to the *Chronicle* building?" Yoshi asked.

"What?" Velvet was surprised by the change in subject.

"At 965 Mission."

965 Mission? Velvet didn't really think that was any of Yoshi's business. "Why?"

"Humor me."

"Fine." Velvet sighed. "If you must know—which I guess you must—I mean, I don't know what it has to do with anything, it's just a medical office complex."

"And who do *you* know there?"

"Artemis McDermid. My shrink. There. Are you happy?"

Yoshi touched Velvet's hand with her own. "Velv, it is not as though I am unaware that you have a shrink. I overheard several detectives talking about a meeting there, this afternoon at two. I would prefer to speak with her first, especially since we are already on the way."

"Oh God, what's she going to tell them? I mean, what I tell her is confidential, isn't it?"

"It will be okay," Yoshi consoled her. "I am sure she will keep your confidence. However, you should probably tell me why you have been seeing her."

"Because I'm a lesbian. Isn't it a rite of passage?"

Yoshi was silent.

"Now?" Velvet made a pointed nod at the driver. She wasn't about to talk about her intimate problems in front of a stranger.

She waited for a sign that Yoshi understood, then remembered about her sight and reached for her hand. Yoshi gave Velvet's fingers a reassuring squeeze. That wasn't what Velvet was hoping for, so she tugged Yoshi's arm to the back of the driver's seat and traced an arrow on her palm. Yoshi nodded her comprehension. They'd discuss it later.

"So, you sent Tuck out on an errand? Cool. I was afraid you'd fired her or something. Not that you would. I mean, she's so cute." Yoshi always had the best-looking assistants, and Tucker—the shy little butchy one with the doe eyes—was no exception.

"Do not go there," Yoshi said curtly.

Velvet feigned innocence. "What?"

"You know what. I would prefer you did not even think about it."

Oh, I've thought about it. I've more than thought about it. Velvet didn't share her glib reply. She believed in right timing, and this wasn't it. "Oh, I see, you want her all for herself," she goaded. She liked to get her friend going.

Yoshi blushed. "That is absurd. It is simply…"

"Doth protest too much."

"Have you forgotten how many assistants you have cost me?"

"Me?" Velvet huffed indignantly. So maybe she'd slept with one or two. But how did that constitute "costing"?

"Yes, you. You date them—"

"*I* don't date," Velvet clarified. Dating was an antiquated patriarchal system designed to constrain women's sexual freedom.

Yoshi ignored her. "Then you leave them."

"I might *get with* a woman, but I'm never *with* her. Not in some kind of going-steady couple way. So how could I leave?"

"If they are not absent from work because they are too exhausted from all night lovemaking—"

"Fucking," Velvet chided. "Or do you prefer 'hitting it'?"

"Then they quit," Yoshi continued to ignore her, "because they simply cannot *bear* to be reminded of you. Or they are so heartbroken that they cannot do their work. They just stare into space pining away. You have blown through four of them."

"*Blown.*" Velvet snickered, doing her best Beavis and Butthead impression.

Yoshi was immune. "Tucker is a great worker and—"

"Too cute to share?" Velvet suggested again.

"Damn it, Velvet. I am serious. In case you have not noticed, my eyesight is not merely deteriorating. It has practically disappeared. There is so much I cannot do. I need—"

"Oh." Velvet gasped as though the wind had been knocked out of her. She couldn't remember a time when Yoshi had admitted to needing anything.

Yoshi declared, "I need someone who can really help—you know, grow with the company and take over more of the field work. Or I need to hire myself a personal assistant like that woman on *Monk*. What is her name?"

"The girl from the pizza shop or Bitty Schram?"

Yoshi crinkled her forehead. "Excuse me?"

"The first season it was Sharona." Velvet launched into her entertainment education voice. "Played by actress Bitty Schram. Since then it's been the girl from *Two Guys, A Girl and A Pizza Place,* Traylor Howard. Both cute, just in different ways."

"I stopped watching it after the first year. But yes, I think I could use someone like her."

"Are you saying you need a nurse?"

"No."

"A seeing-eye person? Why don't you just get a dog? They're more loyal."

Yoshi sighed. "I am on the waiting list, actually, for a seeing-eye dog."

"There's a waiting list? I thought they trained assistant dogs up in San Rafael."

"Yes, they train the dogs there. But then the organization ships them out across the country. I worry that the business may require more. More than Bud—who is permanently glued to the front seat of his Impala—and me." She smiled a small smile. "I know you assist us too. I am not overlooking that."

"Well, I certainly don't want to bad-mouth Tucker," Velvet interjected. "But it sounds like you need another investigator, not a cute receptionist."

"Yes, perhaps I do need to bring on another PI. It is also essential that I have someone who has administrative skills to assist me in that arena. As it is, I just cannot keep from worrying that we might be missing things." Yoshi paused and sighed again. "This time, your life is on the line. Are you not the least bit concerned about Blind Eye's capabilities?"

Velvet scooted over on the taxi's bench seat and palmed Yoshi's knee. Yoshi smiled and covered the hand with her own. Tears pooled in Velvet's eyes and she looked out the window, silently urging them away. She didn't wipe her eyes lest Yoshi hear the movement and ask what was wrong. Velvet wondered if she would ever get used to the idea of Yoshi's blindness. When they were together Yoshi could still see. Oh, her vision was blurry and her peripheral vision sucked, but up close, when Yoshi looked at Velvet's face, she could *see* her. Yoshi could read all the emotions displayed there; Velvet knew that.

Of course she'd always been aware of Yoshi's degenerative eye disease. She'd known that Yoshi would eventually be completely blind. Usually the full effects didn't set in until a person reached their forties. It seemed wholly unfair that Yoshi had a more virulent case and had already progressed to this point when she was only thirty-six.

Velvet and Yoshi had broken up years ago—it had been almost a decade now, and Velvet couldn't remember anymore who'd left whom. They were two very different femmes, but she still liked to pretend that they'd just been too similar and that's why she now stuck with butches. But the truth was, she and Yoshi had just drifted apart while devoting their lives to their careers. They'd both spent seventy hours a week at work and eventually they became ships that passed in the night. Still, their relationship had transitioned into a quiet familial friendship that worked for them.

Unfortunately, the same thing hadn't worked with any of the transitory girlfriends that had followed Yoshi through the rotating door that was Velvet's bed. That was one of the issues she was exploring in therapy. Why couldn't she seem to make a relationship last, why didn't they stay friends with her? And were they right about Yoshi? The post-Yoshi girlfriends eventually formed a loose-knit Yoshi hate club whose members claimed Velvet spent too much time with Yoshi, that she was too intimate with her former lover, that Velvet was always comparing them to Yoshi and that none of them could compete with the specter of that long-buried romance.

Were they right? Velvet didn't see it that way. Hell, she worried when she and Yoshi didn't talk on the phone, especially when Velvet was really into a new girl. There always seemed to be a new girl. Velvet would get bored after a few weeks or get tired of their need for attention or demands for deeper intimacy. Sometimes she envied gay men, who seemed to have those string-free sexual hookups that she would like to cultivate. Really, that was all she had time for in her life anyway.

But at moments like this, when she endured a fierce need for someone, moments when she could appreciate the advantage to having a wife at home—in those moments, Yoshi was always there. Perhaps that wasn't the best or entirely healthy arrangement. Sometimes Velvet felt guilty about the assistance because it didn't seem like Yoshi needed her as often, even though Yoshi had fewer people in her life to turn to. Maybe Yoshi was just more stable.

"I would never doubt your abilities, Yosh. Plus," Velvet took on a more lighthearted tone to tease her friend, "I could solve this myself. I just wanted to spend time with you."

Yoshi smiled. Velvet knew Yoshi was grateful she had not made a big deal of her admitted weakness.

She changed the subject, asking rhetorically, "You know what the worst thing about being in county lockup is?" then answering, "The stench."

Yoshi laughed.

"Honestly. I don't even mean that flippantly. I mean, there you are, locked in this minuscule cell with six other women and you're inordinately obsessed with this pungent odor that doesn't really seem to be coming from any of your fine cellmates—in my case two aging sex workers, an angry shoplifter, and a couple of strung-out junkies. Instead it emanates from the walls or the cement flooring around the tiny cots. I thought at first it was a 'Oops, I forgot where the toilet is' issue, like years of urine had soaked into the floor and attached itself to the cement somehow, on, like, the microbial level."

Yoshi smiled again and allowed Velvet to continue her rant.

"But after a few hours in there, you realize that it's much more serious than that. I mean, I interviewed everyone in the cell last night, collected samples for analysis back at the lab—I'm expecting this to be a cover story, maybe a four-page spread with sidebars and everything. I'm going right in and pitching that to my editor."

"I like it." Yoshi said. "Is there someway we can pin this murder on it? The odor, I mean?"

Velvet was back to her upbeat self. "Exactly. I'm sure it could stand up and move from room to room, and what was it locked up for anyway? You know, my arraignment hearing was nothing like I've seen on *Law & Order.*" She changed the subject, connecting to something she'd thought earlier. That was kind of how her mind worked, like a continuous experimentation in word association. "My experience getting bail was nowhere near what it is like in the movies. Fortunately,

I didn't get just one phone call. I mean, I know you told me to get a lawyer already, but I still haven't seen one."

Yoshi didn't voice disappointment or amusement; she just shook her head and the corners of her mouth twitched.

"At least I asked for a lawyer right away," Velvet argued in her own defense. "As they were putting me in the squad car—they really do put a hand on your head as they shove your handcuffed ass into the backseat. The cuffs, the locked doors, and the metal cage sure make you feel claustrophobic. I thought I might hyperventilate." She felt her chest tightening at the memory.

"When they got me to the station," she continued, "they put me in an interrogation room. After a little while this guy came in wearing this ugly brown suit—where are the fashion police when you need them? So, anyway, he started asking me questions. I told him I wanted a lawyer. You know, they wouldn't even let me make the call. They made it for me. Then another detective—that stocky one from Woodside?"

"Packard," Yoshi supplied.

"Right, Packard. He came in, said the lawyer was on the way and then he sat down and started *telling* me things."

"What, exactly?" Yoshi asked.

"He said they had found a pair of shoes in the *Chronicle*'s Dumpster, and he asked how was I going to explain that. Well, I had no idea. I mean, anyone could use that Dumpster. It's not like it's locked or anything. And what would I be doing with Rosemary's shoes? Well, he told me that I took them from her body after killing her. He asked me why I took them. I told him—"

"Wait," Yoshi interrupted. "You mean you *answered* him?" She shook her head again. This time there was no hint of humor. "*After* you had been read your rights and called your lawyer?"

"Oh, God." Velvet gasped. "I did. Fuck. That was so stupid of me. I can't believe I fell for that. Am I totally screwed?" She held her breath, waiting for the answer.

"What did you tell him?"

Velvet hoped Yoshi's question suggested that there were some things that could be said that wouldn't be a problem. "I told him I wasn't some kind of shoe fetishist and I wouldn't want anything of Rosemary's. Then he asked me what I'd used to strangle her. Said they knew I had had a big ugly fight with her the other night—which is true, of course. I told you about that. Anyway, he said I'd gone to the

Wonderland Park, hidden on a trail until she ran past, and then I jumped out and strangled her."

"How did you reply to that?" Yoshi asked.

"I told him that was crazy, and I said—oh, you aren't going to like this—I said Rosemary's a scrappy bitch and I'd never have been able to take her alone."

"Velvet." Yoshi sighed and shook her head again. "What am I going to do with you?"

"I know, I know, but he was so annoying. But, yeah, after I said that, he sat up like I'd just confessed. He actually asked me who my accomplice was. God, what an idiot."

"Him? Or you?"

"I deserve that. Oh, we're here. You'll have to berate me later." Velvet rummaged in her purse for her wallet.

"Here," she said, waving cash at the driver.

"I am exiting as well," Yoshi reminded her.

"Right." Velvet slid out of the cab and then bent over and reached a hand in to Yoshi.

"Thank you," Yoshi said as she stepped onto the curb. "Will you walk me to your therapist's office?"

"It's just right there—well, I guess I can show you to the door. But then I really must be off. Stan will be in a tizzy as it is, and he's supposed to be doing something for me. I need to keep him happy."

"She will not simply talk to me," Yoshi pointed out. "You will have to give your permission."

"Oh, right." Hastily Velvet found a notepad in her purse and composed a suitable waiver of privacy. She read it aloud.

"I, Velvet Ericksen, give my therapist, Dr. Artemis McDermid, permission to speak with private investigator Yoshi Yakamota of Blind Eye Detective Agency, who is working on my behalf to uncover the truth about Rosemary Finney's death. Please tell her anything that might be relevant." Velvet added her signature, tore the note from the pad, and placed it in Yoshi's hands as they climbed the outdoor stairs to the second floor. "Okay?"

"Thank you." Yoshi was not sure if the note would be of any use, but for some people a piece of paper was all it took to overcome reservations. It provided an excuse.

Artemis McDermid's office was in an older walk-up that was surprisingly quiet inside, given the cacophony of vehicle and pedestrian traffic outside. Though the inhabitants seemed thoroughly modern—Velvet had mentioned a chiropractor, a plastic surgeon, and several therapists—the faint smell of mold and the feel of rough matte walls gave Yoshi an old-world image of the place.

Velvet held the door and ushered her into the waiting room. "She sees patients on the hour. There's a couch here, if you want to sit and wait. It's a quarter till, now."

Yoshi stretched her hand out to feel the couch. It had a soft inviting cover.

"There's a table about a foot in front of the couch," Velvet warned. "It's kind of a tight squeeze."

"Thanks." Yoshi maneuvered into place and lowered herself slowly into the overstuffed cushions that seemed capable of swallowing her whole. "I am afraid I might become wedged in here."

"Thanks for everything, Yosh." A kiss landed on Yoshi's cheek. "I'm so lucky to have you on my side."

Yoshi smiled. "Call me later to compare notes."

"Okay."

"Now take care of yourself. And Velvet?" Yoshi heard the sound of a hand making contact with a doorknob and pictured Velvet hovering.

"Yes?"

"I am the fortunate one—to have you in my life."

"Oh, stop that." Velvet tsk-tsked. "I'll talk to you soon. Good luck."

After the door shut quietly behind her friend, Yoshi wondered what all Velvet had kept from her. Velvet was not particularly secretive, but she was a consummate journalist at heart. Which meant she preferred to hoard potentially useful information—offerings to heap at the feet of the story gods. Yoshi would wager a week's pay that Velvet had not told her everything she knew about this case. In fact, she'd venture that Velvet was either *already* assigned to write a piece on Rosemary's murder or she was on her way to pitch one, right this minute.

Velvet would exploit the fact that she was a suspect as fodder for a compelling article. Which was a problem because she might shield from Yoshi information that would otherwise clear her name, if that meant the paper would have exclusive access. Yoshi would acquire all the relevant facts eventually, but it might not be until *after* they were published in the *Chronicle*.

Closing her eyes, Yoshi made a mental picture of Dr. Artemis McDermid's waiting room. She could smell the printed ink of magazines spread on the low coffee table that pressed against her shins. The smooth cold pressure on her pressed cotton-sheathed legs informed her that the table was metal, not wood. She could hear the stuttering glub of a water cooler against the far wall. In the therapy room, a door opened and closed. As with many other counselor's offices, this one doubtlessly possessed a rear exit, an architectural feature that protected clients from the discomfort of seeing another patient.

Apparently, Yoshi thought, *the last thing you want when you leave your psychologist's office is to witness the person about to take your place on the couch.* Was it about the intimacy? she wondered, having never had occasion to try therapy. Maybe patients desired the pretense that they were the only one, that no others shared that intimate space with their counselor. Or maybe it was about stigma and embarrassment—not wanting to see another human, not wanting anyone else to see that you required such services.

From the other room, a speakerphone rang into the doctor's voice mail. Even after the message began, with the obviously upset voice of a client, the psychologist did not raise the receiver and silence the call. Yoshi hoped only her vastly trained ears could hear through the thin wooden door that separated the inner sanctum of the therapeutic space from potential eavesdroppers in the waiting room. She didn't expect Dr. McDermid to be loose lipped about her patients—by accident or even with a note like Velvet's.

"This is Liz Claiborne. Did you see the news?" A female voice on the recorder cracked with emotion. "She's dead. I have to see you." Sobs emanated. "Please call me, at 863-7384."

Yoshi pulled her special Braille Palm Pilot from her bag and quickly entered the phone number and name. The message ended and there were no others. As the phone clicked off, Yoshi heard rustling through papers, then the dial tone and a number punched in.

"Liz? Dr. McDermid returning your call. I'm sorry I missed you." Artemis McDermid spoke in a cadence that indicated she wasn't connected to a live person. "I usually see my last patient at four p.m.

but I'll make an exception today and stay late, if you can come in. Give me a call and leave me a message confirming what time you'll be here, between five and seven, okay? All right, I hope to see you then."

The phone clicked off and light footsteps—slender legs in kitten heels, Yoshi guessed—shuffled toward the door. She could hear the whisper of fabric brushing against itself as Dr. McDermid entered the waiting room, and speculated that the therapist was wearing a light skirt, probably fashioned from cotton-blend fabric.

Yoshi stood and squeezed past the coffee table to offer her hand.

"Oh," the psychologist exclaimed in surprise. "I was expecting someone else. Can I help you?"

She smelled clean and comforting, as though she had been baking cookies. Yoshi decided, after a deeper inhalation, that the scent of vanilla and chocolate probably originated from Dr. McDermid's use of a cocoa butter–based bath product rather than a plate of cookies. She wondered if the psychologist purchased her personal grooming supplies at Lush, as she did.

"I am here on behalf of my client, Velvet Erickson." For what it was worth, Yoshi surrendered the paper Velvet had entrusted to her and waited a moment for the response.

Artemis McDermid ended the handshake abruptly, dropping Yoshi's hand. "I'm really not at liberty to discuss my clients. A note doesn't change that."

"If you will allow me, I will take just a moment of your time. I do not intend to ask anything that would be confidential."

"Fine." The psychologist didn't make a move toward her office. "You have five minutes."

Yoshi wondered if Dr. McDermid preferred to speak in the public area or was merely waiting for her to enter the therapy room first. Yoshi chose privacy and strode ahead through the doorway. Once they were both in the small inner office, she located a couch and seated herself, resisting the urge to lie down as the patient in traditional psychotherapy. Across from her, a chair's springs squeaked.

Yoshi dove right in. "What time did you arrive yesterday morning, Dr. McDermid?"

The question seemed to surprise the psychologist. She shifted in the squealing chair and said, "Excuse me?"

"My question does not breach your patient confidentiality, does it?" Yoshi asked pleasantly.

Dr. McDermid did not ask "what's it to you?" but Yoshi thought she could hear the question simmering below the surface in the timbre of her reply. "I get in around seven. I like to have an hour to do paperwork, and some of my clients come in before work. Why?"

"Did you notice anything suspicious when you arrived?"

"Suspicious? I don't think so."

"Was anyone else here? Were other cars in the parking lot?"

"Just Dr. Michaelson. He has an office downstairs and drives a silver Mercedes. He's usually here when I arrive. I'm sorry, I thought you had some questions about Velvet?"

"Oh, certainly. What day do you usually see her?"

"It really depends, but I guess it's usually Wednesday afternoons."

"Would you consider her dangerous?"

"Velvet? Oh no, definitely not."

"A threat to anyone?"

"No."

"Did she ever discuss Rosemary Finney?"

The ensuing moment of silence suggested Velvet *had* mentioned her former lover, colleague, and nemesis. The evasive tone when she spoke revealed that Velvet had also made mention of her dislike for the woman.

"Anything my client discussed is confidential."

"Of course. Did you know Ms. Finney?"

Dr. McDermid rose abruptly from her chair. "I'm sorry, but I really must be going."

Yoshi did not move. "Why are the police interested in speaking to you?"

Dr. McDermid drew a deep breath. "How do you know about that?"

"I overheard it when I was bailing Velvet out of jail."

"Jail? Oh, dear." Dr. McDermid seemed to crumple back into her chair.

"Yes, jail. She has been charged with Rosemary Finney's *murder*. So while I respect your commitment to patient confidentiality, please understand that as long as this is hanging over Velvet's head, I will not stop investigating. I will not simply go away because my questions make you uncomfortable. Now, what are the police expecting you to tell them?"

Dr. McDermid's voice cracked. "I don't know, I swear. I can't tell them about Velvet's temperament."

"Why not?" Yoshi asked. "You just said you did not think Velvet was a threat to anyone. Would any statements by you about her mental state not actually help her? Or do you intend to reveal something that would implicate her?"

"No, of course not. I simply cannot break my client's confidentiality."

"Even if she specifically requests that you do?" Yoshi was getting frustrated. She did not believe that Velvet's psychologist was restricted from breaking her confidence in light of her patient's permission. Probing the limits of Dr. McDermid's resistance, she asked, "Would you testify on her behalf—if it got to that?"

"Of course, if I was legally required to. If I were subpoenaed, for example. But even then I would not be at liberty to reveal anything that might break another client's confidentiality."

"Another client?" Yoshi slid to the edge of her seat. "Liz Claiborne, per chance?"

"What?" Dr. McDermid's voice rose in pitch and volume.

Yoshi immediately regretted the question.

"How dare you!" The doctor kicked aside her chair. "You're spying on me? You've violated my clients' privacy?"

Yoshi stood from the couch and held her palms out contritely. "I was not eavesdropping, I simply—"

"I should report you for unethical—" In her anger, Dr McDermid cut herself off. "God, I can't believe you did that." She took two steps and opened the rear door. Cool air rushed into the office, but it didn't serve to cool the psychologist's emotional outburst. Instead, she demanded loudly, "Get out."

"Thank you for your time." Yoshi held out a business card. When it was refused, she dropped it on Dr. McDermid's chair. "If you change your mind—"

"I won't," Dr. McDermid insisted. "Now please leave."

"Not for me." Yoshi added, "For Velvet."

"For Velvet, I won't pursue charges against you."

Yoshi nodded with her head bowed. Before she stepped outside she asked, "Have you ever thrown anything into the *Chronicle's* Dumpster?"

"Excuse me?"

Yoshi strode outside and pointed toward the *San Francisco Chronicle* building. She could smell the trash from the office balcony. "The parking lot here, it butts up against the newspaper's lot, doesn't it? There's a Dumpster, by the fence on their side." It smelled like more than just paper waste. "It would be easy to throw something in there—if you were cleaning out your car or something."

"No."

"I am sure they would not mind."

"I said no," Artemis McDermid repeated curtly. "Now please leave." The air changed as the psychologist started closing the door. "Now really, I must be going."

As the door clicked shut, Yoshi wondered if she had destroyed any prospect that Artemis McDermid would reveal what she knew. Obviously her patient Liz Claiborne had something to do with Rosemary Finney, but what? Had Liz been the one to discard Rosemary's shoes in the nearby Dumpster? Or was it Dr. McDermid? Was the psychologist lying? And if she was, what *else* was she lying about? And why?

To find out, Yoshi was determined to speak with Liz Claiborne directly. From the overheard phone conversation, she knew Dr. McDermid had invited the Claiborne woman to drop by her office later that evening. If the distraught patient did show up, Yoshi would be there to intercept her and extract some answers. There was one thing that Yoshi already knew: she could not simply let it go. Nothing was going to prevent her from clearing Velvet's name. Not even the threat of disciplinary action.

CHAPTER NINE

Before the approaching truck even got close enough for her to
see inside its cab, AJ made out the unmistakable silhouette
of an emergency light bar balanced on the roof and knew that a park
ranger was driving. All the PD units in the area drove sedans. Sure, the
California Highway Patrol had some Ford Bronco–style vehicles, but
those were all unmistakable black-and-whites.

Back home, AJ had never even met a park ranger and she
sure wouldn't fancy them law enforcement. She shook her head in
bemusement. It was the damndest thing, rangers patrollin' suburbia's
streets while rollin' between scattered plots of nothing but dead grass.

She stepped out of her own white sedan and stretched her
arms and legs. By exiting her vehicle, she hoped to avoid the car-69
communication style California law enforcement seemed so fond of.
The cops never leaving their cars, just pulling up to each other like they
was at the McDonald's drive-in. The tight streets of the New Orleans
French Quarter prevented that kind of thing, and in other parts of the
city, like the Ninth Ward, where she'd been raised and patrolled, cops
didn't like stopping too long, even within the relative safety of their
vehicles. They weren't welcome in the hood. Not even by law-abiding
folk, most of them long since lost their faith in NOPD's ability to keep
them safe.

In the hood, gangs and drug dealers ran the show. Most of the
residents got caught up in the street economy, making money off drugs
and prostitution and robbery. When shit happened—as it did on a
regular basis—good folk just hid behind closed doors and the gangs

brought down their own justice. Things were usually resolved down the barrel of a gun.

AJ had been paired with a partner in New Orleans—which made patrols safer, but came at a price, one she hadn't always been eager to pay. During her six-year career, she'd been teamed up with a couple of lazy, ineffectual, homophobic, and in one case downright criminal, partners. In those situations she'd had a choice to make: risk retaliation by breaking the code of silence and turning rat, or remain party to behavior she didn't condone. She hadn't always been proud of the path she'd chosen.

Here in East Palo Alto, the Peninsula's version of the Ninth Ward, AJ not only rolled alone, but there was times when she'd be the only EPA officer riding the streets. The supes on duty were, on paper, the second patrol. But in all the months since she'd started, she never saw one leave the station.

Not that you wanted a supervisor lurking around trying to catch you riding dirty. Or, as she'd begun to fear lately, trying to pin the department's stink on her. The truth was, she'd wanted to get the hell out of New Orleans, least till the Katrina mess blew over. But she'd been lured to this department in part with the understanding that she'd be up for a promotion, making her EPAPD's first female lieutenant. She'd known straight up that they'd recruited her to meet some minority-hiring clause, but every place had its own political bullshit and she could handle that.

During her phone interview the brass told her that the current lieutenant was out on disability leave and it didn't look like he'd be coming back. She hadn't thought to ask what'd happened—being a cop was a dangerous job—so it was only after she'd gotten here that she'd learned the guy was out on psych leave. He'd had a nervous breakdown. Even AJ, as the rookie in the department, could see that wasn't a good sign. It stank, like something fishy was going on. In the last month she'd begun to see why—just around the time the lieutenant recovered and made a surprise return to the force.

The bayside breeze blew over her coiled, closely cropped hair and cut through the fabric of her uniform shirt. She could feel the cool breath on her arms, but the Mylar vest she wore blocked the air from reaching her chest. *Bulletproof.* Bunch of crock. She'd seen what a high-powered rifle could do to the material: tear a hole right through it. The many different layers of fibers crisscrossing each other couldn't stop a .30 caliber round, but at least they could slow handgun bullets and might even stop a knife from getting through to a vital organ.

AJ missed a lot of things about New Orleans, but she had to admit that the East Palo Alto Police had better equipment, even if it was hand-me-downs from Palo Alto, their well-to-do big-sister-city. Because Palo Alto was handing down last year's top of the line equipment, it still totally beat out the decades-old shit they'd been stuck with at NOPD.

When she'd first slid the EPA vest over her head and adhered the Velcro flaps to the front and back panels, she could tell right away that it was two or three pounds lighter than the shit they humped around in N'awlins. That made a big difference, especially on hot days when the dense, nonbreathable material—the same technology that repelled bullets—trapped in the heat and sweat and multiplied them a thousand times. Eventually that crap could kill you, toppling you over with heatstroke.

The white ranger truck that pulled up a few feet from her had a red contraption in its bed, which, AJ had learned, was a portable pumper unit meant to suppress small fires and provide initial attacks until fire department personnel arrived. It could even do mobile attack for areas that required nimble vehicles. The trucks were more like agile quarterbacks than bulky linebacker fire engines. It looked to AJ like the truck was brand new. Last year's model, at the most. Damn, some of the agencies around here sure were stacked. How did she get stuck in the poorest city on the Peninsula? Probably because she was black, AJ thought. When she left New Orleans for the West Coast, she'd thought she was leaving behind the racism of the South. And sure enough, the people here didn't say the N-word to your face, and there were all these rules about "political correctness," a term she never heard back home. But that prejudice shit was still around in her new location. It was just more subtle, so you didn't notice it all the time.

Oh, she'd seen some of those successful homies on television and driving by in their Mercedes and BMWs—less flashy with their money than when the boys back home made it good and rolled by in pimped-out Escalades sporting matching gold grills. Here they'd be some Oreo, talking all proper English and acting like their shit didn't stink, like they forgot where they came from or they embarrassed by the people in the hood. But she'd noticed a deficiency of black faces on the west side of the bay; some invisible force field ran from Marin County to San Jose, keeping all the homeboys confined to the eastern shores.

AJ shifted her concentration to the park ranger who climbed out of the high Dodge Ram cab. She was a petite white woman with long straw-blond hair pulled back from her face into a perfect ponytail. She wore green jeans and a khaki uniform shirt with a gold star badge over her left breast pocket.

"I don't think I've met you," she said, looking AJ up and down. She stuck out her hand. "I'm Lisa Whitman."

Her smiling lips were tinted pink and her ears pierced by small gold hoops. Unlike AJ, Lisa Whitman was trying to look like a woman in spite of the masculine uniform and official gear.

AJ introduced herself and heartily shook the outstretched palm, which was delicate and soft against her own rough calluses.

"Oh." Ranger Whitman's cheeks went a shade darker than her rouge. "I'm sorry. I thought you were a guy."

No, just a dyke. AJ wondered what had tipped Lisa Whitman off. It wasn't usually her gravelly voice. Whatever. She shrugged. "It's okay. I get that all the time."

"It's these vests." The ranger pointed to her own chest. "They smash your boobs and make everyone into barrel-chested unisex. They must be made by men. A woman would design them to accommodate breasts. You can be damn sure that if we had to wear one under our pants, it wouldn't be flat in front."

AJ smiled.

"Anyway, it's nice to meet you. And nice that EPAPD finally hired a woman."

"Yeah? I don't think my coworkers are too happy 'bout it."

"Why? Because of the mustache?"

"Huh?" Was that a put-down? AJ absentmindedly stroked the peach fuzz she carried over her top lip.

"Didn't you notice? All the guys on the East Palo Alto PD have the same mustache-goatee combo. You know, around the mouth and covering the chin." Ranger Whitman illustrated by drawing a finger around her pink lips.

"Ah." AJ *had* noticed how the other officers sported similar facial hair. "What that about?"

"It's stupid, really. The brass made this policy where police officers have to be clean-shaven. This is like their big protest. What*ever*, huh?"

"Ya here about that abandoned vehicle?" AJ nodded in the direction of the trashed Pontiac sedan.

"Yeah. So here's the deal. It's in our lot, so we have jurisdiction. But our supervisors like us to have the local PD write up a police report, too. If it had plates, we'd run those. But since they're gone, let's see if we can find a VIN."

Whitman strode to the vehicle and peered in the broken windshield, checking the dashboard near the steering wheel for the metal plate that carried the vehicle identification number.

"Already ran it," AJ said.

"You did?" The ranger seemed disappointed.

Didn't know I was supposed to save it for ya, AJ thought. "Came back clean. No tickets, tied to no crime, ain't reported stolen."

"Do you have the RO's info?"

AJ nodded and pulled a small notepad from her breast pocket. She flipped through it until she found the registered owner's name and address, and handed it to the ranger.

Lisa Whitman thanked her and jotted down the information in a similar notebook of her own. "If you don't think it's related to a crime, I'll just have it towed, and I'll contact the RO. Otherwise, you can have it impounded."

AJ stared at the remains of the car, trying to decide if it was just an abandoned vehicle or evidence of something criminal. "Seeing how it's so badly vandalized, I think I'm gonna call impound," she said. Better safe than sorry, and besides, the supervisors loved getting paperwork back to prove she'd actually done more with her day than scratch her ass.

Whitman nodded. "Fair enough. Might end up being associated with some other criminal activity and then you'll be happy you hung on to it."

AJ radioed dispatch and requested a tow truck. While she sat in her patrol car filling out paperwork on the trashed vehicle, the ranger wandered around the lot, carrying a five-gallon bucket in one hand and a can-grabbing staff in the other. The garbage stick ended with two fingerlike pinchers that closed around trash when she pulled a trigger on the handle. AJ watched her picking up some litter, thinking about how back home, the city'd have some convict crew doing the job by hand, bent over picking up trash. She completed the triplicate form and then remembered the favor she'd promised to do for Tucker Shade.

Although she seemed done with her task, Whitman walked slowly from one end of the lot to the other. AJ recognized the look. In New Orleans she'd seen guys loafing around on patrol. The job was just about making rent, and cops made less money than the criminals they policed. There'd always be malcontents.

As if she felt AJ's eyes, Whitman pulled the grabber's trigger, lifted it over the white bucket, and let go. AJ didn't see nothing drop from the wand's fingers.

Approaching the ranger, she called out, "Can I ask ya something?"

"Oh, sure." The grabber hit the bottom of the bucket with a thump and Whitman set them down in the dirt.

"That female they found murdered in the park—that one of yours?"

"Oh yeah, that was a big deal. Not ours, though. It was a Woodside park. But it was one of our rangers that found the DB." Whitman used the shorthand for "dead body." "Well, she didn't *find* her. I meant that she was the first responder on scene."

"Y'all handle calls on other properties? For other agencies?"

"Not usually. We have ranger residences on preserves. Wonderland starts down here at the bottom of the hill and climbs up to Highway 35. There's a Midpen preserve across the street. The RP read Midpen's info on the gate there and thought we ran the other park too. So 911 contacted our dispatch, who called up Jenny. Jenny Cooper, she's in the Purissima residence, five miles up the road. She's a friend."

"I'm guessing y'all don't have a lot of homicides in your parks?" AJ couldn't imagine them being anything like the crime-ridden projects she'd patrolled and grew up in.

"We get body dumps, but yeah, not a lot of murders. There was one—back in the seventies, when the Trail Side Killer was ambushing women in parks all over the Bay Area. Most of our medical calls are for vehicle crashes and mountain bike accidents on preserves."

"Was it reported as a 10-87?" When a death was first ruled an accident, then declared a homicide, it could be too late to gather evidence or locate witnesses.

"No, it went out as a medical call for a woman down."

"Y'all hear from your friend about it?"

"Yeah, we talked. Jenny's really upset by it."

"Sure 'nough." AJ nodded. She would never forget the first time she'd seen a murder victim—even though she weren't but six at the time.

Ranger Whitman bobbed her head, then leaned toward AJ and added in a lowered voice, "Especially since she recognized the victim."

"Whoa, hold up. You saying y'all knew her?" AJ's interest was definitely piqued.

"We did, kind of. From a law enforcement stop. Jenny ticketed her a couple of years ago—"

"And she still remembers it?" These guys must not write very many tickets if they could remember everyone they'd ever stopped.

"Yeah, because it turned into such a big thing. See, Jenny stopped her for being on a closed trail in Corte Madera. That's our preserve across the street from Wonderland Park. The funny thing is," Whitman continued, "Jenny's really nice and she'd rather give a verbal warning than a ticket, especially if they apologize. But Ms. Finney didn't even let Jenny explain. She just blew up and screamed in her face. You know that kind of 'do you know who I am?' thing." She paused. "Maybe you don't, working in East Palo Alto." The ranger surveyed her surroundings, as though they made her point for her.

"Unfortunately," AJ replied, "I think I do. I've pulled over some big shots who just rolling through East PA. They'd never own a crib here."

Ranger Whitman smiled and continued, "Right. Well, we get a lot of these new-money guys that come in. You know, Internet whiz kids and Silicon CEOs and they think their newfound wealth gives them a free get out of jail card to pull whenever they want. So Ms. Finney insists Jenny doesn't have the *right* to stop her. We're authorized peace officers under PC 832."

"Sure," AJ affirmed. Although she wasn't familiar with the penal code Lisa Whitman was citing, she understood it to be the state law granting Midpen rangers powers of arrest.

"So, anyway, Jenny's explaining her legal right to make the stop, and that Finney woman, she just takes off. Plows right into Jenny and knocks her over! Which means she's just—"

"Done assaulted an officer!" AJ supplied.

"Right. So Jenny gets on the radio and reports this to dispatch. It's late in the evening by this point, and it's starting to get dark, so a bunch of us rangers responded. It took us, like, two hours to track the subject down, hiding in the preserve. When we finally caught her, Jenny charged her with the assault."

"Yo. It ain't no good to let people off easy for shit like that. You got to have respect or you got nothin'."

"Exactly. So the best part is Ms. Finney didn't show up for her court date."

AJ chuckled. "They issue a warrant?"

"Right, there was a warrant for her arrest. And since it was assault on an officer," Whitman stifled her laughter before delivering the punch line, "the cops showed up at her door in force. Guns drawn."

AJ laughed at the thought of a half dozen uniformed officers stacked backward from the entry door of one of those plantation type mansions she'd seen in the area. "How'd that turn out?" she asked.

"When she finally got to court, she had the nerve to talk back to the judge when he sentenced her to community service. She stood up and bitched about how unfair it would be to make someone like her work with common criminals. She offered to write a bigger check to avoid the community service."

AJ snorted. "How'd that go over?"

"He ordered her to pay a five thousand dollar fine, attend anger management classes, *and* still do the community service. Plus he said her time had to be spent working at one of the Midpen preserves. She was livid."

He should've charged her with trying to bribe a judge, AJ thought. "You sure this Ranger Jenny didn't kill the bitch herself?" She laughed, making light of the question, even though she was curious.

Whitman chuckled. "No. Jenny's the kind of person who hates early morning call-outs. So if she'd done this, I think she would have waited until later in the day. Oh, look at that." She pointed out toward the street at an approaching tow truck. "Guess you must be lucky. Every time I call for a tow out here it takes, like, two hours for them to respond. I think they're afraid of the location."

"He's on contract with the department," AJ explained. "Else I'd be still waiting when my shift end."

Whitman glanced at the thick black wristwatch on her arm, "Shit, it's almost twelve. I've got to go." She pointed at the timepiece. "Butt ugly, isn't it? I hate Timex sport watches, but I got tired of losing expensive ones on duty. If you're interested in the case, you should drop by Wonderland this evening. I heard on the radio that maintenance was going to be up there getting the place ready to reopen tomorrow. They might know something."

"Snap. I might just up and do that." The ranger was right, maintenance might've heard something or stumbled on something while opening the trail. Maybe she would roll up there when her shift ended.

"It was nice to meet you." Lisa Whitman held out a hand.

When AJ went to shake, she found an outstretched business card. She accepted it awkwardly. It seemed like everybody who was anybody out here had their own cards. Soon even she would, but there ain't no way she'd hand them out. The PD's administrative assistant had ordered business cards with her birth name on them. *Angela Joy Jackson.* If they fell into the wrong hands, she'd never live it down.

Rachel Heinz was a twenty-five-year-old Brown University grad who'd been a cub reporter with the *Chronicle* for six months. Although her pedigree was impeccable, her impressive credentials hadn't translated to real-life proficiency. Since her arrival, the golden girl had garnered the ire of nearly everyone in the newsroom. How could someone who'd won awards for her writing, interned at **the** *New York Times*, and run her own highly praised political activist zine, *Altered States,* prove so incompetent?

Rachel seemed only half conscious when on the job, her attention distracted by romantic breakups, money problems, housing issues, and broken-down cars. The revolving soap opera of her personal life conspired with bad luck, natural disasters, and acts of God to trigger frequent late arrivals, unexplained absences, and missed deadlines. To top it off, she absolutely failed to comprehend common words once they were strung together in a sentence and made audible by the movement of Velvet's lips.

It was one thing, Velvet thought, for the girl to misunderstand directions—that could be forgiven. But failing to ask questions beyond the most perfunctory queries? That was unforgivable—that was a mortal sin. The reigning commandment, understood by even the greenest J-school student, was *Ask Questions*. In Velvet's esteemed opinion, the failure of a journalist to ask follow-up questions or clarify assignments was evidence of criminal negligence and should be severely punished. And yet, at the same time, Velvet had a well-deserved reputation for mentoring and cultivating young talent.

In the Rachel Heinz situation, she'd been hoping that the younger woman's life would settle down and her skills would emerge from whatever dark waters lurked below the blank surface. During this particular nurturing period Velvet had resorted to completely rewriting some of Rachel's work and, out of some misplaced sense of loyalty to a fellow journalist, hadn't turned snitch or informed Stan of the problems. All the chief editor saw was the final polished pieces. Which might explain why Rachel was still on staff but could not explain what Velvet was hearing as she sat in Stan's office.

"I can't let you take the lead on the story without compromising the paper's integrity." Her boss sighed and rubbed the bridge of his nose. "Not when you've already been charged with first degree murder." Stanley Wozlawski, managing editor at the *San Francisco Chronicle*, wasn't really the kind of old, grizzled, and jaded newspaper guy from noir film lore. He had an MBA from Stanford, a manga collection in his office, and a husband and two kids at home. But he was hard-assed when it came to the paper.

"You know the charges are crazy," Velvet objected

"I know." Stan leaned back in his plush leather executive. "You made bail. Good."

"No thanks to you."

"I could have put something up, but first I'd need your signature—"

"For my soul?"

Stan nodded.

"Actually," Velvet decided to share her good news, "the truth is, I didn't need your bail money. The judge let me out on my own recognizance."

"In a first degree murder case? What is our justice system coming to?"

"It's not indefinite," Velvet said. "She gave me forty-eight hours to clear my name or surrender to the police. If I still had a current passport

I would've had to give that up too." When he didn't say anything else, she took it as his usual sign of dismissal and got up, framing her final question.

Before she had a chance to form the words, Stan asked, "Where do you think you're going?"

"To find the real killer." She winked.

Stan laughed. "Listen, O.J., it would be irresponsible of me to let you work this story, especially after yesterday morning's public arrest. What kind of example would that give the other writers? They might get ideas, especially on slow news days."

"Wait." Velvet narrowed her eyes at her boss. "I just told you that I have forty-eight hours to clear my name or rot in jail for months waiting for a trial date. And you're seriously going to ask me stay here in the office? When the story's out there? Come *on*."

"You're right. I can't have my best reporter locked away for all that time, unless she's working on a piece about jails."

Velvet, sure now that he'd just been joking, parted her lips and pressed her tongue against her top teeth, forming the *T* sound to begin her gracious appreciation.

But Stan continued speaking. "I wish I could help. I really do. But you know I can't spare you this close to the elections. We're shorthanded as it is."

"But…" Velvet pleaded with her eyes and wondered for just a moment if getting on her knees and begging would help. Probably not, she realized. That probably only worked on straight men.

"You're lucky I'm even keeping you on. *Most* murderers lose their jobs."

"Stan! You know I didn't do it!" Velvet pouted.

"I know what you're capable of," he stated, matter-of-factly.

His eyebrows were drawn down like shades covering his eyes, and deep furrows plowed across his forehead. His mouth was pulled into a frown. If he wasn't being serious, Velvet decided, then it was one good act.

"Of course we'll need to get the dirt on this Finney murder, but…"

Velvet superstitiously crossed her fingers. Here it was, this was going to be the silver lining. Since she was right in the middle of it anyway, Stan was going to rethink and assign the Finney murder to her. That way, when she solved the case it wouldn't just keep her out of jail. The story would break on the front page with her byline front and center.

"I have no choice." He looked sincerely troubled. "I'm going to have to put you on—"

"No!" Velvet gasped before he could finish the sentence. She could see by his face that it was going to be bad. "Not that, please," she begged.

"Fact-checking." Stan finished and banged his coffee mug on his desk like a judge's gavel.

Velvet took the momentary break to close her gaping mouth. She still couldn't believe this was happening. Could the day get any worse? "Fact-checking? That's an intern's job. I'm a journalist, for God's sake." She slid onto her knees in front of Stan's oversized desk, risking additional ruin to the beautiful outfit that already reeked of eau de cellblock. "Give me research, let me copyedit. Anything but *fact-checking*."

"Fine. First go talk with Rachel, she's covering your murder. I want you to fill her in. Background on Rosemary, why you're a suspect, and who else should be."

"Wait. Rachel is doing *what*?"

Stan held up a hand to silence her. "If, *if* Rachel thinks she can use you for research, or anything that keeps you out of the public's eye, then you can work on the story with her."

"Rachel?" Velvet repeated. "Are you kidding? She can't handle this piece."

Stan glared at her. "I don't want to hear it. And I still need you to fact-check that piece on the state initiatives. I expect it by five."

Velvet groaned. "Stan, I need some good news. Tell me you got my film developed."

"Your film?" He sounded vague.

Alarmed, Velvet said, "Duh! The film I gave you yesterday morning. The one I said was important."

He slapped the front of his head. "It'll be done by the end of the day. That's a promise."

Velvet didn't say anything else. She didn't want Stan to know just how important those photos might be. She was almost afraid to look at them herself, afraid in case they were worthless and didn't have any information for her to work with. As she opened his office door she blurted, "With Rachel on the story I'm as good as convicted. I hope you know that. You're sending me to jail."

"I'll be sure to write," Stan quipped.

Still standing in the doorway, Velvet tried one last ploy. She stamped her foot and pouted like Stan's curly-haired two-year-old.

"My hands are tied," her boss said. He buried his head in the papers on his desk. "Close the door after you."

Velvet uncrossed her fingers in disgust. She couldn't believe that her boss was rewarding the most inexperienced journalist at the paper with the most important story of the year. The report on Rosemary Finney's life and sudden death, and the murder investigation, was the kind of thing that could bestow the writer with the recognition and awards that Velvet so clearly deserved. It steamed her panties that an incompetent upstart like Rachel could even acquire a story like this. And she had to admit, it concerned her that the reporter on the case—a case in which Velvet's career, perhaps her very life were at stake—showed no sign of living up to her promise. There was little danger that Rachel was going to help Velvet's cause.

Velvet ambled into the rookie reporter's cubicle and sat without waiting to be offered a seat. "Stan says you're covering my story."

"What story?"

Velvet rolled her eyes and sighed heavily. "I was arrested and I've been charged with murdering Rosemary Finney? She was killed in the Santa Cruz Mountains yesterday morning. She runs *Womyn* magazine? Stop me if any of this sounds familiar."

Rachel continued to stare at her blank-faced.

Wanting to throttle the young reporter, Velvet reminded herself that doing so would mean *another* homicide on her record. Stan would fire her for sure. They'd lock her away, and she'd never find out who killed Rosemary Finney. That was the kind of thing that could haunt a person for the rest of their life. No, she couldn't kill Rachel, and that meant she *had* to help her do her job. It wasn't even about the truth at this point, Velvet joked to herself. It was about escaping hours of mindless research done for this punk kid reporter who didn't even know who she was.

"Remember the cops being here yesterday afternoon?" Velvet asked. "You pointed me out to them? They dragged me out of here handcuffed? I was in jail because the police think I killed Rosemary Finney." She spoke slowly, as though explaining something to a small child. "Rosemary used to also be a friend, one of my best, actually. And an ex-lover, one of my worst. When we were young and idealistic, back when you were a teenager taking ecstasy at a weekend rave, we started a lesbian magazine together."

Rachel's eyes had already glazed over, but Velvet continued describing the magazine's founding.

"We were sexy and snarky and hip and wanted a magazine that reflected that sensibility *and* reached out to the lesbian diasporas. *Womyn* was the culmination of all those hopes and dreams, a magazine that entertained and challenged queer women all across America in a way no mainstream media ever could."

"*Women's* magazine?" Rachel awoke from her stupor. "You mean the one that's in all the checkout lines? Wow. My mom reads that! She loves that Martha Stewart crap. All those recipes and patterns."

Velvet sighed. "No, honey, that's an entirely different magazine."

Disbelieving, she got up and walked back out onto the newsroom floor, where she was met by the usual newspaper symphony, people talking, fingers flying across keyboards, a television blaring in the background, the police scanner, and the distant hammering of the press running downstairs. Yet again, all the noise stopped abruptly and Velvet could feel all eyes boring into her. *Crap.* Her coworkers would never forget the spectacle of her humiliation when she was cuffed and arrested in front of them. By now, even the few who had missed yesterday's show would have heard it lavishly described by their gossipy coworkers. There were no secrets in the newsroom.

Velvet was pretty sure she'd never forget it either. She was further horrified to see Rachel peeking over her cubicle walls. The young upstart would love to take over her job if Velvet didn't recover from this blow to her ego and her career. Even the J-school interns seemed to watch her with barely hidden disdain.

"They let you go?" one guy teased.

"Hey, killer. How'd you do it?" Another laughed.

"Shut up, or you'll be next," Velvet joked back.

As she passed Brad, the Metro editor, he whispered, "Imelda Marcos, if you wanted her shoes so badly, why didn't you just ask her for them?"

"I did, but she refused to fork them over. They were the latest diamond-encrusted Manolo Blahniks—*to die for*." Velvet retorted.

She reflected on the missing shoes. What was the significance of the murderer absconding with Rosemary's shoes? It almost sounded like a serial killer's penchant for collecting souvenirs. She'd have to put in a call to her source at the FBI and have her run the MO through the national crime database and check for any other violent crimes in which the perpetrator took the victim's shoes.

Velvet paused at a window and looked down at the Dumpster in the parking lot below. Yoshi said the police had found Rosemary's shoes in that very bin. Was that just a coincidence, or was someone trying to deliberately frame her? Velvet had to admit that there was a lot of circumstantial evidence pointing her way, and it was making her a little nervous. Even with the best intentions and responsible police work, the justice system could get it all wrong and send innocent people to prison. What if it was the police themselves that were framing her? Then what chance did she have to beat them at their own game?

CHAPTER TEN

D owntown, in the Flood Building, Tucker Shade answered the phone, hoping that the caller was Yoshi. She was disappointed when the voice that responded to her greeting was several octaves lower and carried a different inflection than Yoshi's.

"I got info for y'all." The New Orleans drawl was a dead give away.

"Wow, AJ. Thank you."

"No worries."

"Let me grab a notepad." Tucker set the receiver down and shuffled through the papers on her desk. Not finding blank paper there, she pulled a sheet from the shelf in the supply cabinet, sat down, and thought, *That's stupid, why don't I just type notes right into the computer?* She opened a new Word document and put the phone on speaker. "Go ahead."

As AJ relayed the elements of her conversation with the Midpeninsula Open Space ranger, Tucker typed in the information. "Do you have Ranger Whitman's contact information?" Tucker knew that was something Yoshi would ask for when she arrived.

Yoshi hadn't left a message, and when Tucker called her cell phone it went straight to voice mail. What should she do? She'd tried Bud fifteen minutes ago, but all she got was one of those messages that said the subscriber had left the service area. Where could *he* have gone? Wasn't he supposed to just be going south of the city? This was the Bay Area, for heaven's sake, and Bud had said he would be in Silicon Valley. How could there not be cell phone coverage in the high-tech capital of the world?

"Hold tight, girlie," AJ was saying. "She done give me a card." Through the speakerphone Tucker could hear the sound of rustling fabric that suggested AJ was searching pockets.

When she read the contact information, Tucker's fingers flew over the computer keys. "Okay, how about the other ranger, Jenny Cooper? Did you get her details?" she asked.

"Naw."

"No problem. How about where she lives?"

"Purissima," AJ replied, pronouncing the word like a hissing snake chasing a purring cat away from her mother. Fortunately for Tucker, the policewoman then spelled the name, calling out letters like church bingo.

"Is that a town?" Tucker asked.

"Naw, it ain't. It's one of them Midpen nature preserves."

Tucker typed this information and encouraged AJ to continue with her narrative. When she described Ranger Cooper's previous encounter with Rosemary Finney, Tucker interrupted again. "You know what court that was processed in? The assault case?"

"Didn't think to, sorry," AJ said. "But it'd be in the county she arrested in, I betting San Mateo. Y'all ring up Ranger Whitman, sure's shit she'd be of help. An' I got an idea."

"Oh, yeah, what's that?" Tucker prodded.

"Get you somebody to roll down here and check out that ranger Jenny's pickup. I'm betting she got a five-gallon bucket roped up back there."

"Yeah?" Tucker didn't grasp the relevance.

"That Whitman, she picking up trash and stowin' it in a pail. She say all them rangers carry buckets." AJ paused as though this last sentence confirmed the importance of her previous statements.

Tucker still didn't get it.

AJ tried again. "Cops coulda missed it if Jenny tossed something. Like her latex gloves."

"Oh." Tucker finally understood. "You mean, like she might have used latex gloves when providing first aid, and then she might have just thrown them into her garbage bucket without even thinking it might be evidence? That's great! Thanks, AJ."

As they said their goodbyes and hung up, Tucker thought, *Now I just need to get Bud to call me.* Where could he be? And would she have a chance to tell him AJ's idea before he'd cleared the ranger station?

❖

Yoshi dialed Velvet's work number while she bounced along city streets in the backseat of a cab en route to the Castro. It went straight to voice mail, which was typical; Velvet often had her phone on "do not disturb."

"Hi, Velvet, this is Yoshi. I just wanted to warn you that I offended Dr. McDermid. I hope it does not cause any tribulations for you. I am on my way to talk with the *Womyn* staff. It might be fruitful to check about the Dumpster in the *Chronicle* lot. Will you obtain the number so we can ascertain at what point it was previously picked up? Are you really going to be at the paper all day? The clock is ticking, you know. Do not waste all of your forty-eight hours at work. Not when you were so lucky to get the time. Call me."

The cab stopped on Castro Street, pulling over next to a Bank of America. Yoshi paid her fare and exited onto the busy sidewalk. She immediately smelled the aroma of men. Castro gays were some of the best-smelling men in the city, matching their obsessive cleanliness with generous portions of grooming products and cologne. Even the men that came from the gym up the street smelled fresh.

The pedestrian lights in San Francisco's main gayborhood were not equipped with the synchronized beeps that alert the blind when to walk, stop, or run. Yoshi shuffled to the curb and stopped when her cane dropped in elevation. Even though she could see the shape of large objects, with her condition they often blurred together as though in motion. Her specialist explained it once, the way human eyes perceived the world as though objects were constantly in motion—like images captured by an unsteady camcorder. For those without ocular dysfunction, the brain steadied the image, but for Yoshi it was all chaos. So she listened to the cars, felt for the heat and the odor of exhaust, trying to discern which were idling and in which direction the others were speeding through the intersection. She was not entirely confident in her new skills and was happy that there were people within a few inches of her.

When the light had just changed to red and there was no chance for them to dart out without being struck by vehicles, the pedestrians next to Yoshi physically relaxed. But as it closed in on the next signal, they crouched at the ready, like pumas preparing to spring into motion. The pedestrian light turned to walk without a sound, but the second it changed Yoshi heard the slapping of feet and felt the brush of skirts, hands, jeans, and the breeze of the crowd pressing forward. She moved with them.

Once her feet hit the sidewalk again, she turned left and walked down Castro Street. Smells were a jumble. First a coffee house with espresso wafting out, then a Body Shop with mango soufflé filling the air. There was no mistaking the next aroma. A whiff of Escape to New York Pizza—the best pizza joint outside of Manhattan, or so she'd heard—reminded Yoshi that she had not eaten lunch. Suddenly aware of her hunger, she popped into the crowded joint for a quick slice of their wood-fired gourmet pizza, which used to be served oven warm by a pink-haired girl with a tongue ring and wolf tracks tattooed on her neck. From the sounds of the crowd, little had changed.

Yoshi ordered two slices of "Gourmet," which were topped with feta cheese, dried tomatoes, and artichoke hearts. She knew from experience that Escape to New York didn't take credit cards, but cash transactions presented obstacles for the visually impaired. Unlike the currency of other countries, the United States' bills were indistinguishable to the touch. Printed on the same size paper and bearing no raised Braille letters, one-dollar bills and twenty-dollar bills felt the same in her hands. Yoshi had heard that there was a case pending in the Supreme Court addressing this very issue. In the meantime, she and other sight-impaired individuals were forced to trust that merchants and bankers would not take advantage of the situation.

Yoshi did not have that kind of faith in humanity. She was not comfortable simply unfastening her wallet, allowing a cashier to rifle around and confiscate whatever funds they elected as some blind people did. Instead she had her bills carefully arranged together by denomination, with paper clips located at different locations to indicate their value. Naturally, this required the assistance of a visually able individual—a role Tucker was currently fulfilling, because she wasn't entrusting the job to her financial institution. Tellers could shortchange you too.

Yoshi had recently decided to collect a cell phone photograph of the change she was given—as another layer of protection, so she could later verify she had received the correct amount. Visual impairment added a layer of difficulty to one's life; even the simplest task could suddenly become a convoluted procedure, but she was perfectly capable of devising creative solutions to work around them.

She sat on one of the tall stools at the counter and wondered if the display in front of her had changed since she was last here. It had been years. Back then, there were black-and-white head shots of famous people like Dolly Parton and Matt Groening autographed with short but benign compliments like, "It's all in the sauce, man" and "Keep up the good pizza."

By the time she'd paid and left the bistro ten minutes later, she had decided that the pizza did not taste as exceptional as she remembered. To be fair, nothing did these days. She had heard that this was a temporary response to loss of sight. Once her nasal abilities increased, her taste buds would adjust. The way sight played into taste had surprised Yoshi at first. Before she had begun to lose her vision, she would never have thought that not seeing food would make it harder to distinguish what she was eating.

People in food marketing probably knew, and that's why they colored certain foods a particular shade. Maybe yellow-orange actually made things taste cheesier. Eventually she hoped she would become a connoisseur of tastes, like a wine-tasting champion capable of discerning, from the bouquet alone, the geographic origination and the specific soils the grapes had matured in. But she was a long way from that kind of epicurean talent now.

Three entrances down from Escape to New York, her destination was tucked between a Chinese noodle hut and a sushi joint. Although the metal-barred front door was the type that needed to be buzzed open, Yoshi found it slightly ajar when she reached it. Oddly, the nondescript wooden number behind it was also unlocked. Yoshi pushed it open and found herself at the base of a steep set of carpeted stairs she remembered from a visit twelve years prior.

These led to what had once been the office of Blush Entertainment, a lesbian-owned company that produced erotic lesbian films and had published the first lesbian erotic magazine. The founders had long since abandoned the second-story office, and their once-revolutionary contributions to the sex wars were now barely remembered by the newest generation of San Francisco lesbians. Today the funky little office housed the lesbian magazine *Womyn* and the late Rosemary Finney's put-upon staff.

Yoshi stood at the bottom of the stairs like a hiker regaining her strength before attempting to crest the distant summit. Snippets of the conversation drifted down from above.

"…still can't believe…"

"…Rosemary's not even in the ground.".

Maybe she would not have to climb the stairs after all, Yoshi thought. Maybe she could just stand here and eavesdrop. Even though that was the kind of thing that had just gotten her in trouble at Dr. Artemis McDermid's. The shrill ring of a phone sounded and Yoshi pressed her body against the wall. Slowly, slowly she inched her way up two steps, thinking if she got a little closer she could hear more of the conversation. The phone rang again.

"…she is selling…"

Yoshi crept up another step. She heard the rustle of her clothes brushing along the sheet-rocked walls and froze. Could the *Womyn* magazine staff in the office above hear that?

The phone rang a third time. Was anyone going to answer that? If this were *her* staff, she would be mad as hell. She tried to imagine Tucker letting a phone ring and conjured up a vision of the soft-butch, feet up on the desk, doing her nails. Yoshi stifled a laugh. *As if.*

"*Womyn* magazine," a woman with a Latina accent finally replied brusquely. "Oh, you want to talk with Rosemary Finney? Yeah? What about, asshole? You want to sell her your long-distance plan? Well, sorry jerk, but she's dead. Yes, D-E-A-D dead. She was murdered yesterday. Oh, you don't think it's a good time to call?" She paused. "He hung up on me."

Someone laughed. And kept laughing. A little too long. It verged on hysteria. Everyone dealt with loss in their own way. Yoshi struggled to comprehend why the magazine's staff was back at work when their boss had recently been murdered. Rosemary had accumulated a division of enemies, but surely *someone* would miss her. Surely the psychologically unstable cackling at the head of the stairs was proof that someone was grieving—right?

Yoshi realized suddenly that she was no longer paying attention, and in that moment there was a noise at the door and then a draft as it was pulled ajar and the darkness surrounding Yoshi faded in face of the bright daylight.

"Can I help you?" The woman who'd discovered Yoshi lurking in the shadows of the *Womyn*'s stairwell sounded genuinely surprised, and her voice betrayed no hint of suspicion.

"Who's there?" Yoshi played her helpless tone, stretching out her hands and fumbling into the space before strategically dropping her cane.

"I'll get that." The woman's voice fell and rose as she bent to retrieve the white cane. "Oh, I'm so sorry. You're blind." She pressed the cane into Yoshi's open palm. "I mean," she rushed to correct the potentially offensive descriptor, "visually challenged. I'm Grace Lee."

"Hi, Grace Lee." Yoshi held out a hand. "I'm Yoshi Yakamota."

They shook.

Grace Lee's hand was smaller than her own, with well-manicured short nails. She spoke with the faint accent of a second-generation Chinese American.

Yoshi smiled. It was not every day she met another Asian American lesbian. "I have a meeting here, but I was a little daunted by the stairs," she said, almost feeling bad about her deception.

"Of course." Grace kept hold of her hand. "Let me help you."

They maneuvered the steep staircase with Grace leading the way. Yoshi silently counted the steep stairs as she went, in case she didn't have a chaperone on the way down.

When they reached the landing, Grace asked, "Who are you meeting?"

Here goes. "Rosemary Finney. The editor."

There was more than one harsh inhalation of breath, and the chatter in the open floor office stopped abruptly.

"Is there something wrong?" Yoshi feigned surprise.

Grace fidgeted next to her.

"Didn't you see the news today?" a woman asked from across the room.

Grace stiffened. Yoshi could tell her hands flew to her face. She imagined her running a finger across her throat in the "cut" signal. Subsequently she would almost certainly point to Yoshi's cane or eyes, or mouth the words, "She's blind."

"Sorry," Grace stammered. "It's just that Rosemary, she's dead."

"Oh my God." Yoshi gasped appropriately. "Dead? But I spoke with her a few days ago. How?"

"She was killed yesterday morning."

Yoshi swayed on her feet. Helpful Grace responded by ushering her to a chair.

"Here, sit. Joni? Get her a glass of water."

A moment later, a cool glass was placed in Yoshi's hand and she continued to spin her tale by first "sharing" that she was an old friend of Rosemary's from Brown University, though they had not seen each other in many years. Improvising on the fly like she used to with her father, she revealed that she had come to San Francisco to undergo a cutting-edge, breakthrough therapy that might just restore her sight. In reality, as far as she knew, the treatment she described did not exist and there was no cure for her particular ocular degeneration. She continued with her fabrication, explaining that while she was in town, she had intended to catch up with Rosemary, who was unaware of her visual impairment. Rosemary had found time in her busy schedule to squeeze in a brief meeting and they had scheduled an appointment.

"I guess she is not going to make it." Yoshi offered a weak smile. "Was it some kind of accident?"

"No, apparently she was murdered," the girl who had supplied her with water replied blithely.

"Murdered? Oh my God. How? Where?"

"Well, we aren't really sure about the details, but it seems that she was in some park in Woodside, near her home. A jogger found her on the trail."

"On a hiking trail?" Yoshi shook her head adamantly. "Then it couldn't be her. I mean, what would Rosemary have meant to accomplish on a footpath? She had not gone all L.L. Bean, had she?"

"It's weird, isn't it?" Grace Lee agreed. "But they positively identified her."

Yoshi shook her head again, doing her best to project *stunned friend in denial*. "Who'd want to murder Rosemary?"

From the tense silence, she deduced that Rosemary Finney's employees immediately had a suspect or two in mind. Maybe they had even dreamt of killing her themselves. Yoshi tried to relay how Velvet had described Rosemary, back when the wealthy editor was likeable. "She was such a great woman, dedicated to her friends. A feminist with progressive ideals."

Someone snorted. Another laughed bitterly. "Feminist? Are we talking about the same Rosemary?"

"I suppose everyone changes after college," Yoshi allowed. "You don't think she could have done something that would get her killed? Like drugs? Or making dangerous enemies?"

None of the women responded to her query.

"It is just that," Yoshi dropped her head and let her voice crack, "I thought maybe it would help me to understand. Never mind. I should go."

She stood, wobbled, and then fell forward. As she had hoped, Grace Lee caught her and eased her back into the chair. Was it wrong to prey upon people's guilt and sympathy for the disabled in order to get information? Not if it worked, Yoshi told herself, thinking it was something Velvet would say.

"I don't think you should be going anywhere, not until you feel a little better," Grace said.

"All right," Yoshi meekly conceded. The phone rang again and as soon as it was answered, she said, "You girls are so dedicated. Rosemary was fortunate to have you. Here you all are fast at work, the day after this horrible event. You must be incredibly devoted to your work."

"Are you kidding?" chortled the Latina woman with an accent that Yoshi pegged as Cuban American. She was the one who had rudely answered the previous call. Yoshi could tell she was very angry.

"Becca," Grace cautioned.

"Lay off her, Grace," Joni responded. "Stop pretending this isn't ridiculous. What kind of person makes their staff work when the editor has just been killed?"

"Someone *made* you stay?" Yoshi asked. The astonishment in her voice was not forced.

In the bickering, the phone started ringing again, this time unanswered.

"Yeah, *someone* did." Becca sneered. "That bitch Karen."

"I bet she did it," Joni declared.

"Are you kidding?" Grace's tone was accusatory. "She was always fawning over Rosemary—that's true love."

"Whatever, Grace, you brown-noser," Becca responded. "You going to stand there and defend her *now*? Even though she's selling us to OutNation?"

"That's just a rumor," Grace insisted.

"You think they're going to keep *you* on?" Becca asked. "We are *all* so fucking fired."

"Even *if* that's true," Grace said, "I'm sure it was Rosemary's doing, not Karen's."

"Oh, right, Karen is a perfect angel," Becca taunted. "We *all* know you've got the hots for her."

Yoshi wondered if they had forgotten she was there. She certainly was not going to remind them of her presence, not when their squabbling was revealing so many interesting details.

"Yeah," Joni piped in. Yoshi detected some resentment from the girl. "Maybe *you* killed Rosemary so you could hook up with Karen."

"That's ridiculous." Grace waved aside the accusation.

"Oh, *that*'s ridiculous?" Becca laughed sardonically.

"If it's so ridiculous, where were you when it happened?" Joni asked.

"I don't even know *when* it happened," Grace said, clearly exasperated.

"Around six," Becca supplied.

"So, where were you before six yesterday morning?" Joni persisted.

"Sleeping. Where were *you*, smart-ass?" Grace sighed. "This is stupid, you guys. We shouldn't turn on each other."

"You're right," Becca said. "We should all get together and fight the real enemy."

Becca paused and Yoshi thought she could hear Grace nod in agreement. "OutNati—" Grace began.

"*Karen!*" Becca interjected.

Joni laughed.

"Oh, fuck you," Grace said.

"I think I should depart," Yoshi interjected.

"I'll walk you out," Grace offered eagerly.

As they ambled down the stairs, Grace said, "I'm sorry you heard that. We aren't always—"

"At each other's throats?"

"Yeah." Grace sighed. "It's just hard right now—losing Rosemary and then this rumor going around that we've been sold."

"Do you have any insight into who might have wished Rosemary dead? Is there anything unusual going on at your magazine?" They had reached the base of the stairs.

"Well, there's this newspaper reporter who came around a few weeks ago asking all kinds of questions. Unusual name. Velvet, I think. She might be good for you to talk to if you can find her. Other than that, I don't know if it's anything, but we had an intern a few months ago. Everyone said Rosemary had a thing for her. She was only here for three weeks, and then one day she just stopped coming in. It was weird."

Yoshi was intrigued. "Do you remember her name?"

"Elizabeth Claiborne." Grace held open the door. "Nice to meet you," she said. "Maybe we'll see you at the funeral?"

"Perhaps." Yoshi was noncommittal.

❖

Velvet was not in the mood to fact-check a tedious piece on this year's state initiative that would ban same-sex marriage, but she set about verifying sources anyway, making sure that the Henry fellow who wrote the piece had dotted all his i's and crossed his t's. Stan wanted it by five and she would spend the next three hours making that happen. But she wasn't giving him a thing unless he had her film ready.

While she waited on hold for confirmation from the secretary of state's office, she cracked open a new composition book and wrote a single-word header: "Suspects." Below that on the left side of the page, she listed a bevy of potential killers. Each person clearly had some cause for retaliation against Rosemary. Velvet made another column to express those reasons, "Motive," and jotted down potential motivations.

She added herself to be empirical, and besides, the cops had her at the top of *their* list. If she was going to establish who was really responsible, she'd need to track down and eliminate each person who became a suspect. At least she had Blind Eye on her side. And whatever they found she could, in good conscience, keep from the *Chronicle*. But anything she discovered on the paper's time would have to end up on Rachel's desk. Not that Rachel would know what to do with it—she couldn't write a decent article if her life depended on it. Besides, it was Velvet, not Rachel, whose life was at stake.

So Velvet wasn't about to compromise her leads by sharing information with a cub reporter who didn't give a rat's ass whether she ended up in prison or not. When Yoshi had something solid Velvet would write the article herself and present it to Stan. She suspected that once he was handed a completed and engaging piece he wouldn't be hung up on minor details—like that she'd ignored his assigning the story to Rachel.

At the top of the suspects list was Velvet's friend, *Bend* magazine publisher Marion Serif, who wouldn't speak with her over the phone. Not with a Yuri in the office. Both fans of the movie *Intern* and its insider look at fashion magazines, she and Marion had co-opted the film's snappy slang when Marion began to suspect that *Bend* had a spy, or "Yuri," of its own. Aware that "Yuri" by definition referred to a lesbian in manga and anime, they were amused by the double entendre, and they'd employed the term to describe every spy, tattletale, or backstabber in their lives.

In the months since Marion's suspicions were first raised about a spy in the house of *Bend*, she had become increasingly vigilant, bordering on paranoid. Velvet couldn't blame her. It had to be more than mere happenstance that *Womyn* was constantly outscooping *Bend*. It did seem as though someone was tipping the rival publication off about story ideas as soon as Marion suggested them.

Differing publication schedules meant the newest issue of *Womyn* always hit the stands a week before *Bend,* so there was nothing the *Bend* staff could do to compensate since their publication was already at the printer by the time they discovered the duplicity. For the past three months, the two competing magazines had sat side by side on the newsstands, boasting the exact same cover stories. Lesbian consumers didn't like buying two magazines, not when they essentially covered the same things, so *Bend*'s bookstore sales had plummeted. And since *Womyn* came out earlier, readers assumed it was *Bend*, not its crosstown rival, that was stealing the scoops.

Marion had concluded that one of her staff members was the mole committing corporate espionage, which was why she would only speak freely in person. She had hired Velvet a month ago to smoke out the Yuri but so far, Velvet hadn't had much luck with the endeavor. Now she and Marion were seriously contemplating creating an entirely fabricated magazine, with every word nestled between its covers a complete fake. Perhaps then they could *prove* the other publication had swiped their stories.

It wasn't just the Yuri that could have given Marion a motive to kill Rosemary. There were three million other reasons she might want her rival publisher dead. Three million dollars: that was the amount *Womyn*'s management was asking Marion to pay in their lawsuit. Marion couldn't afford to fight a protracted and costly court battle. *Bend* would be out of business before the suit was proven to be frivolous. Obviously that's what Rosemary had counted on. It wouldn't take Rosemary *winning* the lawsuit to drive *Bend* out of business; all it would take was the lawsuit itself.

Money was always tight in the magazine business, what with distributors who could take twelve months or more to pass along the magazine's share of newsstand sales. In the last decade a stream of the nation's largest distributors had gone belly-up, and they had taken a lot of publications with them. The rise of the monolithic Wal-Mart, bookstore chains like Barnes & Noble, and Internet sites like Amazon and Half.com had permanently altered the publishing landscape, and things were even tougher in the LGBT niche market, especially for publications that targeted only queer women.

Lesbians were too busy trying to keep food on their tables and roofs over their heads to be the kind of consumers gay men were. What kept mainstream magazines afloat, even with three times the pages and half the cover price of *Bend,* was a constant infusion of advertising cash. While mainstream advertisers had warmed to the pink market, they tended to focus on gay men, whose income and spending habits rivaled those of straight households.

Velvet dialed *Bend*'s number and punched in Marion's extension. There was no doubt in her mind that Rosemary and Karen had been hoping to force *Bend* into bankruptcy. Then they could swoop in and buy the competitor magazine, gut it, and use the subscriber list to keep *Womyn* afloat.

"Can we meet when I get off work?" she asked when Marion finally picked up her phone. She didn't give her name in case the Yuri was listening. Besides, Marion knew her voice.

"Coffee?" Marion asked. It meant more than just a cup of joe. She was referring to Velvet's favorite café, the Coffee Klatch.

"Good. See you."

They both hung up and Velvet unlocked the bottom drawer of her desk, withdrew a red folder, and flipped through its contents. Grainy black-and-white photographs of the *Bend* staff were paper-clipped to individual dossiers detailing what Velvet had learned about each employee. In the back of the folder were several computer printouts about surveillance cameras. Two weeks ago Velvet had researched the different brands available and suggested Marion install one at the *Bend* office, but Marion had been affronted at the ethical implications of scrutinizing her staff's every move. She wasn't willing to become Big Brother, not even to save her magazine.

Velvet knew her friend was at her wits' end. Coming on top of the Yuri's damage, the lawsuit must have been a devastating blow. Could it have pushed Marion to murder?

CHAPTER ELEVEN

Bud pulled into the handicapped spot near the entrance of the Midpeninsula Regional Open Space District Skyline Field Office, maneuvered his chair out of the Impala, and rolled up the inviting ramp. At the door he realized that the entrance was positioned so he'd have to make a three-point turn just to get through it.

"Damn it!" he muttered before rotating the chair to face the glass door. From that position he could see that the entrance ahead of him was equipped with neither hydraulics to open automatically nor a ramp over the three-inch lip that separated the cement landing from the linoleum flooring inside. Fucking architects.

As he wrestled with the door it closed against him. With half the wheels inside and half out and the heavy door crushing him, Bud spit out another string of curses. The profanity roused a boy who didn't look old enough to be a ranger.

"Need help?" he offered while grabbing Bud's wheels and trying to haul him inside.

The assistance succeeded only in impeding Bud's way and wasting precious time. Finally he shoved the teenager backward, crunched over his booted foot and rolled into a room ringed by old metal desks and dinged gray file cabinets. Several offices, encased behind glass, lined the far wall, their interiors darkened. Bud located the big round wall clock. 4:35 p.m. He hid a smile. He'd timed his arrival perfectly. He *wanted* to talk to an underling.

The scowling teen hopped in front of him, wearing a full-on ranger uniform, topped off with a gold-plated five-point star badge on his shirt and a brass name tag that read Scott Robbins. *They get younger every year.*

"May I help you?" Robbins asked with a trace of irritation.

"Nice to meet you," Bud said after introducing himself. "Deputy Freeman with the San Mateo County Sheriff's Office told me you might be of assistance. I'm investigating the murder that occurred yesterday up at Wonderland Park."

Bud knew right away that he'd have Ranger Robbins's cooperation. It was clear in the kid's wide eyes and the way he held himself that he had law enforcement dreams. Bud wondered how many times he'd failed to qualify for the police academy before he'd settled on playing park pig. "It's always a pleasure to talk with other law enforcement officers," he remarked. The compliment was distasteful in his mouth, but he knew it would open doors. "You wouldn't believe what a pain it is to work with civilians."

Ranger Robbins nodded vigorously. "Straight up, dude, you don't have to tell me. How can I help?"

"I understand one of the rangers was first on scene yesterday morning?"

"Oh, yeah, Jenny," the kid said enviously. "I wasn't on duty yet," he added as if to explain away his absence from what was surely the biggest event of the year for these guys. He sauntered over to a row of clipboards that hung on the wall between two of the enclosed offices and flipped through several pages before offering one of the boards to Bud. "Here's the IR."

Bud took the incident report and flipped through the two pages. "I'd like to get a copy of this."

"Sure. Want her log, too?"

"That'd be great." Bud couldn't believe his luck. The hour-by-hour log of a law officer's daily activities wasn't meant for public consumption and wouldn't even be submitted to a DA. Yet here was Ranger Robbins, offering Jenny's to him without batting an eye. "So," he continued as Robbins took the clipboard to a copy machine. "The call came in as a medical?"

"Yeah. CDF were like sent to the wrong location. That's how come Jenny got on scene first." He handed the warm photocopies to Bud and returned the clipboard to its designated place on the wall.

Knowing that reports were often condensed and sanitized versions of the real story, Bud wanted to keep the ranger talking. "Did she know right away it was a crime scene?"

Robbins's brow crinkled in thought. "I don't think so. She just found the victim down with no pulse and she couldn't get out on the radio, so she goes and, like, starts CPR." As if embarrassed by the inference of substandard equipment, he rushed to explain, "We've got stupid blind spots up here, 'specially with portables."

"How long was she alone with the victim?"

"Like fifteen, twenty minutes. Why?"

"Just for the record," Bud said with a dismissive wave of his hand, but he was thinking about how a good defense attorney might use that information to raise doubts about physical evidence in the case. "In that time, did she notice anything suspicious?"

Robbins shook his head. "She was hella busy. You know, one-person CPR is super tough, you can't really focus on much else. Except the shoes missing. She was like, 'Who steals shoes from a corpse?'"

Bud nodded. "Anything else?"

"When CDF got on scene and were, like, working on the victim, that's when they finally noticed these marks around her neck. Maybe a ligature situation." Robbins reflexively touched his own neck as he revealed his impressive forensic awareness.

"Did they search for a weapon?"

"Yeah, I guess Jenny poked around a bit, and when I came on duty I did, like, a totally thorough search. Woodside probably sent someone up from the bottom. They kinda don't have rangers, just a maintenance crew. Local PD gives them backup. You know, for law enforcement duties."

"And you didn't notice anything suspicious when you examined the site?" Bud asked.

"No, not really. Well, there was this one thing. Horse tracks on the trail, but I didn't notice them above the murder scene. They coulda just been obliterated by all the EMS traffic up there. But..." Robbins shrugged.

Bud was intrigued. "Could you tell if there was just one set or if they'd come back that same way?"

"Hmm. Now that you mention it, there did seem an awful lot of prints, so they probably did come back that way. Or they could, like, be more than one horse going one way."

Bud nodded. "So there's a parking area at the bottom? Is that where someone would park and unload a horse trailer?"

Robbins bobbed and then shook his head as though he couldn't decide if he agreed or not. "Yeah, there's a lower lot. But they're probably just locals. See, Woodside's straight-up horse central. They don't need to trailer horses, just ride 'em straight from their residence."

"Okay, that's great. You've been a big help." Bud extended his hand.

Ranger Robbins rushed to shake it. "Can I like get the door for you?"

"Sure. If you aren't afraid to be run over again. But first, I need to make a call and I can't seem to get out on my cell."

"Yeah, reception sucks up here. You can use the landline. You don't have to dial nine or nothing." Robbins led Bud down a short hallway and opened the door to a spacious room at least ten degrees cooler than the front office. Floor-to-ceiling windows dominated one wall, looking out at a picnic table under some trees. The wall closest to the door housed shelves of books on medical rescue and native plants of California. Bleached animal skulls and shards of pink glass were scattered around the books. A phone sat on the lone desk next to a tower of stacking chairs. Bud rolled over and dialed Blind Eye's main number.

When Tucker answered, he said, "Put me through to Yoshi."

"Where have you been?" Tucker demanded. "I've been trying to reach you for hours. Yoshi's not here. You haven't left the ranger station, have you?"

He furrowed his brow. Yoshi wasn't around, he was stuck in the fucking boonies, and Tucker was being annoying as usual. "Just put me through to her voice mail."

"No. I have something important to tell you."

"Fine," he said, pulling a notepad from his back pocket. "Just tell me."

"I talked with this East Palo Alto police office I know. AJ Jackson. And she—"

"*She*? What the hell kind of name is AJ for a woman?" Bud chuckled. "Never mind, look who I'm asking."

"You never listen to me, do you? I told you a hundred times—"

"Down, girl. I know the story. Your brother Tucker died, your parents were despondent, they gave you his name. Blah, blah. Get to the point."

"Sorry. The important thing is, she suggested checking the back of Ranger Jenny's truck. Look for a bucket that has trash in it. She thinks there might be some evidence there, like used gloves."

"And how the fuck am I supposed to clamber around in the back of a pickup?"

"Oh, gosh. Sorry, I didn't think."

"Whatever. I'll see if I can get someone here to do it. Now, do you want to put me through to Yoshi's voice mail or write down what I've got?"

"I'll just write it down. Go ahead."

"I've picked up the ranger's report on finding the DB. I'm headed down to Woodside, to Wonderland Park. Maybe I'll swing by the victim's house. We'll see. It'll be another thirty minutes or so before I get cell service again. Got all that? Great, thanks, doll."

Without waiting for more Tuckerisms, he hung up and exited the meeting room. In the hallway he spotted restrooms and rolled into the men's, pushed his way into the handicapped stall, and undertook the lengthy process of relieving his bladder. The bathroom also served as the staff locker room, and no one seemed to think locks were important. Bud opened a locker door at random. It held a uniform, rain gear, and the usual crap. Deodorant, shaving gear, and shampoo.

A knee-high bench ran the length of the lockers, and below it were numerous pairs of dark reddish brown leather boots that laced up over the ankle. Bud stared long and hard at them, his mind processing a possibility that seemed almost too good to be true. He wondered if the women's restroom had the same floor plan.

When he rolled back to Robbins, he said, "I noticed the boots back in the john. Any chance that female ranger—Jenny—might've left hers in the women's room yesterday?"

"We all get two pair, so maybe if they got wet or something, and she changed them. Want me to go see?"

"Yeah, I'd appreciate that."

The kid ducked into the women's restroom and returned a

moment later carrying a pair of boots, their soles encrusted with mud. "Whaddaya know." He held them at Bud's eye level. "Your lucky day, I guess. I think these are hers. They've got 9L6 written inside. That's her call sign."

He held them so Bud could see the faded number on the brushed leather inside of the boot, then set them down on a nearby desk.

"You got a Baggie or something I could use?" Bud retrieved a Swiss Army knife from his pants pocket as Robbins scavenged around in a supply closet. Bud started scraping dried mud samples off the boots with the blade of his knife laid flat to prevent nicks. The boots were the kind of three hundred dollar made-to-order ones firefighters wore. He didn't want to damage them. "That Jenny," he asked when Robbins dropped a handful of ziplocks in front of him. "Her truck wouldn't be out there, would it?"

He knew it was a long shot, what with the earlier lesson about ranger residences, but he asked anyway. It was a reflexive CYA move; it paid to ask questions, even if the answers seemed obvious, if not asking them could in any way come back and bite him on the ass. Like if he stopped by the ranger's house and then found out the truck was here at the station all along.

"P49? Doubt it." Robbins glanced back toward the wall-sized chalkboard. Bud followed the kid's gaze and saw some notations scrawled in white chalk. "Dude." Ranger Robbins whistled in amazement. "You're, like, straight-up *stupid* lucky, man. Jenny's truck is *never* here. She takes it home, you know, 'cuz—"

"She's a resident ranger," Bud completed.

"Yeah. Exactly. But it's going for service tomorrow. That's *sick*, man."

Bud wondered when he'd gotten so old, and who taught these punk kids to talk anyway? He'd never been good at grammar, but *damn*. Kids today. He tried his luck. "Do you think you could do something for me?"

The ranger's baby face pulled into a doubtful scowl. "Yeah?" He pronounced it with suspicion.

"It'd really help with the case if you'd take a look in the back of her truck."

The kid wasn't biting.

"Understandable." Bud exaggerated a shrug. "'Specially seeing as how I'd have to take down all your personal information so I could include it in my official report. And then the chief's always calling people back, you know, to verify everything, and the next thing you know they're embarrassing you with official commendations and—"

"Oh, no." Robbins acted like Bud had misunderstood. "That's no big deal. I mean it's a murder case, man."

"You might be called to testify." Bud pretended he was trying to dissuade the ranger.

"Whatcha need?"

Bud hid his smug smile by wiping at his face. "You guys pick up trash while out on patrol, right?"

"We're not maintenance or anything. There's a crew that does that."

Bud wanted to smirk at the kid's defensiveness. "No, I didn't mean that, I meant small things, like litter from the parking lots."

"Oh, yeah, we do that. Why?"

"Well," Bud drawled, "I was thinking Jenny might've picked up some evidence, just thinking it was garbage. So if you could check the truck bed for litter, there's garbage bags in my trunk."

"Okay." Robbins replied reluctantly. "But, don't you, like, need to check for prints or something? Before I touch stuff?"

"No, that's okay. Just try not to touch stuff too much. Pick bottles up with a pencil in their mouth, that kind of thing. If it's all in some kind of bucket or something, you can just dump it out together."

The kid nodded enthusiastically.

"Catch." Bud tossed his car keys at Ranger Robbins, who had to drop his pack to grab them. "Bag it and put it all in the trunk for me."

❖

Tucker was still alone in the office and not sure if she should just leave work for the night or stay until she located her boss. She tried calling Yoshi's cell again, expecting the voice mail to answer, as it had the forty other times she'd called all through the afternoon. She was actually stunned when Yoshi answered.

Her soft voice sent goose bumps along Tucker's usually baby-smooth arms. God, she'd like to hear the woman whispering her name.

Or shouting it out. Just one night of dipping her pen in company ink, and Tucker knew that it would change her life forever. Trying to focus, she shook the naughty thoughts from her head.

"Boy, I'm glad you're okay. You are, right?"

"I am fine, Tucker. What can I do for you?"

"Oh, sorry, it's just that I'm supposed to be off already, but you've been gone all afternoon and there wasn't a note, and I guess your phone's been off?"

Yoshi sighed. "You are correct. Something unexpected transpired."

Tucker was curious, but didn't pry. "I just wanted to check in before I left for the night."

"Oh. Right." Yoshi sounded almost disappointed.

"I don't have to go, if you need something," Tucker gushed. She'd so like to meet Yoshi's needs. "Really, I don't mind staying late." She wasn't heading home anyway, not for a couple of hours at least.

"Well, if it's not an imposition." Yoshi drew out the first word.

"Not at all," Tucker assured her.

"In point of fact, I *could* use your assistance. I am en route to 965 Mission, where I hope to intercept a person of interest."

"Who's that?" Tucker asked.

"Elizabeth Claiborne. Also known as Liz. She worked briefly for *Womyn*. During today's investigation, I have gotten the impression that Elizabeth Claiborne may have pertinent information." Yoshi seemed cagey. Before Tucker could pose a query, Yoshi said, "Can you do a background search on her and then meet me at the office building next to the *Chronicle*?"

"Of course," Tucker agreed before wondering how she was going to get there. She'd figure it out. She began cleaning off her desktop.

"Good. I originally expected to meet up with Velvet, but I guess she is not at the office."

"I'll see you soon," Tucker bubbled. She was so excited she'd get to spend more time with Yoshi, she didn't even consider what Velvet might think. Nor did it cross her mind that she was more likely to become involved with the investigation than the investigator.

CHAPTER TWELVE

Velvet settled into the cozy leather couch set in the back corner of Noe Valley's Coffee Klatch. The small, lesbian-owned coffee and tea café featured cushy purple brushed-velvet sofas, mocha-colored walls, dim recessed lighting, funky lesbian artwork, and tons of intriguing magazines. To calm herself down, Velvet flipped through the *San Francisco Bay Times* while sipping her skinny, no whip, double mocha. Stan hadn't kept his "promise" until it was too late to get her film back from processing by five. Now she had to wait until tomorrow morning. Velvet was still considering the appropriate response. Maybe she should just resign.

Marion slid onto the seat next to her. "What's up?" she whispered.

Velvet put down the paper. "You heard about Rosemary?"

Marion nodded.

"I've been charged with her murder."

"What?" Marion looked horrified. "You didn't, did you?"

"God, no. But I am trying to figure out who did."

"And you're asking me?"

Velvet smiled, "Not so much, no. But I did want to finish our interrupted conversation. From the other night at the Liberty. What's Rosemary suing you for?"

"You won't believe it. For hiring Kathleen Hillman, among other things." Marion shrugged and shook her head.

"But didn't Rosemary throw her out?" Velvet was incredulous. "Like a year and a half ago?"

Kathleen Hillman was *the* editor credited with turning any queer mag she touched into newsstand gold. Celebrities loved to talk to her, readers loved to gossip about her, and in San Francisco everyone was as enamored with her as Rosemary Finney once was. But when staff tensions grew at *Womyn*, Kathleen got caught in the crossfire, which meant a nasty breakup with Rosemary and getting tossed out by the publisher's legal goons unexpectedly one morning. After a year of solitude on some ashram or something, she had recently reappeared in San Francisco and *Bend* was quick to snatch her up.

"Yeah, she threw her out. It was ugly, too." Marion took a sip of her latte. "Personally, I can't see how *Womyn* has a case, but..."

"But it's expensive to fight," Velvet finished Marion's sentence. She knew from personal experience how difficult it was to go up against Rosemary and her lawyers.

"I tried talking to Karen a few weeks ago, to see if we could...I don't know, work this out somehow."

"Karen? Really?" Velvet was surprised Rosemary's partner would have agreed to speak with Marion. "What did she say?"

"She said no."

"Of course she did," Velvet said sarcastically. *That* sounded like Karen.

"Actually, I got the feeling that Karen wished Rosemary would drop it." Marion stared at Velvet. "What?"

"I didn't say anything," Velvet replied, thinking it was far more likely that Karen had put Rosemary up to the lawsuit than the other way around.

"You had a look. You don't think she could disagree with Rosemary?"

"I'd just be surprised if they didn't show a united front."

"Maybe now Karen will drop the lawsuit," Marion said hopefully.

Velvet wasn't convinced. "I hope so. For you. Maybe the Yuri will stop selling your secrets." She didn't really believe that would happen either. With Rosemary gone, *Womyn* would probably value the insider information even more. "Anything new going on? Anything weird?"

A look of concern crossed Marion's attractive face, and when Velvet prompted her, she said, "Okay. For what it's worth, one of our interns hasn't shown up for two days. It's weird. She's usually so reliable, but I've called her at home and she doesn't answer."

"Well, maybe some family emergency came up or something. Still, I'll look into it if you want."

"Would you? Her name's Liz Claiborne. She's only been with us a month, but I'd hate to lose her. She's the kid I told you about a couple of weeks ago, remember?"

Velvet didn't. She vaguely remembered Marion waxing on about a new addition, but at the time she'd been distracted by a phone call from Tucker, and her mind had wandered to bedroom fantasies.

Marion was silent for a moment, ruminating, her brow pinched in concern. Then she shook her head as if to dislodge the unsettling thoughts amassing there. "Now, what can I do for you?"

"Where were you yesterday morning around five thirty or six?" Velvet had to ask. She needed to verify Marion's alibi so she could cross her name off the list.

"Home, in bed." Marion winked. "Victoria's in town. She can vouch for me."

Marion's lover, a very unproper blond Brit named Victoria, was a pilot with British Airways, and was often away for weeks at a time. When she *was* home, the couple spent days sequestered, making up for lost time.

Velvet smiled, genuinely pleased for her friend. Velvet didn't really see the point of long-distance love affairs. But maybe Marion had the best of both worlds, with some of the perks of a serious relationship, like someone to take to holiday dinners, but without sacrificing her independence. Plus the time the couple spent apart seemed to fuel their passion for each other.

She winked back at Marion. "So, what are you doing talking to me, when you should be home with your honey?"

❖

As Bud slowly maneuvered his Impala around the blind curves of Page Mill Road, he passed more Open Space Preserves and enclaves of the rich and famous. On one hill was a Mediterranean-style mansion that belonged to the founder of the auction site eBay. Around another curve lay the sprawling vineyard of a Hollywood mogul. And under the cover of a tree-topped ridge hid a famous but reclusive dyke musician. Defying gravity, in Woodside money rolled uphill as the wealthy rose above the Silicon Valley's business sprawl. From their high-altitude hideaways, the affluent could look down on the working folk in yet another permutation of feudal systems.

Following the route he'd traced on his *Thomas Guide* map, he meandered down the hill, past townhomes, the wide grassy fields of Palo Alto's Arastradero Preserve, and the sleepy town of Portola Valley. After turning onto Highway 84, Bud pulled into the lower parking lot of Woodside's Wonderland Park.

Woodside was a snooty community tucked against the foothills of the Santa Cruz Mountains, under broad branches of hulking oak trees. The town and its inhabitants set themselves apart from the rest of the Bay Area, and the rest of California, for that matter. Woodside residents were overly educated, raked in annual incomes significantly higher than their fellow Californians, and lived in houses that dwarfed those of other neighborhoods. They kept the riffraff out of their exclusive area—except, Bud imagined, when they needed servants, nannies, and maintenance staff. Those they imported from black and Hispanic neighborhoods on the East Bay.

Bud didn't get the attraction to the place. Surrounded by parks, Woodside felt like a small, country town, except for the sprinkling of what girls would probably call quaint or charming restaurants and stores. Despite its rural façade, it had none of the amenities one would actually go to the country for, like great fishing holes, dive bars, or greasy-spoon diners.

As he turned into the Wonderland Park lot, gravel scuttled away from the Impala's wheels and jingled against the undercarriage. Bud spied a maintenance worker driving a Woodside Maintenance Department vehicle, waved him down, and pulled up next to the battered pickup truck.

"Hey, there, how's it going?"

"Okay?" The driver replied in a questioning manner.

"I see you're with the town. I'm here following up on yesterday morning's homicide."

Bud's direct and officious manner disarmed the young man, who immediately responded to the assumptions that such a statement evoked. Bud wasn't sure what those assumptions were in this case, but if it worked, he didn't really care who the guy thought he was.

"Oh, yeah, what a mess. Just finished cleaning up. They had that trail closed all day with someone posted at each end. Not really sure why, not like the murderer was going to come back. I mean, even the Trailside Killer didn't hang around a day later."

"What all did you clean up?" Bud refocused the conversation on the area of interest to him.

"Oh, uh, I cleaned out the cans and picked up some litter from the lot. Management was worried about line-of-sight issues. You know, after the attack. Thought the trail might be overgrown. Too many blind corners and so on. So after we got the permit, I hiked up and pruned everything back. I just finished opening it up again. Removed the barricades and police tape."

"I'd love to take that trash off your hands," Bud said. "Might have something useful."

"Oh. Sorry, dude, I already gave it to that other guy."

Damn. "What guy?"

"The cop that was just here. You didn't see him on your way in? He just left." The maintenance worker leaned out his window.

Shit. Bud shook his head. "Find anything unusual in the cleanup?"

"Yeah, now you mention it, something strange all right. There was an iPod in the crapper."

"Excuse me?"

"Yeah, you heard right. I'm cleaning the porta-potty and I check to see if the tank's full or not. And there it is. One of those pink ones."

"What'd you do?"

The younger man's eyes drifted upward as if trying to pull the answer from his head. It was a standard liar's tell. "Those things are expensive, so I figure whoever lost it down there probably would want it back. After it's cleaned up, I mean." He chuckled.

Bud imagined that a lot of people, especially the kind to own a pink iPod, actually *wouldn't* be interested in reclaiming it once it landed on a pile of human waste.

The Woodside employee continued his story. "I got my can picker and yanked it out of there. Washed it off with my drinking water. I was going to take it to the lost and found."

Bud didn't buy for a moment that the maintenance worker had meant to turn in the iPod. Maybe he was going to give it to his girlfriend or post flyers in town and hope for a reward from the owner. Even working for an affluent municipality like Woodside, maintenance didn't pay worth shit. Found items were an unofficial perk of the job.

Bud wondered if the iPod had been accidentally dropped in the chemical toilet or ditched there on purpose. If you wanted to get rid of something, what could be a better place to dump it? No one was going to stick an arm in there to get it out.

"I could take it in for you," Bud offered.

"Better not. I got to do a report and everything."

Bud doubted his truthfulness but nodded anyway. "No problem. Would you mind taking a few photos of it for me? Just in case." Once he had photographic evidence of the iPod's existence the kid would probably feel compelled to turn it in. If he didn't, at least Bud would have a picture to show detectives or give to Velvet's defense team. If it came to that.

"You think it could have something to do with the murder?"

Bud shrugged. "Well now, I wouldn't know that. Not without examining it." He held his Polaroid out the window. "A few shots, if you don't mind, with the flash on."

The kid hesitated a moment. Then he accepted the outstretched Polaroid. Lights flashed in his cab as the photos were taken. He shoved the camera and photo cards back at Bud. "It's late. I got to lock up."

"Sure," Bud said. "Let me get out of your way. I'll watch out for that report."

❖

By the time Tucker finished the research for Yoshi and pushed her way through pedestrian crowds over to the *San Francisco Chronicle* office, it was 6:00 p.m. She looked up at the building, wondering if Velvet was up there working late. Then she remembered what Yoshi had said. That she couldn't find Velvet.

Standing in the dark thinking about that woman brought vivid memories to mind, and Tucker experienced them physically. Her stomach tightened and a shiver worked its way down her spine and settled between her thighs. She could almost feel lips bruising her own, a soft body pressed against hers in need, awkward fumbling replaced by bold exploration.

The memory of Velvet pulling her thighs apart with one hand and pinning her back with the other made Tucker feel weak in the knees. How could she be so aroused by one woman when her heart pined for another? She shook the visuals from her mind and consciously slowed her breathing, hoping the dampness in her jeans and the scent of desire wasn't a giveaway. This job could only work if she maintained a distance between her sex life and business. She'd heard that dogs could smell arousal. Could blind girls?

A stream of cars passed by as she continued down Mission Street to the neighboring office complex. Tucker sauntered through the parking lot in front of the three-story building that butted up to the *Chronicle* headquarters and wondered where Yoshi would be and how the blind woman would know it was her approaching.

She whispered, "Yoshi? Yoshi?"

"Over here."

Yoshi's voice was low and Tucker couldn't pinpoint its exact origination, but she wandered in the general direction.

"Under the stairs," Yoshi directed.

In the half-light, Tucker located the cement steps leading to the second floor offices. Beneath it, Yoshi leaned casually against a wall.

"Hi, Tucker, thanks for coming." Yoshi kept her voice low.

"No problem. What are we waiting for?"

"I'm hoping Liz Claiborne is going to show up since Dr. McDermid requested she come by the office this evening."

"Oh, right. I didn't find a lot, but it looks like the Claiborne we're looking for is this journalism student from Amherst College. She's out here in San Francisco doing an internship. It's a requirement of her program. She writes a blog, through Blogger?" Tucker wasn't sure if Yoshi was familiar with the online journaling community. "Anyways, it's funny. She talks about working at a magazine. She never mentions it by name, but I guess you said it was *Womyn*? It's obviously a lesbian magazine, but couldn't it be *Bend*?"

"No, she works for *Womyn*. Or at least she did. One of the employees said she hadn't been around for a month. What else did you find?"

"Just her address. I got it through reverse directory. She lives in the Mission."

"Okay. I'm hoping she will materialize. There was something about her phone message to Dr. McDermid..." Yoshi was quiet for a moment. Tucker half expected the private eye to make a "bing" sound and spit out a fortune teller card like the machine in that movie *Big*. Yoshi continued, "Which I *accidentally* overheard. She sounded more alarmed than distraught by the news of Rosemary's death. And her tone—it gave me the impression that she expected Dr. McDermid to have specific knowledge about the murder. Dr. McDermid seems concerned about protecting Claiborne in relation to this case. If either of them does know something, *I* want to find out exactly what it is."

Tucker remembered watching *Big* when she was a kid. She couldn't remember the occasion, but she must've been at someone else's house, because hers didn't have television. But then, she'd been at other people's houses a lot back then, which she supposed was better than the other option. No kid *wants* to spend all her time at a hospital. They're only there if they have to be.

"Tucker?" Yoshi had her head cocked to one side as though she'd been listening.

"Oh, sorry," Tucker apologized, certain she'd missed something. She was sorry for more than that. She still felt bad about those years, about being healthy when someone she loved wasn't.

"I just asked if you could do something for me?"

"Oh, yeah. Of course."

"Will you go out to the parking area and write down the make, model, and license plates of any vehicles out there? And see if the light is still on in the second-floor office, the fourth one down on the right."

"I'm on it." Tucker brushed her hands over her jacket until she found the small notepad tucked in an inside pocket. Feeling herself up failed to produce a pen, but it did stir up additional memories of Velvet. Tucker felt the heat rise up her neck to her cheeks. She wondered if Yoshi could sense that, like thermal imaging.

"Do you need a pen?" Yoshi held one out to her.

Tucker thanked her and took it. Their fingers brushed and Yoshi jerked hers away, as though electricity had passed between them.

After that reaction Tucker was a little relieved to slip into the darkness. As she traipsed into the middle of the lot, she gazed up and verified that the light was still burning in the specified office. There was even a little movement there, as though someone had been staring out the window and just dropped the shade. It happened so quickly she wasn't sure if she'd really seen anything.

In the far corner of the lot, she located three vehicles. She knew right away what one of them was, even when she was still ten yards away. It had the unmistakable profile of a Volkswagen bus. Tucker thought nostalgically about her own VW, which had served her well over all those thousands of miles and endless nights. She'd bought it in Pocatello, Idaho, and driven it all the way to New Orleans, camping in it at state parks along the way. And she lived out of it while she helped in the restoration of one of the city's youth shelters.

The bus had barely made it back to the West Coast. It nearly blew a head gasket in Houston, and a mechanic there told her it would cost her $1,500 to fix it. She didn't have that kind of money. She'd bought the thing for $600 and done most repairs herself. So she'd just kept driving, plugging away till she reached California, even though she knew she was ruining the engine. She stopped every few hours and added another quart of oil. It limped into the San Francisco Bay Area and expired in Livermore in a final gasp of gray exhaust. Tucker had ended up getting it towed to Oakland. Now its carcass was tucked in the Jacksons' backyard waiting for Tucker to afford parts, find spare time, and learn how to rebuild the engine.

She wondered how the more recent model in front of her handled the hills of San Francisco. Even when hers was in top condition it hadn't had a great deal of power and had crawled up mountains at thirty miles per hour, sputtering all the way.

As she jotted down plate numbers, Tucker was momentarily lit by headlights when a car pulled into the lot. Her first instinct was to hide, so she ducked down between two smaller vehicles. Rather than coming toward her, the car turned into a parking spot near where Yoshi hid below the stairs. The motor sounded rough, like it needed a tune-up. Tucker wondered if the driver could be Elizabeth Claiborne. Still crouched down, she waddled like a goose to the rear bumper and peered across the dark parking lot to the car. The occupants didn't immediately exit. That was suspicious, wasn't it? What would Yoshi want her to do? Creep over there on her belly and jot down the license plate?

In unison, two of the car's doors opened and two figures from the front seat were joined by a passenger from the rear. Tucker ducked behind her shielding vehicle so they wouldn't see her. She heard doors slam closed.

"What the hell?" a brusque, heavily accented voice roared from behind her. Tucker pirouetted to find an angry, balding, middle-aged man pointing a pudgy finger her way. She thought he was probably Italian. "What are you doing to my car?"

"Oh, oh my God, I'm sorry, I'm not doing anything, I swear," Tucker sputtered. "I was just, uh, just…I lost a contact." Tucker was almost pleased at her ruse. A lost contact. It wasn't exactly spy novel material, but for her it was damn quick thinking.

"What?" the guy bellowed.

"I lost my contact lens and I bent over to look for it and I was startled by you."

"All right. But you better not have scratched it," the man said, almost sounding flirty now. "This here is a rare Pontiac."

Apparently taken with Tucker's ditzy act, the hairy-armed guy went on to offer her a night to forget at Olive Garden. By the time Tucker extricated herself, she discovered the suspicious subjects she had meant to tail were no longer visible. Damn. Damn, damn, damn. *Why does this always happen to me*, she chided.

No longer concerned with keeping a low profile, Tucker strode briskly across the lot to the newly arrived vehicle, an aging, Robin's egg blue Honda Civic. She scrawled the Civic's plate on her notepad, finding it difficult to write in the dark. She wondered if she'd be able to read her notes later, or if, in the light of day, it would be a nonsensical scrawl of childlike script written diagonally across the margins of the page. Kind of like Bud's writing. Maybe *this* was why Bud's handwriting was so terrible. Was this what it felt like for Yoshi? Was closing your eyes an accurate, if self-enforced, experience of blindness? Or was there more to it than that?

As she neared the stairs, Tucker whispered to Yoshi.

No answer.

Tucker walked under the stairs, calling her name. "Yoshi?" Her stomach knotted. "Yoshi?" There was no response. "If you are hiding from me, it's not funny." Of course Yoshi wouldn't hide. That was far too juvenile. Tucker knew already that Yoshi wasn't the type for practical jokes.

Her searching became more frantic as the truth became painfully clear. Yoshi wasn't playing some trick on her. She wasn't there. Yoshi was gone.

❖

Velvet was lost in contemplation as she headed out the back door of the *Chronicle*. After her brief meeting with Marion, she'd returned to work and spent some time on the phone, tracking down former employees of *Womyn* magazine. Although several of the women were overly euphoric about Rosemary Finney's untimely death, she'd managed to rule all of them out as suspects. These women freely shared their abject hatred of Rosemary and their glee at her passing but one by one they'd offered solid alibis for the morning of her murder.

Velvet understood that eliminating suspects was a critical aspect of any investigation, but still she felt a little anxious about how little she'd accomplished on the first of her two days out of jail. The clock was ticking, she fretted as she rushed through the dark toward her shrink's office building. What could Yoshi possibly be doing skulking around a parking lot after sunset? Her phone message, left over an hour ago, hadn't given details. She'd just requested Velvet meet her outside Dr. McDermid's office.

Velvet was so lost in thought as she rounded the corner of the medical complex that she nearly collided with a tall figure lurking in the shadows. She started to scream and then recognized her lover's face. "Tucker? What are you doing here?" Then, worrying that the question would be taken the wrong way, she explained, "Yoshi asked me to meet her."

"Oh, Velvet, I'm so glad you're here." Tucker embraced her tightly and moaned into Velvet's neck, "Yoshi's missing."

"Missing?" Velvet disentangled herself. "What do you mean missing?"

"I don't know." Tucker pouted. "We were watching that office up there, the one with the light? We've been waiting for someone called Elizabeth Claiborne to show."

"Did you just say Elizabeth Claiborne?" Velvet recalled the new intern Marion had mentioned back at the Coffee Klatch. "Liz, right?"

"Yeah. A journalism student from Amherst College. She's in San Francisco doing an internship with *Womyn* magazine."

"You mean *Bend*."

"No, *Womyn,*" Tucker insisted. "The staff there told Yoshi about her. Apparently she was working there till about a month ago."

"*Damn.*" Velvet shook her head. The Yuri. She had to be. "Son of a…"

Certainly the fact that Liz had worked at both magazines in such a short time frame was suspicious. Especially in the light of the sabotage of *Bend*. Apparently Marion had trusted her, which meant she'd probably had access to commercially sensitive information. Could she have been sent in by Rosemary to spy on Marion?

Velvet thought about the unidentified young woman whose phone call had triggered her current problems with the law. Thanks to her,

Velvet had gone to Wonderland Park with her camera the morning of
the murder and was now a prime suspect in Rosemary's death. Was the
mystery caller Liz Claiborne? And if so, what exactly did she know?
Suddenly it seemed very urgent to speak to her.

Velvet wondered how much Yoshi knew about the enigmatic intern.
It was time they put together everything they'd each discovered.

"What's this about Yoshi missing?" she demanded.

"Well, see, Yoshi sent me to check if there were vehicles in the lot.
I was only gone a few minutes when this car pulled in." Tucker pointed
at the Honda Civic. "And these people got out and then I got distracted
and now"—she gulped—"now Yoshi's gone."

"And you guys are watching Artemis McDermid's office?" Velvet
pointed up at the one still brightly lit window. "What does my shrink
have to do with all this?"

Tucker raised her eyebrows. "Your shrink?"

Velvet glared at her.

"Sorry," Tucker said, exaggerating a serious look. "I think Yoshi
was expecting the Claiborne woman to show up. She wants to talk with
her."

"So do I. Why is Yoshi expecting her here? It's kind of late for an
appointment with Artemis."

"She overheard a phone call, that's all I know. And now Yoshi's
gone."

"I'm sure Yoshi's fine," Velvet reassured her young lover. "She
probably just went up to the office."

She touched Tucker's shoulder lightly, to calm her. The younger
woman crumpled into her arms and Velvet thought how cute she was, all
worked up and worried in her soft-butch way. She wondered if Tucker
had been crying, and brushed a hand across her cheeks, checking for
dampness. Maybe a little. Such a sweet, naïve gal in many ways, but
when they were in bed together she revealed some surprising skills. In
the dark, she could feel Tucker melting under her reassuring caresses,
leaning in toward her, wanting her. She sensed Tucker had her lips
parted slightly, anticipating a kiss. It sent a little shiver down her back.

Velvet wanted to give in to the moment, but the timing was all
wrong. Besides, Velvet liked to keep her sex and work lives separate,
even if that boundary was occasionally breached, and had, at times,
served as the location of erotic intimacy. It could be so hot to do it in
the office, but not while investigating a story, not outside her shrink's

office, and not while Yoshi was missing. She stroked Tucker's short hair, then gently pushed her away.

"Here's what we're going to do," she said firmly. "I'll go up to Artemis's office, see if Yoshi's up there. You wait here, in case she comes back."

"What if she doesn't?"

"I won't be long. If anything happens, call the police."

Velvet strode briskly up the concrete stairs and down the balcony until she reached Artemis McDermid's office door. She paused for a moment, wondering if this was going to cost her a psychologist. She'd hate to have to find another one, especially when she'd been happy with Artemis's approach. She wasn't a psychiatrist, she just held a PhD in psychology, and Velvet liked it that way. She wasn't fond of psychiatrists, those medically trained mental health professionals who liked to psychoanalyze you or dope you up with Prozac.

Reluctantly, she raised her fist and knocked once.

Before she could knock again, the door swung open and Artemis gushed, "Liz! I've been so worried." She stopped dead, obviously expecting someone else, and stuttered, "Oh, uh, hello, Velvet. This is an odd time to visit."

"Yes, it is an odd time," Velvet agreed. "I thought you left at five." She got right to the point. "Where's Yoshi?"

"Excuse me?" Artemis stepped back as though pushed.

Velvet closed the space between them. "Yoshi, my friend? The PI? I know she talked to you earlier today—where is she now?"

"How should I know? That was this morning."

"Yes. But she came back. Apparently she wanted to talk to Liz Claiborne. She a client of yours, or a friend?" Velvet watched Artemis carefully. A look of consternation crossed her face.

"I'm not at liberty," Artemis protested.

"So, she *is* a patient. Why are you meeting her?"

"That's what I do, meet with patients."

"Are you helping her spy on me?" Velvet demanded.

When Artemis gaped incredulously at her, Velvet wished she could come up with a more subtle way to flush out if it was a coincidence that Liz Claiborne, the *Bend* Yuri, was seeing the same shrink as she. Artemis seemed genuinely stunned by the accusation, but from Velvet's point of view, the circumstantial evidence was beginning to pile up, and it pointed in the intern's direction.

"Maybe you really didn't know, but Liz Claiborne is not only stealing trade secrets from my friend Marion, but she phoned and sent me to Wonderland yesterday morning, when Rosemary was murdered. At least, I'm pretty sure it was her."

The color drained from Artemis' face. "You were there? When it happened?"

"I didn't do it!" Velvet rushed to reassure her therapist. "But maybe your friend Liz was trying to set me up so it would look like I did."

Artemis shook her head.

Velvet eyed her psychologist suspiciously. What was she disagreeing with? What did Artemis know about the case? Velvet continued, "I *swear* I didn't set foot on the trail where Rosemary was killed."

Artemis cleared her throat. "Did you see anyone else there? Do you know—"

"I don't know *what* I saw." Velvet sighed. "Sometimes, when I'm shooting rolls of film, I have this terrible habit of not paying attention to details. I sort of rely on the camera to catch everything and then I go back to the pictures later."

"You took photos but you haven't seen them?" Artemis asked dubiously.

It was just like her shrink to simultaneously show interest in the details of Velvet's life stories while seeming to question both Velvet's objectivity and the subconscious motivations behind her decisions. Artemis probably thought Velvet had seen something at Wonderland but just couldn't admit it to herself. Or maybe the psychologist thought Velvet's odd habit of relying on photographs, and then not looking at the images right away, was a form of self-sabotage.

As much as she liked Artemis, during their sessions, Velvet often found herself psychoanalyzing the psychologist's comments and behavior, wondering, *Why did she ask me that? What does that look mean? What did she think of what I just said?*

"No, I haven't seen the photos because I had to ditch the film with my boss, which was a good thing because after they arrested me the cops sent someone to tear through my cubicle. Anyway, they're still being developed." Velvet fluttered a hand to wave aside the topic. "Can't you tell me what *you* know?"

"You know that my patient information is confidential, Velvet. Even if I wanted to tell you, I can't."

"Look, Artemis, Yoshi's my dearest friend. And I know she wouldn't have been here tonight unless she thought Liz had something to do with Rosemary Finney's murder. I'm beginning to think so too. So where is she?"

"She never showed up." Artemis looked down at the ground.

"I meant Yoshi. Where is *Yoshi*?" Velvet felt anger rising in her chest. Why was Artemis stringing her along? And what was it she didn't want them to know about Liz Claiborne? If her psychologist knew who was really responsible for killing Rosemary, would she protect that person even if it meant Velvet would go to jail for something she hadn't done? *God*, Velvet thought, unconsciously shaking her head, *I really am going to have to find a new shrink.*

"Velvet, are you actually accusing me of doing something to your friend?" Artemis touched her arm. Her knitted brows and the genuine concern in her voice doused some of Velvet's anger. "Do you really think I'm capable of hurting someone? And why? Why would I do such a thing?"

Velvet sighed and threw herself down on the couch. "I'm sorry." She waggled her head side to side. "I know you wouldn't hurt anyone. It's just that I *know* Yoshi was downstairs tonight, so I'm worried. And you're here after hours to meet with this woman and then she doesn't show. What's going on? I assume you've called her?"

Artemis made a small noise of dismay. She looked out of her depth. "I *am* worried." She sank into the seat across from Velvet. For a moment, she rested her face in her hands. "I don't know where she is."

Velvet thought quickly. Obviously Liz was Rosemary's secret agent inside *Bend*, feeding information back to the now-dead editor. Had the Yuri grown a conscience and refused to continue spying? Was she being threatened or blackmailed by Rosemary so that she would betray Marion? Had she finally snapped and killed the awful woman?

If so, maybe she was now on the run. Or maybe someone knew and Liz thought she was in danger. Velvet immediately rejected the idea that Marion could have paid Liz to whack her enemy and was now hunting her down to eliminate the evidence. That plot was more apt for Linda Fiorentino in *The Last Seduction*.

"What are you afraid might have happened? Is someone after her?"

Artemis shook her head. "No, it's nothing like that. I don't know what to think."

"My friends are investigators, and we have reasons of our own to find her. We could help. At least you'd know she's all right. Can you give me her address?"

Artemis wasn't falling for that. "No."

"Artemis, I've been charged with first degree murder in the death of Rosemary Finney." Velvet repeated the phrasing the police had used.

Artemis' face constricted. She shook the expression away, but not before Velvet saw it. "I know. I'm so sorry, Velvet. Is there anything I can do?"

"Well, yeah!" Velvet stood and walked around the coffee table. Standing directly in front of her psychologist, she explained. "If you know something, please spill it before I spend the rest of my life in prison."

"Oh, no, no. I'm sure it won't get that far."

"I've already been arraigned."

Artemis hung her head. "Oh, dear."

Velvet looked down at the Swatch on her wrist. Her long chocolate hair fell in front of her face and she brushed it aside. "In thirty-seven hours and twenty-four minutes I have to appear before that judge again. If I can't clear my name, they'll lock me up for the next three months, minimum, until the trial. Or I'll have to pay enormous bail."

"But how could that happen? You had nothing to do with it!"

Velvet rolled her eyes. "I *know*. It's crazy. But that's why it's so important that you tell me anything you know. I mean, you're not okay with me going to jail for something I didn't do just so you keep your reputation for protecting client privacy intact, are you?"

"No, of course I don't want that, Velvet. It's just that I know you'll be okay. You weren't even involved and you've got friends like Yoshi—who is clearly very devoted to you and who I'm sure will not rest until you are cleared. Can you just give me a little time? I need to talk to Liz first." Artemis's voice wavered and she kept glancing toward the door as if she was still expecting the elusive Liz Claiborne to walk through it at any moment. "Then perhaps I can help."

Velvet wondered what their connection was, exactly. It almost sounded like the psychologist was trying to buy time to bring Liz Claiborne in. Maybe Artemis was already telling her all she needed to know. Could she infer from the shrink's statements that Liz *was* somehow involved in Rosemary's death and didn't have anyone to keep her out of jail—except maybe Artemis herself? Could Artemis be laying the groundwork for some kind of insanity plea? Artemis had said she didn't think Claiborne was in danger from someone else, but what if she was suicidal—was Artemis implying that was a concern, without putting it into words?

As eager as Velvet was to know what Artemis wasn't saying, she could see the psychologist was tormented, and decided it was time to leave. She and Yoshi could track down Liz Claiborne. First they could make sure the girl was okay, and then they would find out what, exactly, her connection was to Rosemary and the murder. Meantime, Yoshi had vanished and Velvet needed to make sure she was okay.

CHAPTER THIRTEEN

Yoshi had not been kidnapped. She had been deep in Spanish conversation with the cleaning ladies responsible for the medical suites where Artemis McDermid had her practice. After assuring everyone that she was *not* with INS, she'd learned that they routinely discarded refuse into the *Chronicle* Dumpster, because the closer Dumpster was occupied most of the time by homeless guys who sheltered between the buildings. She'd also learned that Artemis McDermid had discarded a pair of shoes in the Dumpster the morning of Rosemary's murder. Yoshi wanted to speak to the psychologist about that. So after she'd thanked the cleaning crew, she made her way up to the second floor. Evidently she wasn't the only visitor that evening.

"Your friend was just here looking for you," Dr. McDermid said when she answered her door. She sounded harried, as if she'd been crying.

Yoshi was surprised that Tucker could have that effect on anyone. She reintroduced herself and said, "This is about Elizabeth Claiborne."

"Where is she?" The therapist flung her door wide. Yoshi took this for an invitation and walked in. Even if it was not, few people would order a blind woman to leave.

"Did you divert her so you could talk to her first?" Dr. McDermid demanded. "If you've taken advantage of her emotionally distressed state to—"

Yoshi held up a hand, palm out in the universal sign for stop. "I have done nothing of the sort. I did not encounter Ms. Claiborne this evening." She heard the sound of skin pressed against itself and concluded that the doctor was squeezing her hands together nervously.

Fishing for information, she continued, "You were expecting her tonight, and you're worried."

"Yes," the shrink affirmed with a note of relief.

Yoshi guessed she was thankful that someone else understood her apprehension. "Under the circumstances, I think it is reasonable to be concerned."

She had learned from her PI father that people speak more freely to those who project an air of knowledge. If one appeared to know vital information about an individual, for example, a subject might even become competitive, wanting to illustrate that they knew the person more intimately. Of course, Artemis McDermid was a psychologist and probably able to control immature urges. Still, Yoshi recognized that mental health professionals were just as fallible as anyone else. They had their own emotional problems, their own need to share their stories, and their own psychologists.

Artemis began to cry. "I'm terrified that something awful has happened to her, and I blame myself."

"Tell me about her," Yoshi suggested.

"She...I..." Artemis stammered. "I still feel uncomfortable breaking her confidence."

"We both know she is in trouble and why," Yoshi reasoned quietly. "You cannot protect her forever. That is why I am trying to find her."

Artemis stopped crying. "Protect her?" She laughed a dry bitter laugh that seemed to die in her throat. "I didn't protect her from *anything*. I couldn't save her."

"From Rosemary?" Yoshi took an educated guess and hoped it would pay off.

It did. The floodgates opened as Artemis, relieved to get it off her chest, unloaded. "Well, you wouldn't understand, but that's my job, you know, to save people from themselves—or from the people abusing them. Liz is a very disturbed young woman. She had problems long before she ever met Rosemary Finney. But Rosemary tipped the scales." She sighed and pulled a tissue from the box on her desk, dabbing at her eyes before continuing. "Despite the fact that their affair was rather abusive—emotionally, that is—when Rosemary broke it off, Liz really lost it. She started following Rosemary everywhere. Stalking her."

"That is not a good idea." Yoshi sighed.

"You have no idea. And when she discovered that Rosemary had already moved on to her next conquest, Liz lost it. She desperately wanted to confront Rosemary and have it out with her. I tried to talk her out of it, of course."

"Why?" Yoshi thought shrinks liked to prepare their clients for handling conflict, not avoiding it.

"I was afraid of what might happen if she faced Rosemary alone. I felt it would be safer if the confrontation occurred in the sanctuary of my office."

"If you thought Liz was a threat, did you not have a professional obligation to report it?"

"I wasn't sure," Artemis replied. "I didn't know if she'd be more likely to react violently or just allow Rosemary to victimize her again. Clinically speaking, it would almost be a step forward if Liz were to lash out in response to someone hurting her. And I just couldn't see prematurely committing her to a mental health facility. She had a history of being confined against her will before, first during a rape, and then in a psychiatric facility in Oklahoma."

Yoshi made a sympathetic soothing noise. Liz Claiborne had been through some rough experiences in her young life and Yoshi did not envy her. Gambling, she said, "I assume you are aware that Liz was at Wonderland Park the morning Rosemary Finney was killed."

The psychologist almost sounded relieved. Yoshi imagined this was because she had not made the incriminating disclosure herself. Very quietly, she murmured, "Yes. And it seems that Liz somehow arranged for Velvet to be present, too. Velvet said something to me about receiving a phone call."

"Interesting." Yoshi wondered what else Velvet had been keeping from her. "You were there too, were you not?" she guessed.

Artemis made a soft noise like a hiccup.

"You may relax," Yoshi said. "I am not making accusations. The truth will come out anyway, and naturally I have my own theory. I suggest you tell me your account in confidence so that I can avoid passing on faulty conclusions when I speak with detectives. I would not wish to cause a problem for innocent people." To drive her point home, she added, "To cause an ordeal such as the one Velvet is enduring would be dishonorable. You understand, I am sure."

Artemis reacted with a nervous shuffle. Then it seemed she could not talk fast enough. "There's an explanation for everything. Liz used to meet Rosemary at Wonderland Park."

Yoshi denied herself a satisfied smile. This was the kind of information that could lead to clearing Velvet's name.

"She frequently stayed the night with a friend of hers who lives in the mountains on the Peninsula?" She framed the statement like a question, wanting Yoshi to understand. "From there, she would ride her mountain bike down to Wonderland Park and hook up with Rosemary to talk or have sex. Anyway, Liz let it slip that she was going to meet Rosemary at the park *that* morning. I went there to keep her from doing anything drastic."

"Were you unable to prevent her from going?" Yoshi asked.

"I tried to catch her before she left her friend's house, but when I got there she was already gone. I fucked up. I failed my patient." Artemis was sobbing now, her professional façade entirely shattered.

Yoshi let her cry. After a few minutes Artemis dabbed at her eyes with a handy tissue pulled with a ripping noise from a box on her desk. Yoshi assumed patients wept often.

Artemis began explaining again. "I found Liz on the trail, yelling at Rosemary. Rosemary said something I couldn't hear, and then Liz just jumped her. It surprised the hell out of me. I *really* wasn't expecting that. I tried to break them up, but that sociopath Rosemary turned on *me*. She started hitting me with her fists and screaming about going to the police."

"And the two of you killed her to keep her quiet?" Yoshi postulated.

"No!" Artemis sniffed. "Why would you suggest something like that? Do I seem capable of murder?"

"Contrary to popular opinion, murderers tend to appear much like anyone else," Yoshi said. "Quite frankly, I do not know you. I *do* know Velvet Erickson, and I know *she* did not kill Rosemary Finney. That means someone else did. And I am going to find out who. Now, one way or the other, I just need to hear about your and Liz's involvement. Go ahead with your story."

For a few seconds Artemis appeared unnerved. Then, as if she realized she had gone so far that there was no turning back, she said, "I admit, when Rosemary was hitting me and talking about the police, I was really scared and I decided to make Rosemary give us her shoes so she couldn't chase us. I just wanted to get Liz safely out of there and I wanted Rosemary to cool off. I wanted—"

"To keep her from going to the police?"

"No. No! Just to get out of there."

"Then what did you do?" Yoshi asked.

"Liz gave me a ride up the hill to my car."

"No, I do not think so."

"What do you mean?"

"Firstly, you just said Liz rode her bike to the scene, so how did she give you a ride?"

"Oh, sorry, I mean, that's what she usually did, but not this time, this time, she drove there."

"Okay, let us say that's true," Yoshi allowed for argument's sake. "Does that mean you are actually claiming *you* rode down on a mountain bike? Because I understand there were fresh bicycle tracks on the trail."

"Uh, yeah. That's right."

Yoshi shook her head, disappointed that Artemis would so blatantly attempt to mislead her. "It will not be beneficial to deceive me. You cannot protect Liz this time."

"I don't know what you mean." Artemis played dumb.

Yoshi sighed. "Pardon me if I am misjudging you, Artemis, but you do not strike me as the sort of law-breaking, risk-taking athletic individual who would ride down a steep single-track dirt trail that prohibited mountain bikes. And is that Volkswagen van parked out front not yours?"

"How did you know?" Artemis asked. "I thought you were blind."

"My assistant described it and I could smell it. The odor of oil burning—it is an older model, isn't it? From the 1980s? You have to replace oil regularly, correct? And perhaps it is misfiring?"

"Yeah. Wow. I don't know how you do that."

"I am a PI. You might want to have a mechanic check it out."

"Are you completely blind?" Artemis asked. "See nothing but black?"

"No, actually, not yet. It is more shades of gray. I can still make out large shapes—rough outlines. When everything is pushed together it becomes one big blur. I can tell a person's general size, that kind of thing."

"Is it treatable? Can you have LASIK surgery?"

"No. There are some experimental treatments being tested, but there is no cure as yet."

"And it's degenerative? It's getting progressively worse?"

"Yes."

"That must be very difficult, very frightening to lose your eyesight. I mean—I imagine that it's more difficult than being born blind."

"I cannot say," Yoshi replied. "I know how blessed I was to have those years of sight, because they allowed me to experience the world visually. That is a wonderful gift, to see your father's face, to perceive colors." She shrugged. "Naturally, there is still a great deal of sadness. It is a loss."

"I get the feeling that you don't talk about that much. Maybe you're unwilling for anyone to see your weaknesses, so you don't ask for help." Artemis was falling into therapy mode. "But it might be nice for you to have someone to process those feelings with."

Yoshi laughed. "You are good. I will grant you that. I see why Velvet likes you. However, I am not here to be psychoanalyzed or counseled. I am here to solve a murder and I would like to get back to that. I believe we were talking about your Volkswagen? You were parked at the *bottom* of the hill, in the Wonderland Park lot, were you not? I would wager your vehicle cannot traverse the steep incline to Highway 92—I understand that they are a little lackluster when it comes to hills. It was Liz who parked up on Skyline and rode down the hill, was it not? Was that to ambush Rosemary?"

Artemis's uneasy silence spoke for itself.

Yoshi continued. "Although it is admirable that you are covering for Liz, I do not believe it was you who took Rosemary's shoes." Yoshi smiled at Artemis, hoping to convey a "that's cute, but stupid" look, and then continued her analysis. "But it also makes you an accessory, not just a witness."

"Only if she killed her. And she didn't. I'm certain of that."

"And I am certain you did not scuffle with Rosemary," Yoshi said firmly. "I think if you had, you would have bruises or scratches or some other defensive wounds. Which you do not. I am unable to smell any of the ointments that people typically use to medicate minor wounds, and I know Velvet would have noticed if, say, you had received a black eye in an altercation. You might have been at Wonderland that morning, but I think the whole time you stayed in the parking lot in your van. Maybe you were waiting to talk with Rosemary Finney. Or maybe you were there looking for Liz. I do not know. Regardless, I believe you were in the lot and you witnessed Liz flying down the trail on her bike, carrying Rosemary's shoes. You insist she did not kill Rosemary, but how do you know for certain? Have you asked her?"

After a long pause, Artemis admitted, "No. At the time I had no idea Rosemary had *been* killed. I mean, if she had been at that point, which I'm still not sure of. If I had known, I swear I would have done something: gone to check on her, called an ambulance, something. The funny thing," Artemis added, without laughing, "is that Liz must have thought *I* did it, when the news came out. That I had sent her riding back up the hill via Bear Gulch Road so she wouldn't pass by Rosemary again, and went back and killed Rosemary myself."

"Did she tell you that?"

"Not in so many words, but when we made our arrangements for tonight she was obviously scared." Artemis sniffled. "I think she must have come early, but the fucking cops were here. They *demanded* that I go with them down to the station. I called Liz, but I don't know if she got my message." Artemis shook her head. "I mean, *imagine.* She thinks her therapist—the one person she'd been opening up to and feeling she can rely on—she thinks I killed that woman. Then she finds out I thought she might have done it, that I think she's capable of *that*." She punctuated her words more with her intensifying emotions. "Then she comes here to talk to me and the police are here. She probably assumed I'd turned her in."

"That would explain her staying away," Yoshi said.

"What a blow," Artemis summarized, her voice quiet and wavering. "I hope she's okay."

"You have done everything you can. You will just have to wait until things die down. I am sure she will show up."

"Did I?" Artemis McDermid didn't sound convinced. "I should have seen this coming. Here I thought we were close to a break*through* and it turns out she's closer to a break*down*. I should never have let her go that day. I could have stopped her and I didn't."

"They say hindsight is 20/20," Yoshi remarked. "But I find it far more cloudy than that. When we gaze at past actions, we fail to notice extenuating circumstances. We only focus on one thing. But life is the intersection of a million things, colliding at one particular microscopic point in time and space. It is like a blind curve. You never know what is around the corner."

"Thanks," Artemis offered weakly.

"Tell me how you ended up with Rosemary's shoes." Yoshi prompted a directional change in the conversation.

"You don't miss anything, do you?"

"One of the cleaning ladies saw you throw something in the *Chronicle*'s Dumpster yesterday morning."

"Yes." Artemis sighed. "I threw them in there. I'm so sorry."

Her voice had increased in volume and the scent of her perfume grew stronger. Yoshi deduced that Artemis must have been leaning forward in her chair to emphasize her apology.

"What are you apologizing for?" Yoshi asked.

"I think I've contributed to Velvet's problems with the police. I never meant that. I was only thinking of Liz. Please tell Velvet I'm sorry."

"I am certain that she will understand." Yoshi did not voice her doubts. So far nothing in Artemis's account explained why Liz had phoned Velvet to draw her to the scene. "So, did Liz leave the shoes in your van?"

"Right. I found them when I got to work. I knew I wasn't going to return them to Rosemary." She laughed, but there was no humor in the sound that came out of her mouth.

Winding up their meeting, Yoshi asked if Artemis had anything else to add.

"There is one thing I could do to help, if you'd allow me."

"Yes?" Yoshi was not sure what Artemis had in mind.

"Can you tell me how Rosemary was killed?"

"Strangulation."

"Choking," Artemis mused, before becoming silent in thought. "It brings to mind cutting off someone's voice, silencing them. Did the killer use their hands or something else?"

"I am not sure, yet." Yoshi shifted in her seat. Catching on to what Artemis was thinking the detective was intrigued by what the psychologist might deduce about the killer. "Let us say it was something the victim was wearing."

She knew it would make a difference if the killer brought something with them. *That* could point to premeditation, and Yoshi had the impression that this was not a well-planned attack. Even if she had read the autopsy report and was certain of the details, she would still have kept her answers a little vague. Years of working with the police had taught her discretion when sharing details of a crime, and she did not want to taint Artemis's deductions.

"Not using his hands probably means the killer doesn't want to get his hands dirty, metaphorically. He is not driven to experience the sensations specific to physical contact. Utilizing something at the scene would suggest that it wasn't preplanned." Artemis confirmed Yoshi's inclinations. "Then again, I think there are a whole group of criminals who prefer to use something they find. You understand I'm not trained as a criminal profiler. I've only had one class on the subject. But to me that would seem to indicate that the killer was confident enough to assume he could utilize something at the scene for a murder weapon." She continued to ruminate aloud. "It could be someone who *knew* that Rosemary wore the item. Can I ask you a question?"

"Absolutely," Yoshi said, willing to facilitate Artemis's speculations. You never knew when something could spark an essential insight.

"I assume this was an isolated incident? Not related to other murders."

Yoshi nodded. "Probably not."

"To me, that would implicate someone who was familiar with Rosemary's schedule. I know it sounds like I could be talking about Liz." She sighed again and disappeared into her thoughts. Yoshi heard another tissue pulled from its box. "I don't know if that helps."

"Very much." Artemis *had* said a few helpful things. Yoshi shifted forward on the couch, ready to stand.

Artemis responded by pushing her own chair back and standing up. "I'll call you if I think of anything else."

"Thank you." Yoshi reached for the woman's hand. "One last thing. Have you cleaned your vehicle since the incident?"

"No." As if deducing Yoshi's intention, she added, "I never lock it, though, if that makes a difference."

It might. In court, if they were presenting evidence. There would be no chain of custody, no proof that any trace evidence found inside the vehicle could be linked to yesterday's events. But since Yoshi still hoped to keep the case against Velvet from *going* to trial, she asked, "Would you mind if I looked around in it?"

"No, please do. And, if you find anything that will help Velvet, feel free to take it with you."

❖

Black cast-iron gates and stately ancient oak trees with branches that cast deep shadows on the road hemmed in the Friars-Finney estate. At night, the area looked more like a football stadium than a fancy estate, flooded with hard white beams of security lights. Woodside might have once had more horses than residents, but now it was the domain of spoiled rich bitches who thought just because Daddy made millions they were somehow better than the rest of the Bay Area.

Land that formerly held stables was sold for millions simply to be razed. Once the previous buildings were torn down, the new owners erected enormous, city block–sized mansions so big Bud's own house would probably fit in their washroom. Neighborhood Watch signs were posted every few hundred feet, reminding nonresidents that their every move was being constantly monitored and reported. Although Bud didn't see them, he imagined there were security cameras hiding amidst the branches of darkened trees. He wondered if they were purchased by homeowners or the local police. He'd heard Woodside PD was the most technologically advanced of Silicon Valley's wired cops. Local industry giants like Hewlett-Packard poured money into the community's infrastructure.

The dead woman's house was a three-story sprawling Mediterranean manor silhouetted by lights posted along a circling drive of ghostly white crushed oyster shells. The shades were drawn and lights glowed in several rooms, but no one answered when Bud pressed the drive-up intercom where visitors presumably gave their names to be buzzed through the tall gates. He sat in the Impala for a few minutes watching the house through thick steel bars, looking for any sign of shadows moving. Nothing stirred.

While he was there, Bud thought, he might as well read that ranger's incident report. He'd worked hard enough to get it. He flicked on the overhead light and shuffled through papers to find the photocopy. Since the incident hadn't occurred on Midpeninsula property, the Midpen ranger completed a supplemental report, which differed from other incident reports in several ways, the most critical being that it didn't include a detailed listing of involved parties and their respective addresses, driver's license numbers, and vehicle plates—suspects, victims, and witness all fell in this category.

Bud remembered that Sheriff Deputy Roy Freeman also hadn't

written a primary report, not wanting to be seen as infringing on Woodside's jurisdiction. He wondered if *anyone* had actually gathered the relevant information. He pulled a stapled corner toward him and started reading, skimming the official data until he reached Jenny Cooper's neatly typed "Synopsis of Incident."

> Responded to Dispatch report of hiker down at Corte Madera, gate CM04. On arrival found RP who directed me to the injured individual on Wonderland Park's Huckleberry Trail. Located individual, non responsive. Performed CPR to no avail. Coroner pronounced at scene. Ruled suspicious death, possible murder.

Bud continued to scan.

District Equipment and Supplies Used: Responded in truck P49. Used latex gloves, disposable CPR mouth guard, emergency blanket: covered body with blanket to protect victim's ID from news media.

Risk Assessment: Darkness, slick and muddy trail, trail not properly brushed, poison oak. Poor hand radio reception. Since this was not reported as a crime: risk of perpetrator in the area.

Additional Information:
SYNOPSIS: In the early hours of 10-25-06, Woodside resident Rosemary Finney was found dead on Wonderland Park's Huckleberry Trail. The death was ruled suspicious by the San Mateo County Coroner.

DETAILS: On 10-25-2006 at 0558 hours I was contacted via phone by Mountain View Dispatch and informed of a reported

hiker down in the El Corte de Madera
Creek Preserve. A reporting party was
standing by at the call box by gate CM04.
When I arrived there, the RP directed me
to Wonderland Park, where he had found
the victim on the Huckleberry trail. I
contacted Mountain View, requested Fire,
Ambulance, Woodside Police, and San Mateo
County Sheriff Department.

Carrying my medical bag, I ran down
the trail until I located the victim. She
was lying partially off the trail in the
bushes. The victim was unresponsive, not
breathing and without a pulse. I attempted
to relay the information to dispatch, but
was unable to get out on my handheld radio.
I immediately began one-person CPR, which
I continued until CDF personnel arrived
on scene, approximately 15 minutes later.
The CDF medic and a firefighter continued
manual ventilation, with 2-man CPR, while
I returned to my vehicle at the top of the
hill. There I conferred with CDF Chief
Williams and requested the County Coroner.
As he was delayed, CDF chose to transport
the subject to the ambulance, which had
arrived on scene. With the ambulance crew
and additional CDF personnel, I assisted
in the transportation of the stretcher
down the trail, secured the patient to the
board, and slowly transported her uphill
while 2-person CPR was continued. At the
summit, there was a media crew that was
set up and interviewing the RP. As per
District policy, I declined to speak with
them and referred them to District Public
Relations.

The patient continued to show no
sign of life. She was loaded into the

ambulance. Before the ambulance left, the coroner arrived and time of death was officially declared.

SCENE: Woodside City's Wonderland Park, on the Huckleberry Trail, about 3/5 way down from the top. The victim was partially off the trail, pulled off into the bushes (primarily coyote brush, poison oak, manzanita, and scrub oak). The victim was wearing expensive-looking sweatpants, T-shirt, and a hooded sweatshirt that was partially unzipped. The victim was not wearing shoes. The bottom of her socks were slightly dirtied. There were no signs of trauma (no bleeding).

EVIDENCE: None collected. Saw evidence of recent mountain bike activity on the trail, which is permanently closed to bikes, and fresh horse hoofprints, although the trail is closed to horses for the season. There is a sign to this effect at the trail's upper entrance.

OTHER COMMENTS: At the time, I thought the woman looked familiar. Once I returned to the office I was able to verify that the victim was the same Rosemary Finney who assaulted me several years a—

A short, loud burst from a police siren bellowed. The white paper Bud held in front of his face suddenly glowed rose.

What the— He glanced up and groaned as his corneas were pierced by a spotlight reflected in his rearview mirror. *Damn.* He squeezed his lids shut. Even with them closed, he could see the blue aura tinting everything in his vehicle. *Cops.*

Bud raised his right hand to shield his eyes from the blasting intensity of the spotlight. He'd lost track of time reading the report and now he'd been skulking outside Woodside's richy-rich Friars-Finney estate for forty minutes. No doubt one of the neighbors called 911 to report the noticeably out-of-place vehicle casing the joint. Maybe they thought he was the kind of burglar that scoured obituaries, seeking to target wealthy households distracted by bereavement.

The cops hit the siren again, perplexing Bud. Obviously they weren't asking him to pull over. The Impala was already off to the side of a private driveway. Bud wasn't even blocking the domineering gate that prevented him from reaching the Friars-Finney mansion. Was this one of those "move along" warnings? He raised a hand to signal he understood, then turned the ignition key and the Impala purred to life.

"Stop what you're doing!" The officer's command screeched through the vehicle's megaphone system.

Bud didn't want to be shot again, especially not by some trigger-happy nervous-Nelly patrolman, so he immediately complied, killing the engine. Slowly, very slowly, he slid his hands along the smooth steering wheel until they met at the wheel's apex. Pressing his thumbs tightly against each other like a fat girl's thighs, he stopped moving, aside from the slow rhythmic expansion and contraction of his chest.

The well-aimed spotlight reflected on his mirrors and prevented Bud from seeing the car behind him. He figured that there were probably two officers. This was Woodside, after all, a city with a big enough budget to have two cops doing the job that one San Francisco patrolman handled on his own.

The cops had been silent long enough to call in his vehicle plates, Bud figured. They'd come back clean and these officious jerks would let him go with some kind of warning, or at least drop the intensity of the stop. Right now they were treating him like a threat. Once they figured out who he was, that would end, and in the meantime, since he couldn't see, Bud closed his eyes and tuned his ears to the sounds around him.

Frogs were croaking in the dark. California tree frogs, he thought, and then snorted to himself. "Did you know that the sound of silence in most movies and television shows is actually the call of the California tree frog?" The irrelevant factoid sounded like something Velvet would say, what with her fascination with all things Hollywood. But it had been Tucker who'd shared the tidbit. Maybe you learned that kind of shit growing up a country bumpkin.

Muted mumbling drifted through the window. Was that the radio?

Maybe dispatch broadcasting Bud's private investigation credentials? He'd hear better with the window down, Bud reasoned. He began inching his left hand toward his window.

"Keep your hands on the wheel." The booming megaphone-distorted voice startled Bud.

Why were they still treating him this way? He should have been cleared by now. He returned his wayward hand to rest on the wheel and heard a door open and the crunch of feet on gravel. It would be the guy on the right, Bud thought. *He'll come up to my passenger window, thinking it will be unexpected, and shine a flashlight in my eyes.* That was the usual two-person technique on a stop, leaving a patrolman at the wheel and placing the other more than an arm's length from the source of potential danger, the stopped driver.

He couldn't see the approaching officer, but Bud knew he'd pause for just a moment at the rear of the car, placing one palm flat against the trunk lid, verifying it was secure and no one could burst forth guns blazing. The mandatory hand compulsion, which rookies had to successfully demonstrate in every vehicle stop from police academy to training ride-alongs, wasn't *just* to shut the occasionally ajar trunk. It had a more sinister, more cynical purpose. Every officer touched the vehicle he approached so that if the occupants killed him, there would be some forensic evidence to tie him to the vehicle: his handprint.

This guy placed his hand on the Impala's fin and ran his fingers along the side of the Impala. Bud rolled his eyes. *Way to smudge your print, buddy.* Then the cop was rapping against the passenger window with his metal baton. Bud wondered who'd come up with this tactic. Some egghead somewhere, evaluating statistics? Why did they think it was always safer to approach on the right? Because they expected the criminal to have a gun in his hand, ready to shoot through the door when you came to the driver's side, Bud reminded himself.

Still, here he was, having to stretch all the way across the bench seat to the opposite door. Bud unhooked his seat belt and leaned across the seat, thinking how his outstretched hand could just as easily go to the gun in his glove compartment as the window roll-down handle. *Cops make the best criminals,* he thought out of nowhere, *because they know all the tricks.*

"Evening, Officer." He looked up from the handle after he'd rolled the window down halfway.

He was met with the beam of a flashlight in his eyes. Holding himself up with his right arm, Bud shielded his retinas with the left.

"License and registration," the officer demanded gruffly.

"I'm reaching for my wallet," Bud said, knowing to explain his movements before he made them. "It's inside my jacket pocket." He peeked at the officer for verification.

"Take it out real slow. No quick motions."

"I know the drill." Bud nodded.

He felt the guy tense and heard the snap of a gun hostler being unhooked.

"I used to be on the job," Bud rushed to explain, realizing that the officer had taken his familiarity with the routine as indication that he'd been in the system. He opened the wallet so his driver's license and PI license were both visible, stretched across the cluttered bench seat again, and handed it to the officer.

The patrolman peered at the open wallet, focusing his flashlight on the cards inside. Not saying anything to Bud, he then reached to his shoulder, pressed the button on his mic, and read off the numbers of Bud's license. "Your registration," he reminded Bud while waiting for his dispatch to run Bud's information for warrants.

"Here's the thing," Bud said, nodding toward the glove compartment. "There's a .45 in there. I have a license to carry. Behind the PI card."

The officer jumped two steps back and away from the Impala. His right hand, which had been resting on the handle of his service pistol, drew the weapon in one smooth motion and in another, aimed it at Bud's head.

Jesus, talk about trigger-happy. Bud heard the distinct click of a safety flipped off. He was being treated like a felony vehicle stop, like he'd been flagged with a warrant or something. *What the fuck?* By now they should've been able to verify his credentials. The guy back in the patrol car took over on the public announcement system and Bud played ball, extracting his Colt .45 and dropping it out the window into the gravel. The cop scurried over and retrieved it, then Bud was ordered to toss his keys out the window and exit the car.

He didn't move. With the cold barrel of a gun that was suddenly pressing an indentation into the soft skin below his leftt ear, sitting still seemed wise. "Enough's enough," he said, not looking at the gun's owner. "You guys have had your fun, so let's move on."

The gun barrel jammed deeper into his flesh. "I said, get out."

"So, does Woodside PD treat all PIs this way? Or am I something special?"

"Shut up. This isn't happy hour and I'm not your buddy. Now exit the vehicle."

Bud kept his hands on the top of the wheel and tried to keep his voice calm. "You might have noticed from the handicap plates, or the blue placard hanging over my rearview mirror, or even the wheelchair in the backseat, I'm disabled. If you want to take me into custody, I suggest you provide me with the appropriate accommodations, or I swear to God I'll have a civil rights lawyer crawl up your ass so far that he'll be fucking your ear canal. Now, am I under arrest? Or what the fuck's going on here?"

"We got a report that you're stalking one of our residents. We take that kind of thing seriously, especially after recent events."

"Stalking? That's ridiculous."

"Sorry, sir, but we're under orders to treat you as a person of extreme interest, and to transport you down to the station—*posthaste.*" He emphasized the term as if to reiterate his superiority to the former San Francisco detective. Bud had heard even the cops down here were products of Stanford and other high-caliber universities. 'Course, he didn't think that made for better police. Not if this guy was any indication.

A short while later, after a memorable journey in the Impala, a cop sitting behind him with a handgun trained on the back of his head, Bud found himself in an interrogation room at Woodside PD. "I'll take an attorney, thanks," he yelled as they shut the door behind him.

He pulled vainly at the cuffs that secured each wrist to the metal wheelchair. They hadn't flipped the light switch as they left, and he sat in the dark for the next ten minutes clattering his cuffs and shouting obscenities.

Then the door slammed open, light drenched the room, and a tall, gray-haired man in a suit marched authoritatively up to the table. Bud assumed he was looking at Woodside's Chief of Police, Anthony Barnes.

"Oh, Detective Williams," Chief Barnes sneered. "I remember you from the papers." He pulled a chair out from the table and sat down across from Bud. His smile didn't extend to his eyes. "What ever happened with those charges? What were they? Brutality? No, *corruption*, wasn't it? Funny, as I heard it, you were just about to be indicted, with Internal Affairs breathing down your neck. Next thing you know, you're suddenly injured and all the charges just slip away."

Bud snorted. "You suggesting I got myself shot and paralyzed just to get out of going to court? Brilliant tactic on my part."

"I'm not a doctor. I have no idea what your physical limitations are. But if I recall, they never did catch the guy who pulled the trigger. Meanwhile, three of your fellow officers all go down *hard* like the cleanup after that Rampart shit down in L.A. I heard one guy ate his gun, didn't he? While the other two went to prison? And that doesn't bother you at all?"

"What the fuck do you know about it? If you'd seen the court transcripts, you'd see that I didn't testify against them. I was a fuckin' character witness. The force was my life and those guys *were* my brothers. I straight up bawled like a baby at Mickey's funeral. So, what's it to you anyway?"

The chief turned as purple as an unwanted birthmark. "What's it to me?" He spat at the retired detective. "What's it to me? Mickey Lowman and I went way back. We were friends since the second grade." As he talked, he leaned over the table until he was just inches from Bud's face. "Don't you remember me from Mickey's funeral?"

"Oh, I remember you now." Bud pulled at the cuffs on his wrist again, then pointed his forefinger and aimed it as well as he could. "You were the one with the bulge in your pants. Happy to see me?"

The police chief closed the gap between them with the jab of one arm. His fist closed around Bud's shirt collars and bunched them together, pulling Bud down until the tips of their noses touched. "Listen, fucker, you think you're funny? Yeah, I had *something* in my pants for you that day, but I can assure you, it wasn't my dick."

"That's a relief," Bud croaked, the pressure of the chief's grip cutting off his air.

Chief Barnes whispered hoarsely, "It should have been you that died, not him." He let go of Bud's shirt and pushed him away.

Bud settled back into his chair. He would have rubbed at his sore neck if his hands weren't cuffed. "Is this why I'm here?" he asked. "You gonna kill me?"

"Lord knows I'd like to," the chief affirmed. "I don't know what you did, but I'm sure as shit you were the one to bring those boys down.

But no, today you're here so I can tell you to leave this case the fuck alone."

"What case would that be?"

"You know damn well. The Finney murder."

"Ah, that one. Well, see I'm paid to do a job, so I can't just drop it."

"Let me put this another way. We catch you inside the town limits again, and we'll make your life a living hell."

Bud smirked. "Actually, that takes a lot less than you'd think. And since my client wasn't involved, I think I'll continue to defend her."

Chief Barnes snorted. "That's rich. We both know that your client just happened to be lurking around the crime scene at the time of death. I suppose that's just a coincidence?"

"What are you talking about?" Bud was genuinely confused.

The chief's eyes swept Bud's face, as though searching for deception. Apparently not finding it there, he laughed. "I see, you don't know. She didn't tell you, did she?"

Bud just stared at the man, refusing to give voice to the bad feelings rising in his throat and giving him heartburn.

"You don't believe me? Well, see for yourself." Chief Barnes muttered something into his radio mic. A moment later, a cop came in, handed over a file folder, then unlocked one of Bud's cuffs.

Barnes took an envelope from the folder and pushed it in front of Bud. The photographs it contained were printed on a desktop printer and looked like snapshots taken from a cell phone camera. They showed a Toyota photographed from a distance, filtered through tree trunks and across a street.

"This could be anyone's car." Bud shrugged. "It doesn't prove anything."

Another photo landed on the table, a blown-up image. It showed Velvet Erickson, clear as day, standing next to her car with a camera around her neck.

Bud snorted. "Who took these? How'd *you* get them so quickly?"

"A friend of the town took them. He was concerned about a reporter's presence in our fair Woodside, and when he heard about the murder—"

"Well, that's convenient. If I'm to believe that these photos were actually taken when and where the crime was committed, your friend must have been there, too. What's his name?"

Chief Barnes shook his head. "No, I don't think I'll be telling you *that*. Keep the photos if you like. We have others. But we'll show them again at court. I think we're about done here. Let me just remind you that our town has the benefit of residents and friends who are powerful, not just locally but on a national level. When you fail to clear her, and you will fail, you might want to advise her to plead out. Because there's no way in hell she will ever win in court."

Chapter Fourteen

Although she was in a hurry to get home, it took Velvet nearly forty minutes to make the short drive from the *San Francisco Chronicle* to her Bernal Heights residence. The distraction began a block away from where they'd left Yoshi, who insisted on taking a cab to Liz Claiborne's house and insisted on Velvet and Tucker leaving her there to do her job.

Waiting for a red light to change, Velvet glanced in the rearview mirror and felt bad for depositing Yoshi on the sidewalk at night. Alone. She tried to be open-minded, but she wasn't comfortable with Yoshi's blindness and the vulnerability that came with it. Though it was a long time coming—after all, the diagnosis was years ago—this year seemed different. Yoshi seemed, well, really *disabled* by the change in her sight. It filled Velvet with dread. And guilt.

Her thoughts were interrupted when Tucker turned sideways in her seat and leaned over as if to whisper something in her ear. Velvet felt a breeze rustle through the delicate hairs on her neck as Tucker's ardent breath brushed her skin like midday sun warming the ground. Heat traveled along her nerve pathways and slowly soaked below the surface. Instead of murmuring the sensuous phrases Velvet was expecting, Tucker flicked her tongue along the rim of Velvet's ear, tracing from one side to the other and then engulfing Velvet's lobe.

A horn sounded angrily behind them and Velvet jerked away from Tucker and drove forward, determined to pay attention. Apparently, Tucker was also determined. Although Velvet didn't notice immediately, she was inching her left hand slowly over the space between them on the seat. Her fingers touched Velvet's knee, fondling it through the dark nylons. Then they rounded the curve of her kneecap and ran softly along the inside of her thigh. Velvet's legs weakened as though they were in cahoots with Tucker, and her knees fell away from each other. The pressure of her leg and foot against the gas pedal melted slowly until the Toyota was merely inching along. When another motorist beeped, Velvet stiffened her legs, slammed closed the gates of her knees, and slapped Tucker's hand away.

"Ow." Tucker shook the punished hand. "Meanie." Watching Velvet from the corner of her eyes, she assumed a pout.

Velvet wondered if Tucker was aware just how sexy that full lower lip was. She bit her own lip thinking about it. Tucker's errant hand returned a few moments later to caress Velvet's kneecap. When the touch cracked apart her clenched thighs, Tucker's hand slowly slid up Velvet's leg and Velvet felt her nipples crystallize into hard candies. Steam rose from between her thighs. With one hand on the wheel, she used the other to weakly pull Tucker's hand away from its spelunking.

In response, Tucker pretended to sulk. It was cute on her, Velvet thought, sneaking peeks at the soft country butch from the corner of her eye. She hid a devious smirk from her sexy passenger. *Turnabout is fair play.* As Velvet continued driving with her left hand on the wheel, she ran her right hand along the inside of Tucker's thigh. Her Corvette-red nails were long enough to frighten a less experienced lesbian, but Tucker had seen the amazing ways she could use them or hide them inside her while they made love. Now they grazed the butch's denim-ensconced thigh, causing her to arch in her seat. Feeling the younger woman's response was like a biofeedback loop, giving Velvet a metaphoric hard-on.

When her stroking hand reached the inner sanctum between Tucker's thighs, she rested it there for a moment, reveling in the damp heat that rose from Tucker's Levi's. She then gripped the buttons on Tucker's fly and tugged.

Tucker moaned. Velvet grinned.

"You have to pull over," Tucker begged, in a voice husky with desire.

"Oh? Why's that?" Velvet teased.

"I need you."

"We're almost home, dear. And you seem to be doing quite well as is."

Tucker groaned and released her grip on Velvet's hand. Although Velvet couldn't see at that moment what she was doing, her companion appeared to be searching for something in her front pocket. Just as Velvet was beginning to verbalize some clever observation, Tucker abruptly snatched her hand once more and roughly shoved it down her now-unbuttoned Levi's. All thoughts vanished as Velvet's brain embraced the sensations her palm experienced, sliding across Tucker's taut belly and scratching against the roughness of her pubic hair before being plunged into the damp warmth of her desire.

"Vel!" Tucker exclaimed. "Stop!"

Stunned, Velvet immediately withdrew her hand. What had she done? She glanced up, saw the parked car she was bearing down on, and slammed on the brakes. She and Tucker rocketed forward until seat belts restrained their flight and sent them crashing back into their seats while the tires screeched and the papers from the backseat flew forward and hit the windshield. Finally, the Toyota stopped, resting just a few inches from the other vehicle.

The two women were breathing hard, but now their panting was from fear rather than excitement. Still, adrenaline is adrenaline.

"Did that kill the mood?" Velvet asked. Just because the near crash had heightened her arousal didn't mean it had done the same for Tucker's.

"Hold on," Tucker said as if she wasn't sure. She leaned over and pressed her lips against Velvet's. As their tongues entwined, Tucker slid her right hand inside Velvet's low-cut blouse and fondled one of her mammoth breasts.

Velvet's eyes flew open and she backed away from Tucker's mouth.

"No." Tucker grinned. "I'm good."

"You!" Velvet punched the butch on the shoulder. There was a tattoo inked into Tucker's skin there. It pictured a pinup girl draped across the New Orleans Superdome. Across her busty chest was a beauty queen's banner that said "Katrina." In the background an image of the Mississippi River wound around an aboveground cemetery. One of the mausoleums bore the inscription "RIP New Orleans 2005." A keepsake in commemoration of New Orleans, the tat was an unusual departure from Tucker's rigid thriftiness and hinted at hidden depths, suggesting that she wasn't quite as unworldly as she seemed.

Velvet appreciated such surprises in a lover. "Why don't I stop at the park?" she suggested.

"That'd be nice," Tucker whispered into her ear while massaging her other breast.

"Back off, lady," Velvet joked, swatting her lover away. "Seriously, Tucker, you've got to cool it for a minute or I swear I'm going to wreck."

"Okay, okay." Tucker backed away with her hands up. "Just hurry." She leaned back in the passenger seat and slid one hand sensually down her own tummy toward her own still-open jeans.

"Stop it!" Velvet demanded. "Please."

Tucker looked deflated, but she withdrew her hand and buttoned her fly. "Since you said please."

Twenty minutes later they lay hidden partially behind a tree at Dolores Park, protected from the damp grass by Tucker's jacket spread out below them. Velvet's skirt was hitched up around her hips and Tucker's jeans were bunched around her knees. Breathless and exhausted from their lovemaking, they looked up at the sky. The stars were barely visible, their ancient light obscured by the persistent fog and glowing lights of the city.

Tucker pointed up, directing Velvet's gaze to a constellation. "See? That's Orion. The one you have on your thigh." She rolled on to her side and with a fingertip traced the freckles that she insisted formed the hunter's constellation on Velvet's creamy olive skin.

Velvet, who was embarrassed she even had freckles, pulled Tucker's hand away and kissed the fingers. They smelt of sex. "You ready to go?" She straightened her skirt.

"Yeah, I guess." Tucker pulled up her jeans. "That was nice. Thank you."

Velvet smiled at her lover's odd habit of expressing gratitude after they fucked. Sometimes having sex with Tucker made her nervous. Velvet usually avoided the kind of lesbians who confused casual sex with emotional connection. But when Tucker looked at her with doe eyes spilling over with emotional intensity, she didn't respond in her usual manner—by ending the relationship.

Since Velvet had first explained her rules, which she liked to make explicit prior to all her hookups, Tucker had never violated them by, for instance, verbalizing the L-word. Yet she conveyed the sentiment in the way she traced the features of Velvet's face or, on their increasingly frequent sleepovers, by spooning throughout the night. What frightened Velvet was just how much she was enjoying those aspects of their burgeoning relationship.

She thought about that as they drove back to her place and walked to the door. Reeking of intimate fragrances, Velvet pressed Tucker up against the door frame of her Victorian and turned the key clockwise until she heard the deadbolt click off, then pushed the door open behind Tucker. Their bodies were pressed together, aching for a repeat of their park experience. Velvet walked Tucker backward into the Victorian shotgun's hallway.

Tucker's eyes flew open and her startled look told Velvet something was wrong. She untangled her tongue, but their bodies remained entwined as though unwilling to cooperate. Tucker was speechless. But she was moving away.

"Oh, no," Velvet moaned in dread as she realized that they were falling. They were falling together and she was going to land right on Tucker.

Tucker hit the hardwood floors with a painful "Ow!"

When Velvet landed, her supple, curvy body seemed to engulf the younger woman. Their faces were inches from each other. Tucker's was twisted in pain and she exhaled sharply, but did not speak. *Oh great*, Velvet thought. *She thinks I'm fat.*

"Can you get off?" Tucker pushed at her.

Oh, I don't think so. Velvet replied in her head. *It's over.* She scrambled to her feet. The house was pitch black. She must have forgotten to leave a light on.

"Thank God," Tucker said, rolling onto her side.

Whatever. Velvet opined. She felt along the wall for the light switch and illuminated the hallway. "Oh my God." Velvet was stunned. She leaned against the wall so she wouldn't faint.

"I'm so glad to get off *that*," Tucker said.

On the floor next to her was the unmistakable award statute of so much fame. It was an Oscar. Velvet's Oscar. Well, she'd bought it anyway. It had been awarded to some computer geek special-effects person whose name she hadn't bothered learning, but that was beside the point. She'd won it fair and square on an eBay auction, and now her Oscar was on the *floor*.

"I've been robbed," she declared, making a reasonable assertion.

"Holy shit! Do you want me to call the police?" Tucker lifted the Oscar and held it by the neck as she examined it. "Whoa. Is this real?"

"Of course." Velvet snatched the golden boy away and cradled him in her arms before brushing him off and carefully checking for any wounds. He seemed to have survived intact. "Let's take you back where you belong."

She strode down the narrow hallway to the first doorway, the entertainment room. When she turned on the light, she sobbed. *Everything* was on the floor. Bright rectangles on the wall were blank while the framed movie posters were in a pile on the throw rug. Every disc in her expansive DVD collection had been removed from the tall bookshelf, opened, and thrown in a pile that rose to a small hill on the floor.

The world of film entertainment had always both soothed and inspired her, so instead of using the second bedroom in the house as an office Velvet had set up her desk where she could see the flat-screen TV and her collection of movie memorabilia. The intruder had violated the sanctity of her desk, pulling the doors askew and molesting the contents, which were now strewn on the ground. *What could they have been looking for?*

Velvet wanted to sit down, but the office chair held an assortment of pens, paper clips and Liquid Paper bottles. The cushions of the couch were on the floor and her beloved leather recliner was now home to her collectibles. The autographed photo of Angelina Jolie and her lesbian mechanic girlfriend, the still mint-in-the-box figure of Willow from *Buffy*, which Velvet—to her chagrin—could see was no longer mint-in-box. Even the yellow tennis ball autographed by Martina Navratilova had been damaged and moved.

"Velvet?" Tucker called from the hallway.

While Velvet was absorbing the shock of her battered entertainment room, Tucker had looked through the rest of the house. The other rooms had also been tossed. Tucker was happy to discover that the robber wasn't still in the house. She'd had silly thoughts about protecting Velvet as she searched through the rooms, but she was terrified of coming face-to-face with a real criminal and had no idea what she would have done to defend them. Now, rather than assuaging Velvet's concerns, Tucker was afraid she was bringing worse news.

"Velvet?" she called again as she strode into the entertainment room.

Velvet looked up. "Yes?" Her voice was flat.

"I don't think we need to call the police."

"What? Why? Oh, my God, is he still here?"

"No." Tucker held a piece of paper in her hand. She stretched it out toward Velvet. "It *was* the police. Here's the search warrant, with a little note saying they were here."

"Jesus. They can just do this? They can just come in when I'm not home and trash my place and just leave it this way?"

"It seems crazy. I can't believe they could even get a warrant for this."

"What does it say?" Velvet returned a cushion to the couch and sat down hard.

It took a moment for Tucker to reply. "It says they were looking for evidence in connection with the murder of Rosemary Finney. The murder weapon, clothing, trace evidence. It also mentions photographic film, digital files, CD-ROMs, or photographs related to the crime."

"Those bastards!" Velvet shook her head. "They did this out of spite. It's a fishing expedition. They don't have a case against me, so they're trying to build one so this will get to a preliminary hearing. It's bizarre. I wasn't the only person there that morning and they know it."

"I'm sorry." Tucker carefully stepped over Velvet's things until she reached the sofa. She knelt down in front of Velvet and touched her face. "Can I help you put everything away?"

Velvet shook her head. "No, but thanks."

Knowing Velvet had read her sympathy and would probably push her away now, Tucker made a crooked smile. "I guess this ruined the mood?"

Velvet ruffled her hair. "Yeah. Sorry, sweets. Would you be offended if I took you home now?"

"No, of course not." Tucker smiled, hoping Velvet couldn't see the disappointment in her eyes. Not that it would make any difference. Tucker had learned it was not in Velvet's nature to change her mind to please anyone, not even a girlfriend.

❖

At her Richmond district home, Yoshi stood with her hand on the front doorknob. When the doorbell rang, she called out, "Velvet?" The timing seemed right.

"That's creepy, Yosh," Velvet answered from the other side of the closed door.

"I heard you walking up the steps," Yoshi explained as she let her friend in.

"Yeah? Well, it's still creepy." Velvet hugged Yoshi close. "I'm sorry to bother you at home."

Yoshi gave her a quick squeeze in return, then placed her hands on Velvet's shoulders and pushed her away. "You know you are always welcome, but what brings you?"

Velvet followed her ex into the living room and tossed a bag on the divan. Yoshi heard the bag land with more of a thump than she would have expected from Velvet's purse—even if it was full of recording equipment—and she deduced that it was instead an overnight case.

This was followed by a brief silence and a faint sigh Yoshi often heard when Velvet first entered her home. She supposed that having just come from her own pop-cultural paradise, Velvet found Yoshi's simple, modern, earth-toned living room a stark reminder of their contrasting personalities. Where Velvet had campy movie posters and vinyl miniature collectible toys strewn about her Warholesque loft, Yoshi had abstract Japanese erotic prints and low-slung Asian furniture. Seeing their two homes, it might be hard for a stranger to believe they'd once considered each other soul mates. Yoshi smiled at her own youthful naïveté.

"The police ransacked my house," Velvet lamented.

"I guess that is to be expected, with you being their prime suspect."

"Okay. A search, maybe. But they *trashed* my place."

Yoshi could tell from Velvet's voice that her friend was fishing for sympathy, not rationalization. It was something that had come up in their relationship—although they were both problem solvers, sometimes Velvet just wanted to express her emotions without trying to fix the situation.

"I am sorry, Velvet. That must be really upsetting. Would you like to stay here tonight?" Velvet did have an open invitation, but Yoshi still would have appreciated a little forewarning. Surely Velvet could have called during her half-hour drive through the city.

"Yeah, I would like that." Velvet threw herself down on the sofa next to her overnight bag. "Thank you."

"Martini?" Yoshi asked.

"Of course." Velvet smiled. "Extra dirty, please. Do you want help?"

"No." Yoshi went into the kitchen. She had arranged everything so that she would remember where to find what she was looking for. She opened the freezer and searched around with her hand, locating the rectangular bottle of vodka she kept there. She carefully poured the alcohol and olive brine into an ice-filled glass shaker that she used because an old bartender girlfriend had told her that using a glass container bruised the gin less than a stainless steel one. She mixed in a hint of vermouth, a drop of bitters, and gave it a couple of shakes, then poured the concoction into the glasses and added two giant Basque olives. A moment later she walked slowly into the living room bearing two brimming martini glasses.

"What were the police looking for?" she asked.

"Your balance always impresses me," Velvet said, taking a glass. "You didn't spill a drop."

"Thank you," Yoshi answered politely. Not wanting to get off track, she prompted, "The search?"

Yoshi heard Velvet swirling the contents of her glass before taking a long drink.

She didn't answer the question. She swirled the drink again.

"Velvet," Yoshi said, insisting on a response.

"All right, I need to come clean," Velvet admitted. "There's something I probably should have mentioned earlier."

"I would say so," Yoshi agreed, taking her own sip of the olive-infused martini.

"Wait." Velvet stopped. "You know? How?"

"Oh, I am not sure," Yoshi replied sarcastically. "Perhaps due to my being a private investigator?"

"I should've known you'd figure it out. I'm sorry I didn't tell you sooner. But I can explain."

"You don't have to explain." Yoshi shook her head.

"No, I think I do. See, because I think that's what they were looking for. I have photos."

"You have *photographs*?" Yoshi frowned. "It was not necessary for me to hear that." She was sure heat was flushing her cheeks. "For God's sake, Velvet, why would the police want your private photos?" She shook her head furiously. "How can you be so blasé about this?"

"Blasé? Blasé?" Velvet choked. "I'm absolutely serious."

"Truthfully?" Yoshi wanted to believe it.

"Of course I am. I know what's at stake."

"All right, then, if it is so serious, then where is she?"

"What? Who?"

"You forget I *know* you, Velvet. If you were in a serious relationship, you would not send the girl home. But here it has been only a few hours and you are at my residence, alone. You have never been one to leave a warm bed, so I can assume that she is no longer in yours."

"Whoa. Back up," Velvet interrupted "What do you think we're talking about?"

"Your intimate relationship with Tucker and the appropriation of your personal photos by the police."

"Intimate relationship?" Velvet chuckled. "You mean sex?" She sounded relieved. "You might not think it to look at her, but that girl's got a tight body, and it's no coincidence that her name rhymes with fu—"

"Stop it!" Yoshi covered her ears.

"Yoshi, you're so cute. I think you have a crush on our Tucker." Velvet pinched Yoshi's cheek.

"That is not funny." Yoshi was still upset, despite Velvet's attempted jokes. "I cannot believe you. I asked you to stop having sex with my assistants. It would be one thing if it meant something to you, but I can see that it does not."

Velvet's hand brushed Yoshi's. "I'm sorry. To be fair, we'd already gotten together before you gave me that speech. I just didn't know how to tell you. Besides, you'll be happy to know that I actually *do* like Tucker and I wouldn't have sent her home tonight if not for that little inconvenience of the police ransacking my house."

"Wait." Yoshi wrinkled her forehead in confusion. "What were you talking about?"

"Um, I don't know. After we started talking about my hot young lover I forgot everything else."

"Do not toy with me, Velvet. These photos. Why would the police want them—to discredit you in court?"

"One question at a time. There's something I need to tell you. I have film, I slipped it to Stan yesterday. He was supposed to have it ready for me tonight, but he didn't get it in for processing until it was too late."

"A film of you and Tucker?"

"No, film of Wonderland Park. I'm sorry, Yosh. I should have said something sooner, but—"

"Are you saying you have film that shows who killed Rosemary?"

"It very well might." Velvet did not sound like she was joking at all.

"Oh my God, you were there? And you didn't tell me?" Yoshi was hurt. "I mean, even if you did not think to tell your best friend, did you not think that information might be pertinent to the investigative team trying to clear your name? Why?"

"Well, you know I've been working with Marion Serif over at *Bend*?"

"No."

"Yes, you do. On the corporate espionage case?"

"No," Yoshi repeated insistently. "I did not mean for you to explain why you were there, I meant, why would you keep it from me? What reason could you possibly have? Don't you trust me?"

"Oh, Yoshi, you know I do. I knew you'd be disappointed. You know, getting myself into a position where I make a good suspect. Maybe I worried, just a little, that you might not believe me and you might actually think I'd done it."

Yoshi felt conflicted. Hurt by her friend's lack of faith, she could also hear the depth of emotion in Velvet's voice, the real fear that she might be unable to prove her innocence. She sighed deeply. "Okay," she relented. There had never really been any other possibility. "Tell me why you were at the scene of the crime. I would prefer a reason that has nothing to do with causing bodily harm and or killing Rosemary Finney."

"I was looking for the Yuri."

"You were looking for lesbian anime in Woodside?" Yoshi was baffled.

Velvet laughed. "No. Didn't I make you watch that movie *Intern*? About the fashion magazine?"

The movie sounded familiar. Some people presume the visually impaired did not watch movies. Velvet had never made that assumption. She recommended ones that were heavy on dialogue.

"Is that the film with the young actress you interviewed?" Yoshi asked, having recognized the actress's voice in the film.

"Dominique Swain. Yes. Anyway, as they explained in the movie, a Yuri is a magazine spy."

"That is strange, that the word has such dissimilar meanings. All right, so you were at the park to see a spy?"

"Yes, actually. A woman phoned me and asked me to be there. I think it might have been Elizabeth Claiborne."

"And did you see her?"

"I don't know. I don't think so." Yoshi felt Velvet scoot closer and she sensed Velvet gesticulating, as she had always been wont to do, moving her hands to articulate her story. She described how *Bend* magazine's ideas continually appeared in *Womyn* first and her attempts to find out how this was happening.

"So you determined Rosemary was paying someone for the information? And you reasoned she was meeting that person—the Yuri—at the park?" Yoshi asked.

"Exactly. But I'm not sure I saw the exchange take place. I mean, I saw a middle-aged guy get out of a SUV, you know, one of those Behemoth XLs. He threw something in the trash and then used the restroom and left. Later Rosemary went into the same porta-potty. At first I couldn't believe it, that she would use those kinds of facilities. But then she came out right away, carrying a manila envelope. So maybe the Yuri was the guy with the SUV."

"That sounds more like a bribe than an exchange of information," Yoshi reflected. "It seems improbable that a *man* would be your spy, rather than a lesbian. How would he have access to *Bend* magazine?"

"Exactly. I wish I'd gotten to see what was in the envelope."

"What dissuaded you?" Yoshi couldn't imagine Velvet being easily deterred.

"I looked inside her car after she went for her jog. But I couldn't see it, so maybe she passed it off to someone else."

"It is more plausible that she simply stowed it under her seat," Yoshi concluded. "You expect me to believe that you did not even attempt to jimmy open her car door?"

"Of course I wanted to. But you know how those Jags are. Such sensitive alarm systems. I didn't dare disturb the air bubble around the vehicle," Velvet explained. "And anyway, she didn't go on her run right away, she hung around, doing some stretches and looking at her watch. About fifteen minutes later, a Hummer pulled in and she talked to the driver through the window. I couldn't see if she'd passed off the envelope or not. Then Rosemary took off on her run."

"Did the Hummer depart after Rosemary commenced her run?" Yoshi asked.

Velvet pinched her brow together in thought. "No, I don't think so. Another vehicle pulled in then. A crappy old Volkswagen bus that seemed out of place, what with Rosemary's Jag, the Hummer, and the SUV. And then one of the neighbors came out of their house shaking his fist at me and I decided I had to get the hell out of there."

"What time did you leave Wonderland?"

"Between five thirty and six a.m., but I can't be sure. Do we have a TOD yet?"

"No. I am expecting to ascertain time of death tomorrow when we obtain the autopsy report. Can I also anticipate that you will retrieve your film from Stan?" Yoshi raised her eyebrows and stared in Velvet's direction, hoping to convey the critical nature of her request.

"Now we're on the photos again?" Velvet spoke with mock indignation. "Boy, one time you don't pay attention to a murder scene and then don't get your film processed right away, and you never hear the end of it. I'm on it. First thing in the morning I'll march into Stan's office. Don't worry, after what I said to him tonight, he'll have it ready. Shall I courier it over to Blind Eye offices?"

"No, you most certainly should *not* allow our preeminent evidence to leave your possession. Can I count on you to hand the photographic evidence directly to a Blind Eye staff member?"

"Of course," Velvet said.

Behind the proclaimed sincerity, Yoshi thought she detected a mischievous tone. She confronted her friend. "What dangerous thing are you planning, Velvet Erickson?"

"Nothing," Velvet protested. "I swear. I will hand the photos directly to a Blind Eye staff person."

Yoshi imagined Velvet had a hand over her heart or was raising her fingers in an oath of honesty. *This is about Tucker,* she told herself. Velvet was planning to deliver the film to the Blind Eye receptionist and most likely had in mind to give Tucker something else entirely. For once she wished her friend would focus on the case at hand instead of devoting her energies to arranging her next sexual interaction. Yoshi shifted uncomfortably in her seat as an image of a naked Tucker Shade drifted uninvited into her mind's eye. She winced. She shouldn't be able to imagine her receptionist naked. She threw a sheet over the girl in her mind and pretended not to notice the way it clung to her trim figure.

Speaking of Tucker, Yoshi thought to distract herself, Velvet had not eased Yoshi's trepidation that their affair was nothing more than physical in nature. It really was none of her concern, but she did not want to see the girl hurt when Velvet inevitably tossed her aside for the subsequent conquest.

Truth be told, Yoshi was jealous. It had nothing to do with Tucker Shade. After an eighteen-month romantic dry spell, any woman would be a *little* envious.

CHAPTER FIFTEEN

Have you had that film developed?" Velvet asked Stan Wozlawski first thing the next morning.

"The film you told me to pretend I didn't have? I don't have it."

"You don't have to pretend with me." Velvet expressed her impatience. "Come on, I don't have time for this."

"I'm serious. I figured that film was fair game, seeing as how you work for me. I mean, after you lost your mind last night I had to know if there was a story there that I needed to pass on to another reporter. With you being on fact-checking duty and all."

"Oh, my God." Velvet started to panic.

Stan grinned gleefully. "Gotcha!"

"Jesus, Stan." Velvet clutched at her chest to indicate the heart attack this game was giving her.

Stan chuckled. "Relax. I got it developed." He pulled a manila envelope out of his desk and tossed the black-and-white prints across the desk one by one, as though he were dealing cards. "Looks like a bunch of crap. Don't know why you won't go digital."

"I'm old school, Stan. Remember? That's why you like me."

"Ah, that's it. I knew it was something."

Velvet quickly gathered the photos back into a tight pack. "Thanks."

He waved a hand. "Don't mention it. Really, I mean don't. Not to anyone. Can't let it out that I'm—"

"A softie," Velvet provided.

❖

As usual, Tucker was first to arrive at Blind Eye's office, and she went about her day as she always did, starting green tea, this time in their new kettle, and opening the shades in Yoshi's office—at the blind woman's request. Tucker wondered if opening shades on the eleventh floor brought enough light in to make Yoshi's dark world a little brighter. Or maybe she liked the blinds open for another reason, like warmth or the way the office looked to prospective clients. Tucker didn't know. She just knew she was to open them in the morning and close them midafternoon.

She sat down and opened yesterday's mail. While she sorted she reflected on her involvement in the investigation. Oh, she knew it was just a minuscule contribution, but she loved that she'd been out in the field instead of behind the desk. She'd half expected to think of nothing but the murder case today, but she wasn't. Instead, she kept flashing on being with Velvet and those moments when their skin and lips and hands were pressed tightly against each other's. Tucker thought of Velvet's tugging at her jeans and she shivered. She imagined their bodies, their hearts beating against each other and their mouths yearning toward each other, lips parted, hot breath building up in a layer between them like LA smog. It was the anticipation of touch that turned Tucker on, even more than the touch itself.

She shook her head, trying to force the thoughts from her head. She slowly read the first line on the envelope in her hand. Addressed only to Blind Eye, it didn't reveal who it was meant for. When Tucker slipped her finger under the flap of the envelope it reminded her vaguely of slipping her fingers under Velvet's bra and struggling to unhook it so she could free those luscious DD breasts.

Dammit, she was back there again.

Maybe reading e-mails would hold her attention. All this thinking about last night was spoiling another pair of briefs. Men supposedly thought about sex all the time. How did they get anything done? The phone rang, and that was no help.

"Hi, baby, did you miss me?" Velvet's voice was husky. Was she coming down with something, or had she been thinking about Tucker?

"Good morning, Velvet," Tucker said earnestly. "I was just thinking about you."

"Was I naked?" Velvet asked.

Tucker blushed and looked around the empty office. "Yeah." She lowered her voice. "I missed you last night."

"I did, too. I'm sorry the apartment was uninhabitable. Maybe I can face it tonight."

"You mean you didn't stay either?"

"Nope. I stayed over at Yoshi's."

Tucker felt a cold wrench tighten around her intestines. Well, it was bound to happen. Lesbians never really broke up; they went on sabbatical and got back together. Their liaison hadn't been going on long, but Tucker had known Velvet was too sophisticated and too popular to spend much time with a naïve country girl.

"Tucker, are you still there?" Velvet asked.

Tucker swallowed. "So, you spent the night?"

"Of course. My house was a wreck, remember? I may never go back there. Yoshi says I can stay as long as I want."

Great, Tucker thought sarcastically. Velvet had made it clear from the beginning that she wasn't looking for anything serious and she wasn't the kind of girl to restrict herself to only one special friend at a time. She had said, "There are a hundred flavors of ice cream. Why would you limit your tongue to just one?"

"Oh, that's hella great," Tucker said, hoping it didn't sound like a lie. "So, Yoshi's got a second bedroom?"

"No," Velvet cheerily chirped. "But there's plenty of space. You know I used to live there, when we were together."

"Awesome. What can I do for you?" *Now that you've explained the situation, are we done or do you want something else?*

"I think we should get together this morning. I need to see you."

"Oh." Tucker sighed in relief. *Velvet just said she* needed *to see me!* "This morning?"

"I was thinking right away," Velvet responded.

"What's up?"

"I think it would be better if we met in person. There's something I need to talk to you about, face-to-face."

The wrench was back on Tucker's intestines, clamping down. "Really?" She wondered if the dread she felt was apparent in her voice. Was needing to talk in person *ever* a good thing?

Velvet continued, "Can you come down to my office?"

"I'm at work. I can't just leave. Yoshi…"

"Oh, don't worry about Yoshi, I already talked to her. She's cool with you popping out for a while."

"You talked with Yoshi?" Hadn't they agreed Yoshi didn't need to know about the two of them?

"Of course I did, Tuck. I can't stay in her home and not speak to her, can I?"

"Okay. I'll leave now." Tucker didn't want to be at the office when Yoshi arrived. Right now, she didn't think she could face Yoshi—ever.

❖

AJ rapped a second time on the Blind Eye Detective Agency office door, but didn't get a reply. She glanced down at the two bulging black bags at her feet, the plastic tied closed. Lot of good that did. One of them bags was oozing all over the hall's slick marble floor. She'd found the damn hole after it sat slowly leaking in her trunk all night, rotten garbage juice seeping into the carpet of her Crown Vic. She wondered how she would get the stains out of the carpet. Grandma Latisha'd be all up in her face about not paying attention all them years to her washerwoman secrets. 'Course, her brothers ain't never had to learn that shit, but here she expected to do it and be damn good at it too all 'cause she had a pie. Some crap like olive oil and baking powder. Or was that vinegar and baking *soda*?

The only upside to the damn bags leaking was it wasn't *her* car. She'd never be caught dead in a ride like that, not on her own. It be courtesy the East Palo Alto Police Department. Still, it *had* been assigned to her, and she'd autographed a whole shitload of papers giving up her firstborn if anything happened to the vehicle—especially off duty. *Joke's on them.* She didn't plan on *having* shorties.

After the incident last year when half the EPA fleet got tagged with gang colors and the other half got pinched right out from under their noses, the city came up with the plan to let cops roll their rides home to their own hoods, seeing as how they be safer than areas they patrolled. None of the EPA officers were willing to have cribs in the run-down hood east of Stanford University, and they couldn't afford rent on the rest of the peninsula. So riding patrol cars home made sure they got to work.

Seemed like most San Francisco Bay cities had this problem where their ambulance drivers, firefighters, and PD couldn't afford rent where they worked and instead lived in black and brown hoods of East Bay. Everyone talked about how when the big quake hit, it would knock out all the local bridges and trap emergency crews on opposite sides of the Bay from where they were needed. Imagine if Katrina hit and all PD trapped in a whole 'nother city. Shit would hit the whole west side of the bay all the same. Ain't going to just be lootin' here, neither. The shaking ain't even the worst of it. That'd be all the fires sparked by burst gas lines. San Francisco'd burn to the ground for lack of emergency crews, like it burned in the "big one" of 1906. Hundred years later the locals still went on 'bout it.

Standing here in the hallway with foul-smellin' trash bags, AJ was beginning to think it was stupid to drop by without hearing from that kid Tucker first. She'd thought the Blind Eye offices would open by nine.

Now here she was, and she didn't want to take them stinky, dripping bags back with her. Trying the doorknob, she discovered it unlocked and stepped inside, calling out, "Yo, Tucker? Ya here?" The reception desk was empty.

Light shone under the inner office door. AJ dragged the bags into the reception area, then rapped on the fogged glass with scarred knuckles.

"Yes? Come in."

"Sorry," AJ said as she stepped into the room. "Tucker wasn't…"

One look at the raven-haired Japanese woman with skin the color of grits sitting behind the desk, and her words dried up. She inhaled sharply. Snap. The lovely was straight-up smokin' hot, like a fly Ann Curry. "I, uh…" AJ was unable to think of anything to say.

The woman was staring back at her with piercing blue icicles that seemed to penetrate right through her. Like she was seeing past all AJ's posturing to the scared ghetto kid inside. Everything froze for a second. In that instant AJ felt like her whole world changed. Then the ethereal beauty stood and stretched out her arm.

"Yoshi Yakamota."

AJ was sure this was what angels sounded like. Like the heavenly voice of the gospel choir back home. She leapt forward, and when her meaty hand closed around Yoshi's delicate fingers, she was struck by a sudden desire to be a knight in gold-plated armor, ridin' in on a pimped-out convertible and whisking the Japanese hottie up beside her.

Yoshi's strong and hearty shake upended her fantasy, assuring AJ that she weren't no blushing lotus flower and didn't need no rescuing. They'd both be on modern-day horses, AJ thought, with Yoshi riding a stretched Harley as black and wild as her dark locks. AJ'd bet Yoshi be scrappy in a hand-to-hand fight. AJ smiled. She was down with that. She fancied Heath Bar babes—soft on the outside, with a solid core.

Yoshi's hand still held AJ's. The movement of her slender fingers, stretching away from the handshake, brought AJ's focus back to the moment. Her whole body tingled, the small hairs on her arm straining to meet Yoshi's fingers. But instead of caressing the policewoman's dark skin in parting, Yoshi's fingers stroked AJ's shirtsleeve.

"You must be Tucker's friend AJ." Yoshi's hand slipped away.

AJ searched Yoshi's face. "How'd ya know?"

"Your uniform. I felt the rough permanent-press material of your sleeve. That is a popular fabric in uniforms. And then your walk, of course, with those heavy boots and your hand resting on the gun holster. The leather squeaks." The private eye touched her nose. "And it has a very distinctive odor."

"Did ya just say I smell?" AJ feigned offense.

Yoshi smiled broadly. "The *leather* has a distinctive smell. I did not say it was a bad thing." AJ thought she saw color flushing her new honey's porcelain cheeks. "I am afraid Tucker stepped out to run an errand. Would you like to wait for her? Or leave her a message?"

Did Yoshi think she and Tucker were friends? Or something more? Just in case she did, AJ rushed to clarify. "We only met a coupla times. Me 'n' Tucker. I was just helping out on this case y'all working."

AJ thought she heard Yoshi snort, but it could've been the swivel chair.

"You found something helpful? In this Rosemary Finney situation?"

"I think, yeah. See, I was up that way, near Wonderland Park. I'm rolling by and I see this maintenance guy, loading up these Hefty bags. I just up and asked if I could have 'em. So now y'all have 'em."

"Wait." Yoshi clarified. "You have refuse obtained from the crime scene?"

"Yep. Y'all want it?"

"Of course!" Yoshi laughed.

"Cool. They out there." AJ motioned to the reception area.

"Are you in a hurry? Do you need to leave immediately?" Yoshi asked.

"No, ma'am. I'm not on till ten hundred hours," AJ offered. "That's ten a.m. Y'all need a hand?"

"And a pair of eyes," Yoshi deadpanned and then smiled broadly, to show she was joking. "Would you assist me with sifting through the refuse? At least until Tucker returns?"

"No sweat."

As soon as AJ lifted the first bag, Yoshi knew she'd misjudged the contents and Blind Eye would be hiring a carpet cleaner. She heard the liquid sloshing in open soda cans and half-finished coffee cups soon to be spilling out onto the spread-out newspaper and soaking straight through to the carpet. *Note to self: Have Tucker order a roll of plastic sheeting, the kind they use when painting, for next time.*

"Eww." AJ groaned. "Effin' garbage juice. These bags left a wicked stench in my trunk. I'm so sorry."

"No, I am sorry your vehicle suffered the brunt of this mess. I hope you will allow me to have your trunk cleaned professionally."

"No, ma'am, I—"

"I insist. You are doing so much already. Did it spill on your uniform?"

"Yeah." AJ laughed. "Soaked the left leg."

"Oh, no." Yoshi clucked, pushing AJ into Tucker's swivel chair. "We should get them rinsed right away, before the stain sets. And please don't call me ma'am."

Ignoring her own outfit, Yoshi dropped to one knee and reached out for AJ's knee. She missed. Her hand inadvertently stroked along the cop's uniformed inner thigh. The scratchy fabric clung to Yoshi's palm like Velcro. AJ's taut hamstring muscle tensed, but she didn't move her leg away.

Yoshi was suddenly very aware of her heart beating in the uncomfortable silence of the room. Her cheeks felt awash with crimson and all the little hairs on her skin seemed to be standing at attention. What had just happened? How had she, a respectable businesswoman, ended up kneeling in front of this officer of the law, her hand halfway up the stranger's thigh, ready to pull the pants right off her? She was acting like Velvet, and that was not like her at all.

AJ's strong hand closed around Yoshi's, pulling it away from her thigh and bringing it toward her mouth. The action yanked Yoshi off her knee onto her wobbly legs and propelled her forward until she was standing between AJ's legs. In turn, AJ stood, still holding her hand.

She brushed her dry lips against Yoshi's knuckles. Yoshi wobbled and was pulled closer, encircled in the cradle of a strong arm. For what seemed like hours but must have only been a few moments, the two women stood there, bodies pressed against each other, swaying together to unheard music. Then Yoshi felt AJ's warm breath on her cheek, and thinking they might kiss, she tilted her head and parted her lips. But instead of AJ's lips meeting her own, they pressed against her ear.

In her throaty voice, AJ whispered, "Nice try, miss, but ya ain't getting *my* pants off that easy. Not without no dinner or a movie."

Pressed against AJ's face as she was, Yoshi could actually feel her smile spread. She was suddenly filled with horror as she took in what had almost happened.

AJ released her grip and Yoshi could fairly feel the eyes searching her face. Apparently not finding what she'd been looking for, AJ touched Yoshi's chin, tilting it as though to gaze deeply in her blind eyes. AJ was treating her as though she could see, and it was disconcerting.

Yoshi brusquely brushed the tender hand aside and turned to wipe her eyes. "I am so embarrassed," she said, not looking at AJ. "I do not know what just happened."

"Ya ain't got a need to apologize," AJ quietly reassured her. "Now, do ya want to tackle this mess alone, or can I help?"

"You are not uncomfortable?"

"No, honey. We cool."

Yoshi nodded in appreciation. "All right. Would you take photographs of the process? We have a digital camera that is relatively simple to operate."

"Point and click?" AJ asked.

"Yes."

"Sure 'nough."

As soon as Yoshi retrieved the camera from the storage cupboard and nervously demonstrated the basic features, AJ photographed the collection of empty beer bottles, energy drinks, coffee cups, Clif Bar wrappers, newspapers, and lunch remains. Her hands sheathed in disposable blue latex gloves, Yoshi sifted through the items spread out on the newspaper. Between handling each item and occasionally lifting one to her nose, she was able to distinguish many of the objects. She emptied a paper bag that held sandwich remains, a bag of Lay's potato chips, and napkins.

A small scrap of white paper flitted down. Yoshi picked it up and offered it to AJ. "Anything interesting?" she asked.

"It's a receipt from a Buck's Diner in Woodside."

"Does it have a date stamp?"

"Yeah, both day and time."

"That is great." Yoshi pointed at an empty file box. "Could you set that aside and then pull over a garbage can so we can put trash in it?"

They sorted, the silence only broken with discarding items in the trash.

Yoshi held up another scrap of paper. "Is this a Lotto printout? Or a receipt? I feel the smooth edges on the sides."

AJ took it from her. "Lotto. Late in the day."

"The same date as the murder?"

"Yeah. But afternoon."

"Please keep it too. Some perpetrators return to the scene of the crime, especially if it is a high-profile event with intense media scrutiny. Or it could be garbage of a regular Wonderland visitor. It should be relatively easy to track down where it was bought, if necessary."

The contents of the second bag were quite different. A jumble of branches and plant material tumbled out to be spread around and sifted through.

"You are originally from the South, right?" Yoshi asked as she held a branch up for scrutiny.

"N'awlins born and bred," AJ affirmed. "Why?"

"Poison oak does not grow down there, does it? I think your area has poison sumac instead."

AJ took hold of the thick branch. "This is poisonous? You eat it?"

"No." Yoshi laughed.

"Aww, you're just yankin' my chain."

"No." Yoshi touched her arm. "That is poison oak. The oil on the leaves can cause an allergic reaction."

"That all?" AJ snorted.

"No, that is not all. The allergic reaction causes a spreading, itching rash that can be quite irritating or even send some individuals to the hospital."

"But *this* just a bare branch," AJ insisted. "No leaves."

Yoshi sighed. "You are holding a piece that was recently cut. That is why it is bleeding. Do you see black sap? I can smell it. It tickles my nose. You see, even without leaves, poison oak is still dangerous, and the black sap is exceptionally toxic, even more so than the oil on the leaves. If you touch your skin or wipe it on your clothes, you will most likely get the rash. And you will wish you hadn't."

"You done convinced me." AJ dropped the offending branch.

"Here." Yoshi held out the box of gloves. "You might want to switch."

AJ carefully removed her gloves, peeling them inside out and tossing them in the trash. She pulled on a fresh pair. "What else do you smell?" she asked.

Yoshi wrinkled her nose, posing, "Is there manzanita?"

"Um, like I'd know. What it look like?"

Yoshi described manzanita, the reddish orange shrub with its twisting branches and distinguishing scarlet wood.

"Have you been hiking or camping since you moved here?" she asked the Southern cop.

"No, us black folk, we ain't so hot on hauling our asses up and down hills."

"I used to go all the time," Yoshi reminisced. "I miss it. There are some truly incredible trails in the Bay Area, a surprising variety of ecosystems and terrains. At the crest of the hill there are stunning views of the bay and ocean." She fell silent, thinking about how she would never again experience those views.

"Sounds lovely," AJ said softly. "Maybe you'll take me along sometime." She wielded a branch matching Yoshi's description. "This might be the man's eater."

Yoshi laughed. "*Man-za- nita*, not man eater."

AJ chuckled. "I'm getting scared 'bout these plants. If they ain't poisonous, they'll eat ya. What's up with that?"

"Bag it up for me," Yoshi requested.

"What's it mean?" AJ asked.

"When I was younger my father and I would go hiking in the Santa Cruz Mountains, the hills between Silicon Valley and the Pacific Ocean. He knew a lot about the plants that grew there. There is one species of manzanita, Kings Mountain manzanita, that is endangered because it only grows in very specific soil that exists in small patches. The Kings Mountain variety has a different genetic make-up than the other manzanitas. So, if one of those plants is near the crime scene, it might help us with a DNA trace."

"That's intense," AJ exclaimed. "How do ya test a tree's DNA? There ain't no blood. Do trees have mouths to swab?"

Yoshi chuckled. "Actually, I understand it is a rather involved process. There is a plant lab over at UC Berkeley that has equipment to do it. Recently their scientists have used a similar process to track down the fungus causing sudden oak death. That is a disease that has wiped out nearly ninety percent of Marin's oak trees."

The two women fell silent as they dug through more of the garbage.

"Well, look at this." Yoshi held up an envelope. "It doesn't feel opened." She handed it to AJ.

"Just junk mail." AJ moved to toss it in the trash can.

Yoshi blocked her arm. "No, that is perfect. Someone might have cleaned out their car and discarded the direct mail marketing pieces. What's the name?"

AJ dusted it off with her sleeve. "Ryan Esterhaus. Los Altos Hills. That's not far from the park."

"Can you read the date on the postmark?" Yoshi asked.

"Coupla days ago."

"All right then, I guess we will be paying this Mr. Esterhaus a visit."

"Will ya need a ride?" AJ asked.

Yoshi smiled. "Thanks, AJ, but you have done enough already to help. I should let you get back to your own job."

AJ sighed. "Yeah, guess I oughta be goin'."

"Do I sense some hesitation?"

AJ laughed. "It's that obvious?"

"Well," Yoshi mused, "at first I just thought you wanted to spend time with me, but now I can see that you are just putting off going to work."

"It's a little of both," AJ began.

Yoshi waved the African American woman quiet. They both knew what AJ was going to say, but she thought they'd tactfully agreed not to speak of it here.

AJ nodded. "There's a lot I love about being a cop. Uniforms, respect, brotherhood, but then as a female I ain't so welcome. In

N'awlins, once it got around that I was a dyke, I got shit from other cops all the fucking time. Then things got even worse. No backup when I'd ask for it, giving me the shit jobs, sending me out to get killed, more or less. All these problems kind of blew up with Katrina, and I got me some family out here. They always talking up the Bay Area, so I got a job down there in East Palo Alto…"

Yoshi grimaced.

AJ laughed. "Ya familiar with it?"

"Yeah, once the murder capital of America." Yoshi smiled.

"Well it ain't no more, but still a dangerous hood, high crime rates and all. Gots it's advantages, you know. Ain't never boring. Small town, compared to N'awlins, but I already caught me three murders since I came out here."

Yoshi liked that the policewoman didn't correct herself for acting as though Yoshi could see. She didn't stop, shaking her head and embarrassedly sputtering some apology. It was refreshing.

"But there's some stuff I'm uncomfortable with," AJ said.

Yoshi knitted her brow. "Are you saying that you are being harassed at work?"

"No, not that. It may be nothing," AJ said in a voice that argued differently. "I've gotten the dyke jokes all my time on the job, that ain't no biggie, but last week…" She trailed off, as though unsure if she could trust a relative stranger with her secrets.

"AJ, there are some really strong antidiscrimination laws in this state—"

"It ain't no thing," AJ cut her off. "And you're right, Yoshi, I gotta go."

"All right," Yoshi acquiesced. "But if you ever change your mind, let me know and I will be happy to provide any assistance I can."

From the brisk clomp of her boots, it sounded like AJ couldn't leave the office fast enough.

Yoshi made a mental list of the useful information gleaned from their trash examination. The poison oak and manzanita. The dated receipts that would isolate the trash as belonging to the period of the murder. The unopened mail addressed to Ryan Esterhaus.

The name seemed familiar. Yoshi tried to place it as she moved to the bathroom and washed her hands and face; she was sure the trash odor had clung. By the time she returned to her office, she had remembered the one occasion when the name came up. It had been mentioned by a former client who'd hired Blind Eye to investigate a local talent agent with a penchant for luring teenage girls to the casting couch. Ryan Esterhaus was a movie director, Yoshi recalled, a man who bought his way out of trouble. She knew little about him, but she was sure Velvet could remedy that.

Yoshi picked up the phone. She and Velvet had work to do and photographs to examine, assuming Velvet had done as Yoshi asked.

CHAPTER SIXTEEN

Velvet and Yoshi sat down on rather pretentious and uncomfortable antique chairs in Karen Friars's living room and waited for Rosemary's widow to return with refreshments. Although they'd both denied their thirst, Karen had insisted that a polite hostess would provide refreshments.

When she returned a moment later with a cheese plate and three glasses of iced tea, she said, "It's so good to see you again, Velvet. You look great." She set down the tray and scratched her arms through the thin silk blouse that clung to her delicate frame. "I remember you used to like iced tea."

She held a glass out to Velvet. Her hand was slender, well manicured, and appropriately dainty for the trappings of wealth visible all around them. As Velvet sipped the tea, she glanced down at her reupholstered Louis XV chairs overlaid with Japanese bondage imagery. She wondered if Yoshi would be offended by the cultural appropriation if she knew what was cushioning her posterior. Why was Karen being so polite? Had she poisoned the drinks?

"I'm glad you came." Karen took a seat across from the two women.

"Why?" Velvet asked bluntly. She set the glass down. It didn't taste poisoned. She eyed the cheese plate.

"I would have thought you were instrumental in Velvet's arrest," Yoshi said. "Obviously, someone brought pressure to bear on the Woodside police to secure such a diligent response and focus the attention squarely on Velvet. It strikes me as something you would have been a part of."

Karen tilted her head. "Well, you've got me there." She pushed the cheese plate at Velvet. "Go ahead. I can see you want some."

"Excuse me?" Velvet was flabbergasted. "Did you just admit that you set me up?"

Karen scratched again at her sleeve-covered arm. Her efforts didn't seem to satisfy her. She looked at her arm as though disappointed in its lack of appropriate response. She seemed offended.

"Did you?" Yoshi asked.

Karen returned her gaze to Velvet. "Oh, it wasn't like that." She shook her head. "Oh no, I didn't *need* to set you up. You made yourself a suspect after that public row with Rosemary the other night, and everyone knows you two hated each other. Once I discovered that you were at Wonderland Park that morning, it all fell into place. I just demanded the quick resolution that I so richly deserve. My tax money does pay for that police department, after all."

Yoshi crinkled her nose. "But you certainly didn't bother to inform them that Velvet would never do such a thing."

Karen shrugged. "You would be surprised at what people are capable of, when they are pushed to it." She unbuttoned her sleeve and slid her hand inside to gain greater positioning against the persistent itch. "I assumed the police would do their job and figure things out in due course. Velvet, you always thought I was an ogre." At a murmur from Velvet, she waved a hand impatiently. "Oh, don't deny it. You all did."

"I was going to agree with her," Velvet whispered to Yoshi.

"You thought I changed Rosemary. You thought I *forced* her to change." Karen shook her head. "I didn't. The funny thing is that Rosemary never really changed at all. She was always the poor little rich girl, buried in cash and starving for Daddy's attention. It didn't matter if it was negative attention, just that Daddy noticed. And boy did he notice when she first started sleeping with women. He cut her off."

Karen noted the disbelief on Velvet's face. "It's true. I guess you didn't know. She stayed in school on a scholarship and her mom slipped money into her account. It didn't last long, of course. It wasn't so much out of acceptance that it ended, more like Daddy couldn't be bothered to keep it up. So she went back to being ignored, until she—I mean you." Karen nodded at Velvet in acknowledgment. "Until you started the magazine. I guess one of her father's business partners in New York had a copy, probably to lambaste about the filth, and Daddy discovered Rosemary's picture on the editor's page. It upset him to see, as he put it, 'her illness' in print. All very embarrassing."

Karen shook her head. "May the bastard rest in peace. But then a funny thing happened. The magazine started to make money. And for a Finney, even a conservative like Arthur, a little green always made up for the mortifying things you had to do to make it. They're new money, you see. Not like my family. The Finneys had a history of doing things they were ashamed of, to make the money they had. We Friarses had only done things we *should* have been ashamed of." Karen smiled wryly. She looked around the room and, apparently finding no hint of approval or empathy, shrugged. "So anyway, suddenly Rosemary had Daddy's approval again. Everything became about making money, making a profit, and to hell with the whole feminist politics thing. I admit I came on as a part of that. Hell, those were my values, too. But I didn't make Rosemary go there. When Arthur died she got stuck in this endless need to continue the one thing he had approved of."

Karen was silent for a moment, looking up at the ceiling, as though gathering her thoughts. "But that little rebellious part, that self destructive, self-hating internalization of her father, it started seeping out in other ways. She embezzled from the company. Then she decided we needed to put out a lesbian porn magazine and produce lesbian sex videos."

"There's money in that," Velvet quipped.

Karen shot her a look. "It wasn't the life I had imagined. I want to have children. But how do you raise kids around all of that?" She smiled woefully. "You have no idea what it was like being married to that tramp. I know you thought she'd given up other women for me, but that was far from the truth. She had sex with half the women on those videos. We paid people to be quiet. Hell, I had to settle a couple of sexual harassment suits when she started treating her staff like it was her own private harem. After all that shit I put up with, a few months ago, she announces that she wants a divorce."

Velvet raised her eyebrows and shook her head. She'd had no idea.

"A divorce?" Yoshi's face was taut with concentration.

Karen scratched some more then heaved a theatrical sigh. "I suppose it's time I told you who did this."

Velvet held her breath. She could tell Yoshi was doing the same. Karen's eyes glinted. She had always relished an audience hanging on her every word, even if she normally had to pay employees to provide the silent awe she sought.

Milking the moment, she declared, "The first thing you need to know is that Rosemary was straight."

"Straight? I don't believe it." Velvet repeated.

"It's true!" Karen asserted. "She told me she was never really a lesbian."

"How could that be?" Yoshi asked.

"Well, she said she was just rebelling against her father, then she tells me that she's in love. She's been seeing some actor and wants to end our 'farce.' I was livid."

"Wait," Yoshi interrupted. "She was sleeping with an actor? Who?"

"That bastard Keith Ridger."

Velvet was dubious. Rosemary was one ex she would never have imagined as straight. "What? What about all those years of eating pussy?"

Yoshi and Karen both cringed at Velvet's gauche terminology.

"Isn't that what makes a lesbian?" Velvet demanded. "Or are you saying Rosemary was one of those women who think you can fuck whoever you want and it doesn't mean anything about your identity?"

Yoshi interrupted, hoping to prevent Velvet from further outbursts. "Keith Ridger? But I thought—"

"That he's gay?" Karen laughed. "Those are just rumors."

"But didn't your magazine just out his girlfriend as a lesbian?" Yoshi knitted her brow in puzzlement and didn't ask what she had originally intended. Hadn't Tucker said Keith was engaged to his girlfriend Jennifer?

Karen chuckled. "That was good, wasn't it? I put that in. I wrote that."

Velvet shook her head in bewilderment. "Wasn't that Rosemary's piece? It had her byline."

"I put her name on it," Karen said gleefully. "She was so busy, she wasn't even in the office the week we went to press."

Velvet understood that was the busiest time for a publication and it could be particularly grueling for the staff if the editor in chief wasn't in the office during that hectic period.

Karen leaned forward, her blouse falling away from her pert breasts. She lowered her voice conspiratorially. "I'd heard that *Bend* had a source on record saying that some of the girls on *The Isle of Lesbos* are gay. I just ran with it."

"So *you* know the spy. Who was it? It was Liz Claiborne, right?"

Karen laughed and shook her head. "It's funny how Rosemary is the face of *Womyn*. Even when she's not in the office, everyone thinks she runs, ran, the place. Nobody knows me from Adam. Nobody even notices me. But *I*'m the spy, Velvet. *I*'ve been snooping on you and Marion for months."

Velvet was horrified. "You? How could it be *you*? I'm so careful. I mean—"

"Who are you kidding? You're so predictable. You go to the Coffee Klatch all the time. You always sit at the same table. I pay one of the waitresses to eavesdrop."

Velvet felt violated. "Where else? Did you tap my phone?"

"No, no. Nothing that elaborate. Mostly, I just talk with the *Bend* interns. They have, like, three or four at any one time, and they love to talk about what they do and what they're covering. I'm just the friendly lesbian at the bar who'll buy one more round to keep them talking."

"But wait." Velvet was still trying to piece it together. "I saw Rosemary at the park, picking up an envelope."

"Yes, this one." Karen pulled a manila envelope out of her purse and slid it across the desk.

Velvet opened it. Several thousand dollars in a thick stack of bills fell out onto her lap. "Whoa. What the hell?"

"It's a down payment from Ryan Esterhaus, the director." Karen looked smug.

"Ryan Esterhaus," Yoshi echoed.

"Down payment for what?" Velvet asked.

"He wanted Rosemary to stop sleeping with Keith."

Velvet scoffed. "You're just making things up now, aren't you? Why would Ryan Esterhaus care who Keith Ridger sleeps with?"

Karen smirked. "Long story. Keith had agreed to star in Ryan's next project, but he decided to back out. His excuse was that he's about to get married and he wants to spend more time with his new family, but Ryan knew Keith was blowing smoke up his ass so he got pissed and did something about it."

"All the gay rumors," Velvet mused aloud. "The *Star* interview?"

"Everything. He thought he could ruin Keith's career." Karen shrugged as if she had no *mea culpa* for her own part in the media blitz. "Then he gets Jody Williams—she played that drag king on *Lesbos*—to tell *Bend* that Jennifer is a dyke. Only, *Bend* won't print the allegation because they—"

"Have morals?" Velvet offered.

"Are afraid of being sued," Karen corrected.

"Because they're already being sued by Rosemary!" Velvet said in defense of Marion.

"Right," Karen confirmed.

Her fingers trailed back and forth along her arm, and Velvet wondered if the scratching was a nervous tic. She glanced at Yoshi, who seemed oddly quiet, her face intent as she listened. "So you're saying that the Jennifer Garcia story was totally planted. That it wasn't even true?"

"Oh, I don't know. It might be true. Who cares?"

"That's libel," Velvet pointed out indignantly. She hated journalists who didn't follow an accepted code of ethics.

Karen laughed. "Whatever. That's on Jody. It's all over now anyway."

"What's over?" Velvet asked.

"*Womyn.*"

Velvet was shocked.

Karen smiled. "You think I'm going to run that stupid magazine without Rosemary? Please. I hated that rag. I'm thinking about selling it. OutNation.com is very interested."

"OutNation wants to run a lesbian magazine?" Velvet was surprised that the behemoth would want to delve into that publishing niche.

"No." Karen took a dainty sip of tea. "I think they want to gut it for their online site and the subscriber list."

"You want to destroy the magazine? Were you always trying to wreck it?"

Karen waved the question away. "Rosemary did a good job of that on her own."

"There is one thing I don't understand," quipped Yoshi. "If Rosemary was in love with Keith, why would she accept Esterhaus's money to stop seeing him?"

Karen shrugged. "I'm sure she never really intended to break it off. She just took his money anyway. And why not? Who's he going to tell?"

"How did you determine that Keith was the actor Rosemary was romantically involved with?" Yoshi asked. "Did she tell you?"

Karen harrumphed. "Yes, actually, but only after I'd already caught her in the act. I followed her one time when she said she was going to be away for the weekend on a press junket. I didn't believe her, and as it turned out I was right. She was with some blonde at the Villagio Spa Resort in Napa's wine country. I couldn't get a good look. But I did see the vehicle they drove off in. One of those distasteful Hummers. It turned out to be Keith's vehicle. When I confronted her, she admitted everything."

"I am still not clear on who murdered Rosemary and why," Yoshi said. Her tone suggested that she had found none of Karen's revelations all that astonishing.

Karen looked irritated by this. "I'm amazed I would need to spell it out to a private detective. Aren't you people supposed to be students of human nature?"

"Indeed," Yoshi conceded. "One never stops learning about the depths to which people will sink. Do you know who did it, or are you merely wasting our time?"

"Keith Ridger, who else?" Karen's voice was thin and high pitched, and it shook slightly as if she wanted to scream the information but contained herself because she needed to appear calmer than she felt. "You see, he was ready to give it all up for her, then he found out what she was really like."

"As you did?" Yoshi asked softly.

"Yes, only I lived with it. Apparently he wasn't so…tolerant. He found out about her latest toy and he lost it." She directed a brief triumphant look at Velvet. "That's Liz Claiborne, by the way. A toy, not a spy. Spies have brains."

"Thank you for clarifying all of this, Karen." Yoshi rose abruptly. "I believe we've heard all we need. But I do hope you will have us back later, if we have additional questions?"

Karen looked stunned like a deer caught in the light of an approaching car. Velvet shook her head. They couldn't leave now, not when Karen was giving them the kind of information that might extend her freedom, which was quickly slipping away as the clock ticked down to her surrender deadline. Velvet resisted when Yoshi tugged at her arm, and she was then poked in the ribs.

"I do apologize, but we really must be off." Yoshi turned to Velvet, "Have you forgotten about our next appointment?"

Confused, Velvet gave up the fight and allowed herself to be herded from the room, conscious of Karen staring after them with a mixture of smugness and bewilderment. Velvet had no idea why Yoshi was making vague references to a meeting that didn't exist instead of solving the case, but she'd learned long ago that her dearest friend didn't explain herself as she went along. Yoshi's style was less Matlock and more, well, Buddhist. She gathered endless information, observing, sorting data and emotions, and filtering it all quietly and internally and never really commenting on a case until a decision had been made. When she had all the facts, all the evidence carefully weighed, Yoshi rendered a decision with such thoughtful precision that her analysis was presented like a straightforward verdict, without the meandering explanations and self-aggrandizing "ahas!" that other detectives delivered. To onlookers it was both comforting and oddly disconcerting.

"What was that all about?" Velvet demanded as the Toyota's tires crunched on Karen's white oyster shell driveway.

"To the office, Jeeves," Yoshi commanded. She still felt awkward about Velvet chauffeuring her about instead of using her time to further this investigation. "You do have those photographs with you, don't you?"

"Yes, I told you—"

"Please examine them for me and tell me which vehicles are at the scene and whether you have clearly captured all the license plates."

"You want me to pull over right here?"

"Briefly, yes."

The car slowed. "At least tell me why we had to leave," Velvet said, shifting in her seat, then noisily foraging in her purse. "She knows the whole story. Why not hear her out?"

"If you had paid attention, you would have recognized that Karen had already revealed enough to clarify our next step." Yoshi didn't have time to deal with Velvet's pique now. "The pictures?"

Velvet sighed. "We have Rosemary's Jaguar. A Hummer. A Mercedes SUV. And a VW bus. Decent tail shots of everything. Is this going to keep me out of jail?"

"It will certainly help. You may start driving again." Yoshi reflexively grabbed the door's armrest to maintain her upright position as they peeled out onto the road. She located her cell phone and called Bud.

He answered with his usual grudging respect. "Yeah. What can I do for you?"

Yoshi was quite sure he was gallivanting about, probably reading porn at her expense so he would not have to come into the office. She ignored this behavior because between his episodes of time wasting, he delivered results. Hoping he had one for her now, she said, "I got your message. It sounds important."

"I picked up the autopsy report and I've figured out the murder weapon."

"Really?"

"Strangulation was with a narrow wire or cord, and guess what maintenance just dragged out of the porta-potty?" He paused, evidently seeking something from her.

Yoshi delivered a compliment. "If it's the murder weapon, you may have cracked this case wide open." She refrained from inquiry as to whether he would like a gold star for his mundane efforts.

Evidently satisfied with the lavish praise, he revealed, "An iPod. Pink. I'm guessing she was done with the speaker wires."

"Do you have the iPod in your possession?"

"No, the maintenance stiff wouldn't hand it over. But I got photos."

"I am certain those will be of interest to Detective Fleishman. Where are you presently?"

He sidestepped her question by mumbling something else about the autopsy report.

Yoshi had him go through the general details, then said, "There is one more task I have for you, then I want you to come in."

"To the *office*?" He sounded incredulous, as though that were the most absurd thing he had heard all day.

"It is time that we coordinated the next stage of the investigation," Yoshi said firmly. "Velvet and I are on our way there now."

"What's the job?"

"I want you to interview a movie director named Ryan Esterhaus. He has been implicated by Karen Friars. Find out what type of vehicle he drives, as well."

"Is he our perp?"

"Not necessarily."

"What's the angle?"

"Revenge against Keith Ridger. Karen claims he is the one behind all the gay rumors. We need to know if that is true, and why he would perpetrate such a hoax. And, naturally, his whereabouts when Rosemary was murdered." She didn't go into further detail. Bud would ask his usual questions and elicit both Esterhaus's version of events, and the nonverbal cues that could support or undermine his statements. Afterward, they would determine if his story was supported by facts.

Bud complained but said he would try his luck getting to see Esterhaus and get back to the office in a few hours. Yoshi thanked him and ended the call.

Velvet said, "Well?"

"We haven't yet solved this case, but we are close."

"What's next?"

"We must rule out our remaining persons of interest as quickly as we can."

❖

Leaving the Burger King drive-through, Bud exited onto El Camino Street and then immediately turned into the next business driveway. He pulled into an open handicapped parking space, hung his blue DMV tag on his rearview mirror, and pulled out the autopsy report. Dodging the medical jargon and the indecipherable Latin, he read it again, this time slowly. The gist was just as Chico had relayed verbally—death due to strangulation.

"Lividity fixed in the distal portions of the limbs. Petechial hemorrhaging is present in the conjunctival surfaces of the eyes." That was the big picture, but there were interesting tidbits secreted in the smaller details. For example, the angle of the marks on her neck indicated that the victim had been strangled with a ligature below the mandible, forming a V on the posterior of the neck, consistent with a hanging or strangulation from above with a force that likely lifted the victim off her feet. She had a broken hyoid bone, a fractured occipital bone, and a nearly severed windpipe.

The Finney woman being a lesbian and all, Yoshi said their primary suspects were all women. Bud shook his head. It couldn't have been a woman. Not when the perp needed the physical presence to stand over the 5'7" victim and lift her 125-pound-body off the ground. No way. Bud read further, looking to see if there were defensive wounds that indicated Rosemary had fought back.

Although there weren't many contusions, there was a strange crescent moon bruise on her thigh, scratches on her neck, and skin under her nails. Probably her own, Bud thought, from clawing at the noose around her neck, but they wouldn't be sure until the DNA tests came back. The fingertips of her right hand were cut, as though she'd managed to wedge them between the ligature and her throat for a moment. The scratches on her arms, where the long-sleeve hoodie sweatshirt was pushed up, were most likely from the bushes at the crime scene, but the ME wasn't sure about the etiology of the patch of red bumps on her arm.

There was leaf litter collected from Rosemary's person, and a few hairs of various color and length. Although those could turn out to be critical, nothing sprang immediately to mind. And there were cuts on the soles of her feet. Oh, right, because the perp took her shoes—as a trophy? He wondered. He bet nobody even thought to cross-check the specifics with other unsolved murders to see if this was the work of a serial killer. No, that's right, they'd already pinned this on Velvet Erickson.

Bud called Tucker and asked her to track down his subject, Esterhaus. When she called him back, they spent some time on the phone while she regaled him with superfluous details about the guy: his box office track record, his famed sexual proclivities, even his choice of boxers over briefs.

By the time they were done, Bud was disgusted. He made the drive to Ryan Esterhaus's upscale Spanish manor in Los Altos Hills planning what he was going to say to a guy rumored to like pretty young boys. To his surprise, Esterhaus was not only at home but agreed to speak to him. Bud thought he probably wanted to appear cooperative. People with something to hide often thought they could outsmart investigators, and often assumed that refusing to answer questions made them look guilty.

Esterhaus led him into a sunroom with a wall of floor-to-ceiling windows that was half opened to expose a terraced pool garden. The guy shared Bud's 6'2" height and middle-aged build. His soft features, blue eyes, and full salt and pepper beard gave him a friendly jovial look that seemed at odds with his high-octane action flicks, but probably endeared the son of a bitch to children. As they spoke, he punctuated Bud's statements with phony laughter until Bud wanted to punch him with a similar staccato. He wanted to leap out of his chair and pummel the guy senseless. When Esterhaus started hooting over a comment about the victim, Bud did the next best thing. He threw his drink at the man.

Although splashed by the contents, Esterhaus, apparently more nimble than he appeared, avoided the crystal shot glass that continued on its trajectory and crashed to the floor. No longer snickering, he shook the wet off himself like a dog and stepped toward Bud, who raised his fists in a protective motion. Esterhaus retaliated with his hand outstretched in shake formation.

"Nice throw," he said with no trace of malice as he bumped his palm against Bud's still-closed fist.

Bud, a little confused, reluctantly acquiesced to the handshake. "What was so fucking funny?" The hot blood in his veins still cried out for an answer.

"Oh, I wasn't laughing at you. I was laughing at what you said." The director rushed to explain. "I mean about Rosemary Finney being a helpless broad." He chortled again and wiped his eyes. "That's fucking funny, man."

Bud, who still didn't understand what was so amusing, realized he'd never seen a guy do that eye-swiping move, except in movies. He wondered if the guy was one of those perps who had no real emotions and just acted how he thought he was supposed to.

"Let me tell you about Rosemary Finney." Esterhaus threw himself backward in a trust fall to his chair. "She's a bitch, with a capital *B*. There was nothing, I mean *nothing*, helpless about her. I thought I'd already met the toughest cutthroat women. They're all in Hollywood. But she could put any of them to shame." He looked at Bud expectantly.

"So what?" Bud knew when he was being played. He made sure to project doubt, right down to the steely-eyed stare his buddies used to kid him about.

Esterhaus sighed with resignation, and as though he now hoped to win Bud over with testimonial, he announced, "Rosemary Finney was blackmailing me."

"Oh, really? That's not what I heard. My sources say you were paying her to help you ruin Keith Ridger's life."

"Sure, I was dicking with Ridger, you could even go so far as to say I was trying to break him financially. But it wasn't personal."

Bud rolled his eyes.

"Really. I wanted him for my movie. I wrote the fucking script with him in mind for the character, and he promised me he'd do it. Now he's backing out, telling me he's getting married and wants to spend more time with his family?" Esterhaus made quote marks with his fingers as he said the last word and spat, "Bullshit."

Bud displayed his disbelief. "I'm not hearing a story worth shit, Mr. Esterhaus. If that's all you've got, no one is going to believe Rosemary was blackmailing you. Maybe it's not the best story to tell, anyway. It gives you a motive. See what I'm saying?"

"A motive. You think *I* killed that bitch? Oh, please."

"Can you account for yourself that morning?"

"I can't account for myself two hours ago!"

Bud said, "I'll be sure to pass that on to our associates at the PD."

Esterhaus gave Bud an icy stare. "If you must know, I *was* at Wonderland Park. I saw her not long before it happened."

"Strange time of day for a social occasion."

"It was business. As I said, she was blackmailing me. I gave her money and left. Next thing I know, it's all over town. Couldn't have happened to a nicer piece of work."

"All right." Bud was getting a headache thinking this through. "If you want me to buy that sob story, you're going to have to flesh it out. I need to know what Finney had on you."

In response, Ryan Esterhaus surprised Bud by blushing. *What kind of man blushes,* Bud wondered. This guy was making San Francisco fairies look downright masculine.

"Somehow, I don't know *how*, that bitch found out…" He cleared his throat, turned away, and blurted, "Twenty years ago I was arrested for soliciting a minor. That's just what they called it. I would never…!"

Of all the criminals he'd dealt with over the years, Bud had the most contempt for child molesters. He looked around the room. They were alone. Maybe he should make this guy pay, right here, for what he did to some kid.

Esterhaus put up his hands, palms out. "I swear. I thought the kid was eighteen."

"Sure," Bud said. "That's what they all say."

Ryan's words came out in a rush now, as though the dam that held them in all these years had just broken. Bud wanted to cram something in the man's mouth and block it off again. "It turned out he was sixteen, or fifteen. Who knows. I'm not a fag or anything, I swear. I'm all man. We were filming on location in Pittsburgh, and this hustler, you know, he used to stand out near our set. He was there every fucking evening, offering to blow me as I walked by. He had the biggest lips I'd ever seen."

In Bud's experience, the men who most insisted they were "all man" were the furthest from it. It was his wheelchair. Bud thought, that made a man like Ryan Esterhaus feel comfortable enough to spill his guts. He thought Bud wasn't all man either, and he figured Bud couldn't do anything about his appalling confession. Bud grimaced as he inched it closer to the babbling pedophile. He thought about bashing Esterhaus over the head with the bottle of Scotch, saw the man reflexively lick his own lips, and coughed to keep from gagging.

"This one day, I'd had a really bad day, problems on the set and finding out my major backer was pulling out. And just that once I thought, why not? Wouldn't you know it, the cops were on us before the guy even put his mouth on me." He paused, his eyes aimed at the ceiling, as though recalling that day. Then he looked at Bud, seemed surprised to find him there in the middle of the room, closing the space between them. He held his hand out in the universal sign of stop. "The charges were dropped, I swear."

"Sure. Because you paid him off?"

"It was entrapment," he said indignantly. "Once they realized who I was, they knew it was an isolated incident. They gave me a warning I'll never forget." He tried a rueful chortle, like they were two drinking buddies comparing notes on visits to strip joints.

"Don't bullshit me, Esterhaus. If that was true, what would Rosemary have to blackmail you with?"

"The cops had it on tape. I watched them destroy it, but I guess one of them must've made a copy, because somehow Rosemary Finney gets a hold of it and twenty years after the fact she e-mails me a MPG movie clip. Can you believe that shit? Over the Internet."

"Have you told Woodside Police about the blackmail?" Bud had to ask. He braced himself for the answer.

"No way. They'd never have helped."

"So what happened that morning?"

"I'm stupid," Ryan Esterhaus proclaimed. "I was there, dropping off the blackmail payment. The bitch had me on a monthly cycle. Then I left. But news travels quickly. The woman next door, her husband is in the fire department and she's a big gossip. She tells me about Rosemary the minute I get home. I tried to act nonchalant but I rushed back there as soon as I could to see if the money was still there, in her car. My fingerprints are all over it."

Esterhaus glanced at Bud for feedback, but Bud just stared at him without commenting. He wondered where the film of Esterhaus was— probably at the Friars-Finney mansion.

"So there I am in the Wonderland parking lot, and who do I run into but the bloody mayor of Woodside. He lives just down the road."

Although Bud hadn't known that, he nodded anyway.

"I guess I was acting suspicious," the Hollywood director continued. "Because the next thing I know he's threatening to have me taken downtown and I'm blurting out the whole story."

"But not all of it," Bud reminded him. Esterhaus was sure to have left out the part about liking young boys.

"True. Instead of saying I was being blackmailed, I told the mayor I was bribing Rosemary to take down Keith Ridger. I assured him I had nothing to do with her death and, yes, I pointed him toward that reporter. I mean, here I was worried that she was onto *me*, and taking photographs of *me*, but it turns out she's after Rosemary. What a relief."

"So you told him she had a camera?" That explained a few things. Like the PD smashing up Velvet's place, looking for the film. Bud wondered where the buxom temptress had it stashed. Maybe at Tucker's place. She seemed pretty thick with the kid. Bud didn't want to speculate on why that might be.

Esterhaus was still trying to talk his way out of trouble. He said, "I had to stay out of this mess, so we talked about the city's nine million dollar budget shortfall. I was actually quite glad to help, and I made the arrangements right there. The mayor saw the big picture right away."

Bud squinted slightly, trying to see the big picture himself.

Esterhaus spared him the effort. "Joe Ordinary can be in the wrong place at the wrong time and so what, who gives a shit? But for people like me it's different. We don't have the right to privacy. We're not allowed to make a mistake."

Bud was now at arm's length from the self-serving pervert and ready to take a swing at the bastard when the doorbell gonged loudly, reverberating down the long corridor to where the two men were speaking.

Esterhaus's demeanor immediately changed. He no longer appeared willing to share his thoughts. The oversized vault doors protecting his secrets sealed closed with a loud thud. "I think it's time for you to leave," he suggested coldly.

Damn, what was *wrong* with this guy? Other than his personal desire to beat the crap out of Esterhaus, Bud didn't mind leaving now. On his way in, he had stopped by the garage and taken down the details of Esterhaus's rides, a Mercedes SUV and several sports cars. He now had the guy's admission to being at Wonderland Park around the time of Finney's murder, plus a blackmail motive. He had also assembled a collection of physical evidence from the site, just in case there was key trace, and he had the autopsy report.

Well, shit, he was actually ready for the group hug at Blind Eye.

CHAPTER SEVENTEEN

"Can you really see Rosemary being with a man?" Yoshi posed the question as they drove north.

It was supposed to be rhetorical, but Velvet quipped, "No. Although, these days, what with all the hasbians…"

"The what?" Yoshi wasn't familiar with the term.

"Has-bi-an. Former lesbian. Once a dyke, now with men. Surely you've heard of such a thing."

"Of course I am familiar with the concept, just not the terminology. I thought that was what we called bisexual."

"No." Velvet stopped her. "Totally different concept."

"I simply am not plugged in to lesbian pop culture the way you are, Velvet."

"Don't you even watch *Isle*?"

"No, I don't watch the show."

"What kind of lesbian are you?"

Yoshi ignored her question. "We will be making a quick stop at the Four Seasons before we continue on to the office. Tucker informs me that, according to an Internet blog, Keith Ridger and Jennifer Garcia are currently guests at the hotel. It would be quite useful to interview them prior to our strategy meeting. Unfortunately, it seems that the couple uses aliases when registering to avoid obsessed fans and tabloid paparazzi, and I do not know what names they are using."

"Why didn't you just ask me?" Velvet said. "I've got a girl on the inside. Hold on, I'll call her right now."

Yoshi heard her flip open her cell phone. She hit her speed

dial and held the phone to her ear. Yoshi listened to one side of the conversation.

"Hi, is Tameeka available? Thanks. Hey, girl. Velvet here. I'm great, how've you been? I've missed you too, babe, maybe we could get together sometime soon, if I'm not in jail. Oh, long story. Actually, you can. I'm trying to track down Keith Ridger and...Really? Great. Okay, 302. You're fantastic." This was followed by giggling and frank exchanges about recent sexual activities.

Yoshi whispered, "Wednesday morning."

Velvet patted her, then quickly resumed steering the car. "Were you at work Wednesday morning? Can you ask around? If anyone noticed them Wednesday morning I'd be *very* interested." Velvet laughed. "No, a C-note, if it's reliable. Thanks, doll. I'll call you next week." She closed the phone with a click and returned it to her purse.

"Tameeka?" Yoshi inquired pointedly. "Aren't your hands full with Tucker? Should you be using this other woman?"

"Using *Tameeka*?" Velvet spluttered with laughter. "Are you kidding? No one uses that ebony goddess. She uses you. And good too."

Disco beats interrupted their conversation. Yoshi jumped in her seat and began fumbling with the vehicle's dials. The radio wasn't on, and as Velvet reached for her purse again, Yoshi realized that must be the new ring tone on Velvet's cell phone. Last month it was Ozzy Osbourne's "Crazy Train," and the volume had been set at a deafening level. Every time it rang Yoshi imagined Velvet tossing her hair in head-banging rhythm while holding her hand aloft, middle fingers tucked against her palm, forming horns with her fingers. She smiled to herself. Velvet was nothing if not colorful.

"It's Tameeka," Velvet hissed as the call progressed. "She found someone that saw Kennifer Wednesday evening."

"Kennifer?" Yoshi shook her head.

"Keith and Jennifer? You know, like Brangelina. Anyway, they got together for dinner after Keith arrived back in town. The bellhop got photos. Those guys sell shit to the tabloids whenever celebrities are in town."

"Dinner. And anything from the morning?"

Velvet asked her ebony goddess then ended the call. "Only Jennifer in the Hummer, coming back from her fitness training. That's all. Anyway, they're at the hotel now, if we want to go bust in on them."

Yoshi thought carefully. She was not perfectly ready to interview the couple, but it was unlikely that a more judicious moment would present itself. Velvet's news confirmed Yoshi's darkest suspicions about Karen. Eager to confirm that Velvet had drawn a similar conclusion, she announced, "Rosemary was not dating Keith. I think she was having an affair with his fiancée."

"But Karen said—"

"And you've never known her to lie?"

"Her story was a little far out, but what would her motive be?"

"She's hiding something."

"Yes, but—"

"I imagine that an inheritance is more attractive than a divorce settlement," Yoshi affirmed.

"She's trying to frame Keith for the murder using jealousy as the motive, when she's the one who was jealous?" Velvet sounded pensive. "That's ironic."

"Your photographs might prove Keith's car was at the scene," Yoshi said. "But not that he was driving it."

"Jennifer Garcia was there."

"As was Liz Claiborne," Yoshi said. She avoided mentioning Artemis McDermid's name despite her knowledge about the psychologist's presence at Wonderland that morning. "It seems that all of Rosemary's dirty secrets were there at the same time, which must have made for a quite volatile situation."

"And yet they arrested *me*!" Velvet's disgust was palpable. "What do you suppose actually happened?"

"I won't be certain until I have spoken with Bud. But we do know one thing. There are enough suspects and enough physical evidence to provide reasonable doubt. Perhaps even enough to get the case against you dismissed."

"Well shiiit, if it isn't Bud Williams!" San Jose Police Chief Jesus Hernandez stood from behind his large chestnut desk as Bud rolled up to the open door. "Come in, come in." Jesus rushed over, pumped Bud's hand a couple of times, and then darted back into his office, shoving seats against the walls to make room for Bud's chair. Once he was sure his old partner was comfortable, and shut the glass door, Jesus parked himself down into his executive chair. "What the hell brings you to San Jose?"

"I need a favor."

"Of course you do," Jesus laughed.

"Let me show you something." Bud fumbled around in his jacket.

"I don't want to see it," Jesus joked.

"Here." Bud pulled a small package out and passed it across the desk.

Chief Hernandez picked it up. "It's a tape recorder," he said, stating the obvious. "I've seen one of these before, Bud."

"Listen," Bud insisted.

"It better not be fart jokes." The tape was already rewound. He pressed the Play button. A man's voice crackled from the box. "Who is this?" Jesus asked.

"Ryan Esterhaus—the director,"

"This a new movie idea of his or something?"

"Just listen." Bud played the tape through to the end, occasionally rewinding it to listen more intently to a section.

Jesus no longer made jokes. "Wow. Did he know you were taping him?"

Bud shook his head.

"Who's your client?" Jesus knew Bud well enough to know that there would be a client involved in this.

"Velvet Erickson, she's a reporter with the *San Francisco Chronicle*. She's been charged with Rosemary Finney's murder."

Jesus cleared his throat. "Well, honestly, Bud, I don't think this *proves* anything." Bud started to cut Jesus off, but the police chief held up his left hand and kept talking. "He never says *he* did it. Okay, so he claims he bribed the police to ignore him, but that doesn't clear your client. He witnessed her at the scene of the crime."

Bud shook his head. "Amigo, I'm not here to clear Velvet Erickson, I'm here about the kid. I want Esterhaus for doing the kid in Pittsburgh."

Jesus Hernandez stared at his friend for a long time. "Does your boss know what you're doing?"

Bud shook his head impatiently.

"Fine, I can see you don't really want my advice. What *do* you want?"

"A search warrant for Rosemary Finney's house, to find the film of Esterhaus with the kid."

"Jesus, Mary, and Joseph," the chief swore. "And you think I can pull that kind of thing out of my ass? In case you didn't notice here, we're in San Jose. You're talking about a Woodside residence. That's a whole other county, for chrisssake."

"You expect me to go to Woodside PD and tell them their mayor elicited a bribe? I was a visitor in Woodside's fair police station just the other day, and let me tell you, they don't want to see me again."

"Okay, granted. But what about San Mateo County?" Jesus asked, suggesting the sheriff's department.

"Oh, sure that's great," Bud complained sarcastically. "The sheriff is a good buddy with Woodside's mayor. And I know the San Mateo DA personally called San Francisco about pulling Velvet in."

"Fine, what about a San Mateo judge?" Jesus pondered.

"Yes, exactly, that's what we could do."

"*We?*" Jesus rubbed his brow. "Shit. No way. Do you have any idea what kind of political hailstorm this could unleash? We're, like, a week away from the elections."

"*I* can't do it, Jesus," Bud said. "No one's going to listen to a washed-up detective with a stake in the situation. I need you."

Jesus sighed. "You always pull this kind of shit. Just tell me straight out exactly what your crazy plan is. All of it. I don't want to be surprised by anything in five minutes. Got it? Spill."

"Fine." It was their history that Bud was relying on to pressure Jesus into going along with his plan. But it was the same history that led to situations like this. Jesus knew all of his tricks. "We go to Judge Weinstein—"

"Weinstein?" Jesus chuckled. "Let me see if I've got this right. You think that because Harold Weinstein is friends with Jeffrey Travis, who is running to replace the current San Mateo sheriff in next week's elections, he'll be open to this? Didn't you used to always say 'Don't mix politics and police work'?"

"Sure I did, but don't you see, it's already mixed together. You got the Woodside police chief and the mayor deflecting interest away from a suspect in a *murder*. Then you add all that money."

"The money that was donated to Woodside for its new life flight helicopter? Even if Esterhaus did donate that money, that's far from proving bribery."

"Yeah, but don't you see?" Bud pointed at the tape recorder. "If you listen to it, Esterhaus says that the mayor told him it was a *nine* million dollar shortfall, right?"

"Right."

"But look." Bud spread open a newspaper he'd picked up earlier in the day. He pointed at a headline about the anonymous seven million dollar gift. "See?"

"If that's right, where did the other two million go?" Jesus had obviously drawn the same conclusion as Bud.

"Right? I'm wondering if it has anything to do with those slick campaign commercials. All of a sudden, they're interrupting the news every five minutes so that jerk can tell us how to vote."

"Okay." Jesus could finally agree with Bud's assessment. "So they'll need to put a special prosecutor together. You're talking about weeks or months."

"That's why I need *you* to help speed things along. If you approach the right judge and explain that some of the evidence is in jeopardy and throw in the Woodside mayor and San Mateo sheriff, that could speed things up. Especially if you already had an investigative team in mind." Bud pushed a scrap of paper at his friend.

Jesus glanced down at the short list of names jotted there and chuckled. "Um, Bud? I think they'd notice that Chico's my son."

"I figured. That's why there's a question mark after his name. Add a San Jose detective."

"What makes you think they'd take this list?"

Bud shrugged. "It could work."

Jesus stared at the list, shuffled the recorded tape around his desk, and didn't speak. Bud let him think. Jesus would have to decide for himself that this was a good idea before he'd pursue it.

Finally Jesus got up. "First I'm getting the techs to make a copy of this tape. Just in case. Then we'll go see if I can get myself fired."

❖

Keith Ridger answered the door of the presidential suite. He seemed surprised and then immediately pissed off at their presence. Even while angry he was gorgeous. Velvet had wondered if he would be, in person. But there was no doubt, with those striking blue eyes framed by the longest lashes she'd ever seen. His blond hair was tousled and his high cheekbones were touched with a brush of opaque pink. If any man could turn her, she laughed to herself, this would be it. He was the new Brad Pitt and everyone knew it. But he looked off, and Velvet wondered if he had been fighting with his fiancée.

Sensing his retreat, she jammed a size seven foot in the doorway, sacrificing precious Manolo Blahnik footwear to stop the door from being shut in their faces. "Listen, Keith, we're here about the murder of Rosemary Finney."

"Sorry. Don't know her."

"Oh, I think you do. You and Jennifer both. You can talk to us or we can go to the police and tell them about it. See, we know all about the romance."

Yoshi elbowed Velvet to keep her from wasting all their ammunition before they were even out of the hallway. She pushed a business card through the cracked doorway. "We are here representing Blind Eye Detective Agency," she said. "I am sure we would all be more comfortable speaking about this inside."

Keith glanced nervously down the hotel corridor as if checking for rabid fans or paparazzi. "Does anyone else know we're here?"

"Just the hotel staff. For now." Velvet made it a veiled threat.

Reluctantly, he ushered them in and led them through a formal entry, past a dining area and pantry into the suite's living room. The walls were a shade of butter with hints of gold highlights. The furnishings were suitably decadent: ebony sitting chairs, eucalyptus lounge chairs and matching love seat surrounding a glass-topped gold leaf coffee table. Floor-to-ceiling windows offered an impressive view of Yerba Buena Gardens.

Keith pointed them toward the plush ottoman as Jennifer Garcia, wrapped in an oversized white bathrobe, stepped into the room. "Who was that?" she asked before noticing the women. She shot Keith a disapproving look but he made no effort to introduce them.

Velvet said their names and held out a hand that was received with an icy glare from Jennifer. Velvet covertly directed Yoshi toward the sofa and sat down next to her.

"So you were saying?" Keith prompted.

Neither he nor Jennifer sat. They remained standing in opposite doorways.

Yoshi nodded. "We're here regarding Rosemary Finney."

Velvet thought she heard Jennifer inhale sharply, but it happened so quickly that she couldn't be sure. Maybe she was a better actor than Velvet had given her credit for. Neither Jennifer nor Keith responded. They just stood in their respective locations, blithe smiles undermined by the glint in their eyes.

"Rosemary was murdered two days ago," Yoshi said.

"What?" Jennifer gasped as if she lived in such a rarefied realm she had not seen news of this real-world event. "I mean, I'm not sure what this has to do with us, but how dreadful. Murder."

"Let me step in here." Velvet opened her bag and, as she and Yoshi had discussed, pulled out the manila envelope she'd been guarding all day. Slowly, theatrically, she dumped the envelope's contents onto the coffee table in front of her. The pile was topped off with the color shots she'd gotten from the bellhop. As Jennifer craned slightly to see, Velvet drew one of the black and whites from the stack and held it up.

"This is a picture I took Wednesday morning. I think that's your Hummer, right?" She held it out to Keith, who accepted it reluctantly. "This was taken at Wonderland Park around the time Rosemary was killed."

He glanced at the photo and then walked it over to Jennifer, handing it to her without comment.

"Here's a close-up." Velvet drew another image and raised it. "See? You can see the license plate in this one." She held up another. "Oh look, here's a photo of Rosemary. It looks almost like she's talking to the driver of this Hummer."

"What do you want?" Keith's voice had a hard edge.

"Even if you can prove that's Keith's car, you can't prove who was in it," Jennifer said flatly.

"We want the truth," Yoshi said. "Once we leave here, I will be meeting with a detective who is quite interested in these photographs."

Velvet picked up some of the color images. "Now, these were taken right outside the hotel here. See, that's you, Jennifer, getting out of this Hummer. Oh, here, I bet if we blew this one up we could see the plate again. There's this time stamp here—huh, this is just an hour after Rosemary was killed. You don't look very happy."

"What do you want?" Keith asked again, angrily.

"The truth," Yoshi answered.

"I think it's time we called our attorney."

"That's up to you," Yoshi said. "But you will leave me with no choice but to go public with this. My client wants the murderer caught, so if I have to resort to such tactics to smoke her out—"

"Are you saying this can be kept quiet?" He sounded wary, like a man who had been bitten too many times.

Yoshi said, "If either of you is guilty of the murder, or of being an accessory, I won't be able to help you. But if you are innocent, it would be wise to speak to me before this is all over the Internet. We know for a fact that one of you was involved with her sexually. Now Rosemary's partner, Karen, claims it was you, Keith."

"But—" Keith started.

Velvet interrupted him. "But *we* know better, don't we? You've been up in Canada. So that leaves you, doesn't it, Jennifer?"

"I don't know about you," Yoshi said to Velvet, "but I would be rather perturbed to discover that my fiancée was cheating on me with another woman."

"Did that threaten your manhood, Keith?" Velvet asked smugly.

"Fuck off."

Velvet pulled a copy of the recent *Womyn* magazine from her bag. "I suppose you've seen this?"

Neither Keith nor Jennifer reached for the offending publication. Jennifer put her head in her hands and started to cry. Keith put an arm around her and pulled her close to him.

"I love Jennifer," he said. "We love each other."

They paused for a tearful hug. Velvet watched carefully. They were *both* better actors than she thought. Or they weren't acting.

"Sure, she's had some experiences…with that woman," he went on. "People experiment. She's playing a lesbian character. This just started out as research. You probably don't know this, not being in the business, but for actors, the line can get blurred between reality and fiction when you really get into a character. You become that person, but that doesn't make it *real*."

"It was nothing," Jennifer said emphatically. "I broke it off, but Rosemary didn't want it to end. And then she had the *nerve* to publish that." She pointed at the magazine as though it were kiddie porn.

"She didn't, actually," Yoshi corrected. "It was Rosemary's partner who ran that story. Apparently there is some type of smear campaign against Keith."

"Against me?" Keith snorted.

"Yeah," Velvet interjected. "Orchestrated by Ryan Esterhaus."

"Ryan? No way."

"I guess," Velvet continued, "he felt like you'd breached a verbal contract?"

"You see?" Jennifer exploded, waggling a finger at Keith. "I *told* you he was behind that *Star* shit. And you wouldn't believe me. I can't believe you wouldn't believe me. Is it any wonder that I had to..." Jennifer swallowed her words as though she had just thought better of what she was saying.

"I'm sorry, baby." Keith shook his head. "I just can't believe he'd do something like that, I mean, hurt you to get at me."

"Anyway," Velvet prodded, "it's a whole lot of motive."

"I didn't kill her," Jennifer insisted. "I swear. And neither did Keith. He wasn't even in town. We didn't even know she was dead."

Keith nodded again. "We don't watch the news. It upsets Jennifer. We were booked all day yesterday doing press stuff. This morning we slept in and then just hung around together. We haven't had a lot of time together lately." He pulled his bride-to-be closer to him.

"Maybe it was Esterhaus," Jennifer suggested. "Maybe he killed Rosemary to frame us."

"Why were you at Wonderland that morning?" Yoshi asked.

Jennifer sighed and took Keith's hand. In a low voice she said, "I was trying to protect him. If people think he's marrying a lesbian, it'll be the end. So far, he's had the benefit of the doubt from his studio, but you can't imagine what it's like. I just wanted to reason with her. I thought I might be able to get her to print a retraction."

Keith kissed her. "Thank you, baby. God, when I think about what could have happened. It could have been you killed down there..."

They cried some more and Velvet felt Yoshi shuffle impatiently. She said, "Keith's right. Weren't you worried about being down there at dawn, with no one around?"

"I had no choice. I knew I had to go somewhere like that, where no one would see us. She told me that's where she goes jogging."

"Did you get to talk to her?"

"Yes, but only for a moment, then she got angry and walked away. I waited for a while, then I just gave up." She stared at Velvet. "Maybe I could have saved her if I'd walked down the trail."

"You don't have anything to feel guilty about, baby." Keith placed a protective hand over her belly. "Anyway, you had two people to think about."

Velvet wasn't sure what to say to the idea of a little Kennifer. A love child or a smoke screen for two actors who needed one? She had no idea.

Yoshi had it covered. "I assume I can call you to confirm any other information?"

"Yes." Keith's drawn face relaxed. "I'll authorize my publicist to put you through."

The two women left as gracefully as they had entered.

"Do you believe them?" Velvet asked Yoshi as they walked down the corridor from Kennifer's suite.

"That they didn't kill Rosemary? Yes. That they're a happy couple? No."

CHAPTER EIGHTEEN

Several hours later, after a meeting Yoshi described as fruitful despite the absence of Bud, who had phoned in with his most feeble excuse yet—a flat tire—Velvet, Yoshi, and Tucker drove up the long crushed-shell driveway back to the Friars-Finney estate. There were no other vehicles parked there, in particular no baby blue Impala and no sign of Bud as they neared the house.

"So where is he?" Velvet wondered aloud. When neither woman responded, she asked Tucker directly. "Tucker, when he called, did it sound like bullshit?"

"No, I don't think so. I mean, he sounded excited, like he was going to show you something." Tucker twisted in her seat and pressed her face against the small side window in the car's cramped backseat. "Horses!" she exclaimed, sounding much younger than her years. "You didn't tell me she had horses." She touched the window with her fingertips. "Can we stop?"

"No, we can't stop, Tucker." Velvet laughed.

"Why not?" Tucker demanded like a kid in a candy shop.

"Didn't you have horses growing up?" Velvet asked, knowing Tucker was raised in a rural environment.

"No, we couldn't afford anything like that," Tucker lamented. "But I used to do odd jobs at the Green Pasture Stables, so I was around them a lot. Why can't we stop? Bud isn't here yet. Come on, can't we just for a minute?"

Velvet slowed the car to a near crawl.

"Wait," Tucker insisted. "There was a horse at the murder scene. I saw it in Bud's notes. The ranger saw fresh hoof tracks."

Yoshi laughed. "Sure there was a horse on the trail, but—"

"You see? There was a horse there, and Rosemary's wife just happens to own a horse? What're the odds?"

Yoshi turned around in her seat so she was facing Tucker.

The younger woman wasn't looking her way, still entranced by the horses.

"Do you know where we are—the town?"

"Woodside?" Tucker answered. "So?"

Yoshi sighed.

Velvet placed a comforting hand on Yoshi's shoulder and whispered, "She's not from here."

Yoshi nodded. "Okay. Tucker, Woodside is a town as famous for its many horses as its rich residents. It has the nation's highest number of equines per person. In fact, until about ten years ago there were more horses in Woodside than there were people. Horses are a dime a dozen."

Tucker sounded dejected. "Let's just go."

"It wouldn't hurt to look, would it?" Velvet asked, squeezing Yoshi's shoulder a little to ask her friend's permission.

"Fine," Yoshi sighed in resignation. "Go, have a little field trip if you must. I'll be here if you need me."

Tucker was out of the car before Yoshi had finished speaking, darting across the dry grasses to the split redwood log corral.

"Thanks," Velvet said. "Where'd you put that camera? I might as well take it with me, just in case."

Yoshi pulled the small digital camera from her purse.

"Oh, right. It's digital. Damn. What do I do?"

Yoshi laughed at her Luddite friend. "Slide open the lens, look through the viewfinder, and press the button down a little bit until it focuses. Then push the button down all the way."

Velvet held the device as though it were ticking.

"A child could do it," Yoshi joked.

"Today's kids could program a cruise missile. That means nothing to me." Velvet pushed open the car door. "Wish me luck."

She turned toward the horse corral, where Tucker was now sitting on top the fence. Two brown horses sauntered toward the country girl.

Velvet held up the camera and snapped what she hoped would be a photo. Maybe a technician could decipher it even if it was fuzzy, Velvet thought, before reminding herself that Blind Eye didn't have its own *CSI*-like forensic lab.

"Velvet!" Tucker called, waving. "Come quick."

❖

As Velvet trotted off toward Tucker, Yoshi's cell phone buzzed and vibrated on the floor near her foot. She must have dropped it out of her bag earlier. She fumbled around on the floor, relieved when she found it and located the Talk button before the caller hung up. It was voice activated, Yoshi knew, but she took pride in memorizing the key locations and only occasionally had a mishap like deleting a client's voice mail message instead of just hanging up.

"Yoshi Yakamota," she said professionally into the phone.

"Good morning, Yoshi Yakamota." Karen Friars's waspy, pinched voice startled her. How had Karen gotten her phone number? "Are you waiting for an invitation?"

"Excuse me?"

"Come on now, Ms. Private Eye, we both know you're sitting in my driveway. Why don't you come up to the house and join me? I so enjoyed your previous visit." Karen's voice dripped with sarcasm.

"Well." Yoshi wondered if she should call Velvet.

"Leave your friends," Karen said ominously as though she'd read Yoshi's mind. "I'd rather speak to you alone."

What the hell, Yoshi thought, wondering what Karen was up to. She agreed to walk to the house. It was time for her to push through her fears and regain a modicum of independence. During this entire case she had relied far too much upon the others. Velvet and Bud were talented investigators, and Yoshi was trying hard to appreciate her new role in facilitating a team effort. Still, she could not deny that she felt envious and wanted a chance to pull her own weight. Blind Eye was *her* agency, after all. On some level this felt like a showdown, but she wasn't sure who the other person was behind their mask with their ninja stance. Was her foe Karen Friars or her own limitations and fear? There had been enough excuses; now it was time for her to fully integrate and employ her investigative instincts and her fledgling sensory skills.

Yoshi sensed danger, but she welcomed the feeling. In her own way, she knew she could be a match for this woman, and she concealed a power Karen would not be expecting.

Her opponent was standing in the doorway when she arrived. The private eye wondered how long she'd been there. Had Karen monitored her the whole way up the driveway, weaving back and forth and employing her cane to avoid wandering into the narrow creek that ran alongside it?

"It's so nice to see you." Karen offered her hand but not her sincerity.

"My pleasure," Yoshi replied with equally fake sentiment.

Karen led the way down the long hallway, passing the lounge where they had spoken earlier.

Yoshi paused at that doorway, a little nervous. Risking that she might sound paranoid, she asked, "Isn't this the room?"

"I'm taking you somewhere more intimate," Karen offered, doing nothing to ease Yoshi's concern.

As Yoshi was led farther along the hallway, her feet shifted from hardwood floor to a long expansive rug. From its musty smell she imagined that it was likely from the same period as the other furnishings, but rather than feeling threadbare under her shoes, it was quite cushiony. It probably had a thick pad underneath. As they penetrated the depths of the palatial house, the rug ended and the natural light faded away, replaced by shadows and lights strung from the ceiling. Although Yoshi could only see the changing light, she had some sense of the house's architecture from the sounds and smells of the rooms they passed.

"Would you like to feel around and familiarize yourself with the room?"

Yoshi couldn't tell if the woman was being facetious or genuinely hoping to put her at ease. "I'm fine," she said, using her cane to locate the furniture and her hand to find an appropriate seat.

Karen took a seat next to her and lit a cigarette.

"I didn't know you smoked." Yoshi thought it was strange that she had not smelled the distinct smell of tobacco smoke earlier. It could quickly permeate every material and was one of the most difficult odors to get out of a room or clothes.

Karen sucked on the cigarette and then coughed. "I don't. I quit five years ago."

Yoshi knew that stress could start a person smoking again. But was it the stress of losing her lover or of *killing* her lover? She still was not absolutely positive.

She heard Karen scratching through fabric, apparently still itchy. This confirmed Yoshi's initial suspicions. "I know why your arms itch so much," she offered.

"It's just a rash." Karen scratched again.

"No, I am pretty sure that it isn't. You're making it worse by scratching."

"Are you stalling? Where's Velvet?" Karen asked suspiciously.

"She's looking at your horses."

"Why? What does she want with them?" There was a change in the tone of Karen's voice. What was it? Yoshi wondered. Was she nervous?

"I am very interested in your rash," Yoshi corrected. "Especially since it suggests you were on the trail where Rosemary was killed."

"You're making that up." Karen asserted.

Yoshi heard distant chiming and wondered if it was the grandfather clock they had passed or the doorbell. Maybe Velvet and Tucker were here. "Actually, Karen," she continued, "it's an allergic reaction to poison oak. Scratching it is merely spreading the oil around. You get it under your nails and the next thing you know, you've spread it to your face."

If it was the door, Karen made no move to answer it. "So I picked up poison oak. Big deal."

"You encountered it on Huckleberry Trail," Yoshi said. "The trail where you attacked Rosemary."

"Nonsense. When Rosemary was killed, I was putting Paisley through her paces."

Yoshi chuckled at the alliteration. "I presume that's your horse?" She could practically hear the wheels clicking into place in her head. "That's why you don't want them looking at your horses. You *were* there. You were on Paisley when you killed Rosemary! That's why the lacerations angled up. Because you were so far above her." Yoshi snapped her fingers. The crescent moon bruise Bud had mentioned. It was all coming together now. It was a hoof imprint! "Your horse kicked her or stood on her during all the commotion. That's the type of evidence juries find memorable."

Karen was suspiciously quiet. Then Yoshi heard the floorboards creak. She leapt to her feet, her hands out in front of her, not knowing what to expect next.

❖

When Velvet got close to the horse run, Tucker jumped down from the fence and ran up to her, her eyes wide. She grabbed her sleeve and began pulling Velvet along.

"Look. She's hurt." Tucker pushed Velvet against the rough wood poles and pointed at the closest horse, whose dark black eyes were shaded by shaggy maroon bangs.

Velvet was surprised at how big the creatures were up close. She decided to call the horse Tucker was pointing to Star, not because the stripe on the horse's forehead was shaped like one, but because she'd always liked the name but was sure she'd never be able to give the name to a kid. On a person, Star was a stripper name. You just couldn't get around it. But on a horse…

"Do you see?" Tucker indicated the scratches and black welts on Star's foreleg.

"What is that?"

"Dried blood."

Before Velvet could respond, Tucker vaulted the fence and landed on her feet with a soft thud. Star didn't seem to notice. She'd pushed her nose through the bars of the fence and was nibbling on Velvet's blouse, her lips tickling Velvet's skin. Velvet nervously reached out to touch the horse, moving her hand slowly until she brushed against Star's cheek. Wow. She was surprised at how soft the horsehair was against her hand. Maybe $800 horsehair weaves weren't such a bad thing. They didn't have to kill the horse to get the hair, right?

Star abandoned the blouse, leaving it damp but not torn, and mouthed Velvet's hand. Velvet jumped back. "She tried to bite me," she warned Tucker. "Be careful."

"She was limping earlier. I just want to look at her foot." Tucker stepped up to the horse and brushed her side.

"Are you crazy? You'll be kicked. Get away from there, Tucker, I mean it."

Tucker chuckled. "Calm down, Velvet. You like it calm, don't you, yes you do," Tucker said to the horse in a cooing voice. "I know what I'm doing," she assured Velvet.

Apparently animal husbandry was the one arena in which Tucker showed absolute confidence. As she continued whispering baby talk into the horse's ear and kept a hand on the horse, she gradually moved down the horse's belly, onto the flank, and down the leg.

"I can't look," Velvet muttered, covering her eyes with her hand. She was sure Tucker was going to be kicked or trampled. When her lover didn't scream in pain, Velvet ventured a peek through parted fingers.

Tucker was holding Star's back leg bent, with the hoof resting on her knee.

"Are you crazy?" Velvet whisper-screamed.

Star stared at her through the fence, seemingly oblivious to Tucker.

Upside down as the hoof was, Velvet could see now that the horse wore metal horseshoes. She'd played horseshoes in the park but never thought about them really being worn by horses. Velvet looked down at her own fashionable shoes and was glad she didn't have to wear metal clunkers secured to her feet with nails.

Velvet peeked again at Tucker, who was now holding a pocketknife in her right hand while holding the hoof, which was the size of her fist, with the other. Velvet recognized the knife. It was one of those red army knives that boys seemed so fond of. Tucker carried the thing with her all the time. So much so, in fact, that it had worn a spot in her jeans, like a guy's wallet. Velvet had made fun of it at first, wondering what a girl needed a knife for in the city, but Tucker insisted that she needed to be prepared. The young nonsmoker carried a Zippo lighter for the same reason.

In a move that made Velvet gasp, Tucker seemed to plunge the knife into Star's hoof, inside the area not covered by the shoe. Tucker flashed her a look and returned to her task, scraping at the hoof with her knife.

Now Velvet could see that Tucker had something on the ground below her—maybe a paper bag from the car—and stuff came off the hoof and rained onto the paper with a rustling sound. It looked like Tucker was cleaning the mud out of the horse's shoes. Oh, cool. Velvet remembered the camera in her hand and snapped pictures of Star,

Tucker, and the scratches on Star's leg. She was glad the flash didn't go off, thinking that was the kind of thing that would make an animal mad.

"Snap!" Tucker exclaimed, holding something aloft between her thumb and first finger.

"What is it?" Velvet queried.

Grinning triumphantly, Tucker folded her knife together, picked up the paper bag of dirt, and bounded to the fence. "It's an earring!"

She passed it to Velvet, who carefully took it and held it in her palm until Tucker climbed the fence. Then she handed it back to Tucker.

"You found it," Velvet said. "Besides, it's not my type. I don't wear studs."

Tucker tucked it in her front pocket and patted her thigh as though verifying that it was there in her jeans. "I don't think the horse does either. How about Rosemary?"

"Hmm?" Velvet was saying good-bye to Star. "What about Rosemary?"

"Did she wear studs?"

❖

Yoshi stood in a defensive stance, her feet shoulder-width apart, knees slightly bent and left leg back. Her arms were outstretched in front of her, held out nearly half an armsbreadth from her chest. Her father had made her take years of defensive moves, so Yoshi hadn't just learned karate. She'd learned karate and kickboxing and judo and jujitsu. For her, that meant she knew a little about a lot of martial arts but had never become a master in any of them. She wondered if she could defend herself now with her eyesight nearly gone. Certainly her instructors would have insisted she could. The art of hand-to-hand combat entailed many of the same skills she was employing to complement her dwindling sight.

She saw a shadow move and braced herself.

"Ms. Friars?" A Latina voice radiated from the doorway.

Yoshi didn't waste much time sighing in relief. She immediately sprinted toward the doorway and bumped full speed into a table. Shooting pain in her shins doubled her over at her waist.

"*Ah, mi Díos.*" The woman rushed to help Yoshi.

"What is it, Selima?" Karen demanded.

"The door, ma'am, visitors." She sounded frightened. At this moment, Yoshi didn't blame her.

Karen sighed heavily. "I'll go handle it. Get our friend some ice, Selima, and do stay put, Yoshi."

Yoshi had no intention of staying put. As soon as she'd regained her composure, she limped after Karen. She had nearly caught up with her when she heard the door open and Karen inhale in surprise. It was not Velvet and Tucker.

"Good evening, ma'am," said a masculine voice with the officious tone that suggested a badged member of the law enforcement community. "I'm sorry to bother you, but we have a warrant to search this house."

"A warrant? What for?"

It was a question Yoshi wanted answered as well. What was happening? Had Bud found reason to call the police? Was this why he'd asked them to meet here?

"It's all in the warrant, ma'am," another gruff voice chimed in. "Please step aside."

From the commotion, it didn't sound like Karen was complying with the request. Yoshi wondered if they would physically push Karen aside.

"How dare you!" Karen hollered. "Wait until my lawyer hears about this!"

"Feel free to call, ma'am. In the meantime, we'll get started."

Yoshi heard heavy footsteps in the hall and doors opening as the search began.

"All this might go faster, ma'am, if you'd just tell us where to find what we are looking for."

"What *are* you looking for?"

Yoshi heard the rustling of paper as someone consulted the warrant itself.

"Well, see, this isn't even me," Karen Friars insisted. "It says right here that you're looking for some kind of film belonging to Rosemary Finney. That's not me. I'm Karen—"

"We're aware of who you are, ma'am. Your name is on the first page."

As another set of footsteps started down the hall toward her, Yoshi, who'd been leaning against the wall listening, hurried toward the front door.

"Just show them Rosemary's office," a familiar voice muttered.

Yoshi smiled. It sounded like Bud was behind this after all.

"Yoshi? Damn, girl, you okay?" Footsteps rushed forward and strong hands closed gently around her arm. "Did she hurt you?"

It was her lady cop in shining armor.

"AJ!" Yoshi exclaimed, letting her weight fall against AJ's stalwart body. She inhaled AJ's reassuring scent. "I am delighted it's you. But what brings you here?"

"That'd be a long tale, enough to call it Bud's doing. Come, my lady, let me get y'all a seat. I want to check your leg."

CHAPTER NINETEEN

Just as Yoshi and her police escort reached the living-room door, Velvet and Tucker rushed into the house. "What's going on?" Velvet asked, breathless.

"Some kind of search," Yoshi said. "I'm hoping AJ or Bud will explain better."

"AJ? What're you doing here?" It was Tucker's turn to ask.

AJ smiled. "Bud—" she started to say in her Southern, honey-dipped, husky voice.

"Bud?" Velvet asked. "Where is Bud? For that matter, where is Karen Friars?"

"I'm in here," Bud called from the living room. "Wondering how long it'd take you to get here."

The four women hurried into the room to find Bud casually helping himself to the Friars-Finney liquor cabinet. He was noisily searching through the bottles, no doubt hoping for the type of Scotch he would never purchase for himself.

"Bud!" Yoshi chided.

"What?" he asked innocently.

"Put that down!" Yoshi demanded.

"Who told?" he asked, looking around accusingly. The other three women shrugged in unison.

"What is going on?" Yoshi was all business.

"Karen's giving some officers a tour," Bud offered. "Have a seat."

"Just talk." Velvet insisted.

"Uh-uh," Bud insisted. He lowered his voice. "First things first. Is there anything you'd look for—you know, if you were searching for evidence to tie Karen to the murder?"

"Bud!" Yoshi exclaimed in the same tone she had employed in regard to the alcohol. "From what I gather, this warrant is not for us, it's not even related to the case."

"Right," Bud agreed. "I can explain."

"Riding boots," Tucker said. Bud looked at her and raised his eyebrows.

Velvet nodded. "She's right. Riding boots, especially if they're muddy. And a single stud earring."

"Yeah." Tucker pulled the earring out of her pocket and held it aloft. "I found this stuck into the horse's hoof. Awesome, huh?" She held it out to Bud.

Not accepting it, Bud shook his head. "AJ, you should probably get going, before you get in trouble."

"Ya got that right, T Spokes. Catch y'all later."

Bud ignored the nickname but thought to himself it wasn't too bad. "Tucker, go with her," the retired detective directed.

"No, Tucker, don't," Yoshi demanded.

Tucker hesitated, looking back and forth between the two, not knowing what to do.

"Don't I still run the agency?" Yoshi asked. "Or did something change?"

"We don't have time for this," Bud insisted.

Velvet could see the anger rising in Yoshi's expression. She didn't envy Bud making Yoshi mad. AJ stooped and whispered something in Yoshi's ear, which seemed to soothe the private eye. "Go ahead, Tucker," Yoshi said, a half smile on her face.

Tucker looked at Velvet as if still unsure.

Velvet nodded her assurance. "C U," she signed.

Tucker smiled and followed AJ out of the room.

"What the *hell* is going on?" Yoshi demanded as soon as the two left the room.

"Long story short, this afternoon San Mateo County Judge Harold Weinstein created a special task force to investigate allegations of Woodside officials accepting bribes."

"Fascinating." Velvet scribbled notes. What a great story.

"What does that have to do with a search here?"

"Well, one of the bribes was from a director. Ryan Esterhaus," Bud moved closer and lowered his voice conspiratorially. "He claims he bribed the Woodside mayor to keep his name out of this investigation, right? But then he admits to being involved in this sexual assault of a juvenile. It was twenty years ago, but—"

"But they've changed the statute of limitations on sex crimes," Yoshi concluded.

"Right. Anyway, Esterhaus claims that your friend Rosemary, somehow, got a copy of the tape showing the assault. I convinced the judge that the videotape is part of the larger case against the Woodside officials."

Yoshi wasn't sure she entirely understood, but she wanted to bring the conversation back around. "How does this help us do our job, which today is to clear Velvet's name? You remember Velvet, right?"

"Hi, Bud." Velvet waved.

"Yeah, how dare I care about anything else?"

"Does this have *anything* to do with us?"

"Yes, Yoshi, it does. I managed to get your friend AJ assigned to the task force so we could have a *man* on the inside." Bud emphasized the word as if he deliberately got it wrong. "Now she and Tucker are using the cover of the search to do a little searching of their own."

"But won't that disqualify any evidence they find? Fruit of the poisonous tree and all that?" Velvet asked, concerned about the possibility of going to trial now that her deadline was creeping ever closer.

"It would," Yoshi agreed, "if the police do it. But if a private citizen, like Tucker, were to wander off on her own and accidentally stumble upon something... But you sent AJ with her."

"Just to get her upstairs past the other cops and point her in the right direction, I swear."

"Shouldn't we join her?" Velvet wondered aloud.

"No," Bud said with conviction. "Karen would recognize you two."

"And having an accused murderer find the evidence that exonerates her really doesn't look good," Yoshi pointed out.

❖

"Well, isn't this cozy," Karen muttered, walking into the living room to find Bud, Yoshi, and Velvet conversing there. "Is this the whole gang? Are you all the reason for the brutes tearing up my place?"

"The jig is up, Karen." Velvet smiled.

"I don't think so. The officers assure me this has nothing to do with Rosemary's murder."

"You're right, I suppose," Bud said. "But that could all change in the blink of an eye if someone stumbles on evidence of another felony. You are aware of the plain-sight rule, aren't you? The exception to the search warrant requirement that says if you see it, you can collect it? You know, I think I might have mentioned exactly what that evidence might be, in this case."

"Like what?" Karen hadn't yet fallen for it.

"Um, I don't know." Bud continued the attack. "Say, muddy riding boots."

"Right." Karen smirked. "What am I supposed to fear you'll do with my boots?"

"It's not the boots so much," Yoshi explained. "We think the mud might place you at the scene of the crime."

"Oh, sure." Karen rolled her eyes. "I'm supposed to believe that you can prove when and where I have been from the dirt in my shoes? I hate to rain on your parade, but the Wonderland Park is just down the road, and I'm sure its dirt isn't any different than that on my property."

"Actually," Yoshi continued, "we are expecting the mud collected from your boots to be exceptionally telling. We expect that it will match the dirt from your horse's hooves."

At the cue, Velvet held up the paper bag and shook it lightly to show it wasn't empty. It was sealed with a strip of red evidence tape, so she didn't worry about it spilling.

"You wondered what they were doing with your horse," Yoshi reminded Karen, pointing toward Velvet.

Velvet smiled and theatrically waggled the bag at their suspect.

"I don't believe you." Karen didn't sound as sure this time.

"You know," Yoshi continued, "I found out that the parking area of Wonderland is covered with gravel that was brought to the site from the quarry down off Stevens Creek Reservoir. So it's rather unique in this area. Still, I think Karen might be right…"

Karen looked relieved.

"I think the dirt itself might be less important than a pollen analysis of the material *in* it. When we have that sample analyzed"— Yoshi pointed toward Velvet again—"I bet we'll find Kings Mountain manzanita. You know, it's a threatened species that occurs only in elevations much higher than your backyard. Our assistant, Tucker—you haven't met her, have you?" Yoshi paused for effect, not really waiting for an answer.

"She spoke with the people at Woodside Parks and Recreation, and they informed her that there are only two patches of Kings Mountain manzanita in Wonderland Park. By a strange coincidence, one of them happens to be where Rosemary was killed. Well, it's not so strange, actually. See, Rosemary was attacked on a blind curve, where the bushes had obscured the trail. Those bushes are Kings Mountain manzanita, which the parks department did not realize when they first built the trail, but now they cannot even trim it back without a permit from the state."

"Manzanita?" Karen laughed. "I have manzanita in my landscaping." She pointed out the window.

"But not the Kings Mountain variety, Karen," Yoshi continued her lecture. "*That* type is notoriously difficult to propagate; apparently even native plant nurseries struggle to grow the plant. And they are simply unavailable for commercial landscaping."

"Got what ya need." AJ's husky voice sounded from the doorway, where the police officer was holding up a pair of mud-splashed riding boots.

"So I was at the park," Karen admitted in light of this new evidence. "Sue me. I went there yesterday to mourn my wife."

Behind Karen's back, AJ winked at the Blind Eye team. "Y'all excuse me while I stow this evidence in my trunk. Don't be letting her leave."

"Nice try, Karen." Yoshi shook her head. "The rangers closed the trail down right after the incident, and they didn't completely open it until this morning."

When AJ's burly frame left the doorway, Karen's eyes followed as if the suspected murderer was thinking about darting out after her. Her unspoken hopes were dashed when Tucker replaced AJ in the doorway.

"Oh, hi, Tucker," Velvet called, "Come in and join us."

Tucker came in looking sheepish. "Um, I—"

"Excuse me?" Karen snapped.

Tucker's eyes widened. "Gosh, sorry. Did you guys know Rosemary had an iPod?" Tucker waited for the appropriate timing for the delivery that Bud had requested by way of AJ. "We found an empty charger, but no iPod. You wouldn't happen to know where it is, would you, ma'am?" She directed the question to Karen.

"I don't know, I think it was stolen," Karen said belligerently.

"Oh, did you file a police report?" Bud asked.

"They're so cheap we thought we'd just get another."

"So it must have been stolen recently?" Yoshi asked. "Because she hadn't replaced it yet?"

Karen, who had been standing near the doorway, came farther into the room and collapsed onto a chair.

"Did you ask about the earring?" Tucker asked.

"What earring, dear?" Velvet asked, hoping Tucker would play it up as well.

"Well, see, when I was cleaning the mud out of that horse's hoof? I found this earring. It's like she stepped on it? And then stepped in some more mud, so it was down a layer? Anyway, I thought maybe it belonged to Miss— I'm sorry, I don't know your last name."

"Friars," Karen spat.

"But I can see that you like to wear hoops, like Velvet. This is a stud, more like what I might wear." Tucker fiddled with the earring, twirling it between her forefinger and thumb.

Velvet was impressed with Tucker's performance. Maybe those hours together with *Law & Order* playing in the background while they were screwing had paid off. Either that or this AJ was one quick teacher and had infringed on her territory.

"Didn't I tell you?" Bud interjected. "The medical examiner mentioned an earring in her report. I think she said Rosemary only had one in. Yeah, that's it, she was missing one."

"That *is* interesting," Velvet agreed. "But not as interesting as this." She hoisted a cell phone over her head. "I picked this up during all this commotion—"

"That's mine," Karen screamed and snatched at it. "You have no right."

"Probably not," Velvet agreed, holding it out of reach. When the enraged widow lunged at her, Tucker rushed in and pulled Karen away. Tucker, holding a kicking and screaming Karen with arms wrapped around the woman's abdomen, looked positively horrified. Still, the butch's reaction thrilled Velvet, who smiled at the protective move.

"But you know," Velvet got back on point, "I was fiddling with this phone while we've been sitting here and I think I've just stumbled on your call history. For example, look, this says you received a phone call the morning Rosemary was killed, just about the same time, too."

Velvet pointed the small screen at Karen, as though the sight of the LCD numbers would be the key to disarming her. She was pleased to see that Karen did stop kicking Tucker's shins, even though her eyes were still bright with rage.

"She phoned you?" Yoshi was intrigued. "She called to ask you to pick her up, didn't she? Because Liz Claiborne had just stolen her shoes and she was upset. But you rode over on your horse instead of taking your vehicle. Was that because you wanted her to drive her Jaguar back, or was it because you already planned to kill her?"

"So I was there," Karen suddenly admitted, to Yoshi's delight. Once a small admission was made, it was a crack in the veneer and it was only time until the rest of the façade crumbled. "But I didn't kill her." Karen now hung in Tucker's arms like a rag doll.

Tucker dragged her over to an empty seat and dropped her in it.

Yoshi waited for Karen to mention taking a pair of shoes with her; Rosemary must have asked. Asking a leading question would only alert Karen to the revealing hole in her account, so Yoshi remained silent. If Karen did not take shoes, that spoke volumes of her intentions.

"So, what was it, Karen?" Velvet asked. "You see Rosemary talking with Keith Ridger? Or should I say Jennifer Garcia? Was that it? You realized she was lying to you about the whole straight thing?"

"It was Keith, not Jennifer, that Rosemary was fucking," Karen insisted. "It's his fault she's dead, you know," she posited. "He might as well have killed her himself—or maybe he did. I don't know. I swear she was alive when I left."

"Why don't you explain everything to us," Yoshi urged softly.

Karen nodded. "You're right, she called me. She was really upset."

"About Liz?" Velvet asked.

Karen waved the suggestion aside. "About Keith. He'd just broken up with her and she was devastated."

Velvet and Tucker shared a look of disbelief. If there was any chance that Karen was innocent, she was disproving it with every lie she told.

Calmly, Yoshi said, "You can stop lying now, Karen. Keith was not in town when Rosemary was killed, and that can be proven. So, please, just forget the fiction and tell us what happened."

"You might not believe this," Karen continued, accurately gauging the mood of the room. "But I was still in love with her, even after all she'd put me through. And all I wanted to do was comfort her."

"So you killed her," Bud interjected gruffly. "That's comforting."

Yoshi waved at him to shut up.

"She was completely despondent." Karen started along a fresh track. "She hated herself. Work. Personal stuff. We'd stopped communicating, so I don't know much more than that. She was very depressed."

"Are you saying this was an assisted suicide?" Velvet was incredulous. Was Karen a compulsive liar or just desperate to try any story in case one of them struck a chord?

"Yes, that's exactly what I'm saying. She begged me to kill her, but I just couldn't. She even suggested that I use the wires from the iPod she was wearing. She was completely hysterical, and I couldn't calm her down. She begged me until I finally said I'd do it. And I tried, I squeezed the wires around her neck, but I just couldn't keep at it. I was crying and begging her to let me stop, and I guess I must have cut off her air a little bit because she passed out."

"She died," Bud offered.

"No." Karen looked up belligerently, her eyes red from crying. "I swear she was still alive when I left. She was still breathing, it was just like she was sleeping. She was so beautiful. So I laid her down by the side of the trail and I left. I figured she'd wake up and she'd put this whole nonsense behind her. The only thing I can think"—she wiped at her eyes and sniffled—"is that after I left, someone else must have come…maybe it was Jennifer, maybe she was jealous of Rosemary, or her plaything Liz. One of them must have come back and killed her. It's so awful." She hung her head and sobbed. "I feel so guilty."

When she stopped speaking Bud clapped his hands together. "Brilliant! That's the best fucking story I've ever heard!" He stopped clapping, and his voice turned serious. "What a load of bullshit."

Karen looked up, stunned, as though not believing what she heard. She reached a hand out toward Velvet. "You believe me, though, don't you?"

"Sorry." Velvet shook her head. "I'm going to have to go with Bud on this one." She held up her hand as though quieting objections. "I know, it seems wrong to me too, for me to side with Bud, but there you go. I did believe *some* of what you said, Karen. But you went a little overboard there at the end. Yoshi?"

Yoshi paused. Reflectively, she said, "I am curious about something. What happened to the spare pair of shoes you took out there with you?"

"What shoes?"

The reply was quick and automatic, telling Yoshi all she needed to know. "Yes, it is as I thought. Why would you take a pair of shoes to a woman who would not be needing them?"

Yoshi heard a small gasp, then Karen reiterated shrilly, "I said I didn't kill her. You know I couldn't do that."

"I'm sorry, Karen, but that's not what the evidence is telling us. See, there was only one set of horse prints on the trail because it is officially closed to equestrians for the season. One of the only methods someone could have used to strangle Rosemary and leave behind the markings on her neck that angled up would be for them to be above her. For example, on a horse. I think you were on Paisley and when you got to Rosemary, you just grabbed the headphone wires and twisted. Something a psychologist said—I believe she may have been speaking to you, telling you something, and you just wanted to shut her up." Yoshi shook her head. Even when the life of an annoying woman was snuffed out, it was a terrible waste.

"Well," Karen snorted. "You don't have to believe me. You all have no right to be here, and I want you to leave." She stood up, her cheeks blazoned with anger and marked with streaks from crying. She pointed at the door as if demanding Blind Eye's departure.

"Maybe so." San Francisco Detective Ari Fleishman's stern voice sounded from the door as he stepped in from the hallway. "But I have the right to be here, and from what I've heard there's more than enough for us to take you in."

"Who are you?" Karen's mouth was agape. "You're not with the Woodside PD."

"No, no, I'm not. I'm Detective Ari Fleishman with the San Francisco Police Department," Ari said, closing in on the suspected murderer. "Thanks to our friend Bud here, bribes from a Hollywood director, a couple of San Mateo justices, and several apprehensive politicians, this case—like the one in connection with the videotape the boys upstairs are looking for—has been severed from Woodside's jurisdiction due to fears of political corruption."

Facing the wealthy woman, Ari pronounced, "Karen Friars, you are under arrest for the murder of Rosemary Finney. Please put your hands behind your back." He began reading her the Miranda rights.

"No!" Karen insisted, stepping away.

A tall, good-looking Jewish man with a mop of black curls, Detective Fleishman easily placed Karen into a restraint hold and began cuffing her, all the while reciting the litany of rights.

Velvet was having a hard time not dancing around and chanting the rights with Ari. She was beginning to think her nightmare was over.

Once he finished cuffing the suspect, Ari smiled and addressed the Blind Eye team. "Well, gang, I always knew you weren't to be taken for granted, but I'd never expected you'd take down an entire city government."

He laughed heartily and, pushing Karen Friars ahead of him, directed her out the door to his waiting squad car.

"Not bad for a day's work," Yoshi agreed.

Velvet sang out, "Free at last!" and hugged Tucker.

"How about you, Bud," Yoshi called out to the retired detective. "Your thoughts? Are you pleased with the way this day has wrapped up?"

"Not yet," Bud grumbled.

"You *will* be," AJ offered, sauntering into the room with a broad grin on her face.

"They found it," AJ added gleefully.

"What?" Yoshi asked in Bud's stead when he didn't answer.

"They found the videotape," AJ explained.

"Really?" Bud rolled closer. "They found it?"

"Yep, one of them other officers, under loose floorboards in a bedroom. Guess y'all lucky he stepped down on that spot and creaked the board. When they done yanked up that board, they found the tape an' a stack of Benjamins."

"And you're sure it's the one?" Bud demanded.

"Yeah, they say they sure."

Bud was so excited he practically skipped his chair out of the room.

Velvet turned to Tucker. "Do you want to go after him with me? I want to get the scoop on this story." Velvet leaned in and whispered in her ear, "This could be my Pulitzer."

Tucker nodded.

"Or just my excuse to get you upstairs into a bedroom." Velvet licked Tucker's ear.

Tucker turned red in embarrassment.

"You ever do it in a mansion before?"

"Velvet," Tucker said insistently. "Stop it."

With her arm around the younger woman, Velvet walked toward the door. "Come on," she said, "it'll be a celebration of a job well done. You really impressed me today."

A moment later the living room was left to Yoshi and AJ. AJ offered Yoshi her hands and pulled her out of her sitting position.

"Nice." AJ offered a word of congratulations.

"Thank you." Yoshi blushed. "You were pretty handy yourself."

"Y'all done here?" AJ asked.

"I believe so," Yoshi admitted, reluctant to leave.

"I just got dismissed for the night." AJ cleared her throat. "Wondered if ya might want to go out with me. Dinner or the like?"

Yoshi smiled from ear to ear. "I think I would like that, AJ. Do you like sushi?"

"Never tried it." Sounding nervous, she asked, "Ain't that raw fish?"

"You have much to learn." Yoshi smiled and tugged on AJ's shirtsleeve. "Will you wear your uniform?"

"You'd like that, huh?" AJ laughed. "No, I got a shirt in the squad car."

On their way out, Yoshi jotted a note and dropped it inside Velvet's car. From the way Velvet and Tucker were conspiring, Yoshi assumed it might take them some time to make their way back to the car. When they did, Velvet would find a small, delicately handwritten note that said, "Any advice for dating a cop?" and Velvet would smile, knowing exactly what she meant.

CHAPTER TWENTY

Yoshi blew out the candles on the vegan chocolate cake that Tucker had brought from the Rainbow Grocery Co-Op in honor of Yoshi's nonbirthday. It was not that Yoshi didn't want to celebrate another milestone year, but she understood that office parties were more about Blind Eye coworkers and professional friends than the celebrating individual. As Yoshi's exhalation extinguished heat from the flames, Tucker shoved a rectangular package into her hands and squealed, "Open it!" sounding more like a fifth grader on Mother's Day than an employee.

It was almost as though the Rosemary Finney case had brought the Blind Eye team, and its honorary members, closer than ever. Bud seemed to have softened somewhat and was being less gruff than normal. AJ and Velvet had been around the office so much in the weeks after the case was solved that they were acting like full-fledged members of the team. Although AJ's presence was not purely professional, Yoshi enjoyed the attention immensely.

"Open it, my lovely," AJ needled Yoshi, who was carefully removing the Scotch tape from her birthday package so as to not tear the paper. Just because she couldn't see the design did not mean that it had been chosen haphazardly. She would later obtain a visual description.

When Velvet could stand it no longer, she muttered, "Let's get on with it," and reached over Yoshi to give the paper a good, strong tug. It tore in half and made everyone, even a rather stunned Yoshi, laugh.

She shook her head. Count on Velvet to be the impatient one. Yoshi fingered the lightweight rectangular box and discerned that it was most likely some kind of software. They all seemed to come in similar packages. She shook it and heard the confirming rattle of CD-ROMs.

"It's Dragon Naturally Speaking," Tucker said rather proudly.

"What's that?" AJ asked.

"It's speech recognition software for your computer," Tucker explained to a rapt audience. Yoshi did not spoil the moment for the young woman by mentioning that she was well acquainted with recognition software. "It's really cool. It means you can just talk into your headset normally and the computer will automatically type what you say. And you can use it for the case reports or e-mail or the budget spreadsheets, even IMs."

Yoshi raised her eyebrows. Although she could not read others' facial expressions, she'd learned that they still looked for hers.

"Instant messages," Velvet filled in the blanks.

"Tucker, I don't know what to say," Yoshi admitted. She had wanted the software for some time but hadn't justified its expense. She banished the critical voice in her head that asked why she required taking care of and why she was no longer able to receive light or entertaining presents. "Thank you." She made sure none of her mixed emotions tainted the expression of gratitude.

"Hello?" a voice from the outer office sang out, and there was a shuffling of feet as those gathered around the large desk strained to see who was coming. AJ remained standing by Yoshi's side, and with the others distracted, she caressed Yoshi's shoulder. Yoshi smiled, appreciative that AJ respected her disinclination for public displays of affection.

"We're in here, Artemis," Velvet called and a flirty little skirt rustled in the breeze of the central heat as Artemis strode in. Another person, whose perfume pegged her as a woman, trailed in more slowly, as if she were apprehensive.

Artemis made the introductions. "After all you did to put Karen away and make it safe for Liz to return to the city, she just wanted to meet you in person. She'll be there in court to testify when it comes to trial."

"I appreciate that, Artemis, and thank you for your insight on the case, it was quite helpful." Yoshi extended her hand in the women's direction and Artemis grabbed it but pulled Yoshi in for a hug instead.

"Thank you *so* much," she whispered.

Yoshi stiffened uncomfortably. The intimacy was disconcerting, and she couldn't wait to get out of the embrace. "So, this is the enigmatic Liz Claiborne." She held out a hand.

"Miss Yakamota?" Liz's voice was barely audible. She had a delicate and hesitant handshake that seemed to fit naturally with what Yoshi had come to know of her. "I'm so sorry for the trouble I caused."

"It's Velvet you should apologize to," Tucker interjected without tact. There was a soft thud and a yelp that Yoshi imagined was Tucker's response to a well-placed kick by Velvet aimed at improving the young woman's social skills.

As Tucker and Liz stumbled over apologies, Yoshi raised her voice and asked if the others could give her and Liz a moment alone in her office. It took a few minutes for AJ to strong-arm the reluctant partyers, who were eventually led away with promises of cake and ice cream. As soon as the door closed behind them, Liz Claiborne began to talk. And talk. And talk. Apparently she had been talking all day and the Blind Eye office wasn't her first stop.

"The police were really nice," Liz said. "I told them I'd testify. The thing is, I saw everything up there that morning. I was just so scared, and I was quite a long way from where it happened. I wanted to stop Karen but I didn't know how to, so I just hid. When she left, I ran to help Rosemary but...she was dead."

Liz began to cry softly. Yoshi wouldn't have known except she had begun to suck in her breath for long moments of time then heave slightly, each time letting out a sentence or two. Yoshi felt for her, this sweet, corn-fed young Midwesterner caught up in Rosemary and Karen's twisted world and resorting to manipulation as the disempowered often did.

Artemis was quick to assist her patient. "Liz has been in hiding at her grandmother's house this whole time. She was afraid she'd been seen by Karen and thought she might come after her as well. Then when she was trying to meet with me and saw the police, she was convinced that Karen was intent on framing her for murder. Not to mention the terrible psychological trauma of witnessing the crime."

"I can certainly understand that, Liz," Yoshi said calmly. "What convinced you to come forward?"

"I love Rosemary. Loved Rosemary. I know everyone thinks that's deluded but I think she may have loved me, too. I just didn't want there to be no one in court to tell her side of the story."

Yoshi wanted to accept this at face value. Through this whole ordeal, she had never considered that there would be someone who really did love Rosemary unconditionally. It must take a special person to have that in her. Of course, Liz was very young. But Liz had also made certain choices that spoke of more complicated motivations. Obviously she was conflicted about Rosemary, and jealousy could drive people to uncharacteristic behavior.

"You phoned Velvet the night before Rosemary was killed," Yoshi said. "Why did you do that?"

Liz was silent for a long time, then she sounded ashamed. "I had this idea that I could make her give up everything and be with me. It probably sounds stupid to you, but I thought if I talked to Velvet and she did a story about Rosemary…you know, exposing her and Jennifer Garcia and the stuff I knew she was doing to destroy *Bend*…then she would change her life."

"You thought you could be a part of that change?"

"I just wanted her to realize she couldn't keep on treating people like she did." Impulsively, she added, "And I suppose I kind of wanted her punished, too. I mean, for what she did to me."

Yoshi thought through the young woman's revealing words. One small but important detail was missing. "Do you carry a cell phone?"

"Yes."

"Then why didn't you call 911 when Karen attacked her?"

An edge of defensiveness slid into Liz's tone. "I don't know exactly. The police asked me about that, too. It's hard to explain. It was like it wasn't really happening." As if trying to convince herself as much as anyone else that she was a helpless witness, she explained, "I was standing there watching, and it seemed like a bad dream. I just didn't think about making a phone call."

Yoshi tried to imagine seeing a person being murdered and doing nothing. Shock could have immobilized a young woman like Liz. Yet there were other possibilities. Yoshi's thoughts returned to Liz's admission about wanting Rosemary punished. The complicity in her one-time lover's death could certainly have been unwitting and unconscious. Or darker emotions could have been at work that morning. Yoshi suspected they might never know the entire truth. Rosemary had played with fire when she used and misused other people. Arrogantly, she had imagined she would never be burned.

Yoshi asked nothing more of her unexpected visitor. There would be a trial, and perhaps some of her remaining questions would be resolved when Liz and Karen testified. She exchanged some parting words with the two women, and after they had left her office, she welcomed the others back in, hoping to finally get a piece of that vegan cake.

"I have something for the Blind Eye team as well," Yoshi announced and handed a small stack of envelopes to AJ to distribute. There was one each for her, Bud, Tucker, and Velvet.

"What is this?" Velvet asked without opening it.

Tucker ripped into hers and gasped audibly. "Wow. This is awesome!"

AJ pressed her envelope back into Yoshi's hands. "I ain't be needing this from y'all. I was just doing my job."

Yoshi explained, "We received a substantial reward for solving the Finney murder."

"From who?" Velvet demanded suspiciously as though she thought Yoshi was making this up to cover for her own generosity.

"From the Finney family, of course. They were delighted that Karen's arrest means she will not be entitled to the whole of Rosemary's estate and inheritance."

Velvet chortled, and Yoshi knew she would feel that taking Finney money was some small recompense for all Rosemary had put her through.

As they worked their way through the remaining cake, Velvet mused aloud, "It's weird. I thought I was going to Wonderland Park that day to catch Rosemary red-handed in the ultimate case of corporate lesbian espionage, but it was so much worse."

"A murder like that, it's personal," Bud said.

Velvet sighed. "She was a viper, but she also helped pioneer lesbian publishing. She didn't deserve what happened." In response to the silence that followed, which had less to do with lack of interest and more to do with a skilled bakery, she changed the subject abruptly. "Have you guys ever heard of Pioneer School? It's this ex-gay school that is right here in the Bay Area—can you believe that? They've had a couple of kids run away from the program and just disappear. Probably living on the street at Haight Ashbury or something. Anyway, my editor wants me on it, so, I've gotta run. Gotta chase a new story."

Soon they'd all be chasing something new, Yoshi thought—a different career, a deeper relationship, a fresh case that could change them more dramatically than they'd ever imagine.

About the Authors

Diane Anderson-Minshall has been writing as long as she's been reading. Her first work, published when she was eight years old, was printed in *Highlights* magazine. It was about a circus. Since then she's covered everything from the mundane (regional dog shows and Egyptian irrigation procedures) to the sensational (Hollywood's A-list and female serial killers). Diane's writing has appeared in dozens of magazines including *Passport*, *Bust*, *Bitch*, *Venus*, Utne, *Seventeen*, and more, and she is the executive editor of *Curve* magazine and the founder and former editor of *Girlfriends* and *Alice* magazines. A journalist since she was thirteen (her first job was covering the school beat for the *Independent Enterprise* in Payette, Idaho), Diane has received a handful of honors for her work including a 1998 Visa Versa award for her celebrity journalism, a finalist for the Women in Periodical Publishing's Woman of the Year Award in 2000, and Power Up's Ten Amazing Gay Women in Showbiz Award in 2006. Some day she hopes to write a true crime novel that looks at infamous lesbian murders and a sensational novel as great as her three favorites: *Punish Me With Kisses*, *The Grounding of Group Six*, and *Fear of Flying*.

Jacob Anderson-Minshall has been many things: farm boy, carny, artist, activist, park ranger, and lesbian. He grew up on a small farm in southeastern Idaho, where his mother fostered his love of reading and mystery with bedtime stories like Edgar Allen Poe's *Pit and the Pendulum* and 5,000-piece puzzles obscuring the dinner table for weeks at a time. His grandmother, a librarian, sent boxes of books, which he consumed during long winter months and years without television. For nearly four decades Jacob was a girl named Susannah. During that time he received a M.A. in Rhetorical Criticism, cofounded Idaho State University's LGBT student association, ran for homecoming king, cofounded the lesbian magazine *Girlfriends*, and began his life's romance with his wife Diane, who has been his partner for seventeen years. Jacob writes the syndicated weekly column TransNation, which runs in queer publications from San Francisco to Boston, and is a frequent contributor to *Bitch* magazine. As a former park ranger and law enforcement officer, Jacob is familiar with both the parks and open spaces of the San Francisco Bay Area and the procedures involved in enforcement duties. His interest in crime was intensified with the 2000 murder of his brother-in-law, Tom Sherwood, in Pocatello, Idaho. To this date the case remains unsolved.

Books Available From Bold Strokes Books

Blind Curves by Diane and Jacob Anderson-Minshall. Private eye Yoshi Yakamota comes to the aid of her ex-lover Velvet Erickson in the first Blind Eye mystery. (978-1-933110-72-1)

Dynasty of Rogues by Jane Fletcher. It's hate at first sight for Ranger Riki Sadiq and her new patrol corporal, Tanya Coppelli—except for their undeniable attraction. (978-1-933110-71-4)

Running With the Wind by Nell Stark. Sailing instructor Corrie Marsten has signed off on love until she meets Quinn Davies—one woman she can't ignore. (978-1-933110-70-7)

More Than Paradise by Jennifer Fulton. Two women battle danger, risk all, and find in each other an unexpected ally and an unforgettable love. (978-1-933110-69-1)

Flight Risk by Kim Baldwin. For Blayne Keller, being in the wrong place at the wrong time just might turn out to be the best thing that ever happened to her. (978-1-933110-68-4)

Rebel's Quest, Supreme Constellations: Book Two by Gun Brooke. On a world torn by war, two women discover a love that defies all boundaries. (978-1-933110-67-7)

Punk and Zen by JD Glass. Angst, sex, love, rock. Trace, Candace, Francesca...Samantha. Losing control—and finding the truth within. BSB Victory Editions. (1-933110-66-X)

Stellium in Scorpio by Andrews & Austin. The passionate reuniting of two powerful women on the glitzy Las Vegas Strip, where everything is an illusion and love is a gamble. (1-933110-65-1)

When Dreams Tremble by Radclyffe. Two women whose lives turned out far differently than they'd once imagined discover that sometimes the shape of the future can only be found in the past. (1-933110-64-3)

The Devil Unleashed by Ali Vali. As the heat of violence rises, so does the passion. A Casey Clan crime saga. (1-933110-61-9)

Burning Dreams by Susan Smith. The chronicle of the challenges faced by a young drag king and an older woman who share a love "outside the bounds." (1-933110-62-7)

Fresh Tracks by Georgia Beers. Seven women, seven days. A lot can happen when old friends, lovers, and a new girl in town get together in the mountains. (1-933110-63-5)

The Empress and the Acolyte by Jane Fletcher. Jemeryl and Tevi fight to protect the very fabric of their world...time. Lyremouth Chronicles Book Three. (1-933110-60-0)

First Instinct by JLee Meyer. When high-stakes security fraud leads to murder, one woman flees for her life while another risks her heart to protect her. (1-933110-59-7)

Erotic Interludes 4: Extreme Passions. Thirty of today's hottest erotica writers set the pages aflame with love, lust, and steamy liaisons. (1-933110-58-9)

Storms of Change by Radclyffe. In the continuing saga of the Provincetown Tales, duty and love are at odds as Reese and Tory face their greatest challenge. (1-933110-57-0)

Unexpected Ties by Gina L. Dartt. With death before dessert, Kate Shannon and Nikki Harris are swept up in another tale of danger and romance. (1-933110-56-2)

Erotic Interludes 3: Lessons in Love ed. by Radclyffe and Stacia Seaman. Sign on for a class in love...the best lesbian erotica writers take us to "school." (1-9331100-39-2)

Sleep of Reason by Rose Beecham. Nothing is as it seems when Detective Jude Devine finds herself caught up in a small-town soap opera. And her rocky relationship with forensic pathologist Dr. Mercy Westmoreland just got a lot harder. (1-933110-53-8)

Combust the Sun by Andrews & Austin. A Richfield and Rivers mystery set in L.A. Murder among the stars. (1-933110-52-X)

Tristaine Rises by Cate Culpepper. Brenna, Jesstin, and the Amazons of Tristaine face their greatest challenge for survival. (1-933110-50-3)

Too Close to Touch by Georgia Beers. Kylie O'Brien believes in true love and is willing to wait for it. It doesn't matter one damn bit that Gretchen, her new and off-limits boss, has a voice as rich and smooth as melted chocolate. It absolutely doesn't... (1-933110-47-3)

Passion's Bright Fury by Radclyffe. When a trauma surgeon and a filmmaker become reluctant allies on the battleground between life and death, passion strikes without warning. (1-933110-54-6)

Justice Served by Radclyffe. Lieutenant Rebecca Frye and her lover, Dr. Catherine Rawlings, embark on a deadly game of hide-and-seek with an underworld kingpin who traffics in human souls. (1-933110-15-5)

Justice in the Shadows by Radclyffe. In a shadow world of secrets and lies, Detective Sergeant Rebecca Frye and her lover, Dr. Catherine Rawlings, join forces in the elusive search for justice. (1-933110-03-1)

A Matter of Trust by Radclyffe. JT Sloan is a cybersleuth who doesn't like attachments. Michael Lassiter is leaving her husband, and she needs Sloan's expertise to safeguard her company. It should just be business—but it turns into much more. (1-933110-33-3)

Broken Wings by L-J Baker. When Rye Woods, a fairy, meets the beautiful dryad Flora Withe, her libido, as squashed and hidden as her wings, reawakens along with her heart. (1-933110-55-4)

Of Drag Kings and the Wheel of Fate by Susan Smith. A blind date in a drag club leads to an unlikely romance. (1-933110-51-1)

Stolen Moments: Erotic Interludes 2 by Stacia Seaman and Radclyffe, eds. Love on the run, in the office, in the shadows…Fast, furious, and almost too hot to handle. (1-933110-16-3)

100th Generation by Justine Saracen. Ancient curses, modern-day villains, and a most intriguing woman who keeps appearing when least expected lead archeologist Valerie Foret on the adventure of her life. (1-933110-48-1)

Distant Shores, Silent Thunder by Radclyffe. Dr. Tory King—along with the women who love her—is forced to examine the boundaries of love, friendship, and the ties that transcend time. (1-933110-08-2)

Beyond the Breakwater by Radclyffe. One Provincetown summer, three women learn the true meaning of love, friendship, and family. (1-933110-06-6)

Safe Harbor by Radclyffe. A mysterious newcomer, a reclusive doctor, and a troubled gay teenager learn about love, friendship, and trust during one tumultuous summer in Provincetown. (1-933110-13-9)

Battle for Tristaine by Cate Culpepper. While Brenna struggles to find her place in the clan and the love between her and Jess grows, Tristaine is threatened with destruction. Second in the Tristaine series. (1-933110-49-X)

Honor Reclaimed by Radclyffe. In the aftermath of 9/11, Secret Service Agent Cameron Roberts and Blair Powell close ranks with a trusted few to find the would-be assassins who nearly claimed Blair's life. (1-933110-18-X)

Honor Guards by Radclyffe. In a wild flight for their lives, the president's daughter and those who are sworn to protect her wage a desperate struggle for survival. (1-933110-01-5)

Love & Honor by Radclyffe. The president's daughter and her lover are faced with difficult choices as they battle a tangled web of Washington intrigue for...love and honor. (1-933110-10-4)

Honor Bound by Radclyffe. Secret Service Agent Cameron Roberts and Blair Powell face political intrigue, a clandestine threat to Blair's safety, and the seemingly irreconcilable personal differences that force them ever farther apart. (1-933110-20-1)

Above All, Honor by Radclyffe. Secret Service Agent Cameron Roberts fights her desire for the one woman she can't have—Blair Powell, the daughter of the president of the United States. (1-933110-04-X)